Praise for William Jack Sibley and **SIGHS TOO DEEP FOR WORDS**

"Sibley (*Any Kind of Luck*, 2002) blends skillful storytelling with a sharp insight into human nature in this darkly humorous, intricately plotted tale of a prison inmate who, through years of correspondence, falls in love with a woman he has never met—a woman who turns out not only to be a gay man, but a closeted gay minister.

Lester Briggs is serving a five-year prison term for stealing—of all things—a church. Out of prison early for good behavior, Lester leaves behind his cellmate and lover of convenience, "Little Ray," and heads for the small town of Rockport, Texas, where he hopes to find Laurel Jeanette Yancey, the love of his life. He finds instead the closeted gay minister who has been writing to him; the minister's lesbian sister; a kindly, old gas station manager who offers him advice and later a job; and a whole host of other colorful characters (most of whom end up having some bearing on the plot, however minor). Plotlines reach levels of mistaken iden¬tity, confusion and startling coincidence not often seen outside of farce or soap opera, but this infuses the events of the story with a genuine humor and insight that keeps the material fresh. Sibley deftly handles his characters' emotions, from the brief connection between a distant father and son, to the emotional roller coaster Lester Briggs finds himself on—in love with the mind of a man and the body of that man's lesbian sister, all while struggling to adjust to the realities of life outside of prison. It's to Sibley's credit that the emotional reality of the characters never suffers for the sometimes outlandish convolutions of the plot. Readers looking for an entertaining book with surprising touches of depth and emotion are sure to enjoy this fresh, dramatic tale.

Funny, touching, heartbreaking and insightful."

–Kirkus Review, www.KirkusReviews.com, November 20, 2012

D0043647

Sighs Too Deep For Words

William Jack Sibley

ISBN: 1-4776-6417-3
ISBN-13: 9781477664179

"Spirit intercedes with *sighs too deep for words.*"—Romans 8:26

chapter

ONE

It had been almost four and a half years since Lester Briggs had sex. Old-fashioned sex. Sex with someone of the opposite sex. He was feeling a tad restless.

Everything he saw on that highway leaving Corpus Christi reminded him of something or someone he hadn't had in a while. Like that orangey-pink housedress flapping away off on the trailer house clothes line. Made him think of fried sweet potatoes his daddy used to make in a skillet with molasses and cooking oil. They were good eating. Course, no one ever served him fried sweet potatoes in prison. And he hadn't seen his daddy since he was nine. And actually, now that he looked at it, that housedress was more an orangey-brown than an orangey-pink. Still, everything he saw that first morning of his new redemption made him horny and hungry.

The Texas Gulf Coast was rank with sex in August. Driving past a Dairy Queen, he saw a carload of high school girls get out in short shorts, tank tops, and long legs the color of lightly baked bread. They shrieked and shoved one another like sparring seagulls, oblivious to the passing ex-con lying low in the pickup bed before them. Lester eyed their callow perfection and self-absorption and shook his head in dismay, "God-a-mighty, bunch a dimwits wouldn't know how to kiss a baby's butt."

Raw beauty was OK in its place. Lord knows Lester had made love to those prison centerfolds hanging in his cell a jillion times over. But they never bothered writing him back. Not one of them ever sent him new socks or a San Antonio Spurs sweatshirt. None of them called him "Angel Cake" or wrote a poem in his honor like the one that began with, "My Love is Number 298345 of the Texas Department of Criminal Justice, Diboll Unit—a number worth waiting for." No one anywhere had ever done anything close to that except for one individual, Laurel Jeanette Yancey. Laurel Jeanette Yancey of P.O. Box 416, Rockport, Texas, to be exact. She was the only person on earth who truly, deeply, and passionately cared about Lester. And though they'd never actually met, he had over 315 letters in his grip that testified to their remarkable and unparalleled love. And soon he would surprise her with his presence, and nothing would ever be the same for either of them. Of that, he was certain. A man had to take chances. Laurel Jeanette would understand that.

Leaving the town of Orange Grove, the truck clipped along at a pretty good speed. The farmer who picked him up had said if he didn't mind riding in back with his two black mouth curs, he'd be glad to give him a lift. Lester was much relieved. His conversational skills had wasted away to practically nothing in prison. After guns, sports, women, and drinking, everything else men said in the "dick domicile" was an even bigger lie. All Lester wanted was to sit quietly in the hot Texas sun and think about Laurel Jeanette. Occasionally he contemplated the hard-on he'd been transporting since daybreak, and a smile would cross his face. Life was almost good again.

He'd shut his eyes for only a couple of seconds when it came back to him, beating like a red cardinal flapping and scratching to get in the window. Little Ray's face, his cell mate at Diboll. The look on that boy when the "Badges" took Lester from the cell was something he didn't want to have to remember. It was like seeing a little kid get punched in the gut. Or a dog run over. Lester didn't want to keep thinking about it, but it kept coming at him every time he thought he might be clear of the notion. Little Ray was twenty-one and doing four years on a state felony for controlled substances. He'd gotten busted with a half gram of cocaine outside a west Texas beer joint. The son of a hardware store manager and a grade school teacher, he had about as much business being in prison as a pond duck. Didn't make any sense putting a kid like that in a place like Diboll. He'd done a stupid thing, it was true, but to wall him up with every kind of degenerate and malicious outlaw that had ever sucked air nauseated Lester. It wasn't right. And he didn't know how to fix it. And he was scared for Little Ray.

The pickup came to a halt so fast it threw both cur dogs into Lester's lap. They'd been up on the toolbox road surfing and got pitched against the rear window and then tossed backwards. One of them stuck a foot on Lester's crotch and came about a hair or two from causing him some grave uneasiness. Lester glared at the old farmer in the rearview mirror and thought about saying something, but he decided otherwise. Not today. He shinnied out of the back of the truck, pulling his duffel bag.

The farmer rolled down his window: "I'm making a left here. You got about another ten miles into Rockport."

Lester tipped his cowboy hat. "Much obliged."

The farmer spit and shifted into first. "What'd they lock your ass up for anyway?"

Lester looked at him, surprised. "Who says I was locked up?"

The farmer grinned, "Son, I done a year and a half up in Huntsville back in the '50s. Look at them shoes you're wearing. Department of Corrections issuance if I ever seen it."

Lester stared down at his cheap, white "Asian Keds" and suddenly felt ridiculous. He mumbled, "Theft."

"What'd ya steal?"

Lester glanced at the farmer, scratched his head and sighed. "Church."

The farmer bellowed, "A church?"

"Just the building. It belonged to my granddaddy."

"What kind a goddamn building?"

"Barn. They took his barn when he lost the place. Moved it into town and turned it into an Assembly of God. Never sat right with me. I went and put it on the back of a flatbed and hauled it off one night, pews and all. Third-degree felony theft, five years—six months off for playing nice with the other boys."

Mouth open, the farmer stared at Lester and then suddenly burst out laughing. "Crazy sumabitch, you ought to run for governor. They could use a toot like you up in Austin." He then jammed the truck gears and lurched off, nearly dumping the black mouth curs.

Lester picked up his bag and started walking. He looked down at his ugly sneakers and dropped the bag in disgust. Despite it being almost noon and already close to a hundred, Lester sat on the pavement, took off the offending footgear, and hurled them into the bushes. He then reached into his grip and pulled out a pair of moldy, scruffy cowboy boots. He struggled getting them on his feet, and even though they'd been in "state storage" a total of 1,642 and a half days, they were a damn sight better looking than those "kiddy tennies" he'd been wearing. Lester stood and began walking again. Slowly. It'd been a long time since he'd worn heels. His steps were deliberate; he moved his hips gradually at first and then propelled each leg with an easy, rolling gait. It was coming back. The way a man's supposed to walk in boots. Even prison can't take away everything.

After about a hundred yards, Lester took off his T-shirt and stuffed it into his back pocket. Now he felt good. Real good. His arms and chest were pretty pale, but he'd made good use of those jail weights. Fact was, at twenty-eight years old, he was in the best shape he'd ever been. Six foot one, 176 pounds, and, in spite of the starchy slop served in prison, he'd managed to transform an already acceptable chassis into a frame of highly toned excellence. With his giveaway-Cajun lineage of gleaming black hair, blue eyes, fair skin, and lightly freckled torso, Lester had spun more than a few heads in prison. It was inevitable. Bunch of wild-ass, horny guys always scoping each other out, Lester had been seriously freaked in the beginning. He was young, pretty, and naïve, and he fully grasped the consequences. After a couple of harrowing pillow biters that were essentially four- or five-guy gang rapes, he learned the ropes quickly. No fool in his right mind would keep fighting those "hoe check" beatings day after day. He knew he'd be hurt bad, or most likely be "accidentally" dead in a month. He was introduced to "Fat Beto," the man who got the protection money to keep the serious animals away and "Eddie B.," who became his "war daddy." Eddie B. was a two-hundred-thirty-pound, forty-year-old, ex-professional wrestler who went "nut up" one Christmas morning and strangled three people in an old folks home while visiting his mother. He said he could never remember why he did it, but that he knew it was something just had to be done. Being a war daddy meant he basically looked out for you—for favors. In Lester's case, it was extra money, cigarettes, candy, plus the occasional hand job. And once in a blue moon, a little further attention as well. Lester became a speed master at doing the "may tag" (fellatio). In fact, he became largely philosophical about the whole thing: eat or be eaten. Eddie B. had four other boys who did him favors as well, which for Lester meant that after those initial rapes he'd kept the rest of his semi-cherry intact for the next four years. In prison, it was no small feat.

He'd even discussed it with Laurel Jeanette. He could talk to her about anything—food, politics, TV, animal husbandry, prison rape. Nothing was off limits. Laurel Jeanette had said the main thing about his "skirmishes," as she called the rapes, was that he'd physically survived it unscathed and God would heal the rest in time. It didn't seem to faze her. She was unusually sympathetic and wise in that way. Although she rarely offered advice, when pressed she nearly always said the right thing. Lester had never met a woman quite like her. Within a month of their first correspondence, he fell hopelessly, deeply, and very consciously in love. She was his light: never failing, never indefinite, always steady.

Lester didn't hear the car approaching from behind. He was so deep in his head, he thought at first it was just the wind whirring up. He turned around to see a convertible stopped to a crawl fewer than twenty feet behind him. A foreign car, red. Some kind of high-class jazz music was coming from inside, and a man was singing in a language other than English. A blonde woman, maybe a little younger than Lester, was driving, and some guy who looked like her junior counterpart was seated next to her. Lester stopped walking, and the guy whispered to the woman. The car immediately sped up and raced around Lester. As he watched it careen off, he shook his head. Then, about a quarter mile down the road, it came to dead stop in the middle of the highway. More words were exchanged between the two, and then the car quickly shifted into reverse and squealed back toward where Lester was standing. He stepped to the side as the car grated to a halt beside him.

"Hi." The blonde woman, who was wearing sunglasses and a scarf, smiled at Lester.

"Hi."

"Need a ride?"

Lester looked at them as if he were seeing Martians for the first time. They stared back at him like two polite tigers. "I…I'm just going into Rockport. I can make it."

The young man spoke: "That's where we're headed. Come on; we'll give you a lift."

Lester didn't move. "You from around here?"

The woman removed her sunglasses. "Our folks have a summer house on the bay. We've been coming down here all our lives. Hop in. We'll take you where you're going."

Lester studied the pair one more time, then started to put his T-shirt on. The young man grinned, "That's OK; you don't have to dress for us. We're the informal type." Lester, looking embarrassed, pushed his shirt back in his jeans pocket. The young man opened the car door and scooted closer to the woman. Lester got in beside him, and the car sped off so fast again his cowboy hat blew off. The woman laughed and braked, causing Lester to jolt forward, hitting his nose to the dash.

"You might want to hang on to that hat, cowboy. These convertibles are hell on costumes." Lester opened the door and reached out to pick up his cheap straw hat. Once again, they sped off, this time the wind neatly parting Lester's hair. He resolved to hold the hat in his lap for the duration.

"Melanie Wheelwright," said the blonde. "My baby brother, Daniel," she nudged her brother then held out her hand and shook Lester's, direct and strong, like a horse trainer. Or a public defense attorney. Lester then shook Daniel's hand, who indecisively extended it as if it were being remote controlled. "Lester Briggs. Where ya'll from?"

"I live in New York. My brother's in his last year at Rice University. We're from Dallas originally. You?"

Lester shifted the bag between his legs. "Well, I'm from a little farm town up near Texarkana. Ya'll never heard of it."

Daniel grinned slyly. "I know Texas geography really well. Where?"

Lester shrugged. "It's just a little old bend in the highway. Nobody's ever heard of it."

"Daniel knows every back road in Texas. It's like a hobby of his. Try him."

Daniel spoke excitedly, "Let's make a bet!"

Lester glanced at him and smiled. "Nah, that's OK."

"Come on. I'll ask you three yes-or-no questions, and I'll bet I can guess where you're from. Bet me something. Anything."

Lester looked at Daniel again and casually appraised his rich-boy uniform: Italian loafers, linen shorts, knit silk shirt, lizard belt with a silver concho buckle. He shook his head and laughed out loud. "All right. I'll bet you that belt you got on you can't guess my hometown in three guesses."

"You're on!"

Melanie suddenly interrupted. "Wait a minute, Danny, what are you betting of Lester's?"

Daniel turned his gaze on Lester and pondered his physique like it was something being offered on a cafeteria line. Lester instantly wished he'd put his shirt on. He was feeling unusually pale next to these two sun babies.

Finally Daniel looked up into Lester's eyes. "I think I want… your pants."

"My pants?"

"Yeah."

"What do you want my jeans for?"

Daniel shrugged. "I…collect them?"

Lester was uneasy. "They're not real clean."

Daniel narrowed his gaze. "I've got a washing machine."

Lester looked at him a second longer and then shook his head. "Fine."

Melanie laughed and screamed, driving even faster. "Whisper the name in my ear, Lester." Daniel leaned forward in the cramped front seat and Lester sided towards Melanie, cupping his hand around his mouth. He stopped a few inches from her ear. He suddenly couldn't fathom being this close to a woman. A very beautiful woman. He stared at her skin. It was beyond perfection, like some kind of golden, honeyed fruit. He studied her ear. Perfection. Small, delicate, and adorned with a pale pink pearl. Her blonde hair was cut to the middle of her neck, and it flipped and shone like a thousand silk threads. He closed his eyes and breathed in. She smelled like some exceptional combination of suntan lotion, woman, and a sweetness Lester had never known. Daniel, tired of leaning forward, suddenly threw himself back in the seat, bumping Lester.

"Oh, sorry! Are you still whispering the name? God, I'll never guess if it's that long."

Melanie shoved Daniel forward. "Go ahead, Lester."

Sex was everywhere in August. Lester felt a sudden need to reposition his privates, but decided against attracting attention. He leaned in once again, whispering. Melanie looked at him. "It's called *what*?" Lester whispered once more. This time Melanie threw her head back and roared, "Oh my God, it's too good to be true! Daniel, if you get this one, I'll give you *my* pants."

Lester sat back in his seat, and Daniel turned to him, very serious. "Is this town within an hour's drive of Texarkana?"

"Yes."

Melanie shouted, "First question!"

"Is this town south of Texarkana?"

"Yes."

"Second question!"

Daniel bit his lower lip and stared straight ahead, concentrating intently on the horizon. Finally, he asked, "Is this town a one-syllable word?"

Lester had to think for a second and then nodded. "Yes."

Melanie took off her scarf and held it high above her head, letting it whip deliriously in the wind. "Wheee! The last question—and the answer is…?"

Melanie and Lester stared at Daniel who shook his head slowly, smiling. "This is so-o-o easy; everyone knows the answer to this. You're from Hoot!"

Melanie screamed wildly and blew the car horn, weaving back and forth across both lanes. She then motioned for Daniel to take the wheel as she stood up in her seat, unzipped her pants, yanked them off, and tossed them on Daniel's head. Breathless with excitement, she regained the wheel, and she and Daniel turned to Lester expectantly.

Lester stared at both of them, stunned. "Have you ever been to Hoot?"

Daniel blinked. "Twice."

"Wh—Why?"

"It's on the way to Sulphur." Lester couldn't believe it. Sulphur was an even smaller knothole than Hoot. As much as Melanie and Daniel were enjoying this little game, Lester felt downright queasy. Not only was he wearing an old pair of dingy prison briefs, he was obviously sporting wood. The brief interlude with Melanie had fossilized his member. He was now convinced something was definitely wrong with him. An intermittent six-hour erection—how could it be? Melanie and Daniel continued gaping. Lester sighed and slowly picked up his bag, handing it to Daniel. Carefully, methodically, he began removing his boots in the cramped front seat. He felt exceptionally awkward, like a Great Dane squatting in a Radio Flyer. Sitting the boots aside, he glanced furtively in the rearview mirror and instantly wrestled his pants down both legs in one blurry, frenetic movement. Balling up the jeans, he tossed them to Daniel. Lester hugged his knees and stared out the passenger side feeling like a complete idiot. Twenty-four hours ago he was dreaming about freedom, and here he was virtually naked and trapped in a toy car with Donny and Marie Headcase.

"Who's 'L.R.'?" Daniel was burning a hole in Lester's arm, staring at his tattoo. Four and a half years in prison, and Lester had managed to escape with just one tattoo. Two letters—big letters. Most of the guys at Diboll were so illustrated, watching them was like reading a newspaper. Who an inmate was, what he'd done, and where he'd been were all encoded on flesh. With just a hollowed-out ballpoint pen, some guitar string, a nine-volt battery, and a slot-car motor, a person had his very own "tat machine." And it was a flourishing business—till you got caught. The spread of disease made the guards go mental if you got busted. Lester determined early on, his one tattoo would be a sufficient enough memento of his "East Texas sabbatical."

"Just a friend." Lester rubbed quickly at the four-inch ornate lettering on his left bicep.

"Girlfriend?"

"No."

"Boyfriend?"

Lester turned to Daniel, unsmiling. "I don't know any guys with boyfriends."

Daniel lasered him back: "Guess you haven't been to Houston in a while."

Lester started to speak when Melanie interrupted, "You're very fair, aren't you, Lester? I guess you must be worried about skin cancer. I should be, but I'm not for some reason." Melanie smiled and idly pulled a strand of blonde hair from her mouth. "You're in terrific shape. Where do you work out?"

Lester wished they'd get off this whereabouts inquest. "Just… the gym."

Daniel was off again. "Which one? World? Bally? Gold's?" He peered at Lester and slowly began nodding his head. "Wait a minute, hold the phone. Now that I really get a good look at you, it totally makes sense."

Busted. Lester could see the Rockport city limit sign up ahead. At least it wouldn't be that much farther to walk.

Daniel giggled, "You know what you are?"

Lester nodded and grimaced at the sign. "Most of the time."

"You're a 'Y' boy! Am I right?"

Lester turned to Daniel, baffled. "A what?"

"A 'Y-guy.' You work out at the YMCA, right?" Lester barely moved his head.

"I knew it! I'm always right about this stuff. You *so* have the look."

"Look?"

"Yeah. White, daddy, suburban, two kids, khaki Dockers, stock portfolio, racquetball goggles. Where's your Beemer? Pop a fan belt back down the road?"

Lester looked bewildered. "Uh-huh."

Daniel snickered, pleased with himself. He and Melanie glanced at each other and burst out laughing. Melanie leaned forward, "You know, we almost didn't stop and pick you up. We thought you might be an ex-con or something."

Lester grinned back.

***

Stepping out of the Exxon restroom, Lester pulled his pants legs over his boots and stuffed his T-shirt in. Melanie had thoughtfully stopped at the gas station so he could change into his only other pair of pants, the bottom half of a dark-gray polyester suit. As Lester approached the car, Daniel threw his blue jeans at him.

"What's this for?" Lester asked.

Daniel looked bored. "She thinks I should give them back to you."

Melanie smiled, "It was just a game. He wasn't really going to keep your pants."

Daniel didn't look so convinced. "Yeah, a game—Pop Goes the Weasel."

Lester put the pants back in his duffel bag. "Well, thanks for the lift. Maybe I'll see you around."

Melanie looked surprised. "Don't you want a ride to where you're going?"

"Actually…I'm not real sure where I'm going."

"What do you mean?"

"Well, I'm here to meet someone I've never met before. All I know is her name. Her address is a post office box."

Melanie shook her head. "I don't understand."

"Thanks again."

Opening the car door quickly, Melanie jumped out and hurried to Lester. "Wait a sec. You're going to be here a while, right? Maybe you can come out to our place. We're having a barbecue this weekend."

Lester, suddenly shy, stared down the street. "I don't know. I'm kinda…Maybe. We'll see…"

Daniel slid down in the car seat and stuck a bare leg out the window. "Say yes, Lester. She's not going to let go of your shirt till you do."

Lester looked down to see Melanie slowly twisting the material just below his navel. He coughed, clearing his throat. "Yeah, OK."

Melanie released his shirt, and the knot unwound. "So, who is this special someone? Maybe I've heard of her."

"Her name's Laurel Jeanette. Laurel Jeanette Yancey."

Daniel suddenly sat up in his seat, slapping his forehead. "Laurel Jeanette Yancey? Are you shitting me?"

Melanie rolled her eyes. "Stop it, Danny."

"I know Laurel Jeanette! My God, why didn't you say something? Isn't she that chesty redhead that drives the sanitation truck every Wednesday and Friday on our street? Oh, she's…*distinct*."

Melanie tried not to smile. "He's not really my brother. He just plays one to please my parents."

Lester nodded. "That's OK. I'm not a Y-Guy either." He turned to Daniel, smiling. "You got it partially right, though. I just left four years of prison behind yesterday. Thanks for the ride. You can find me at the homeless shelter if you're looking." Lester picked up his duffel bag and started walking across the street. Melanie and Daniel stared at him. Their expressions shared an uncanny likeness to that of a crocodile having just had its jaw broken from the swift kick of a departing zebra.

Lester walked around downtown, what there was of it, and tried putting the encounter with Melanie and Daniel out of his mind. Maybe he was out of practice. Maybe he was still too naïve. Or maybe they were just too slick. Whatever it was, it left him jumpy and moody. They had it way too easy, Lester thought. That easy seductiveness, the arrogance and certitude money bestows. Of course, he knew either one of them could be had, no question. But that was just as troubling. He was pretty close to wanting exactly what they were selling.

Crossing the street from the H-E-B grocery store, Lester made his way over to the post office. The small Gulf Coast community had a quiet, unassuming feel to it—families with kids in wet swimsuits being hauled about, old couples walking Pomeranians, amateur artists displaying amateur paintings of seagulls and native, windswept live oaks in every storefront window. Judging from the preponderance of seashell wind chimes and Texas flag geegaws for sale, these were the number one summer keepsakes to haul home from the Coast. Everything seemed slow, simple, and sedate. Perfect for a recovering felon.

In the post office, Lester stood in line behind a young Mexican American mother holding an infant. A full head of jet-black hair and two tiny onyx eyes protruded from a blanket over the mother's shoulder. The baby was so small and fragile, it seemed to Lester it could've been born that morning. An impassive little Buddha from space. Lester wondered if he'd ever have children. Was there any need? Did the world necessitate his offspring, or was it just another scam to keep the social security roles filled? The relentless desire-to-procreate gene seemed not to have been deposited in Lester's amalgamation. After his own melancholy childhood, he figured fatherhood was best left to egotists and homesteaders.

Stepping forth in line, he faced a pleasant-looking, middle-aged woman with the name Mirtie pinned on her blouse. "Can I help you?"

"Yes, ma'am, I'm looking to find the address of one of your box holders."

"A box holder?"

"Yes, ma'am."

"You mean you want to know where they live?"

"Yes, ma'am."

"Well, we can't do that." The large female clerk standing next to her stopped counting postcards and looked up.

Lester continued, "Well, we've been corresponding for almost four years now, and I'm just trying to make contact is all." Lester pulled out the neatly wrapped bundle of 315 letters tied with a shoelace and held them up. The two women stared at the collection of envelopes suspiciously.

The clerk with the postcards spoke up. "Have you tried the telephone, hon?"

Lester nodded. "She doesn't have a phone."

The women looked at each other. Finally, Mirtie held out her hand. "May I see one of those envelopes?" Lester handed her the bundle, and she stared at the return addresses. Her coworker came over to gawk as well.

"They're all from here. You can see from the postmark."

The women shared another look, and Mirtie handed the letters back. "Why don't you try writing this box number a postcard and tell them you're in town?"

Lester looked appalled. "No! It's supposed to be a surprise. I've been planning this for a long time. Listen, can you just tell me if you recognize this face?" Lester dug into his bag again and pulled out a fake leather wallet the chaplain at Diboll had given him on his last birthday. In it was the only picture of Laurel Jeanette he had. After two years of constant pleading, she finally gave in and sent him a 2×2 color photo that showed her in a sleeveless dress with a snowy winter background, courtesy of the Walmart photography studios. He loved it dearly. Lester thought she looked a little like Pamela Sue Martin from *Dynasty.*

The women stared at the picture at length. The postcard clerk then turned abruptly and went back to serving another customer. Mirtie smiled somewhat embarrassed. "I'm sorry. It's against postal regulations." Lester stared crestfallen. He started to turn slowly. *Regulations? What damn regulations? I've had nothing but REGULA-TIONS up my ass for the past four and a half years. Does she think I've come all this way to be put off by some lame-ass postal regulation?* Lester suddenly turned back to the clerk, but she'd already put up a next window sign and exited. Provoked, he stuffed the letters and his wallet back into the bag and left the building.

Outside on the lawn, Lester kicked at a petrified dog turd and began walking toward the park by the bay. He needed time to think. What now? Something would come to him; it always did.

As he was about to cross the street, he heard a sharp "psssst!" emerge from a row of parked cars behind him. He turned to see Mirtie stooped down between a van and a camper in the Burger King parking lot. She was motioning him toward her. Lester scanned the boulevard for traffic and ran across the street.

Mirtie pulled his head down so as not to be visible. "Listen, I got no business doing this, but I figure if I'm off post office property, it's none of their concern." She then pointed down the street. "Walk six blocks that way, and make a right. They may be able to help you."

"Thanks. What's there?"

"A church."

Lester felt his neck muscles tighten.

"That's all I'm going to say. You just head on down there and keep your eyes open. You'll understand when you see it. How long were you in for, son?"

Lester pulled back, startled. "In where?"

Mirtie smiled. "It's OK, shug. They gave the same gym bag and polyester gray suit pants to my boy when he got out of the Ramsey Unit. I swear, you kids spend more time in jail nowadays than you do anywhere else. I don't know what's happened to you all. Must be the drugs."

Lester shook his head. "I don't do drugs."

"No, course not. None of you do. Well, go on and good luck."

Lester took her hand. "Thank you, ma'am. I appreciate it."

Mirtie called as he was about to walk off: "Hey! You need any money? Have you eaten?"

Lester smiled. "Yes ma'am, I'm all right."

She suddenly reached over and stuffed a bill in his pants pocket. "Here's five dollars. Get yourself a hamburger, and don't buy any beer with it. And if you ever run across a tall, sandy-haired fellow named Darryl Schuhart, tell him..." Her voice faltered to a whisper, and she looked away. "Tell him...his mother loves him." She then turned and crouched back to the end of the camper, walking off. Lester idly scooted a cigarette butt with his boot. God's little helpers. You never knew, just never knew when they might turn up.

Lester stopped long enough in a convenience store to buy a Coke, two bags of peanuts, and a gigantic turkey leg sitting in a hot box next to the register. The two breakfast burritos he'd eaten at the Circle K in Goliad were long gone. He'd ravished that bird leg like they were sharing a honeymoon. Nothing in prison came close to being that immediately satisfying. That was the thing about freedom: *gratification!* The only gratifying thing about prison was that the freaks inside would still be there when you finally got out.

Lester turned the block, wiping his hands on the paper sack from the store. He tossed the bones and Coke can into a street drain. Replenished, he saw the whitewashed Episcopal church down the street and smiled. It looked nothing like his granddaddy's barn, and that was a great relief. Lester felt no great love in his heart for most churches, and the sooner he could find out what he was there for, the sooner he'd be on his way.

Standing on the front walkway, he saw no signs of life about. The building was a one-story affair with shingle siding and an aluminum steeple inadvertently tacked on. Texas-generic, Gulf Coast standard-issue, lower-end, pious architecture, except for the grounds. As Lester looked around, he could see that someone had a pretty remarkable green thumb. The lawn and beds were as groomed and laden with flowers and shrubs as any plant nursery he'd ever seen.

Lester pulled on the front door. Locked. He walked around the building. Every door locked. Not a car in the lot. Sitting on the curb in front of the church, he opened his last bag of peanuts. "Laurel Jeanette, you're not making this easy. If you want me to find you, give me a little help, darlin.'" Lester wolfed down the salty nuts in about three bites and pondered his next move. He was thirsty. He looked around for a garden hose and spotted one off to the other side of the building. Walking in that direction, he noticed for the first time the church sign framed on three sides by azalea bushes:

St. Michael's and All Angels Episcopal Church, 8:00 a.m.

Rite One Holy Eucharist, 9:30 a.m.

Adult, Youth, and Children's Sunday School, 10:30 a.m.

Rite Two Holy Eucharist and Children's Chapel with prayers for healing immediately following the service, 6:30 p.m.

Contemporary Service Worship theme: "Does Jesus know your e-mail address? He's online and ready to chat."

Lester smiled. He started to read again, and then he froze. A chill in his leg had run up his spine and numbed his lips. He blinked and squatted down to touch the glass pane. Silently he thanked Laurel Jeanette as he read again:

Sunday's service delivered by the Reverend Philip... *Yancey.*

chapter

TWO

"Father Phil? Yeah, lives up on Agarita Street. Big old, light green house with a porch running round it. You a friend of his?"

Lester looked at the elderly black man hosing off the drive in front of the gas pumps at the Chevron station. "No. I just...I think he knows a friend of mine."

The old man nodded. "Probably so. Old Phil knows about everyone." He slowly twisted the nozzle of the hose till it stopped spraying, and then he peered up at Lester. "You ever see a bullet in a man's leg?"

"No, sir."

The old man pulled up a wet, khaki pant leg and, just over the top of his leather work boot, pointed to an inch-long ridge of nubby flesh. "What you think about that?" But before Lester could formulate a response, the old man interrupted, "Know who give me that?"

"No, sir."

"Course ya don't. Not even a smart fella like you would know a thing like that. And I know you ain't dumb neither 'cause you and I gone to the same finishing school. He grinned. "Ain't I right about that?"

Lester stared at the man, mystified. Did everyone in town know he was an ex-con? Was it stamped in a metal plate on the back of his head?

"Now I got a question for you," he continued. "What finishing school?" The old man cackled, spit, and pulled his pant leg down. "She-yut, Buster Brown, you come walking up here lookin' paler'n Duz detergent, got on them cheap-ass suit drawers they give every bird gets sprung. Hell, I still got mine up the house—got big ole arms from doing nothing but working them iron cousins in the bull pen *gimnasio* all day. But the real deal is you got the look... right here," he said, pointing two fingers at his eyes. "You *stupid-fied*! That's what I call it. Look like you been turned loose in a cat house with your willie on backwards. Hell, you don't know whether to sit or shout, toot or poot! I know! Took me six months on the outside 'fore I got to lookin' like a actual human being myself."

Lester stared at him expressionless. Then he laughed. "You're crazy. You all crazy round here."

The old man smiled broadly, "That's right. Crazy as two owls in a shit house—but then I ain't lost lookin' for no preacher." He pointed to Lester's duffel bag. "And I sure as hell ain't toting around no Department of Corrections satchel like a goddamn billboard for the po-leece to peruse."

Lester looked down at his grip, frowning. Maybe he did stick out like a rat in a rain barrel. What could he do about it?

The old man scratched his jaw and pointed. "Listen, Casper, why don't you go into that crapper over there, change them pants, throw your bag under my desk in the office, and splash some cold water on your face—least ways you won't look like a ghost no more."

Lester nodded, relieved. "I appreciate that. Name's Lester Briggs."

"Otis McCloud."

The two shook hands and Lester motioned to his leg. "So, who did put that souvenir in your leg?"

Otis beamed again. "A preacher done that. Ain't that a terrible thing?"

Lester flinched. "Why?"

"'Cause I killed his sorry ass, that's why!" Otis whooped like a madman. "Sunavabitch got to foolin' round with my woman, so I stuck my pocketknife in his ribs, and damn if the old God fearin' bastard didn't pull out a pistol and shoot me right 'fore he fell down deader than Moses." Otis shook his head. "Some kinda bad-shit world when the 'good' Christians got bigger weapons than you got."

Lester nodded in accord. It was a hell of a note, indeed. "Well, I'm just gonna change and be on my way. It's real good of you to help me out like this, Mr. McCloud."

"Otis. Nobody call me Mr. McCloud 'cept my parole officer, and she got her pointy head so high up her butt, she tell everybody I'm her African American proviso. Do I look like some African pro-vee-so kinda shit to you? Hell, I ain't hardly been out of Texas. Only thing I know 'bout Africa is Tarzan and that seven-foot mutha for the Houston Rockets, Hakeem Olaju-who-who. Sunavabitch can play ball, cain't he?"

"Yes, sir." Lester stood there smiling. He was torn between leaving and just shootin' the shit all afternoon with Otis. He got a kick out of the old man.

"Well, go on. You don't need to be wasting your time around here with a no-count like me. I'll watch your valuables, go on."

Lester nodded and walked towards the men's room. Inside the dark and tiny vestibule, he gazed into the cracked mirror over the sink and examined himself. He was sallow looking and disheveled, and Lord knows a twelve-dollar, strip-mall haircut wouldn't have hampered his confidence any, but—hell with it. It wasn't about *appearances* between him and Laurel Jeanette. Theirs was a relationship based on *consequential* things. He smiled at his reflection: "It ain't the clothes and the haircut. That's the ad, not the car." Wetting his face and hair with water, he rubbed his cheeks till they stung and combed his black strands into a shiny, respectable do. He then put on his plaid, cotton shirt, shook out his jeans, and scrubbed his mouth with warm water and an index finger. Best he could do. He was certainly no show pony at this point, but no hound dog either. He felt reasonably assured he'd make an agreeable impression.

Stepping outside the men's room, Lester saw Otis cleaning the front windows of the station with a squeegee. Otis winked, "Sa-a-ay, now that's an improvement. You don't look like you been sleeping down the morgue no more."

Lester grinned. "Which way's Agarita Street?"

"Walk up this road here 'bout a quarter mile, make a left on Hackberry, go two blocks, and you're there. It's on the right—light-green house with a porch running round it."

Lester watched as Otis sloshed his squeegee in the mop bucket. "So tell me why you never got that bullet taken out of your leg?"

Otis straightened up, spit, and wiped his brow with a sleeve. "'Cause maybe…maybe that's just the place God wants it to lay." Lester waited for Otis to offer more explanation, but instead he went right back to scrubbing the window.

Lester pondered Otis' reply, then shook his head and stepped off towards the street. Otis called to him, "Hey, Casper! Hope you find what you come for. If it ain't here, maybe you ain't lookin' hard enough!" He hooted loudly and Lester waved, continuing on.

Lester waited for the light at the intersection. *People are damn funny. Here this SOB kills a preacher for practically nothing, and yet he'd probably give you his last wedge of Bit-O-Honey if he heard your stomach rumbling. People are damn funny.*

Lester walked under the spooky live oaks that lined the road, which grew sideways from the constant Gulf winds bending them over. It was an unusual phenomenon that Lester found entirely appropriate to the nature of this small, eccentric town. Rockport revolved in its own singular orbit. Funk, charm, and some real oddball-ness tied up with oleander, seagull shit, and fishnet. That it pulled itself together without becoming a freak show of country-cute, potpourri hell was no small achievement. Considering most city-bred people's mania for turning everything real into *insta-quaint*, Lester figured Rockport had beat the devil. For now.

The position of the sun told him it was somewhere between four and five in the afternoon. Lester hadn't worn a watch since that first day at Diboll. Time was solely a matter of expansive conjecture for an inmate. Could be morning, could be afternoon. You ate, you slept, you stood at a machine press in the license shop. What did it matter what time it was? Time was a free man's obsession. A prisoner didn't give a shit. All you cared about was your release date.

Lester began whistling, a simple thing he couldn't remember attempting for a long, long time. It was beautiful to be out in the fresh air, to look up and see sky and clouds and birds. He was so grateful, a little ball of sadness formed in his throat. Never again. Never again would he be the "guest" of any correctional institution anywhere, anytime. Of that he was certain.

Turning onto Hackberry Street, Lester started getting anxious. *This preacher's got to know of Laurel Jeanette. How many Yanceys can there be in a town this size? Maybe she's his daughter, or maybe they're cousins.* He stopped and absently snatched a few leaves from a nearby photinia bush. *God, if she's there, please don't let me be clumsy or stupid. Work with me on this. How 'bout it?*

God was his usual taciturn self. Lester could feel his palms getting wet, his mouth going dry. His head started to ache, so he sat down on the curb, taking several deep breaths. *What's the worst that could happen? She'd refuse to see you? Never. Find you repulsive? Hell, she's seen my picture. She's met somebody else?* Lester held his breath. The thought hadn't occurred to him till now. *I'll kill the bastard!* He stood quickly. His mind was playing games with him.

Did it all the time in prison. *Let it go. That's old shit. Let it go, Lester!*

From the street corner he could see the pale green house with the wraparound porch. Just like the church, it too was profuse with greenery and plants and vegetation, the likes of which Lester had never seen. It was as if a piece of Eden had fallen down along this scruffy side of the Gulf of Mexico, and the angels just decided to leave it there. "Let the locals get a whiff of paradise," they'd said. "Won't hurt 'em to see what they're missing."

He could see a white, four-door Chevrolet parked in the drive. Some kind of grass wreath was attached to the mailbox pole (a wreath, in August?). Birdbaths and fountains and wind chimes and little rock sculptures were scattered about like way stations for elves and fairies. Fantasyland! That's what it was. Lester made his way up the walk, slowly taking in each new sighting with the thrill of a kid. It was as if his eyes were being exercised after a long, monotonous slumber. Here was a small pond with huge goldfish skimming the surface, there a birdcage hanging in a magnolia tree with half a dozen yellow finches skittering about. A rope hammock, a sundial, an enormous silver gazing ball perched on a marble pedestal. It seemed to Lester the most peaceful, amiable place he'd ever been.

From inside the screen door on the front porch, he could hear classical music. Someone appeared to be cooking. He heard the sound of running water and pots and pans dully clanking. The smell of something frying wafted from the kitchen window as Lester reached for the front doorbell. Fried chicken, shrimp— and hush puppies? It *was* hush puppies! Real cornmeal, chopped onion, and fried-in-bacon-grease hush puppies. How long had it been? The house, the yard, the smells. It was if he were coming home to a home he'd never had.

As soon as he'd taken his hand off the bell, a man appeared at the end of the hall and stared at Lester. He held a cup towel and appeared to be drying a plate. "Can I help you?" The man didn't move.

Lester cleared his throat. "Yes, sir. I'm trying to locate someone I'm hoping you might know?"

"Who you looking for?"

"Name's Laurel Jeanette—Laurel Jeanette Yancey."

The man stopped wiping the plate. Lester couldn't make out if he was perturbed, interested, or just plain listless. From the shadows of the hall, Lester could see they were about the same height.

Lester spoke again: "You wouldn't happen to know where I might find her, would ya?" The man didn't speak, didn't move, didn't appear to breathe even. Lester rubbed his knuckle against the doorframe and chuckled softly. "Sorry to bother you like this. I saw your sign down in front of the Episcopal church. Just figured ya'll having the same last names, you might be related or something. Maybe a daughter or sister..." Lester paused for a second and then laughed again nervously. "I sure hope she's not your *wife!*" The man flinched imperceptibly, and Lester suddenly lifted his hand from the door. In a sickening flash, it banged him upside the head like an errant Frisbee. Jesus God, Laurel Jeanette was this man's wife!

Lester abruptly stepped back from the entry as if it were on fire. The spit in his mouth vanished, and he croaked, "E...Excuse me." Turning, he stumbled into an enormous potted fern perched atop a pedestal. It flipped and clattered onto the floor like a sack of walnuts. Stooping to restore plant, gravel, and peat moss into some form of coherence, he glanced up to see the man standing behind the screen door. "I don't think it's broke. Sorry to have bothered you." Lester kicked the last clump of dirt off the porch and jumped down the steps, running.

"Wait." But Lester didn't turn. He wanted to get as far away from Agarita Street as his worn-out boots could truck him. "Wait! I might be able to help." Lester slowly eased his flight and came to a halt in front of the mailbox on the curb. He warily turned back to see the man now standing on his front porch. Under one arm he'd stuck the plate, and in the other he held the cup towel wound in a ball. He looked older than Lester, maybe eight, ten years. At first glance, he appeared nonthreatening enough. A nice-looking sort. He reminded Lester of one of those smooth TV game-show hosts: clean-cut, wavy hair, dimples, good teeth.

Hesitant, Lester spoke, "Y...you know her?"

The man nodded. "Come on back."

Lester felt suddenly ridiculous. What was he? An adult or some thirteen-year-old clown? He idly poked his boot toe in a pile of pea gravel by the walk. "You look like you're fixing dinner. I...I can come by later."

"I won't be eating for a while."

Lester stood motionless. Something made him uneasy. Finally the man opened the screen door and motioned him inside: "I may have an address for Laurel somewhere. Would you like to come in?"

Lester exhaled and stared off down the street. "Yeah...OK." The garden had somehow become less appealing during his second trip to the door. Why had he not noticed the crumbling barbecue pit, the overgrown ivy choking the life out of several hackberry trees, the rusted lawn furniture? He stopped on the steps beneath where the man stood facing him and stuck a hand out. "Lester Briggs."

For a moment the man seemed to hesitate, and then he took Lester's hand anxiously. "Philip Yancey."

"You're the pastor, right?"

"That's right." He stared at Lester for a moment and then laughed nervously. "I'm sorry. You caught me by surprise here. I wasn't...I wasn't expecting anybody."

"I shoulda called. I didn't know how to reach you. I hope I didn't ruin your plant here."

"No, no! It's..." Philip hastily stroked the fern leaves. "They're pretty indestructible long as you don't overwater. Hate wet feet. Like a rosebush. Do you garden?"

Lester looked at him oddly. "No."

He nodded. "Well...come on in." Philip held the door open for Lester. It was the first private home Lester'd entered in over four years. He instantly surveyed the cut-glass chandelier hanging over his head, the carved grandfather clock down the hall, the marble fireplace, the high-back leather chairs in the living room, the elaborate paintings of flowers and dogs and horses—he was awestruck by the refinement of it all. People really do live like this, he thought to himself. Unexpectedly, a well fed, inquisitive Golden Retriever came padding down the hall toward him.

"That's Windsor; he won't bite. He'll just sniff you to death." And sure enough Windsor made a round-robin of Lester's entire person with meticulous proficiency.

Lester scratched behind Windsor's ears. Then he glanced up at Philip. "You have…a beautiful place. Really do."

"It was my mother and father's house. When they died, I took it over."

Lester's eyes darted around the hallway as he peeked into each room. It felt as if he were walking through the pages of a book filled with fantasy pictures. "So much stuff. Where did you buy all this?"

Philip laughed, "I couldn't afford this on my salary. Dad was a lawyer; Mom was the collector—Persian carpets, Chinese porcelains, Japanese enamels, French *om-peer* bibelots."

Lester shook his head. "I don't know what any of that is, but it sure makes you feel like you're inside a department store at Christmas."

Philip watched as Lester continued scanning the interior. "Would you like something to drink?"

"Drink?"

"Coke, tea…beer?"

Lester smiled. "I didn't think preachers drank beer."

"How many Episcopalians do you know?" Philip smiled. "It's not against the law to have it in the house, is it? Preachers get a lot of visitors, and sometimes people want something other than tea."

Lester eyed him, unconvinced. "Sure, OK."

"Come on back to the kitchen. I'll see if I can find that number." Philip walked down the hall while Lester continued exploring his surroundings. He picked up an ostrich egg cradled in a small easel on a table. He shook it, sniffed it, and sat it back in its stand. Opening a music box, he smiled as a miniature, dancing bear revolved to a classical tune. So much…*stuff*! It worried Lester just having to keep track of it all.

"I've got Lite and I've got regular," Philip said, standing at the end of the hallway holding up two beers.

"Uh…Actually, I probably should pass. I haven't been drinking much lately. My stomach's been a little upset."

Philip looked concerned. "Is it serious?"

"No, no. It's just that I haven't had beer in a while. I used to drink a lot, maybe too much, ya know? I'd better pass, but thanks."

Philip nodded. "No problem." Returning to the kitchen, he called out: "I've got some sun tea with a little mint in it. That ought to fix you up."

Lester made his way down the hall toward the kitchen. "Listen, I don't want to take up much of your time. If you've got that number, I'd appreciate..." When he reached the kitchen, his mouth dropped. He'd never seen anything quite like it. It was *Better Homes and Gardens* on growth hormones. Never had he seen so many pots and pans, appliances, enormous ranges, double-wide stainless refrigerators (two), cutting boards, butcher blocks, hanging knives, sinks (four), canisters, cookie jars, stocked pantries, an ice machine, and food! There were baskets of fruit: apples, lemons, limes, figs, pears, and bananas. A ham hung from an overhead hook as well as salami, bologna, and some kind of cheese on a rope. He saw cakes, pies, cookies, bread, and noodles strung on a rack. There were jars of olives, strands of garlic, bowls of tomatoes, corn, broccoli, cabbage, and asparagus, and, sure enough, an enormous plate of hush puppies arrayed on paper towels like some still life of normalcy.

"Cooking's my hobby," Philip smiled.

Lester stared glassy-eyed at the hush puppies. "No shit—'cuse me."

Handing Lester a glass of tea, Philip motioned to the plate. "Would you like to try one?"

Lester hesitated a half second. "Well...I don't want to eat your dinner or nothing." Philip lifted the platter, and Lester politely took two of the still-warm fritters. Barely stopping to chew the first one, he drew breath, knocked back some tea, and eagerly devoured the second. "Man, you don't know...how fine these...truly are. I haven't had anything this good in years."

"Why's that?" Philip queried.

Lester stopped chewing, wiped his mouth on his sleeve, and shrugged. "Just because. I appreciate all your hospitality and everything. You think you might know where Laurel's number is?"

Philip peered into Lester's eyes, probing for some further explication. Then he turned toward a small desk in the corner. "Sure, sure…Let me look in this drawer over here. I'll have to do a little digging." He turned on a small lamp, put on his glasses, and began shuffling through a pile of papers. Lester couldn't help himself; he reached over and filched another hush puppy. Philip spoke without looking up: "Help yourself to more of those if you like. I'm making a bunch to bring to the church later on."

Lester swallowed and said in a garbled mumble, "'ank 'ou."

"I don't know if I kept it…her number."

"Is she kinfolk?"

"Distantly. She was here for a while then left not too long ago."

"Where'd she go?"

Philip shrugged. "Dunno. She's her own girl, that one. We go years with hardly a word sometimes." Philip sighed and removed his glasses. "Nope, it's not here. I thought I'd saved it, but it's gone."

Lester looked stricken. "You're sure?"

"I'm sorry—are ya'll…good friends?"

"More'n that," Lester said. He stared at the floor, crestfallen. "Lot more. Well, thank you for lookin'. If you should hear from her, tell her Lester came by. You've got a real nice place here."

"I'm sorry I couldn't be more helpful."

Lester nodded. "So long." He turned and walked back into the hallway. About halfway down the corridor, he saw something out of the corner of his eye. Perched in a tiny frame on a bookshelf was the exact same picture of Laurel Jeanette he had in his wallet. Standing next to it was a photograph of Philip. Lester froze. "She give you that?"

Philip saw the picture and immediately reached for it. "Yes, yes she did. I'd forgotten about that. Nice picture, isn't it?" Lester took the photograph from him, gazing at Laurel's image. He spoke in a soft, clear voice. "She's the only person I've ever known who really *knows* me. All my problems, hang-ups, fears…dreams. I could tell her anything. I could be exactly me. Not some liar or fake. How many people can say they've met their highest good?"

He handed the photograph back, turned, and walked toward the entry. Stopping at the screen door, he mumbled a faint "bye" and then hurried outside.

Philip shouted to him just as he reached the street, "How can I get in touch with you...if she calls?"

Lester called back over his shoulder, "I'll be around," and then he vanished behind a neighbor's dense green hedge of ligustrum. Philip, staring down the empty street, lowered himself into a wicker chair by the door. His heart was beating so fast he thought for a moment he might pass out. He put his head in his hands and rubbed his throbbing temples.

***

Just how long he'd been sitting there, he wasn't sure. The sun had nearly set, and the hint of a cooler Gulf breeze had drifted down Agarita Street, ruffling the collar of his blue cotton shirt. The evening grackles had returned to the live oaks rooted in the yard and were now noisily preparing their twilight repose. Windsor was asleep on the porch landing, twitching his nose at some pestering gnat.

Philip's body had gone completely slack. He felt drugged, lethargic—comatose. What had just happened? He tried piecing it together in his head again: the doorbell, turning off the stove, the body behind the screen, edging closer, confusion, and then seeing...*him.* It was like some preposterous dream. Did it really just happen? Here. He was *here?* Philip exhaled deeply. The tension in his forehead had eased somewhat. What in God's name would he do now?

The VW van pulled into the drive clunking, sputtering, and whirring like some industrial revolution diorama. Seven o'clock. Entire railroad schedules could be platted around the arrival time of that van in the driveway each evening. The occupant of the vehicle would automatically get out, stretch, and stroll over to the side with the sliding door and immediately begin unloading multiple canvas bags filled with paints, brushes, smocks, and drawing paper. Windsor would amble forth to welcome the returning wayfarer, who asked the same invariable question, "Hi, Win, ya miss me?"

Turning to trudge up the walk, lugging the unwieldy bags, and dodging Windsor's tenacious scent patrol, the arriving personage would then stop at the top of the steps, sigh, and announce—

"What are you holding my picture for?"

Philip, stirring ever so slightly, emerged from his interior labyrinth. "What?"

"My picture, you're holding my picture?"

He looked at his hands. Indeed he was still holding the small, framed portrait Lester had handed him. "I...I was just...looking to see how much you favor...Mother..." His voice had faded off. "More and more."

"Well, that's odd, isn't it? I am her daughter. Are you OK?"

Philip nodded.

"What's for dinner? I'm starved." Luz Yancey opened the screen door and walked in, Windsor following at her heels. She dropped her bags in a heap and began rifling through the mail in a straw basket on the hall table. "Bills, bills, bills. No love letters today, Winster. Come on, boy. Have you had your supper yet?" Luz disappeared down the hall into the kitchen, humming.

Philip, with great effort, stood from the chair and walked slowly to one of the porch columns. Leaning against it, he tried to stifle the welling that was now blurring his vision. Nervously he rubbed his eyes and stared into the paling twilight. "Welcome home, Lester Briggs."

chapter

THREE

"I don't like what you're wearing." Yvonne Wheelwright looked up from her morning paper and squinted at her daughter's ensemble.

Melanie Wheelwright replied apathetically, "Oh Mother, I hate for you to be uncomfortable with my fashion choices. I guess the good news is, you don't have to wear it!" She grabbed an orange from a bowl and headed for the front door.

"Where are you going—*like that?*" Strikingly pretty, nothing about Yvonne was incidental. From the coiffed, highlighted tresses, the tasteful gold hoop earrings, and the filigree Bvlgari necklace to the burnished plum nails, crisp linen shirt, suede leather belt, beige silk slacks, and Ferragamo loafers, she had the overall appearance of an indestructible Gucci saddlebag.

Melanie turned, glaring: "Where do most people go in a swimsuit? The beach, the pool—High Mass? I'm going to get some sun on the dock."

"I think some men are down there working on the boat."

"And your not-so-vague inference?"

Yvonne dropped her paper and stood. "In case you weren't looking, save for three strips of colored cotton, you're practically naked, dear. This is small-town Texas, not Ibiza."

"Would it make you feel better if I went upstairs and put on my Annie Oakley vest?"

Yvonne smiled serenely. "You know what I'm driving at."

"Yes, in your Sherman Tank way. Let's see, 'We must avoid at all costs any possible indiscretions on Melanie's behalf with the local riffraff.' At least until she's pawned off to her New York investment banker. Then she can screw whoever she likes."

Yvonne crossed her arms. "Is this the part where I gnash my teeth and rend garments over your contemptuousness? It's your life, sugarplum; you have every right in the world to screw it up." She handed Melanie a beach towel. "But not on my dime. As long as you're in *my* house, eating *my* food, sleeping on *my* fine white linens, you'll behave like a proper guest and do as your hostess requests."

Melanie stared at her mother, barely containing her ire. "You really hate that you can't run my life anymore. You know, your little rules and social blueprints died the day Amy Vanderbilt jumped off her penthouse. This is going to shock you, Mother, but I have my own life, my own career, and my *own* money. Maybe I should just get a room down at the Cactus Motel. They're a lot less particular about who sleeps on their fine sheets. Maybe I'll just discuss it with Daddy, see what *he* thinks?" Melanie exited, the screen door slamming hard behind her. Yvonne stared after her daughter, a look of distress marring her mostly faultless features.

Daniel entered the room wearing silk pajama bottoms and an undershirt. He yawned and then smiled. "Did I miss another heartfelt mother-daughter moment?"

Yvonne was silent. She saw Melanie waving to one of the workers mowing the lawn.

"It's obscene watching people squander potential," Yvonne said. "They beat it away like flailing at a piñata. My God, lift the blindfold—you could have it all!"

"And that would be called *cheating*, Mother." Daniel poured some milk into a bowl of Cheerios and scratched himself. "I need a banana."

Yvonne turned from the door. "They all went bad."

Daniel shrugged. "Story of my life." He moved to a chair in the living room and propped up his feet. Yvonne sat across from him, scowling. He glanced at her and then mumbled with his mouth full, "Wha?"

"What time did you get in last night?"

He stopped chewing. "What do you mean? I'm still at the disco, swinging from the silver ball."

"What lucky parents we are to have such witty children."

"Hey, it could've been worse. What if I'd been straight?"

"Or a genius? What if, what if..."

Daniel shrugged. "You're the one that was on painkillers when you were pregnant with me. You're lucky you didn't give birth to Phyllis Diller."

"Without those painkillers, sweetheart, you'd have ended up with Phyllis Diller for a mother. If you must know, they were Seconals, and I'd kill for one right now."

Daniel stopped chewing again and put his spoon down. "Are you depressed about something?"

"Damn right. I'm a mother! Your sister's this close to actually settling down with a highly suitable mate, and she's running around here acting like Jennifer Lopez in heat. Her fiancé's a prince, but no man puts up with that kind of outlandish behavior for long."

"Excuse me, but how is Brian—who's in New York as far as we know—supposed to establish what Melanie's doing down here anyway?"

Yvonne scrutinized a stray thread on the cashmere sofa throw.

"Mother, are you...? You're not talking to Brian are you?"

Yvonne folded the throw carefully and placed it over the arm of the couch. "He's practically my son-in-law. And spare me the outrage; on you it looks like bad irony. I haven't told him anything damaging. I'm not totally remiss. But I will not facilitate in another hapless marriage of cynicism, prevarication, and provocation."

Daniel held his spoon aloft. "Whose marriage are we talking about?"

"Mine!"

"What cynicism and prevarication?—tell, tell!"

Yvonne stroked her chin impatiently. "All I'll say is this: there were certain things about your father that were deliberately kept from me. I won't let it happen to someone else."

Daniel sat his bowl and spoon down and moved to Yvonne's side. "Mother, you can speak freely and without embarrassment. It'll be our secret."

Yvonne looked at him, surprised.

"Daddy's small for his size, isn't he? I know, I've seen."

Yvonne was indignant: "There is nothing wrong with your father's dimensions!"

"O-K."

"What are you anyway? Some magnitude freak?"

"Interesting way of putting it."

"Honestly, I don't understand this gay male obsession with proportions. You think all that matters is *size*."

"It's not...*everything.*"

"What about love and fidelity, loyalty and nurturing?"

"That's why we have pets."

Standing now, Yvonne turned to leave. "I'm not having this conversation. You're too flippant about something I consider very sacred."

"But back to Daddy—"

"*Finito!*" she interrupted. "Your sister's throwing her life away with a shovel and a thong bikini, and all you want is to talk about bulk. What did I do to deserve these kids?"

"I hesitate to bring up the Seconals."

"Enough!" Yvonne, distraught, turned back to the window.

Daniel went over to her and put his hand on her shoulder. "Mom, Mel's a big girl. She will or she won't; she has or she hasn't. You can't make people dance just 'cause you're holding the CD.

Can't you see she's having her last summer of freedom? She's going to marry Brian."

Yvonne pulled a tissue from the pocket of her slacks and dabbed at her nose. "You think so?"

"No. But if it makes you feel better…"

She swatted Daniel's chest. "I don't guess there's any chance of getting you married?"

"Are you kidding? I'd get married tomorrow! Help me find someone. My youth is melting like wet cotton candy. What about your hairdresser in Dallas? Sebastiano, Septien—What's his name?"

"He's married with five kids."

Daniel shrugged. "I'm not the rigid type. We could work around that."

Yvonne smiled. "I seriously doubt your father would approve."

"Daddy doesn't *approve*, Mother. He *endures*."

Yvonne shook her head and looked up to see Rosa, the Guatemalan housekeeper, carrying a large vase of gladioli into the room. "Rosa, please! I don't want you carrying anything heavy in your condition."

Rosa sat the vase of flowers on a nearby sideboard and beamed. "It's OK. He's not jumping so much today. When he kicks, I sit." Rosa, from all appearances, was nearing the end of her pregnancy. Her stomach was so huge in proportion to her tiny frame, it was hard for Daniel to figure out exactly how she could sit, much less get her arms around that mountain of a middle.

"You're looking all bright-eyed this morning, Rosie. Finally get a good night's sleep?"

"Oh, yes," Rosa giggled. "I had another dream about George Clooney. That man, he puts me crazy!"

Daniel excitedly tucked his legs under himself. "Where did you go this time?" he asked. "Skiing in the Alps, New York, the Academy Awards?"

"He came right here to this house!"

"Stop!"

"He wanted to see where I lived. I made him dinner and afterwards…we went to my room."

Yvonne and Daniel both waited expectantly. Finally Daniel asked, "Where was I? What was I doing? Did he say anything about me?"

Rosa shook her head. "He just said he wanted me to meet his mother one day."

Daniel looked disappointed, and Yvonne shook her head. "Can a person get a migraine in their stomach? 'Cause that's what I'm getting listening to you two. Rosa, have you seen Mr. Wheelwright? He's supposed to be driving me to the chiropractor this morning."

"I think he was down on the boat earlier."

"Oh God, if he starts with the Brasso on those horns again, I'll never get out of here. There's some hamburger in the freezer. If you'll put it in the fridge to thaw, I can throw us together a meat loaf for dinner tonight. Oh, and don't forget to water the banana trees out by the cabana; they're looking a little ragged. *Muchas gracias.*"

Yvonne turned to Daniel and pointed upstairs with her thumb. "You—put some clothes on." She then aimed for the front door and headed down to the dock across the road.

Rosa stared after her, rubbing her stomach. "Why does she always say *muchas gracias* like she's apologizing to me?"

Daniel picked up his cereal bowl. "I think it's her way of making you feel more comfortable."

Rosa looked at him and then moved the flowers to another side of the table.

"She really likes you, you know."

Rosa nodded.

Daniel studied the bowl in his hands. "Have you…made up your mind when you're going to tell her?"

Rosa stood back and studied the flower arrangement. "No."

"Don't you think it should be before the baby's born?"

She answered distantly, "Um-hmm."

"What are you waiting for?"

Rosa picked at a few wilted stems. "I think your father and I should tell her together."

Daniel laughed nervously. "Are you crazy? She'll have a seizure. *He'll* have a seizure."

Rosa turned to face Daniel. "'Mrs. Wheelwright, your husband is the father of my baby, and would you like me to wash your new sweater separately from the stockings?' If you were me, when would be the best time to bring this up?"

Daniel sighed, gazing out the window. "I wish…you'd never told me."

Rosa walked towards him. "No. Your father is very sweet to me, but he doesn't understand. A rich man doesn't have to. You're the only friend I have here. I had to tell someone."

Daniel looked at her sadly. "What a mess. He'll never say anything to my mother. He can't; he's incapable of hurting her. What did you tell your family in Guatemala?"

"I met a man."

"And Mother still thinks he's some roughneck on an offshore drilling rig?"

Rosa nodded, rubbing her stomach again. "Why does she have to know more?"

Daniel frowned. "Rosa, this is my half-sibling you're about to give birth to. This is…*your*—my family! I'm many things, but deceitful I'm not. *You* could tell her, but my father…never. It's like she allows him his proclivities, but she can't stand to face them. Hey, it's not my arrangement, you know. Oh, she'll scream bloody murder and threaten every kind of deadly act, but I'll stand by you. You've just got to do it, Rose. You've got to."

Rosa stared at the dry, withered leaves in her hand and slowly, gently, closed her fingers around them till they crackled and snapped into tiny, dusty pieces.

***

Yvonne stepped onto the dock of the boathouse that her husband Bob had constructed in 1987, the year he finally unloaded all his junk bonds before the market went south in October. To celebrate his lucrative timing, he bought a 60' Chris Craft and built an elaborate New England-style barn and dock to berth his floating fiberglass palace, *El Amor Descolorado*. Tourists driving along

Bay Road frequently stopped and gawked, asking passersby if there were some kind of historical museum inside. It amused Yvonne and, if queried, she frequently answered, "Yeah, I married him."

As she approached the yacht, Yvonne saw Eddie Frye, a tall, brooding, thirty-nine-year-old, beer-joint lothario, hosing the deck and staring with rapt attention toward the bow of the boat. Moving closer, she noticed Melanie lying topless alongside the boat railing. Stopping just behind Eddie, she yelled out, "What are you doing?" Eddie turned frantically, nearly spraying Yvonne in the process.

"I said, what…are…you…*doing?*"

"Hosing the deck! Jesus, Yvonne, you nearly scared me to death."

Yvonne crossed her arms, incensed, "Only because I know you better, Mr. Frye, you keep your eyes off my daughter and on your job. Understand?"

Eddie grinned slyly, twisting the nozzle on the hose. "Looking at an almost-naked person freely showing themselves in public ain't against the law."

Yvonne wanted to slap that smug expression off his face. "Are you trying to deliberately irritate me, Eddie? Do you want to cause trouble? Is that what you want?"

Eddie sighed, squinting into the distance. "I wouldn't necessarily say I'm looking for trouble, Yvonne, but then I ain't overly worried about it finding me neither." He winked at her and went back to hosing the deck. "'Sides, your husband needs me around here. You don't want to make Bob unhappy, do you, Yvonne?"

She stared at him as he calmly splashed water before them. If she despised anyone on the planet, it was this shiftless, obstinate, coarse, immoral travesty of a louse before her. He made her skin crawl. Very few people got to Yvonne the way Eddie Frye did. Very few people ever attempted.

She stepped around him, muttering, "You've been warned." As Yvonne ascended the boat ramp, Eddie looked up to catch a glimpse of her round, still-firm ass retreating into the cabin. He shook his head and wondered why so many bitches like her managed to keep their figures when his own wife was easily three of her put together. He leaned over the side of the dock and blew his nose into the water.

Bob Wheelwright was screwing in the final bracing gear to his new depth sonar as Yvonne stepped onto the bridge. After thirty-two years of faithful observation, she never tired of admiring her husband's robust, masculine features. He was simply the best-looking man she'd ever laid eyes on. From his crinkly, clear blue eyes, ruddy complexion, strong nose and sandy brown-gray hair to his athletic physique, Bob Wheelwright was a walking ad for the good life. His construction firm, Wheelwright Ltd., had been involved in some of the Southwest's most high-profile building projects. Life had indeed been fortuitous.

"Hey, Skipper."

Bob turned, grinning. He was like a kid with his first Tinker-toy set. "Hey yourself, Matey."

"Has it occurred to you that your daughter's lying naked in front of a bunch of prison cowboys?"

Bob looked at her, confused. "You mean Eddie? He's got three kids, a second wife, and back problems. He's harmless."

Yvonne shook her head. "Aren't they all. I don't see how you can be so oblivious to her behavior."

"What behavior?"

Yvonne threw up her hands. "See what I mean?"

Bob looked toward the front of the boat and shook his head. "Honey, she's lying on her stomach reading a book, on her father's boat. Where's the felony?"

"Fine. You two are the team. I have no say in the matter, as usual."

Bob reached out and put his arm around Yvonne's neck, kissing her. "Hey, ease up. She's a beautiful woman, engaged to be married. Let her enjoy her last summer at the bay house."

Yvonne turned back to Bob. "You realize she's the only child we have that will ever feasibly get married?"

Bob stared at her.

"In a *wedding dress*!" Yvonne continued. "I want her to be happy; I want her to have a good life. It's a nightmare of confusing signals out there for young people today. If a person isn't mindful, life sucks them up and deposits them on the wrong side of forty, scratching their heads and wondering where it all went. As her mother, I shouldn't be concerned?"

"Trust her. She's an adult." Yvonne stared into Bob's eyes and leaned against his chest. He stroked her hair. "How come you don't get this wound up over Danny? There's your laundry list of confusing signals."

Yvonne smiled. "Because deep inside that birdbrained head of his lies a mind like NASA Mission Control."

Melanie suddenly appeared at the top of the steps. "Here they are—Rockport's own Rob and Laura Petrie." She pranced before them, delivering a flawless Mary Tyler Moore impersonation: "*Raaaahb*, do you think this outfit's appropriate to wear to dinner with Buddy and Sally?" Bob grinned good-naturedly. Yvonne sighed, tugged at an earring and stared across the harbor.

"Very cute. But your mother's got Mary Tyler Moore beat all to hell in the looks department." Melanie glanced at Yvonne and adjusted the fragile filaments restraining her thong. Bob, appraising her outfit up close, scratched his chin. "You know, sweetheart, that swimsuit might just be a bit much for the local set."

Melanie rolled her eyes in exasperation. "Oh God, not you too. Can't I spend half a morning at my own house enjoying a little solitude without the Moral Majority instigating a lynching?"

Yvonne demurred. "I don't think a lynching is what Eddie has in mind."

"Who's Eddie?"

Yvonne gestured beneath them. "The man who's been spraying the same spot with the garden hose for the past thirty minutes."

Melanie scoffed. "Oh please, Mother. By the time Jethro screws up enough courage to say 'hi,' I'll be a grandmother."

"Yes, it's the *quiet ones* that are usually so reassuring."

Melanie looked at Bob, wide-eyed. "Would you do something with her, please? She's obsessed with me turning into the whore of Babylon."

Yvonne looked indignant. "I never said such a thing,"

"You're acting like it!"

Bob threw his hands up. "OK! I don't want to spend the rest of *my* summer refereeing you two. Mel, would you do your retro parents a favor and put on something slightly more modest?" He then turned to Yvonne. "And would you—short of finding your daughter naked on Main Street—just ignore it?" The two women turned away, simultaneously scowling.

"Great. Now I've got a broken bilge pump to fix."

Yvonne put her hand on his shoulder. "Whoa Captain, you're driving me to Corpus to the chiropractor, and then you're buying a new blazer for the dinner party at the Larrabees' next week, re-member?"

"Oh hell…today?"

Yvonne nodded.

Bob sighed as he reached for his canvas tool bag. "I'm gonna go one more summer with a disintegrating boat and no time to repair it."

"The White House isn't any better maintained than this! Take half a day off; it won't sink."

Bob grumbled as Yvonne whisked the teak shavings from the drilled hole into her palm and deposited them swiftly off the star-board side. Melanie, pulled her hair back and held it tightly in a fist on the back of her neck, She spoke softly, "I'd like to invite someone to the barbecue on Saturday."

"Who?" they both asked at once.

"An ex-con—is that all right?" Melanie smiled.

Yvonne turned to Bob. "You see?"

Bob shook his head. "Fine. Invite your ex-con. We'll just have Rosa follow him around to make sure he doesn't lift any silver-ware."

Yvonne tried again. "Who is this person?"

"Really, does it matter if it's an ex-con or Prince William? He's a friend of mine. I've invited him to come."

"Of course, why even ask? It's all apparently a *fait accompli*."

"Because, Mother dear, I was raised in the school of etiquette that predicates a hostess must be informed of any sudden guest revisions. Otherwise…it's not cricket." Melanie turned and descended the stairs.

Yvonne called to her: "What's his name?"

"Lester."

"Does he have a last name?"

Melanie stopped near the stern and glanced up at Yvonne, smiling. "Boy Toy."

***

After leaving Philip Yancey's, a dismal Lester had wandered around Rockport thoroughly muddled. Where was Laurel Jeanette? Why had she left? What was it about Philip that kept him all jumpy and wary? None of it made sense. For Laurel Jeanette to up and run off like that? No—not likely. Lester was miserable. He'd tasted his first day of freedom and found the whole experience somewhat akin to utter emptiness.

Returning to Otis' gas station well after dark, Lester was surprised to find it closed. After prison, "civilian" hours were difficult for him to grasp. Here Otis had a brand new 24-hour ATM machine installed right beside his front door—and yet, you had to go somewhere else to buy anything. Kinda open, kinda shut. Lester reckoned this was mostly the world's problem at present—couldn't make up its mind.

He stood back and studied the transom over a side door. He figured he could shimmy up the edge, slip in quietly, get his valise, and be on his way. Not a problem. Moving a few old batteries to stand on, Lester pulled himself up through the window and landed carefully inside the unlit storage room. Dark as it was, he could make out a small portal, which he determined must lead to the front office. Quietly opening the door, he started to enter when he felt a sudden, hard compression on his lower back.

"I don't believe I'd take another step, 'less you want a new ass made outta lead."

"It's Lester, Mr. Otis—I came for my bag."

Lester felt the cold nozzle of the rifle lift from his rear. A light was switched on. "Boy, you don't know how close you come to getting your entire backside reconfigured! What the hell you doing breakin' in my enterprise?"

"I just wanted to get my belongings and leave."

"At half past two in the goddamn morning? I oughta call the pleece right now."

Lester turned to face Otis. He was wearing an old undershirt, baggy boxers, and red knit cap on his head. "Don't do that, Mr. Otis. I wasn't going to steal anything, honest."

"Jailbirds all alike. Get that first smell of freedom, and you back to breakin' the law faster than a hog can shit corn."

"You got me wrong, really. I didn't know you were here."

"Course ya didn't! That's why you decided to just come on in and help yourself. Why you think I sleep down here at nights? Ever lowlife in Texas has tried to break into my outfit."

Lester tried changing the mood. "I guess I didn't realize this was such a hot spot for treasures."

Otis snapped back, "That some kinda crack? You don't think I got anything here worth stealing? It'd frost your gizzard if you knew what all I got in here."

"What?"

Otis nodded slowly. "Yeah, you a smart little peckerwood all right. You must think I'm dumb as dirt. I'ma call the pleece; that's what I'm gonna do."

Lester stiffened. "Now, Mr. Otis, you don't want to do that. I told ya I came just to get my bag. Now I'm getting it, and I'm going. And if you try to stop me, I'll hurt ya, so help me I will."

Otis squinted at Lester, then frowned and spit. "Where you been? Out at some roadhouse carrying on?"

"Walking."

"Walking?"

"Helps me to think."

"Shite. You a worse liar than a thief. " Otis spit again, scratching his head. "Where you staying at?"

Lester shrugged. "Hadn't found a place. Guess I was gonna see if there was a church shelter or something."

"Hell, you'll get bedbugs big as tomato seeds at one of them charity holes." Otis mulled the situation momentarily. He spit again. 'Spect you better just bed down here. That way I can keep an eye on ya, and you won't be up all night beatin' off head lice."

Lester looked at Otis, surprised. "You mean that?"

"I don't say nothing I don't mean. Get your duds and come on back here. I got a cot next to the washroom. You can scrub yourself off, and then maybe we'll all get some shut-eye round here."

Lester picked up his bag and followed Otis to the back of the building. Pulling an overhead chain, Otis scooted a small cot out from under a table. "Army surplus. Best damn stretcher tax money can buy." He pulled an old wool blanket out of a grocery bag on the shelf, shook it off, and handed it to Lester. "Probably won't need it, but case you do, here it is. There's a wash towel and a bar of soap in the toilet. Goodnight." Otis started to leave for an adjoining side room. "Oh, and if Mildred gets into bed with you, just scoot her off."

"Mildred?"

"The guard cat. Hadn't caught a mouse in years, but she gives 'em a good workout." Otis shut the door to his quarters.

Lester stared around the anteroom. It was stacked floor-to-ceiling with tires and cases of oil, brake fluid, antifreeze, fan belts, and old inner tubes. It smelled like the world's largest rubber boot. He sat his tote down and began pulling off his T-shirt. Sniffing his pits he was immediately grateful for soap and water. He was grateful for a lot of things—a place to stay, the lady at the post office, Otis, people who pick up hitchhikers...even hush puppies.

He stood naked in front of the tiny lavatory and rubbed himself with a corner of the towel in one hand and an orange bar of Woodbury soap in the other. The smell reminded him of his grandmother's old house, back when he was just a kid and the world was still good and safe. When did it stop feeling trustworthy? He wondered if there was a precise moment when the good fell away and the unknown entered.

He sat the bar of soap down and rinsed himself off with another edge of the towel. Dousing his head under the sink, he rose up to study his reflection in the mirror. His skin was bright pink from the cold water. Gazing intently, he couldn't identify that gleam people used to notice about him. No doubt it had vanished, along with a number of other clever characteristics he'd acquired along the way, right after entering Diboll. Funny, he hadn't noticed their absence till now. Could a person regain his or her goodness? He looked at the initials on his biceps: L and R. He wondered if Little Ray was asleep right now. Was he up pacing like he usually did when he couldn't relax his mind? Who was his new cell mate? Did they get along? Were they…doing it? Lester imagined Little Ray lying next to the new prisoner, arm around his middle, his slow breathing tickling the back of the new roommates neck hairs. He rubbed his eyes and hung the towel on a wooden bar. What could he do about Little Ray now? That part of his life was over. It happened. A lot of things happened in prison. What could he do about it now? He wished him well. Mostly, he wished he didn't think about him as much as he did.

Lester turned off the overhead bulb and lay naked on top of the cot. The room was just right: coolish but not chilly. He yawned, stretched, scratched his balls, then held his cock in his hands. Maybe just a quick wank, something to help him sleep. He started to enjoy himself, letting his mind wander, when something large and hairy pounced on his feet. Lester yelped and jumped off the bed like he'd been shot. Grasping for the pull chain, he yanked on the light to see the fattest, hairiest cat he'd ever seen. Mildred stared back at him with a vaguely bemused expression. Lester took a deep breath. "God almighty—cat you just scared the living Jesus out of me. You can stay long as you don't purr. You purr and you're history." Lester pulled the light chain and lay back down. All thoughts of self-gratification vanished as he waited for his thumping heart to settle back down. Gradually, gently, and soundly, he drifted off to a deep, motionless sleep. Mildred crept her way up to a warm spot between his long legs and purred contentedly for the rest of the night.

chapter

FOUR

"Ain't you pretty!"

Lester squinted, opening one eye and blinking at the shaft of light pouring down on him. For a brief moment, he had no idea who was speaking or where he was.

"I see Miss Mildred kept you all nice and cozy during the night. She quite the social one." Otis chuckled as Lester lifted his head and stared at Mildred perched on his chest, whirring like a sawmill. He shooed her off and tugged at the blanket now wrapped around his middle.

"What time is it?"

"Time to get your hiney outta the sack and get to work."

"Work?"

"You got some other job you need to be at? If you're gonna stay here, you need to earn your keep. Ain't no free rides in this world."

Lester sat up and scratched his head. "Am I staying here?"

Otis looked at him, bemused. "Damn, you the slowinest person to get a fix on a situation I ever met. Where'd you get your schoolin'?"

Lester stared at Otis with his mouth open. Somehow, in the course of one night, he'd gone from breaking and entering to employee of the year. Baffled, he glanced around the tire repository. It was certainly no worse than his suite at Diboll. Definitely.

"Mr. Otis, I appreciate your offer, and I believe I'll just take you up on that. I do have one stipulation though."

"What's that?"

"I don't know how long I'm gonna be here. There's somebody I gotta find, and if I don't—well, I'm afraid I'll have to move on."

Otis spit. "This ain't no lifetime proposition! Hell, I may be gone 'fore you. Now get your idle ass outta bed and help me change a flat. There's a pot of coffee in the office." Otis turned and walked outside.

Lester slid off the cot and put on his jeans and last clean T-shirt. *World's sure got a peculiar way of doing things..* Stopping in the washroom to splash water on his face and comb his hair, he glanced at Mildred squatting in a corner. "You're not sleeping on top of me tonight. I let you get away with it 'cause I was too tired to mess with you. You hear me?" Mildred looked at Lester blankly, and then she stuck her hind leg in the air and began licking her anus.

He shook his head. "Show off."

Walking outside the front door of Otis McCloud's All Purpose Chevron, Lester glanced at the wall clock. Even though it wasn't yet eight o'clock, the temperature was already creeping up towards high muggy. Still, it was bright and sunny, and the persistently humid Gulf breeze splayed a lively sheen on all who ventured into the alfresco sauna.

"Roll that jack over here," ordered Otis, "and let's get this old Ford set right." Otis motioned to the portable hydraulic lift. Lester wheeled the contraption over, and together they began removing a large ten-ply radial from a 4 × 4 pickup. Between grunting, coughing, wheezing, and spitting, the two men worked mostly in wordless accord. Finally, Lester stood back as Otis tightened the wheel nuts with an air drill.

"I just want you to know, Mr. Otis, I wasn't trying to steal nothing last night."

Otis turned around and squinted at Lester. He wiped his forehead with a sleeve and continued securing the tire. "I know that. Wouldn't a let you stay if I'd thought otherwise. Hand me that can of WD-40. Got a rusted bolt here." Lester handed him the container of spray oil. Otis spritzed, tightened some more, and finally stood. "So, how was your first day in Rockport?"

Lester crossed his arms, sighing. "Confusing, I guess."

Otis laughed. "Ain't that the shittin' truth."

"I don't know. I can't get my bearings or something. Everything feels like it's wound up differently than before."

"Before prison?"

Lester nodded.

Otis shook his head: "Nah, it's the same old joke it's always been. Same fools leading the same dumb-shit lives. *You* the one that's different. Gonna take a while 'fore you remember what the rules are."

Lester bit the inside of his mouth and frowned. "Maybe. Or maybe I'll just go someplace they don't have stupid rules."

Otis laughed again. "You find it, and me and Mildred'll go along with you!" Otis yanked on the electrical plug. "Son of a bitch!"

"What?"

"Pulled the damn socket off the cord. Ain't that a dirt sandwich." Otis stared at the frayed plug and reached into his pocket, pulling out a five-dollar bill. "Here, run on over to the True Value and get me one of these plugs. It's down about a half mile on the right, back of the drug store."

Lester took the five dollars. "You don't want me to drive?"

"You got a license?"

Lester looked at his shoes. "I 'spect it's expired."

"I 'spect you can walk then."

Lester nodded and shoved the five in his jeans. As he turned for the street, Otis called to him: "And bring me one of them little fried peach pies from the Petronilla Bakery next door. Get one for yourself. Don't take all day; we got work to do!"

Lester nodded and waved back to him, bounding across the intersection.

He hurried at a fast clip, when it gradually dawned on him he wasn't on a time clock anymore. "Hell with it. I'm done marching to somebody else's docket." He breathed in the sweet oleander-scented air and began strolling as if Jesus had just handed him a new smile. "Mr. Otis'll get his thirty-nine-cent plug. He can just keep his drawers on till I get back, too."

Lester rambled past the parking lot of the post office again and thought about Mirtie and her wayward boy, Darryl. No telling what kinds of grief and regret those two had brought on each other. "Mothers and sons—there's a big sack of fire ants," Lester mused. "Just leave 'em be. No point stirring that mound up." Least ways, that's how it had always been between Lester and his own mama. They were just better off in separate counties. Too much alike—and too much unalike.

Lester was hungry. He didn't know if a fried pie would be enough to hold him till lunch, provided he even got lunch. Up ahead he saw a large brick restaurant—The Keel Boat—with lots of cars parked around it. He had a few dollars of his own. Why not just get some real eggs and toast and start the day off proper? It wouldn't take that long, he reasoned.

The bustling restaurant was filled with chatter and darting waitresses. Lester stood patiently next to the PLEASE WAIT FOR HOSTESS sign. A middle-aged redhead zoomed by and called out to him, "How many in your party, handsome?"

"Just me."

"Come on." Lester followed her into the dark, excessively air-conditioned restaurant and immediately felt out of place. He wished they'd had a front counter he could have sat at. Maybe this was a bad idea. It seemed as if everyone were staring at him. *Why do people stare all the time?*

"You need some coffee or juice, hon?" the waitress asked, handing Lester a menu.

"Coffee."

"You got it. Who do people tell you you look like?"

"Me?"

"Uh-huh."

"I don't know."

"It's somebody famous. I'll think of it. It's not Patrick Dempsey...I'll think of it..." She turned and hurried back to the kitchen.

Lester looked at the menu again, hiding behind it. *Do I look funny? Do these people think I'm an ex-con, too?* Lester tried concentrating on the menu, and eventually the jumble of printed words began to register in his brain. Food! Shrimp, steak, Mexican plate, pancakes, cheesecake—cherry pie a la mode! Lester was paralyzed. What could he order? No, what *should* he order? There was nobody there to decide for him. His arms and knees began to quiver from the chilly blast of air aimed directly at him. His stomach was hurting now. He glanced up to see a table full of men looking at him. This was a surefire mistake. He lowered the menu and stood. Again, the entire room seemed to be concentrating solely on him. He started walking purposely towards the front entry, but light-headedness gradually overtook him. For just a second, he felt he might stumble and fall...

"Lester?"

Grabbing the side of a chair, Lester turned to see a shadowy figure in a corner booth staring at him. "Lester—it's Philip Yancey. Would you like to...join me?"

Lester was completely confounded. He stared at Philip as if they were both emerging from cloud banks. He couldn't determine what his emotions were exactly. Part of him wanted to leave; part wanted to eat; and part just wanted to sit with Father Phil and deconstruct Laurel Jeanette. "Uh...I was...um...leaving."

Philip replied, "I'm almost done here. Can I give you a lift?"

The waitress suddenly appeared behind Lester, holding out his mug of coffee. "Here ya go, sugar. Couldn't find you. You sitting with Father Phil?"

Philip smiled and motioned for Lester to sit.

"I...can't stay long." Lester sat slowly in the booth, uncertain.

"We'll get ya out in no time. What'll ya have, hon?"

Lester didn't answer but stared at Philip's plate. Philip smiled and said, "The pancakes are awfully good here. How 'bout a stack with some eggs and bacon?"

Lester nodded.

The waitress stopped writing and stuck her pencil in her hair. "Lord love a duck. I know who you look like! John Payne! You ever see *Miracle on 34th Street*? That cute little Christmas movie with Maureen O'Hara and darlin' Natalie Wood? He was in that. She turned to Philip. "Don't he look like John Payne, Father Phil?"

Philip smiled and nodded. "Yes, I believe he does."

"I couldn't live without my old movie channel. Only thing on cable worth watching. You know what's on tonight? *Damn Yankees!* with that gorgeous boy Tab Hunter! Father, you need some more coffee?" Philip shook his head, and the waitress hurried away.

Philip looked at Lester, who stared at his place mat. "So...found a place to stay, did you?"

Lester nodded.

Philip struggled on: "We have our regional arts and crafts show coming up this weekend. Rooms get kind of scarce this time of year. Some people have to stay all the way in Corpus..."

Lester suddenly looked at Philip, eyeing him intently. "Where is she?"

Philip stopped mid-sentence, his mouth open. "I...I told you..."

"Actually, you didn't. You told me nothing. You've got her picture. She lived with you...And now she doesn't want to see me, is that it?"

"No."

"She's mad?"

"No, Lester—"

"Then what? I *need* to see her!"

Philip shook his head, slowly. "You can't."

"Why?" Lester pounded the table with his fist. People turned once again to stare.

Philip smoothed his paper napkin and spoke in a calm, reasonable voice. "I need to show you something after you've had your breakfast."

"What?"

"I'll show you."

The waitress approached again, carrying a coffeepot. "OK, handsome, don't beat a hole in the Formica. I was just on my way to bring you some more." She picked up Lester's cup and poured as Philip smiled solemnly back at the roomful of curious faces.

***

Philip parked his white Impala under the shade of an expansive ash tree and Lester followed him to the back door of the Episcopal church. Fumbling briefly with his keys, Philip opened the door to admit Lester into the dark cocoon that was his office. He switched on a desk lamp and turned to Lester.

"Why don't you have a seat?"

"I can't stay long. I'm working at the Chevron station, and I need to get back."

"Otis McCloud?"

Lester nodded.

Philip sat behind his desk. "He's a good man. I guess that means you'll be staying a while?"

Lester shrugged. "The main thing is, I got to find Laurel Jeanette."

"Why?"

"I told you—I love her."

"How much...do you love her?"

Lester spoke in a voice that seemed to come from the bottom of a deep well—muffled, distant, lost: "With everything I got, everything I hope to have, all of me."

Philip gazed at him and turned his head quickly. He finally cleared his throat and said, "I hope...what I tell you will be treated with complete discretion. I have…a position in this town and…do I have your word that what I'm about to say will travel no further than this room?"

Lester, perplexed, nodded his head "OK."

Philip looked at Lester again and then slowly turned to a nearby filing cabinet and opened it with a key. He pulled out several large, ribbon-tied manila portfolios and placed them on the desk.

Lester stared at them, and then at Philip.

"Open them," Philip stood and moved to the window, his back toward Lester.

Lester tentatively picked up one of the parcels, undid the string clasp, and reached inside. Pulling out a handful of letters, he immediately recognized his own handwriting. "Wh—What is this?"

Philip continued to stare, motionless. When he finally spoke, his voice was monotone. "Why couldn't you have just stayed away?"

Lester's hand began to tremble again, and he let the half dozen or so letters he was holding drop to the table. "Where's… Laurel Jeanette?"

Philip turned to him, his face a tight, gray mask. "I…*I'm*… Laurel Jeanette."

A sudden swooping sensation hit Lester's gut, as if he were falling from a steep cliff. He stared at Philip, struggling to concentrate. Suddenly the familiar ache in his stomach resurrected, and his face grew hot and prickly. He started to speak, stopped, and then leapt to his feet shouting, "Where is she?"

Philip, unflinching, repeated his words: "I'm Laurel Jeanette."

Lester lunged for him, grabbing his shirt and slamming his head against the wall. The two men stared at each other in horror. Lester leaned in and whispered into Philip's ear, as if somehow raising his voice again might thoroughly render his sanity. "Who… is that picture of?"

Philip swallowed with difficulty. "My…sister."

Lester rammed his knuckles deeper into Philips's chest. "What is her name?"

Philip choked out the words, "Luz. Luz Yancey."

Lester's mouth brushed against Philip's ear as he wheezed imperceptibly. "And *where* is she?"

Philip turned his head to the side. "She…she lives with me."

Lester was dazed. His shaking hands caused the unbuttoned collar on Philip's shirt to flutter wildly. Suddenly, as if jolted by electricity, he pushed Philip away. Turning aside, he tucked his jittery hands under his arms and faced the wall. "Does she know about me?"

"Nothing."

Lester took a deep breath. "Why?" He turned back to face Philip. "Why me?"

Philip stood, taut with anguish. "I began writing to the inmates when our local diocese started a prison outreach program – started prison out reach three years ago. You sent me your picture. I couldn't get you out of my mind. I kept asking God, 'Why is he there? What has he done that couldn't be forgiven?' You told me how much you wanted someone to love, how lonely you were, how lost, sad…You were describing *me*. I…*we*…needed each other."

Tears welled up in Lester's eyes. He'd never experienced such intense feelings of rage and contempt. "You lied. You took advantage. You cheated me out of the most true thing I've ever known."

Philip shook his head. "No, I gave you something to hope for! And you gave me back my *faith*." He pointed to the pile on his desk "Those letters are the only proof I have that I'm still—*alive*. That I can feel…love."

Lester spit out the words bitterly: "But I *don't* love you!"

"Yes" Philip nodded slowly. "You love the person that wrote those letters."

Lester was dumbfounded. How had this madman so methodically subverted his life? How had he let it happen? Lester suddenly panicked. "I've got to get out of here."

Philip took a tentative step towards him. "Laurel Jeanette didn't ask you to come here. I was happy the way things were. What choice did I have? A closeted minister in a small town…What choice is there?"

"I just got out of *my* prison. Find your own way." Lester started to exit and turned back at the door. "I want to meet her."

"That's impossible."

"Nothing's impossible, Phil. You figure out a time and a place. I *will* meet her." Lester walked out of the office and into the burning sunlight.

Unconsciously, Philip began scooping the scattered letters on his desk. He stopped and glanced down at his hands. In an instant he seized the bundle and flung it across the room. Dozens of paper silhouettes flapped to the ground like mortally wounded birds.

***

See her he would. It didn't matter to Lester that she didn't know who he was. He knew who *she* was. He could *convince* her that he was worthy of her love. Once she met him, once she could see for herself the truth, regard, and sincerity in his eyes, how could she fail not to be *spellbound?* It was their fate.

And Philip? Lester could only muster pity for the sorry bastard. To deliberately dupe another man's desires in that way? It was beneath disdain. He felt only rebuke for such a despicable lowlife. He vowed he would not be defeated by Philip's outrageous violations of ethical behavior. A "Man of God" no less! Lester congratulated himself for suppressing the urge to thrash him. He'd already seen too many prison beatings, and they had never fixed anything—only left a bigger hole in the perpetrators head. Three years of his life had been spent in maintaining a consummate vision of undiminished love. He would not be defeated. Miss Yancey just hadn't had the great good fortune of meeting him yet. Strangely enough, Philip's pathetic revelation had only reinforced his will.

Lester suddenly stopped walking. Without realizing it, he'd been jogging nearly all the way from the church. His entire body was wet from nerves and heat. He squinted ahead and saw the Chevron station. Otis was leaning across the hood of a big, long Cadillac.

"Damn!" Lester pivoted on his boots and began racing back up the block. He'd forgotten the plug and the peach pies. Bad enough being late, but he figured Otis would for sure be pissed if he came back empty-handed. Since Otis might be the only friend he was liable to scrape up at this point, Lester wanted to be good to the old man.

He stepped into the street without paying attention and nearly got his leg run over. A red sports car squealed to a halt within a pocket comb's length of his zippered fly. Lester put both hands on the side of Melanie Wheelwright's Porsche and exhaled uneasily. "You trying to get my attention?"

Melanie smiled. "I'm sorry. I guess my mind was somewhere else. I'd hate to mess up that pretty face of yours."

"You nearly got me killed."

Melanie smiled and shook her head. "No—I rarely miss my mark. You need a lift?" She leaned over and opened the passenger door. "You can be nice to me; I'm just trying to get to know you better."

Lester studied Melanie and then glanced back towards the gas station. He nudged the car door shut with his knee. "Can't. Don't have time." He turned and started off down the sidewalk. Melanie drove slowly alongside him.

"Why are you being so mean? Did I make you cry or something?"

Lester shook his head. "I don't have time to play, that's all."

"Man on a mission. You gonna run for mayor?"

Lester stopped walking and stared wearily at Melanie: "Has anyone ever told you being a smart aleck is not one of your better qualities?"

"That's why I work so hard on developing inner beauty, so people will overlook those little peculiarities." Melanie smiled. "Come on. It's not nice to make a girl beg."

Lester stared at her. Here was this blonde, long-limbed, and completely desirable Texas beauty practically dragging him into her Porsche! Was he so indoctrinated to the idea of Laurel Jeanette that he couldn't appreciate any other possible likelihood? He rubbed his index finger along the top of the windshield trim. "You know where the Petronilla Bakery is?"

"Oh my God, they make the best fried pies in Texas. Get in."

Lester opened the tiny door and slumped down on the seat, feeling like he was back on some kiddie park ride.

Melanie roared off with her standard eagerness, and this time Lester stretched his arms out to brace himself.

"I'm gonna be fired 'fore I even get in my first hour on the job."

Melanie turned. "You got a job?"

"At the Chevron station."

"Mr. McCloud?"

Lester nodded.

"Oh, he's the best. I think he's the only man left in Texas who still fills up your gas tank for you." She squinted at him and asked, "When did this happen?"

"This morning. I should've been back an hour ago."

"I'll put in a good word for you. I buy all my gas there." Melanie smiled. "Had any luck finding...What's her name? Lauren, Lucy?"

"Laurel. She doesn't exist."

"Excuse me?"

"Somebody made up the name so they could have a long-distance relationship with me."

Melanie looked at him, alarmed. "Are you serious?"

Lester nodded. "Pretty funny, huh?"

"Not really. I'm sorry."

Lester shrugged. "Some people have pretty peculiar ideas about love. I guess I always thought it was something *honorable*."

Melanie pulled into the parking lot of the bakery and turned off the engine. She stared straight ahead, neither of them moving. "What are you going to do now?"

Lester rubbed his jeans with his palms and smiled. "Buy a couple of fried peach pies and go back to work." He started to exit the car, and Melanie put a hand on his arm.

"I really would like for you to come out to the house on Saturday. We'll have lots to eat and drink, and you'll meet some really boring people. And then we can go sailing on the bay. Does that sound like a totally awful proposition?"

Lester frowned and rubbed his chin. "No one would deny you're a very attractive woman, Melanie, but if you're thinking we're going to start something, I can't."

"I never said—"

"You didn't have to. I don't see myself getting involved with anyone right now."

"I'm not asking for your hand in marriage. This might surprise you, but I'm engaged to be married myself. I'd like to have a new friend, that's all."

Lester grinned at her. "Fine. Do you mind if I still don't believe you?"

She smiled back. "I was hoping you wouldn't."

They both walked inside the bakery. Melanie's short, white miniskirt contrasted agreeably with her flawlessly long, tan legs. An exiting customer turned to admire the more noteworthy aspects of her receding posterior and then winked to his buddies awaiting him in an adjoining vehicle. "Jesus Christ, if my old lady had a butt like that, I'd tie her to the front of my jeans and we'd go round as Siamese twins." The men hooted as their beat-up plumbing van growled into reverse and spun out of the lot.

The glass door to the shop had squished shut behind them. Inside the small room, the fragrance of baking bread, warm doughnuts, and a German chocolate cake being frosted assailed Lester's senses. He felt a sudden, primal need to linger beside the stooped-over woman behind the counter, adorning her dense masterpiece with voluptuous swirls. A German chocolate cake! Had anything ever looked so incredibly enticing to him? The warm, sticky gumbo of coconut, pecans, butter, and brown sugar made him want to stick his tongue in the bowl and lick till his fillings hummed.

And then he felt it—that surging accomplice between his legs, Mr. Congenial. Mr. C was as unfailingly predisposed to gratification as the three fundamentals of immediate escapism: Coke, popcorn, and a movie ticket. Stub held high, Mr. Happy anxiously awaited the show to start. Hungry and horny, horny and hungry: the double dependables of his life. Coupled with a preposterous craving to gorge himself, Lester desperately wanted to sit somewhere and ease his overtaxed brain.

Melanie idly picked up a bag of Mexican wedding cookies and stooped to peruse a tray of exotic candied sweet potatoes, *camotes*. A classic, south Texas Mexican bakery contained as much perplexity and provocation within its walls as the ubiquitous Catholic Church, which nearly always stood nearby. Both shrouded in parochial lore and mitigation, they were equal parts solace and persuasion…and *all* marketing.

A brunette stood at the front counter talking with the cashier. She held a small biscuit in one hand and a cup of coffee in the other.

"I can't make up my mind. The cheese is good, but maybe the garlic's better."

"Take both?"

"Oh God! I'm getting as big as a house. Just give me a half dozen of the cheese and one of those *empanada* things over there."

"The guava?"

"You have guava? Now I'll have to have some of those. Give me three…no, six! You know, Delia," she smiled, "you're the worst thing that ever happened to a diet." The brunette turned and smiled at Melanie, now standing alongside her, peering into the glass case. "I'll be out of your way in a sec."

"Take your time. I can't make up my mind either."

"Isn't it awful? Every time I come in here, I realize how deprived my life is." The two women smiled in accord.

"I can barely drive past anymore without my face breaking out," Melanie laughed, shaking her head and gazing covetously at the *cajeta* fudge bars.

The woman icing the cake suddenly looked up and blinked toward the others standing at the cash register. Lester watched as she shook her salt-and-pepper curls and blew little puffs of air. From the expression on her face, it seemed she was rising from some deep well of "cake-frosting oneness" somewhere in her head. "Everybody complains; nobody *restrains*. I guess that's why we're in business some twenty-odd years."

"Oh, I wasn't complaining, Miz de la Rosa. It's just that when someone's 'the best,' it's hard to buck temptation." The brunette swallowed the rest of her biscuit.

"You want to know the secret to owning a bakery? Make sure people get what they *don't* need. And who wants to live without fat anyway? We'd all look like bugs or something," Mrs. de la Rosa replied.

Lester continued staring as the salt-and-pepper-haired woman scooped up a flat knife loaded with candied goo and resumed cake layering.

The cashier finished filling the woman's bag of goodies and rang up the sale. Lester swallowed hard and then slowly turned to face the street. He modestly adjusted his unwieldy manhood into a less conspicuous position. Naturally, he hadn't worn any underwear this morning. Didn't have anything clean. Anyway, he'd gotten used to bare-balling in the pen. A burlap bag was about as agreeable as the "prison panties" they were assigned.

Melanie turned to him. "Lester, you said you wanted the fried peach pies?"

The brunette handed the cashier her money and leaned close to Melanie. "Enjoy your fat quotient. A bug's life isn't long." The two women giggled as Lester walked over, edging past the indulgent displays of pastries, pies, and sweets. Surrounded by such provocation, he felt as if his dick had swollen into bread-loaf proportions. If he were to so much as bump into a cookie, he was convinced he'd ejaculate all over himself.

Mrs. de la Rosa suddenly looked up and noticed him for the first time. She slowly licked the corners of her mouth, grinning. He turned away from her and decided to concentrate on the cash register ahead. Commerce, enterprise, sales receipts—anything to detract him from food and sex.

From behind Melanie, Lester saw the cashier shut the register drawer and turn to move a tray of pralines. As he exhaled, Melanie unexpectedly bent forward to examine a pie on the middle shelf. Her white miniskirt bumped solidly against the front of Lester's jeans. The firmness of her ass, the astonishing, spontaneous thrust of her butt against his pelvis instantly sucked the remaining oxygen from his lungs. Suddenly he was bungee jumping off the top of the world.

The brunette turned at exactly the same moment and stared at him. It was Laurel Jeanette. (Or Luz. Or God.) He never even blinked. Mouth agape, eyes distended, pelvis shuddering, Lester left his body. Right after coming all over himself.

chapter

FIVE

When he opened his eyes, Lester's ear was throbbing like hell. He could vaguely make out four faces peering down at him.

"There. I told you he'd be all right. Just pinch their earlobes hard; they come round." The cake lady removed her clenched fingernails from his ear.

"What happened? You sounded like you were dying." Melanie, still in shock, stared down at him.

"I...I...Oh my *God!*" Lester rose abruptly on his elbows to stare at the front of his pants. He was drenched with...coffee!

"I'm so sorry. When I turned around, you let out this really grisly yell, and I guess I got scared and spilled my coffee in your lap." Laurel Jeanette/Luz was kneeling beside him. "I've got some napkins here if you'll—"

"*No!*" Lester scrambled to his feet, mortified at his unimaginable behavior. Did he or did he not just shoot his entire wad in front of a roomful of strange women? Prison stories were rarely this outrageous! He looked down again at his jeans. Saved by Folgers and Equal. "I'm OK. Fine. I just hadn't eaten anything...I got light-headed. That's all." The women continued staring, not entirely convinced another awesome performance wasn't forthcoming. "Really," Lester insisted. "I'm fine."

They all rose hesitantly, and the cashier handed Lester a wet dishtowel. "I never knew those little Styrofoam cups could hold so much coffee. You got soaked, boy!"

Lester eyed the woman nervously.

"I'd like to pay for your dry cleaning. Here's seven dollars. You think that'll be enough?" Luz held out some cash in her hand.

"Forget it."

"No, really. I'd feel better if you'd at least let me pay for the cleaning."

Lester shook his head, too humiliated to look at her. "Nope."

Luz folded the money in her hand. "I am so sorry. I feel like such a klutz. You sure you're OK?"

"Yep."

Luz turned to Melanie. "Well, it was nice talking to you."

"Same here."

Luz turned to leave. As she exited, she heard a strangling growl behind her.

"I-I-I-I-iiiiiiiiiiiiiiiii..."

All four women stared at Lester; no one dared to breathe.

"I-I-I-I-I...changed my mind. I think I would like you to...pay for my cleaning."

Luz looked at him, unsure. "O-K." She reached into her pocketbook again to pull out the bills.

"No...!"

No one moved.

Lester took a deep breath to calm himself. "How 'bout...I... bring the pants to you?"

"To me?"

Lester nodded. "If you have a washing machine, I'd prefer that."

The women glanced at each other, perplexed.

"Oh, OK. A washing machine…fine." Luz tentatively dug for a pen in her shoulder bag. "I'll write down my address…"

"I know!"

Again, the women stared in alarm.

"I mean…you live *here*, right? Just give me your phone number, and I'll call…if that's OK?"

Luz studied Lester's face for a moment. "Yes, I live with my older brother. He's a minister here in town. Everyone knows us." She scribbled on a piece of napkin and put the pen back in her bag. "Just call when you want them cleaned," Luz told him. She quickly handed Lester the number and exited the bakery. "Good-bye…again."

Lester watched from a window as she got into her van, started the ignition, and drove off. Glancing down at the paper napkin in his hands, he studied this "new" handwriting. He was astonished when a bead of sweat smudged the ink.

"Did you need to get something?" Melanie asked softly.

Lester blinked and quickly stuffed the number in his pocket. Turning toward the bewildered cashier, he smiled shyly, "Two fried peach pies to go."

Melanie tore into Otis McCloud's Chevron station and braked the engine before Lester had time to fasten his seat belt.

"So, you coming or not?"

"Huh?"

"To the party on Saturday night? Say yes. Pretty please?" Melanie's smile was a beguiling fake, a box of zircons spilled across a dressing table. Fetching but somewhat suspect.

"What time?"

She clapped her hands and blew the horn.

Lester shot her an acrid grimace. "Why'd you do that? You want him even more pissed at me?"

Examining herself in the rearview mirror, Melanie sighed. "*Calme vous.* I told you he's a sweetheart."

Like a February groundhog, Otis emerged from the door of his office blinking and sputtering. He glared at the two, not recognizing them yet, with a look that could bend iron. "This ain't no goddamn drive-in. You want a gal in short pants serving corny dogs, get that skinny-ass, foreign car over to the Sonic!"

Melanie rose up in her seat and waved. "Hi, Mr. McCloud. It's Melanie Wheelwright, remember? I bought four new tires from you last year."

Lester, feeling extremely odious in his damp apparel, closed his eyes and contemplated spontaneous dissipation.

Otis scowled at Melanie, and then he switched from frown to delight. "Well, it sure is! Where you been, honey? I hadn't seen ya round in a while." He hobbled toward the car when he inadvertently caught sight of Lester scrunched down in the seat. "Son of a bitch! I sent you for breakfast, and here it is damn near Easter!"

Before Lester could open his mouth, Melanie interceded: "Mr. McCloud, you'd be so proud of Lester!"

"For what, not getting his head blowed off ?"

Melanie purred, "I was on my way to the Wednesday social hour at the Palm Aire Nursing Home—you know where it is?" Otis hacked and spit. "And as I was carrying in my tape player and my box of doughnuts, I realized I'd forgotten *the coffee!*" Lester turned to look at Melanie, recognizing the signs of a humongous Texas whopper being whelped. "So, I got back into the car and raced over to the Handy Andy, and since I was *way* late, I just went ahead and rented a big old party percolator already filled with hot coffee. You know, the big ones?" she gestured for effect. "Well, when I got to the nursing home, just how do you think a hundred and fifteen pound, near anemic like me was able to get that big barrel into the building?"

Otis eyed her cynically and pointed to Lester. "Him."

Melanie nodded. "Here were these poor, pitiful old people just standing around in their nightclothes looking out the window, waiting for a sugar doughnut and their bossa nova lessons. I tell you, Mr. McCloud, I don't know when I've ever been so grateful to see anyone in my life. I practically threw myself at his mercy. I said to him, 'Won't you please carry this big coffeepot into the building so those little old people standing up there will have one more day of knowing someone, somewhere cares enough about their shabby, depressed lives to make just the tiniest difference in an uncaring world gone horribly mad with apathy?'"

Otis stared at her, then at Lester, then at Melanie again. "What kind of horseshit is this?"

Melanie got out of the car, moving briskly to the passenger side. "I'll tell you what kind, Mr. McCloud. You don't believe me—believe this!" She flung open Lester's door and pointed righteously to his coffee-stained crotch. "This poor man got attacked by a deranged mob of senior citizens waiting for their java fix! You're lucky he made it out of there without his arm being torn off."

Otis glanced at Lester's grimy jeans and shook his head. "Jesus Herbert Christ. I still don't see how that took three and a half hours?"

Melanie threw up her hands. "Somebody had to dance with them, Mr. McCloud! You can't just leave old people alone all hopped up on sugar and caffeine and "The Girl from Ipanema" throbbing in the background. My God, you'd have to call the national guard out just to break up the orgy." Melanie stood with her arms crossed defiantly.

Otis removed his tattered baseball cap and scratched his head. "Well...that's about the wildest sumabitch story I've heard in a long time." He put his cap back on and sighed. "Orgy, huh?" He allowed himself the tiniest of grins. "You think they might be needing some more volunteers soon?" Melanie smiled, and Otis turned back to Lester, rumbling, "Go change them nasty britches, Ricky Ricardo, and meet me out back at the grease pit. We got work to do."

Otis walked off to the rear of the station, and Lester slowly began extricating himself from the Porsche. "Where'd you learn to be so deceitful?"

Melanie slid back into the driver's side and smiled. "Sunday school. One should always learn from the best. I'll bring you by the directions. Six o'clock sharp, Saturday." Melanie pressed a button raising the canvas roof on the convertible. "Oh, and wear something vulgar." Melanie lowered her head. "Republicans love being offended." She peeled out of the station.

Lester folded the top of the pie bag he was holding. Contemplating his first full morning in Rockport, he quickly arrived at a conclusion: routine it wasn't.

Standing once more in front of the sink, Lester wiped himself clean with the wet towel. It occurred to him that it would not be entirely unlikely he might end up attacking Mildred the cat if he didn't get laid soon. And what was Luz's reaction to this unsettling episode at the bakery? Were there any signs of perception on her part? Some awareness? A single thread of discernment? It was impossible to know. Everything had happened so god-awful fast. Lester reached into his pocket for the crumpled napkin she'd scribbled her number on. It looked nothing like "her" handwriting. The characters were messy, jumbled, and loopy. Laurel Jeanette's handwriting was as neat and orderly as a phone bill. He slid the napkin back into his pants pocket. Didn't matter. A person's faith could not be dismembered with a single, regrettable incident. He would meet with her, soon. Alone.

Slipping on the gray prison trousers, Lester eyed a bottle of Dove dishwashing soap on the shelf above and squeezed some on his jeans. He then filled the sink with warm water and soaked the pants. Watching as the dried flakes of sperm disengaged and floated to the top of the water, he thought of Little Ray. He figured he'd be folding sheets and towels in the prison laundry about now. How many millions of pounds of sweat, tears, spit, puke, shit, piss, blood, and semen did he and Little Ray haul in their daily rounds in the laundry? Enormous cloth mountains of physical waste surrounded them like great Andes of Anguish. And yet, he'd liked working in the laundry best of all. Water and soap brought purification. Redemption in a wash bubble. At the end of each day, as the last pile was sorted, folded, stacked, and discharged, Little Ray would inevitably glance toward Lester and smile. He was the one person in the entire prison purgatory that gave a damn. A friend, a helpful friend, a confidante. *What the hell did it matter they were both men?* Prison was hardly the place for moral fastidiousness. Consolation was welcome in any form.

Lester stared at his submerged hands. Would anyone or anything ever satiate this persistent need for consolation? The jagged, massive yearning for human contact that wrapped itself around so many conflicting likelihoods. The coffee stains billowed and clouded the water, vanquishing all past transgressions.

He dried his hands, put on a shirt, combed his hair, and started to exit when he stopped and suddenly rammed his fist against the side metal paper towel dispenser. It swung perilously for a few seconds and then dropped sideways, crashing to the floor. Lester stared at the mangled container. He slowly pointed a sneaker toe toward it and slid it behind the commode. Glancing in the mirror a final time, he feigned a look of outrage: "St. Michael's and All Angels Episcopal Church, I do believe you have a devil in your midst!"

***

Rosa sat crying at the kitchen table while squeezing jalapeño cheese rosettes on English crackers. The party wasn't for another couple of hours, but already she was behind in her preparations. Wiping her cheek, she tried concentrating on the "flourish" of her artistry that delighted Mrs. Wheelwright so. "Rosa, what you do with a pastry sleeve is nothing short of magnificent. I think you should design our Christmas cards this year!" It pleased Rosa to please Mrs. Wheelwright. Actually, it didn't take much to make either of them happy: a little attention, some encouragement, nice shoes—the touch of Mr. Wheelwright's hand.

Rosa felt the baby kick, and she shifted on her stool. Reaching into her uniform pocket, she retrieved a tissue and blew her nose. Her mother had warned her that Americans were a ruthless, uncaring, amoral lot. She didn't, however, specifically caution her against older Texas men with easy laughter, gentle arms, and shiny blue–green eyes the color of *quetzal* feathers. Their affair had started about six months after Rosa joined the Wheelwright household. For a nineteen-year-old virgin from a remote village in Guatemala, her initial liaison with *Roberto* was as natural and pleasing as a warm, spring bath. She knew immediately that he cared for her. The way he held her, the smiles, the small, silly gifts she'd find in her room. He was a boy—a foolish and tenderhearted boy. It seemed as if their roles were reversed somehow, that *he* was the virgin, she the adult. When she told him of her pregnancy, he beamed as if he'd just won a shiny new medal. Her fears eventually dwindled into a kind of vague repentance. Even her strict Catholic upbringing couldn't rend from her the appropriate remorse. It simply never felt like sin to Rosa. God would have to assess the consequences, not she.

And yet the tears fell, sometimes hourly. She couldn't bear to hurt him, or her. They'd truly been lifesavers. But without a green card, a job, a car—someone to help interpret the crazy events that passed for routine in this new land—Rosa felt singularly paralyzed.

And what of the other one? It was true; Bob had not been the only man. In her rush to partake of American freedom, she'd done the only natural thing: acted impulsively. Dave Gonzalez was a handsome, energetic offshore rig worker who wandered into her life as matter-of-factly as a summer Dirt Devil. And he vanished just as quickly. Her tiny act of autonomy, on the evening of her one and only American date, never even hinted at a likelihood of further expectation. It was over before it had begun. Forgotten but for the child's DNA. How could she explain that complication—least of all to Bob?

"Have you ever seen a baby cottontail?" Bob Wheelwright stood in the kitchen doorway, holding something in his hands. He was freshly showered and dressed for the party, looking even younger in his linen Bermudas, sandals, and short-sleeved silk shirt.

"A what?"

"Baby rabbit, *un conejo.*"

Rosa rose from her seat. "Ahhh, let me see. Where did you find it?"

"On the lawn. One of the dogs must've smelled the nest while the mama was out shopping for groceries."

Rosa picked up the tiny ball of fur and nuzzled it against her cheek. "So little. How can something so small survive in this world?"

"Numbers. There are a lot of little baby rabbits."

Rosa stroked its ears with her finger. "But I only care about this one."

"Come on. Let's take it to its mama." Bob put his hand on Rosa's shoulder and started for the kitchen door.

"I'm not finished cooking!"

"We won't be long." Rosa stared at his imploring smile, hesitated slightly, and then turned to lower the burner on a simmering double boiler. They exited the kitchen and walked across the lawn now glimmering with hundreds of lanterns, candles, and twinkling lights. Bob waited until they were behind the garage and then glanced furtively toward the house. Turning back to Rosa, he brushed his fingers against her cheek. "Have you been crying again?" She nodded. Bob put his arms around her. He kissed her ear and cheek and then softly on the mouth. "*Rosalina*—please don't worry. I'm going to take care of you and the baby. You know that."

She nodded. "I don't…feel good about hiding around Mrs. Wheelwright."

Bob touched his forehead to hers. "I love you—and I love my wife. What should I do about that?"

Rosa gazed at the horizon. As usual, she was unable to fully comprehend this mingled proclamation of shared devotion. What did it mean ultimately, for her, for the baby? It made her dizzy contemplating such unknowns. She turned to Bob. "Your son knows. He asked me, and I didn't lie. He said he already knew anyway. Maybe your wife does as well."

Bob sighed. "And did my son say when he thought it might be the appropriate time to tell his mother? Tonight at the party? After church on Sunday? Perhaps the next time she and I make love, I could whisper in her ear."

Rosa glared at him and turned to walk back to the house, but Bob took her arm. "You're going to have to trust me, Rose. I don't want to hurt this woman any more than I already have. Can't you understand?"

Rosa nodded, but she wasn't sure of anything. Bob then opened her hand cradling the sleeping cottontail. He lifted the squirming animal and smiled. "I think it's a boy. He's looking at me like he already wants to punch my lights out." Stooping before the tall grass and brushy weeds bordering the yard, Bob gently placed the rabbit in a cluster of lantana flowers and shoved its rump. "Go, find your family. *Mas comida.*" After a moment's hesitation, the cottontail squeaked and vanished into the thicket.

Rosa stared sadly. "So many baby rabbits in the world, but only one for me to worry about." Bob put his arms around her, kissing her again. This time Rosa placed her hand behind his head and held him close to her. They clung to each other like two strays in a gale.

***

Daniel sat in the dark under the mimosa tree, finishing his joint and vodka grapefruit juice. He nonchalantly watched his father and Rosa caressing across the lawn. Daniel marveled at the old man's friskiness. "Big horn dog. Let's hear no more crapola lectures about 'curbing our base instincts,' shall we, Pop?" Daniel took one last toke and tapped the burning end on his shoe. What did he care? He was glad Daddy-o was getting some. Rosa was a sweetheart. But Yvonne! Mother was just not good with "domestic disturbances." The woman wasn't designed to deal with any life anomalies. All he could hope for was to be back in school before the shit hit big time. It was cowardly, he realized, but he also knew he didn't have it in him to survive the counseling, therapy, and hand holding she'd require when the "baby bombshell" exploded around them.

Daniel downed his drink and brooded about his own romantic life. Zilch. All summer and not even a fifteen-minute zip fuck with some navy slut from the base in Corpus. Most distressing. Was he ill? Bored? Or, God forbid, just getting older? He stood and placed the dead joint inside his sock. Tonight he'd get laid if it meant sleeping with horny old Dr. Caraway, the eighty-year-old family podiatrist. "Toss your cares away with Caraway!" the old lecher had whispered into Daniel's ear at a drunken yacht-club frolic earlier in the summer. You wish, granddad. As things were progressing, tragically enough, it might just be the unrivaled offering of the season. Daniel shuddered and slouched back to the house, mumbling morosely into his empty cocktail glass, "Party time!"

***

"Yvonne, *where* did you get this marvelous chutney? It tastes like Trader Vic's meets the Ponderosa. Fabulous!" Grace Baldwin dragged a celery stalk down the middle of a cream cheese wedge glazed with chutney, and popped it in her mouth.

"Do you like it?" Yvonne smiled. "It's a chipotle/teriyaki blend. Isn't it heaven?"

Grace nodded blissfully.

"Be sure and try one of those oysters in bacon cognac butter next."

Grace moaned and continued chewing.

Yvonne turned to scrutinize the rest of her guests. She'd be the first to admit it; she'd never find an antidote for anthrax, lead a social revolution, or govern a small country, but she for damn sure knew how to throw a party! She thought sadly of her contemporaries who had simply given up or had never fully grasped the wonderfully beguiling art of entertaining. And an art it was. A bag of chips and a six pack might make for a lively gathering, but one certainly lacking in charm. And charm was such an elusive component nowadays. It took a true master to blend illusion, taste, and generosity, seasoned with a precise amount of audacity and seduction to make a party exceptional. It was a constant balancing act, toeing the cellular-thin line between stuffy and raunchy. A true hostess could "feel" her room like she felt her shoes. Were they tight or comfortable? Appealing or frumpy? Complementary or ruinous?

"Douglas, I think you need another drink. Let me get you one."

"Lenora, that is such a beautiful blouse on you; I feel younger just watching you wear it.

"Oh! Don't tell me—wait a minute—from that divine cologne you're wearing, this has to be the handsomest doctor I know: Martin Caraway!" Yvonne whirled around to see Dr. Caraway, old goatboy himself, wearing his regulation burgundy velour blazer and cream turtleneck (in August!).

"That's my girl. Always sniffs out the rose in a roomful of cabbages!" Everyone tittered at the doctor's contemptuous wit, and the two of them threw their arms around each other, cooing like teenagers.

Gazing from afar, Daniel assessed his mother and Martin objectively. Why do so many women like *her* have so many elderly gay friends like *him*? It was fascinating. He'd noticed it among a number of his mother's contemporaries: thin, high-strung, wealthy, clotheshorse *heterosexual* women who attracted bald, successful, wealthy *gay* men. Like diamonds and platinum, rice and beans, Merrill and Lynch. One of life's corroborated equations. Was this his future, too? Sunset years of waltzing fragile belles from party to party like heedless moths hitting all the bright spots before dawn. True, he adored women and, yes, he was sufficiently entertained by the entailing "man drama" that enveloped so many of their lives. But an existence as a coterie attendant? Could there perhaps be some other vision foreseeable for him rather than imminent walker?

He turned to see Melanie slinking down the stairs and wearing what looked to be a beige lamé hand towel. Her hiney was almost covered by a sparkly thong that appeared to have most sensibly come as a match set. Daniel shook his head. The girl had titanium ovaries to attempt such drag at one of Yvonne's soirees. He envisioned the ensuing tumult with glee.

Bob, still in the kitchen, lifted a tray of artichoke, fennel, and Gruyère cheese puffs and winked at Rosa as he exited for the dining room. Stepping into the lively inner sanctum of mirth, smoke, alcohol, Fracas perfume, and the subdued tones of Sarah Vaughan, Bob winced as one melting hors d'oeuvre rolled to the edge of the platter and pitched heedlessly onto the carpet. Anxious to avert a traumatized pout from Yvonne, he quickly booted the offending appetizer behind a floor vase of pampas grass blooms. Looking up, he was suddenly aware of all eyes transfixed on the staircase—all but Yvonne's. She kept her back turned, aware of some impending crisis transpiring behind her. Whether she'd caught Bob's contretemps with the cocktail morsel was hard to discern. Her eyes had taken on a kind of remote, anesthetized stare, similar no doubt to that of the mother cobra watching helplessly as one of her offspring is carried off, thrashing and biting in the jaws of a mongoose. Slowly she unhinged and pivoted to see Melanie hitting the last few steps. A tight, chiseled smile etched Yvonne's face. With great effort she resisted the urge to run and throw a bedspread over her daughter.

"Hi, everybody. It's just me." Melanie grinned and waved indolently to the crowd. Daniel could tell she'd probably had a little inhalation therapy upstairs from her loopy demeanor. As she started across the room, a stiletto heel snagged in a loop of the hall berber, and she fell sideways into the arms of the Pfefferlings, a wealthy banking couple from Houston. Trying to lift her, Mr. Pfefferling nearly pulled Melanie's scant chemise completely over her head. If it had somehow not been apparent previously, everyone now knew for certain that a bra was not a component of Melanie's ensemble. Daniel couldn't help himself. He nearly bit a hole in his cheek to keep from howling with laughter.

As Mrs. Pfefferling frantically yanked at a piece of fabric to girdle Melanie's butt, Bob quickly entered the fray. Babbling nonstop, he thrust his pastry assemblage at the nearest gawking bystander. "Who'd like hors d'oeuvres? Jim, have you tried these artichoke things?—out of this world. Julia, if you'll pass these to the Lewises over there. Who needs another drink?"

Yvonne, gathering her strength, immediately sized up the entire regrettable occurrence with precision and shrewdness. *When tossed a sow's ear, look for a dog to feed!* "My goodness, Melanie, how very *New York* of you! I should have worn my strapless Carolina Herrera, and we could have come as a team!" Yvonne turned brightly to the crowd, rallying the troops. Immediately they all joined in *ahhing* and *oohing* over Melanie's bold fashion sense. Crisis temporarily averted.

Daniel rolled his eyes. *Bunch of frauds.* If it had been anyone else but Bob and Yvonne's progeny, they'd have chained her to the back of a pickup truck for a country road trip.

Pouring another *Pouilly-Fumé*, Daniel tried ignoring the doorbell faintly chiming in the background. He doled out the golden liquid until it spilled from the top of the glass. Carefully leaning in, he then lapped at the surface of the goblet like some oversized spaniel in Ralph Lauren. What the hell—it was just another night of boorish behavior from the Wheelwright "no-neck monsters." Lifting his head, he suddenly proclaimed in a theatrical voice, "Ooh, Brick! Sometimes I feel just like a cat on a hot tin roof!"

Rosa, hoisting a wicker basket of miniature croissants on her shoulder, passed Daniel and stared. "Cat? *Que* cat?"

Energized, Daniel immediately invoked the role of "downwardly spiraling alcoholic actress," one of his favorite "Sybil" personas. Fluttering eyelids and scratchy voice, he dragged on an imaginary cigarette: "Oh honey, it's *s-o-o* not about the cat. Can't you see it's just *s o o* much more than about the goddamn cat!"

Rosa shook her head. "*Igualmente.* The sister—and now you."

Stella Kowalski suddenly made an appearance: "Say no more about Blanche! You didn't know her as a girl. No one was as sweet and trusting and—"

The doorbell rang again, and Rosa cocked her head, sighing. "Can you get that, Dolores del Rio? I've got to bring in the cheese." She marched off toward the buffet, and Daniel hoisted his glass, irked at the abrupt suspension of his dramatic prowess. Lumbering toward the entry, he waved perfunctorily to Dr. Caraway, now sitting in a corner with Mrs. Fentiman, the widow of a former state senator. "Hello, Daniel! I need to talk to you later. I'm getting a little fishing party together for next weekend."

Daniel nodded, murmuring to himself, "Goody, goody. Trekking for trouser trout with Martin Caraway." He smiled blankly and proceeded down the hall.

Opening the front door, Daniel blinked and nearly dropped his glass. There stood Lester, wearing tight jeans and a smallish T-shirt with the words Texas Department of Corrections emblazoned across the front. He looked exactly like something ripped from the cover of *Unzipped Magazine*.

"Hi."

"Hel-lo."

"Your sister told me to wear something vulgar. This is all I had. Is it a costume party?"

Daniel nodded slowly. "In many ways, yes. Come in."

Lester entered the house as Daniel eyed him like a seagull on a bag of Fritos. "You are something, you know that?"

"Why?"

"Trust me. If you were looking from this direction, we'd be expecting our first child by now."

Lester stared at him.

"Would you like to meet the rest of the cannibals?"

Entering the living room, Daniel made certain Dr. Caraway was the first to spot Lester. Martin glanced up, nearly choking on his spinach *empanada*. "Dr. Caraway, Mrs. Fentiman, I'd like you to meet a new friend of mine and Melanie's. This is Lester. Lester…"

"Briggs."

"That's right. How could I forget? I guess my mind was somewhere else. I wonder what makes our minds wander so, Dr. Caraway. Dr. Caraway?" Martin Caraway's expression resembled something between a frightened bunny rabbit and an eighty-year-old Rottweiler holding a salami between its paws.

"P…pleased to meet you. Briggs? Did you say Briggs?"

"Yes, sir."

"You're not related to the Stephen Briggs family from Lubbock are you?"

"No sir, I doubt it."

"I went to school with old man Stephen. I say 'old man' because he was a few years older than me, *heh-heh*. What did you say you do?"

Daniel took Lester's arm. "He didn't. But maybe he'll tell us all about it on that fishing trip you've got planned." Daniel turned Lester toward the others. "And my, my…here comes Mother." Yvonne approached the two men with the wary stealth of a phobic ocelot.

"Mother, I'd like you to meet Lester Briggs."

"Hello, Lester Briggs. Welcome to our home." Clenching her teeth, Yvonne zeroed in on the T-shirt. "That's an interesting shirt you're wearing. Did you get it at the Gap?"

Lester shook his head. "No, ma'am. I earned it."

Yvonne looked momentarily surprised and then smiled brightly. "How clever! What do you do?"

"He's in oil and gas, Mother. Can't we just offer him some bread and water before the Inquisition starts?"

Daniel started to shove Lester toward the dining room when Melanie looked up from a cluster of middle-aged men and squealed. "He's here!"

By now, everyone in the room was focused on the lanky stud in the prison T. Their looks varied from mild disapproval to virtual molestation. Melanie, sloshing her champagne, teetered toward Lester and flung her arms dramatically around his neck. "You look fffffucking great!"

Yvonne's smile was so fixed, Daniel feared she might have detached a nerve. Resolute as ever, she chirped, "All right everyone, shall we move to the patio? I think our grilled snappers are almost done. Rosa, can you help me transport some of these appetizers?"

They all aimed en masse for the back doors. Melanie took Lester's hand, leaned into his ear, and bit it softly. "You know what makes you so sexy?" She didn't wait for his answer. "Everything. There isn't one part of you I wouldn't want to take a bite of."

Lester blushed nervously. "Looks like you've got a head start on me here. How much of that fizzy stuff have you had?"

Melanie held up her finger. "One! One little baby glass." She drained the champagne and put her finger to her lips, whispering, "And two teensy-weensy, *pequeño* Valium—just to get me through another Mother Extravaganza." Melanie rolled her eyes. "You don't know what I go through." Bob passed by carrying two chairs from the dining room. "Oh Daddy, have you met Lesss—ter?"

Bob sat the chairs down and extended a hand. "Pleased to meet you, Lester. Glad you could make it. Will you help me keep an eye on my girl tonight? I'm afraid she might have just one too many, and I'll really catch hell from her fiancé up in New York. She's told you about Brian? Great guy, investment banker, big boating fanatic like me. Do you boat?"

Lester shook his head. "My uncle has a bass boat. He's let me borrow it a few times."

Bob laughed agreeably and patted Lester's shoulder. "Great. Good man. We'll talk." He shuttled off to help Yvonne.

Melanie leaned her head on Lester's shoulder, pouting. "Poor Daddy. I wish you'd met him before he discovered…water."

***

Dinner seemed to last an eternity. After Melanie passed out in a chaise lounge halfway through the blood orange sorbet, Lester began conversing with the guests. Most of them were genuinely curious, intrigued even. He decided to sit on the prison tales and just stick with stories about his funny relatives from Hoot. Everyone seemed entertained enough. And he was truly enjoying himself. A few beers, good food, lively conversation—it was the simple things that made life tolerable. Finally, Yvonne decreed it time for Melanie to be put to sleep in her room. Daniel led the way while Lester carried her up the stairs into her bedroom.

Flicking on the light switch, Daniel gestured, "And here's where Miss Life of the Party hangs her lampshade."

Lester put her down gently on the bed and gazed at her comatose splendor. "Why does she get so wasted?"

Daniel shrugged. "Why does anyone? She's unhappy."

"About what?"

"The usual—poverty, war, famine. That and she's never really liked her feet."

Suddenly Melanie rose from the dead and stared at Daniel. "Sweetheart, bring me one more glass of champagne so I can sleep."

Daniel, incredulous, said, "Honey, if you can't sleep on that pool you drained downstairs, nothing's going to help."

"Pleeeeeease. Just one."

Daniel glanced at Lester, shook his head, and left the room.

Lester sat beside Melanie. She smiled at him through half-shut eyes. Suddenly she began pulling him toward her as if to whisper in his ear and instead stuck her tongue in his mouth. Lester's heart began racing so fast, he was afraid he might've broken something. "Whoa! You're drunk."

"Uh-huh."

"You've got a boyfriend."

"Uh-huh."

"Your parents are down—" Melanie pulled Lester on top of her with one hand while simultaneously pulling her dress over her head with the other. "Hurry, before he gets back."

Lester stared at her perfect breasts as she closed her eyes, gasping. Undulating in all her naked splendor, she was exactly like every airbrushed, impeccable jail-cell pinup on the walls at Diboll. He couldn't believe this was happening. Slowly, he traced his middle finger on one nipple and then leaned forward and put his mouth on her skin. Melanie sighed, clutching his head. "Hurry!" Lester put an ear to her chest listening to her heartbeat. His body ached to make love. To hold and be held. To feel flesh, breath—wet and warmth—over and over and over. Lester heard laughter coming from the lawn. He heard Daniel talking to his father. He listened to the murmuring noises in Melanie's throat. And then he stood up.

"No."

Melanie opened her eyes wide. "No?"

"Not this way."

"What way?"

"I don't...love you."

"I don't love you. So?"

"I can't."

Melanie couldn't believe it. Slowly, tears welled in her eyes.

The hurt and perplexity in her face was tangible. The last thing he wanted was to hurt her.

She spoke in a whisper: "Once...before I get married and completely, *hopelessly* turn into my mother, I want to know what real passion is. Just once." She rolled slowly to her side and faced the wall.

Lester felt sick. Looking at her exquisite naked back, he wanted very much to touch her skin once more. Instead, he pulled at the afghan at the foot of the bed and covered her shoulders. "I'll call you tomorrow, Melanie." As there was no answer, he walked out, closing the door gently behind him.

Lester walked numbly down the hall. When he reached the stairs, Daniel was ascending with the glass of champagne. "What happened?"

"She's asleep."

"Great." Daniel put the glass to his mouth and drained it. "This whole thing was making me thirsty."

Lester continued around him.

"Where you going?"

"Home."

"Already?"

"I have to work in the morning. Tell your parents thanks. I had a very nice time."

"That's not very gentlemanly. You tell them."

"I can't right now."

Daniel glanced toward Melanie's bedroom. "That bad, huh?"

Lester continued for the front door. "Night."

"Hey," Daniel called.

Lester turned.

"You need a ride?"

Lester shrugged and continued walking down the stairs and out the front door. Daniel sat his drink down and followed him outside.

Standing on the lawn, they both gulped in the night air rolling up off the bay like a wet fish fry. "Come on. I'll drive. Least I can do for you sticking it out at the House of Wax all evening."

Daniel got into the Porsche and opened the passenger door. Lester slid in beside him.

They were both silent as they drove along the estuary. Daniel reached for his prized Nina Simone CD and inserted it into the player. Mouthing the words to "My Baby Just Cares for Me," he suddenly glanced over at Lester. He shifted the Porsche into first and then turned onto the beach road, away from town.

"Where you going?"

"Just a quick swim."

"I told you, I gotta work early in the morning."

Daniel smiled. "Everybody has something to do in the morning. We spend our whole lives 'doing stuff in the morning.' Right now, I want to go swimming, and you're going with me."

He parked the car on an isolated stretch of beach. Turning off the ignition, he turned to Lester. "Come on, I'll show you my smallpox vaccination if you show me yours."

Lester frowned and stared off into the distance.

Daniel shrugged. "Suit yourself. I won't be long." He took the keys and shoved them in the crotch of his underwear, smiling at Lester. "Just so I don't lose them." Then he stripped down to his civvies and ran into the water, yelping like a six-year-old. Lester watched him splashing and leaping about like a clown and shook his head. *Where are these people from anyway?* Daniel stood on his hands and did upside-down splits. He then ran to the edge of the surf and reached into his underwear. "Uh-oh," he said dramatically, smiling toward Lester.

Lester rose up in the seat. "You lost the keys!"

Daniel shook his head. Then he held up the keys, jiggled them, and flung them into the ocean. "*Now* I have," he said, laughing.

Lester jumped out of the car. "You stupid idiot! We've got to walk all the way back into town?"

Daniel shook his head again. "Cute and dumb are not scientific equations, you know. I have an extra pair hidden under the car. You'll have to come swimming for one full minute if you want me to look for them."

Lester sighed wearily and gazed toward the lights of the town. "I don't have a swimsuit."

"Neither do I."

"I'm not wearing underwear."

Daniel pulled off his shorts and flung them into the surf. "Neither am I!"

Lester stared at Daniel. He put his hands on his head and yelled as loud as he could: "Is everyone in this fucking place crazy but me?"

After a brief silence, Daniel replied, "Actually, the jury's still out on you, dude."

Lester yelled again. Then he stood and ripped off his shoes, shirt, socks, and jeans and went running into the surf naked as an egg. The water felt incredibly, amazingly good to him: bristly alkaline and pungent, honest-to-God Gulf of Mexico brine. Texas embryonic soup. From oil spills to sea turtle piss, it's all in there—teeming with more life than a seesaw loaded with five-year-olds.

Lester made as much of a scene as Daniel had. He did back-flips and somersaults. He tried bodysurfing. He and Daniel cuffed great tsunamis of water in each other's eyes. Daniel tossed a nasty wreath of seaweed on Lester's back, and Lester tackled him, tying it around his neck. Daniel picked up an abandoned bucket, scooped sand into it, and dumped the whole thing on Lester's head. Lester pursued him down the beach for about a hundred yards, but Daniel outran him. Finally, Lester lay down on the wet sand and stared up at the stars.

"Truce?" Daniel came trudging back and collapsed beside him.

"Truce."

"God...I'm so out of breath. How can I be in college and breathe like I'm a hundred?"

"You just ran a three-minute mile, that's why."

Daniel nodded and laughed. "I'm fast. At least until I want them to catch me."

They both lay there, gasping. Daniel covertly studied Lester's long, handsome body stretched out in the sand. Here was *People* magazine's "Sexiest Con of the Year" lying naked beside him. He shook his head, thinking, *Why me, God?*

Clearing his throat, he turned to Lester. "If you don't mind my asking, what does a guy *do* in prison for four years? You know, for release."

Lester rose slowly and walked toward the surf. Daniel watched him striding gracefully through the shallow water. Lester kicked at some small rollers and then turned back to Daniel. "I'm not gay, if that's what you're asking. I like women."

"OK."

"I've been with guys. It's no big deal. So, what's the big deal?"

Daniel shrugged back at him.

"Look, I've been *obsessed* with this woman for nearly four years now. I love her. She's all I had to keep me going. I...I've never been able to talk with anyone like her before." Lester walked back toward Daniel, sitting down again. He spoke softly: "You know what I'd like to know? What do people do when everything they believe turns to shit?" Lester sighed, pushing his hand through his hair.

"I guess they find some other shit to believe in."

Lester picked up a chipped sand dollar and sent it skittering across the water.

"And what if...a person weren't absolutely sure about everything he thought he was once absolutely sure about?"

Daniel squinted, focusing on the horizon. "That depends. Are we talking about potato salad or...sexual preference?"

Lester looked straight ahead, motionless.

Daniel finally spoke. "You know, it's not really that difficult. What makes your dick hard, Lester?"

He laughed. "*Everything*—and nothing."

Daniel grinned. "See? That was easy. We're down to two things!"

Lester rolled over on his stomach. "You've always known you were gay, haven't you?"

Daniel shook his head. "I got confused once in third grade when I kissed Cindy Rushing. She threw a ball like a guy, so that might have been it. Yeah, I've always known I was *sexual.* Hey, I've never fully ruled out women, but then I've never fully ruled out Clydesdales either."

Lester lifted his chin and propped it on his fist. "I had a... friend...at the state pen. His name was Little Ray. In prison talk, he was my 'bitch.' But he was more than that. You know, I went as long as I could without sex, and then I just woke up one day. Hell, I needed it. Everybody gives you shit, and everybody does it in prison, so what the fuck? I got a *boy—friend*. At first it was just releasing tension. But then, I guess he got under my skin." Lester rolled onto his back. "I liked him. Loved him...I dunno." Lester stared at the stars. "Prison does some strange stuff."

"What if Little Ray were here right now?"

Lester continued gazing and then rolled over to face Daniel. "I miss the way he feels; I just don't feel that way about other guys. Maybe I'm a 'one-guy' gay?"

Daniel smiled, stood, and walked toward the water, brushing the sand off his ass. "So, did you find Little Ray attractive when you first started...doing it?"

"He was OK."

"When did that change for you?"

"When did *what* change?"

"Your feelings for him."

Lester put his hands behind his head, thinking. "He told me he loved me one night. No one had ever said that to me before."

"And then you began to feel for him back?"

Lester nodded.

Daniel kicked a clump of sand impatiently. "Don't you see? It's not about *who* you have sex with; it's about *here*," Daniel said, thumping his chest. "Are you truthful in here? Fuck society, fuck religion, fuck the government. Are you an honest person in *here*?" Daniel dropped to his knees in front of Lester: "Love a woman, love a man, love a seashell. But don't cheat yourself out of loving *something*."

The two stared at each other until Daniel finally stood awkwardly and began walking toward the car. He opened the hood of the Porsche and groped around for the key in the darkness. He suddenly felt Lester's hand on his shoulder. Daniel shook his head nervously. "I swear to God, Lester, unless this means something real to you, don't go there, 'cause it's incredibly real to me right now."

Lester put both hands on Daniel's shoulder and turned him around: "I'm looking at you. Really looking. I need...someone."

Daniel slowly put his arm around Lester's waist, and the two men embraced. Falling to the sand, Lester closed his eyes and thought of nothing. Heavenly nothing. All he knew was the present—the taste, the touch and the smell of *now*.

chapter

SIX

"Neither death, nor life, nor angels, nor rulers,
nor things present, nor things to come, nor powers,
nor height, nor depth, nor anything else in all creation,
will be able to separate us from...love..."—Romans 8:38–39

Lester reread the Bible verse over and over again. Romans 8:38–39. It adhered to his brain like a form of solace glue. "Nor anything else in all creation will be able to separate us..."

Looking up, he rested the tattered, paperback Bible on the box beside his cot. He'd found the Holy Book buried on a shelf behind Otis' desk and asked if he could borrow it. It was soon apparent to Lester that Otis was the nonproselytizing sort of Christian who didn't give a rat's ass about your spiritual well-being unless you showed some inkling toward redemption, in which case he turned into a font of encouragement and advocacy. "Best damn book ever written! Old Bible's got more whoring, thieving, and blaspheming then all the trash on TV combined. Them old Pharisees, Moabites, and Hittites all a-whomping and smiting each other—if they wadn't a bunch of hell-raisin' outlaws, I don't know what is."

Lester yanked the chain on the overhead light. Lying back on his cot, he stared in the darkness at the red glow from a smoke detector fastened to an adjacent wall. Mildred crawled up and settled in her preferred spot between his legs. After her ritual back-and-forth pawing of the bedspread, she settled down and began to purr. Lester tried sleeping. He tried thinking about the "just after the rain" interval on his granddaddy's farm—the smell, the stillness, the lacquered gleam of wet. It had the effect of quieting him down enough in prison to be able to sleep. He tried counting backwards, repeating the Lord's Prayer, rocking his right foot, but nothing seemed to work. As much as he sought the narcotizing effects of sleep, it wasn't happening. Daniel, Melanie, Laurel Jeanette, and Philip consumed his thoughts. Who was he now? Had there been a shift? A "new view" partially obscured by some hidden dread and distrust? What was happening to him?

He threw off the bed covering, sending Mildred sputtering under the racks of tires. Sitting on the side of the cot, he scratched his head, exhausted. Sex with Daniel had been fast and greedy. They'd consumed each other. As with Little Ray, there was the same lusty abandon and carnal response. But what appeared to be largely missing was any sentiment. Of the many emotions Lester felt afterwards, love was not among them. And whether it was a form of love that he experienced with Little Ray, or whatever other feeling it was, it was definitely not there with Daniel.

Who am I now? Straight man who desires sex with women, and one other man only. Straight man who *thinks* he desires sex with women, and one other man only. Straight man who *thinks* he desires sex with women, and *possibly* one other man only. Bisexual male. Bisexual male with preference. Bisexual male who really wants to be with only one man. Bisexual male who really wants to be with only one man, and perhaps one woman, but open to possibility. Gay man. Gay man who wishes he loved women. Gay man who desires sex with women, and one other man only. Colossal fuck-up in need of intensive counseling.

Lester hobbled to the bathroom, his bare feet sensitive on the cold, concrete floor. Standing at the toilet, he wondered why it even mattered. Labeling, categorizing, this senseless pigeonholing of something as esoteric as sexual desire. You're either a vegan, left-handed, dyslexic, Native American, Catholic, transsexual, hemophiliac, dwarf—or you're not. What's to be done about it? The initial answer for him was that, of course, it *did* matter. Very much. A fluid, pliable, mutable existence was perhaps a wonderful thing to aspire to, provided that's who you were and provided that's what you were able to attract. But this, he knew in his heart, was definitely not who he was. All things to all people seemed to be to Lester all wrong. The desire, wherever it came from, to affect and be affected by *one* individual in *one* exceptional way was consummate to his being. Somewhere, somehow there had to be an answer to his predicament because what he most genuinely felt at present was a staggering lack of love: love in any form, of any kind, with any degree of tenderness.

Shuffling back to the cot, he collapsed in a bewildered ball. Did everyone find intimate human bonding this perplexing? Was he the requisite freak of natural law?

Comparing himself to the others in prison was pointless. There were the numerous fathers of offspring in the "outside" world who nonetheless kept two or more boyfriends strung along "inside" for their exigent needs—all seemingly raucous heteros who blathered incessantly about their wives and girlfriends and who, regardless, he spied repeatedly either on their knees or on their toes in the mortal press of another man. Sure there were those who abstained. There were those who wore their dicks raw from masturbation, too. Sex is to prison what hymns are to church. Keeps the place humming.

And before prison? Lester was for all intents and purposes a lapsed virgin. He'd done all the high school make-out sessions and felt the girls up and down. But gone all the way, hit a home run, shot under the goalpost? Only once. A couple of months before going to prison, he'd met a schoolteacher from Tyler, Texas, at a local dance. She was pretty and kind, but it was over too quickly, and he sensed she was ticked off about something. He was probably too shy, or clumsy, or…something. And with guys? Some early Boy Scout exploratory sessions, one or two overnighter, grabby-goosey male episodes that didn't amount to much. He figured it would all come together with the right one. Actually, he really didn't think much about it. He'd been a fairly serious boy and a fairly subdued man. Prison had only added a few alterations to his overall character.

And Laurel Jeanette or Luz, or whoever she really was—he did love her. Of this he was certain. The incident with Melanie only reaffirmed his belief that the wrong person was, as expected, the wrong person. Regardless of attraction or desire, a new pair of gloves will work only if they fit. He resolved that Luz was the answer to his present torment. He'd let himself get sidetracked. Though others might seek to prevent his aim, he knew in his heart what was real. So what if Luz wasn't who he once thought she was? She was definitely who he needed her to be. And for now, it was enough for him until they could meet again.

Lester closed his eyes and rolled over. Sleep eventually came, intermingled with warm tuna breath and tremulous whiskers sharing his pillow.

***

Luz stood at her back door appraising Lester with a confused half-smile on her face.

"What did I think? I thought you were a true-blue, nine hundred percent, foam-at-the-mouth nutcase. Are you?"

"No, ma'am. Not at all."

She wasn't convinced. "How do I know I can trust you?"

Lester shrugged. "No problem. I'll sit out on the curb here and wait till the pants are done. I'd sure appreciate it if you'd visit with me some though."

Luz studied him a moment longer and pushed open the screen door. "Come on in."

Lester hesitated briefly. After checking the driveway and garage for Philip's Chevrolet, he wanted to be certain they were alone.

"If you've got company or obligations, I can come back another time."

"No. Just me. I don't teach on Wednesdays in the summertime, and brother's at church working on the grounds."

Lester stepped inside, and Luz smiled brightly. "But just so you'll know, we've got guns in every room, and I'm conversant with all of them." She turned around and walked into the kitchen.

Lester followed behind her, once more transported by the smells and incredible array before him. Luz walked toward the utility room, talking over her shoulder. "You're probably thinking this is where Julia Childs hangs when she's not liberating France of excess truffles."

Lester stared blankly. "Who?"

Luz glanced back at him. "My brother's an amateur chef. He's the 'Eydie Gourmet' around here, not me. I'm happy with peanut butter and saltines." Luz held up her arms: "Toss me those pants, and I'll stick 'em in the washer."

Hesitantly, Lester pitched her the jeans, feeling as if he were offering his dirty underwear up for some kind of civil inquiry. Luz dumped them and some other garments into the machine. "They'll be done in a few. How 'bout some lemonade? We can sit on the front porch and swap yarns."

Lester smiled and nodded.

Luz walked to the fridge, removed a plastic pitcher, and began pouring two glasses. She suddenly made a face. "Eww, I think he put blackberry juice in here." She sniffed the container suspiciously. "God, the man can never leave well enough alone. Do you know any other living human being that puts candied lavender in their coffee?"

Lester shrugged, not entirely certain he knew what candied lavender was.

Luz handed him a glass. "Well, maybe this cures ringworm or something. Shall we?" Luz led the way to the front porch, and Lester once again followed.

Watching her move down the hallway, he studied her figure. She was a little heavier than he'd expected: more solid, fleshy. And she definitely possessed the traditional hallmarks of female fertility with her "child-bearing thighs." But she was also a little taller than he envisioned and definitely more physically imposing than her dated picture revealed. Overall, she bore the ripeness and fullness of a lush persimmon—a large, female persimmon. And when she smiled, Lester thought his chest would split. She was still so beautiful and desirable to him—and so painfully removed.

"Come here, Windsor. Come here, boy." Luz plopped onto the porch swing, stretching her bare legs beside her. The dog bounded up the front steps, momentarily sniffed at Lester's shoes, and then jumped in the swing next to Luz. She scratched his head. "This is my baby, Mr. Windsor L. Canterbury Yancey. I got him when he was still about the size of a house slipper. He's almost ten now." Luz hugged his neck, and Windsor emitted a throaty groan, placing his head contentedly in her lap. Luz turned to Lester. "Do I know you from somewhere?"

Lester nearly dropped his lemonade. He looked at her. Was she playing with him? Was this some cruel ruse she and her brother devised to torture dumb jays like him? He stared at his drink. "Why do you ask?"

"No reason. I get a lot of students in my classes over at the community college. Thought I might've seen you around before."

Lester bit his lip. "Nope. I've never been to college." He looked up again. "You a teacher?"

Luz nodded, quickly stifling a yawn. "'Scuse me...yes, art. Oh, I didn't sleep well last night. Theory, drawing, history of—been doing it for five years now. Love the students, hate the bureaucracy. I mostly daydream about living in Paris on a houseboat on the Seine." Beaming, Luz held up her hands dramatically: "'The Luz Yancey Lifetime Movie—French intellectuals thunderstruck by Texas girl and her bluebonnet paintings!'"

Lester stared at her, bewildered. She'd lost him completely.

Luz, unconcerned, lifted the hair on the back of her neck. "Awfully humid, even for August. Downright hateful." There was a pause in the conversation.

"Is Luz your real name?"

She turned to him, surprised. "Uh-huh, why?"

Lester again stared at his glass. "I dunno. It's different."

Luz suddenly pushed the floor with her foot and started the swing swaying. "Mercedes McCambridge. That's who my folks named me after. Actually it was the character she played in the movie *Giant.* Rock Hudson's older sister?"

Lester again looked at her vacantly.

"You have seen the movie *Giant?*"

He shook his head.

"Oh my God, every Texan by law has to see *Giant!* We wouldn't know what to do when our first gusher came in if it wasn't for James Dean!"

Seeing no response in his face, Luz's smile faded. "So what *do* you do…and what, by the way, *is* your name? You've never even told me."

"Lester. Lester Briggs."

"So much nicer when you know someone's name, don't you think? Are you from around here, Lester Briggs?"

He sat upright. "I'm from northeast Texas, a little old town 'bout the size of a baseball field. Right now I'm temporarily employed down at Otis McCloud's gas station."

Luz nodded slowly. "Oh, you're working for Mr. Otis? Well, he's practically the unofficial mayor of Rockport. Not much goes on around here he doesn't have the final bead on." She drained her glass and sat it on the porch. "What brings you down all this way?"

Lester shifted uneasily in his chair. After the endless days and nights in prison, the untold hours spent in utopian conjecture—the fantasy, schemes, and resplendent future he'd devised for the both of them—*never* did he *ever* come up with a meeting as unlikely as this one. "Well, I…I've come to look for someone."

Luz again nudged the floor with her foot. "Oh…who?"

He felt his face begin to flush, his heart jabbing at his ribs. He wanted to leap from the chair, take her in his arms, and press her against him. He wanted more than anything for her to recognize him, to stop this nightmarish farce and just acknowledge his presence. Nervously, he cleared his throat. "I don't think they know me anymore."

"Really?"

Lester stared at her. "Seems like…they forgot me, or something."

The swing halted, and Luz rubbed her arms, intrigued. "How awful. What are you going to do?"

Lester thought for a second. "Wait, I guess. I don't give up so easy."

Luz studied him briefly and then rose from the swing. "Well, I just hope you're not disappointed. Seems like you give people half a chance, and they go right ahead and break your heart in two." She passed Lester, lightly placing her hand on his shoulder. "I'm gonna check those clothes."

He shut his eyes and focused on her touch. In an instant, the past four years of his life compressed into a small, trifling notion of inconvenience. It had brought him to this place. One lone tear slid down along the corner of his nose, and he felt himself spiraling into a deep, deep well of anguish. After a pause, he opened his eyes. Out on the street, a tiny bird was pulling loose tobacco from a discarded cigar and ferrying it up into the trees. A nest created from the most random of possibilities. The startling synergy of make-do and circumstance. He exhaled deeply and looked at Windsor dozing on the swing. He was a free man for the first time in years. Whatever opportunities or hindrances awaited, *he* was now the engine of his destiny. Excuses were entirely pointless. He stared a moment longer and then placed his lemonade on the porch, stood, and entered the house. Moving toward the back laundry room, he stopped just inside the hallway and watched as Luz inserted wet clothes into the dryer. Without thinking, he stepped behind her and put his hands on her shoulders. Luz jumped with a shriek, terrified.

"I…I have something to ask you."

She gaped at him, speechless.

"Would you like to go to the picture show with me?"

Luz stumbled backwards, clutching a damp T-shirt to her neck. Finally she inhaled and steadied herself against the wall. "Jesus Chri-i-i-st! You scared the living shit out of me. Don't ever do that again!"

Lester shook his head, immediately contrite. "No."

"You want to give someone a coronary? Get your head knocked off ?" Luz pointed an indignant finger: "*Don't* try that anymore." She glared at him, shaking her head. And then, much to Lester's amazement—and her own—she started to laugh. She laughed so hard, she knocked the box of Tide over, spilling it across the surface of the dryer. Luz glanced at the heap of white detergent and laughed still harder. She then grabbed a handful and flung it at Lester, deliriously. "*Picture show?*"

Embarrassed, Lester brushed the powder from his hair.

"Are you from Mars? Nobody goes to the *picture show.*"

"They do in Hoot!"

Luz nearly choked. "*Ho-o-o-t?* What in God's name is 'Hoot'?" She seized another clump of soap and hurled it at Lester, whooping with hilarity. This time Lester reciprocated with his own handful of soap flakes. Luz squealed in protest as she shook the residue from her hair.

"That's where I'm from—Hoot, Texas. Don't you know anything?" Lester began laughing with her.

Luz immediately shot back another blast of soap powder, shouting breathlessly. "There is no such place as Hoot! There's no Hook, Hawk, Hoop, or Hype, either—liar, liar, pants on fire!" Gasping with laughter, she grabbed the box of Tide and halfheartedly banged Lester on the side of the head before collapsing to the floor, exhausted.

Startled, Lester seized the now-concave box and emptied the entire contents on top of her. Luz howled in outrage and reached over to bite his leg. Tumbling beside her, Lester immediately examined his calf for blood.

"You trying to cripple me? That hurt!"

"Serves you right for scaring me."

98

They both sat there on the laundry room floor, giggling and sputtering like a pair of three-year-olds. Lester watched as Luz swatted at her shiny brunette hair, sending the soap dandruff flying. He thought she was the most extraordinary thing he'd ever seen. It suddenly occurred to him how amazingly resourceful God could be when he truly needed one's attention.

Luz was still snickering and shaking her head when she inadvertently glanced up to see Philip standing at the door. His horrified expression immediately produced the image of a large, gray pickle in her head. She smiled at him. "Hello."

"Wh...What are you doing?" Philip sputtered.

Luz blinked at him and held up a fistful of detergent: "Laundry." She began to laugh again. Philip glared at Lester and turned back toward the kitchen. Luz mumbled, "I'm in deep shit now. That's my older brother."

They both stood and shook themselves. Lester gently swept the back of Luz's blouse with his hand. "He doesn't have all that much to be mad about."

Luz shook her head. "Oh, he has a temper when he gets worked up." She then shrugged. "Whatever. It's my house, too." She leaned in and whispered, "He can't afford to buy me out."

Together they walked into the kitchen. Philip, standing ramrod straight, seemed transfixed by a bowl of fruit before him. Luz started to speak when he suddenly spun around and beamed at them both. "Who'd like a kiwi daiquiri? Doesn't that sound like a good idea?"

They both stared blankly. Then Luz walked to the sink and filled a glass with water. "That's quite a switch. I was expecting to get my head bitten off."

"Oh, life's far too short to carry around a grudge, don't you think?" Philip approached Lester, smiling. He extended his hand. "Philip Yancey."

Lester, motionless, eyed him for what seemed an eternity. Luz turned from the sink and stared at them both curiously. Finally, Lester accepted his hand.

"Lester Briggs."

Philip exhaled, shaking his hand. "Pleasure to know you, Lester Briggs. How did you and my sister come to…meet?" He watched Lester apprehensively.

Luz drained her glass. "I sat his crotch on fire several days ago. I seem to have that effect on people."

Philip turned to Luz. "In plain English."

"In plain English, I spilled coffee all over him at Petronilla's. So, I offered to wash his pants for him." Luz affected a Southern belle drawl: "Honestly, your honor, it's the truth!"

Philip turned to Lester, a small smile on his face. "Will you join us for a daiquiri then, Mr. Briggs? Fresh laundry and demon rum—such charitable consecrations don't happen every day."

"I've got to get back to my job. I'm on lunch break."

Luz jiggled her blouse, dislodging the last specks of soap. "You shouldn't pass this one up. Reverend Yancey rarely breaks out the grog before sundown." She turned to Philip. "And what is the noteworthy occasion, may I ask?"

Philip picked up a kiwi fruit and began peeling in a bowl. "Oh, the splendor of summer, the never-ending mystery of life, the glory of God to transcend our humble tribulations—it's all worthy of a good, stiff pour."

Luz smiled, "Works for me. I don't have to be anywhere."

Lester brushed some residual specks off his shoulders and turned to Luz. "Thanks for the lemonade. It's been a pleasure."

"What about your pants?"

"I can pick them up later. So will you…go?"

Luz looked at him for a moment and then shrugged. "When?"

"How's Friday?"

She grinned. "Why not."

Philip, listening intently, turned to Luz. "Making plans? Isn't Friday when you said you'd help me start painting the assembly hall in the Sunday school building?"

"That's in the afternoon. Lester and I are going to the 'picture show' Friday night."

Philip stared at Lester with a frozen smile on his face. He turned back to peeling kiwis. "I see."

Lester approached Luz and held out his hand. "I'll be looking forward to it." He pointed a thumb toward the laundry room. "Need some help sweeping up?"

Luz shook her head. "Forget it. Two minutes with a Dust-Buster—I'm done."

Lester massaged his head. "You've got a strong right hand."

Luz grinned. "I'm pretty tough for a girl. No one would ever play with me at recess."

Still holding her hand, Lester replied, "I would've." After a pause, he turned on his boots and started to exit. Stopping at the back door, he called to Philip, a tiny smile on his face, "Reverend." Lester clomped down the back steps and whistled down the driveway.

Philip, stone faced, continued with his kiwi peeling.

Luz reached for the portable vacuum hanging under a cabinet and laughed. "Funny guy. There's something so…I don't know, naïve about him. He's sweet."

Lester concentrated on his bowl of fruit. "Does he know about you?"

"Know?"

Philip was silent. "What you are?"

Luz laughed again. "What 'I are'?"

Philip suddenly dropped the knife and scowled at Luz. "Oh, come on, Luz. Did you tell him or not?"

"Tell him *what* for God's sake?"

"That you're gay!"

Luz blinked in astonishment. "Uh…And what reason would there be for bringing *that* up?"

Philip sighed and looked out the kitchen window. "Because has it occurred to you, sis, that he might be interested in you… sexually?"

Luz was thoroughly bewildered. "Oh, come on! He's some hillbilly bumpkin from Poop or Shoot, or God knows where. He's *so* not into me."

Philip scraped his stool back from the counter and marched toward the sink. Exasperated, he tossed the kiwi peels into the garbage disposal. "You always do this, you know. This 'clueless' thing around men. And then you can't understand why there are repercussions down the line when the hurt feelings and resentments start to appear."

"What are you talking about? First of all, I don't care a thing about this, this Lester—"

"That's it! That's exactly it. You're oblivious to anyone else's reaction except your own. I've seen it happen over and over again. That math professor, the veterinarian you had over for dinner…"

Luz stared at him, dazed, shaking her head. "The math professor was ten years ago. The veterinarian is married with two kids and a wife who was in the hospital getting a hysterectomy. I offered to feed him."

"You never see it! Both of those guys were lusting after you, and you treated them like…like yesterday's newspaper."

"Like I'm supposed to go to bed with every guy that gets a little horny or something?"

Philip crossed his arms, staring at her. "Luz, you're not unattractive. Some men find you very attractive. You send out mixed signals all the time, and it only leads to confusion." He sighed and turned to wipe the counter with a dishrag. "I'm just saying you might find you'd have better luck with those women you're interested in if you didn't cross so many boundaries all the time."

Luz stood there, nodding her head. "Oh. Uh-huh. I get it. Actually, what you're really saying is, you're hot for Lester yourself, and now you're going to make me suffer because he treats *you* like yesterday's newspaper. Right? You know you're the one who's chosen to live your life in a 'holy closet,' not me. So before you go accusing others of 'conflicting gestures,' maybe you ought to take a good look at your own screwed-up life, and ask yourself why *you're* so god-awful lonely."

Philip patiently folded the dishrag and neatly laid it over the faucet. Finally, he turned to face Luz with an outstretched arm: "Luz…"

"No-no-no! Please, not the older brother/pious preacher crap. I'm not in the mood." Luz sat the DustBuster on the counter and started to leave. She stopped at the back door. "And you're wrong, you know. Boundaries just keep people out. It's a little hard having a relationship of any kind when all you do is build walls, Philip." Luz walked outside and called for Windsor.

Philip stared at the bowl of neatly peeled kiwis before him. After a brief moment, he methodically opened a counter drawer, removed a box of plastic wrap, tore off a precise amount of covering, sealed the fruit neatly, and placed the container on a shelf in the refrigerator. He then poured himself three fingers of dark rum and sat alone in the kitchen.

chapter

SEVEN

"Bernice O'Daniel. That was her name." Otis stood under the Jeep Cherokee, gazing up at the busted and leaking oil pan. "Sonofabitch must've run over a barbecue grill to do all this damage. Ain't no armadillo gonna cause this wreckage." He shook his head. "Damn city people think every scrape happens to 'em driving in the country caused by a armadillo or some rock the size of Shreveport. Hell, half of 'em so juiced on *piña coladas* and beer, they wouldn't know if they'd run over Mary or Jesus or both. Raise her up a foot."

Lester pushed the lever on the hydraulic lift and slowly the SUV ascended on its platform to about five feet off the ground. Otis began loosening the mangled oil reservoir. "Hand me that crescent wrench over there."

Lester passed him the wrench. "So, Bernice—she was the love of your life?"

Otis grunted. "I didn't say that. She the one nearly *ruined* my life. Hell, I've loved 'bout a million gals, but she the only one left her tag on me."

"How's that?"

Otis peered up at a rusted and crooked bolt obstructing his progress. He lowered the wrench and spit. "You some kinda sigh-ky-triss or somethin'?"

Lester shook his head. "Just curious. Seems like everybody's got at least one sad story to tell."

Otis muttered. "Yeah, some of us got five or six. Anyway, she was just an old gal I let get to me. It's over and done, lo-o-o-ng time ago."

"How'd she nearly ruin your life?"

Otis snorted, shaking his head. "You is the insistent-est fella I ever know'd! You 'bout like a rat terrier with a sock in its mouth." Otis glanced at him. "Get your standing-around-butt over here and hold this wrench."

Lester moved next to Otis, and the two of them began twisting and jerking the unyielding oil pan. "I met her when I was in seminary school."

Lester dropped his arms and gaped at Otis. "Where?"

"You heard me. Hold this thing!"

Lester returned to his grip.

Otis continued: "Ever since I was a boy, I wanted to preach the word of God. Well, I saved up my money, and the good Lord took me down to a little old preaching school for colored people, yonder round Beaumont. It wadn't but three or four classrooms, but I thought I was all the way to 'Hoe-vad' and gone. Welp, first day I was in that Jesus-school, in walk this fine lookin' species of a gal—got red hair and coffee-green eyes, and she just standing there all tall-like with her big titties and long legs, and I say to myself, 'Oh thank you, Lord, for showing this sinner to heaven!'

"She come down to learn how to nurse and midwife for the poor, and we began hittin' it off right away. Now Bernice was on the fair side 'cause she being a quadroon an' all, and back in them days, I was partial to light-skinned gals 'cause I figured, you know, they got somethin' I ain't got." Otis hacked and spit, grumbling, "What they got is mostly fear of the sun and shit-don't-stink airs 'bout 'em, but that's another story. Anyway, we was getting awful serious with one another, and one day she tells me she's pregnant with our baby and I better get serious with the marriage license. Well, you know, I always figured I'd be hitched sooner or later, and Bernice was the best-looking gal around, and I just reckoned everything right happens at the just-right time. So, we high-tailed it off to some lil ole church in the piney woods and done the deed. And we was happy as two squirrels on a peanut log. For about nine months."

Lester gaped at him. "What happened?"

"What you think happened? Bernice had a baby!" Otis finally loosened the busted oil pan, and the two of them lowered it to the ground. Standing, he wiped his forehead with a crumpled hankie. "I walked into that bedroom up at her kinfolks, and she was bawling and squalling like somebody'd just sat on a puppy or something. I looked over in the baby bed to see Otis Jr. and—God help me—there was Herbert Hoover lookin' back at me! Little poot was pinker than Shirley Temple. Now I ain't saying I couldn't contrive a light-skinned baby, but this papoose was nearing on Norwegian!"

Otis walked over to the outdoor sink and stuck his head under the faucet, dousing himself good. Taking a long swallow of water, he shook himself off and dabbed his forehead with the hankie. "*Ooo-eee!* Hot, hot, hot." He tied the hankie around his forehead and started beating on the dented basin with a mallet. "What was I tellin'?" He nodded. "So, Bernice snuffs and snorts that she don't know how such a thing could happen 'cept that *maybe* she mighta had a minor transgression with some white preacher down in Port Arthur right 'fore she met me. I said, "Fore you met me? Woman, you been carrying this baby over a year now! I don't believe so, you iniquitous Jezebel.' So I go pay a little visit to that fine, white Church of Christ *padre* that done her so, and damn if he don't have some sorry, broke-down old lady hisself. An' eight little tit hangers besides! Meanest, most poor-ass looking tribe I ever laid eyes on. Well, he gets to jumpin' and shoutin' about what kinda nigger did I think I was coming into his parsonage and sullying his good name. I told him he was a no-count, scum-filled, lying sacka shit, and I pitied his half-breed baby gonna grow with no daddy and a mendacious mama to boot. Damn if the old reprobate didn't pull a pistol from under the sofa and aim it right at me. I wheeled around and stuck his nasty self good with my pocketknife." Otis' eyes grew large as bottle caps. "And then the raggedy bastard shot me right back!" He pointed to his lead-filled leg. "And there she lay, *muchacho*. Pride, lust, anger, ten years in the pokey…and the last vestige of Bernice."

Lester blinked, engrossed. "Whatever happened to her?"

Otis shrugged. "Hell do I know? She lit out for newer pastures when I went off to the pen."

"And the baby?"

Otis scratched his jaw and gazed into the distance. After a pause, he said, "He a doctor out in California."

"How do you know?"

Otis squinted at Lester. "I raised him, that's how. When his mama run off, my sister Cornelia kept him and brought him up till I got out of prison. Otis Jr.'s a fine man. Good man. We may not look alike, but in here"—Otis pointed to his heart—"we just the same."

Lester shook his head. "But why raise somebody else's kid after what they did to you?"

Otis finished beating on the oil pan and held it up to admire. "All it needs is a little soldering—better'n new." He eased up slowly on his arthritic knees. "I raised that boy 'cause that's the way God planned it. God give everyone a road map and some loose change when they starting out. All I did was give that boy a lift."

Lester studied Otis as Otis spread some solder paste on the scuffed metal. Here was a man who probably never owned more than two pairs of shoes at a time, but he'd acquired more heart and wisdom than any person Lester knew. It wasn't every day you got to meet a real human being.

"You're a good man to be acquainted with, Mr. Otis. I guess God put you right in my path."

Otis eyed him sideways and spit. "Either that or the devil needed some entertainment. When you're done holding your Johnson there, you can go fetch me a case of that 10W30 Quaker oil up on the shelf in the office."

Lester grinned and turned, walking toward the front of the garage.

Out on the boulevard, tourists were gliding by, hauling their boats, trailers, Jet Skis, and other personal philosophies of escapism. And it suddenly occurred to Lester he was truly content here. Nothing approximating ecstatic yet, but he was slowly gathering up steam on "happy-with-a-vengeance."

He whistled to himself as he hauled down the box of motor oil. Mildred was napping atop a nearby candy machine, and he gave her a mindful glance. "Milly, either you been eating more mice than usual, or you're 'bout to have yourself a little surprise." Mildred stared at him with all the care of a glutted Roman emperor. She yawned and licked herself.

Lester shook his head. "Don't come looking for me when you got a roomful of kittens crying behind you."

Lester headed out the door again when he noticed from the corner of his eye a powder-blue Jaguar crawl into the station and honk its horn. He looked over to see Yvonne Wheelwright in the driver's seat, staring straight ahead behind enormous "Jackie O" sunglasses. He sat the box down and approached the car. After a moment, Yvonne lowered the glass on the electric window and smiled demurely. "I'm so sorry. I didn't mean to honk. Old habits die hard."

"No problem. Need a fill up?"

"Supreme. Thank you."

Lester walked around to the pump and began filling. Yvonne casually stepped out of the car and stretched her legs, appraising the station curiously as if she'd just stumbled onto a Greek ruin along the Aegean. In her crisp cotton shirt, cashmere sweater slung loosely round her shoulders, toreador pants, sandals, brown Coach leather bag, and gold belt, she looked as if she'd been antiquing in the Hamptons. Or, possibly lunching with her attorney.

She removed her dark glasses and bit one plastic stem with her teeth. "It's Lester, isn't it?"

"Yes, ma'am. Lester Briggs."

"I'm so glad you came to our party the other night, Lester. I feel terrible I didn't get a chance to visit with you more."

"No, ma'am. It was a real nice party, thank you."

Yvonne laughed. "I think you absolutely enchanted quite a few of my guests. You must come back and visit with us again. Soon."

Lester smiled at her quizzically. "You need that oil checked?"

"Please."

Lester moved over to the driver's side and popped the hood. Yvonne followed him around to the front and glanced at the engine, her voice growing suddenly alarmed. "Oh God, what is that?"

"What's what?"

Yvonne pointed, "That thing there, that pile of…weeds."

Lester bent in closer to look. He stuck his finger in the small pile of grass, string, and hair lying beside the battery. Inside were three baby mice no bigger than Jordan Almonds. "You've got traveling companions."

"What are they?"

"Field mice. It happens. Mama builds her nest in a warm, dry place. She's just not always too picky about the neighborhood."

Yvonne was stunned. "Will they get into the car?"

"They could. But then they probably won't live that long. You want me to get rid of 'em?"

Yvonne flung her hands on the car hood, horrified. "Good Lord, no! Household murderess heaped on my pile of transgressions would be complete overkill. You think the mother will return?"

"Possible." Lester squinted at her. "You might want to leave out a cheese plate and some red wine just in case."

Yvonne stared at him blankly. Then she nodded her head, smiling. "Right. Some Brie and a good *Cotes du Rhone*. Roger."

Lester slammed the hood shut. "Oil's fine. Need anything else?" Lester began removing the gas hose when Yvonne sidled up beside him.

"You know, I was just wondering. I hope you won't think I'm prying, but…How much do you make here?"

Lester looked at her, surprised. "Nothing yet. Why?"

Yvonne grinned. "Well, I'm just going to lay this all out for you to decide. My husband's been working on his boat for nearly three years now—adding stuff, removing things. I couldn't begin to tell you all the alterations he's done. And I'm afraid he's getting completely despondent about ever seeing the light of day on finishing all his improvements. And I just thought, well, you seem like such a capable young man. Perhaps I might be able to hire you away from Mr. McCloud's establishment for at least a few days a week to come help Mr. Wheelwright?"

Lester looked at her. "Whose idea was this?"

Yvonne raised her eyebrows. "Mine. Oh, Mr. Wheelwright would *never* dream of asking anyone else. I'm sure he's convinced he could re-float the Lusitania and refurbish her if he just had a clean stretch of weekends."

Lester placed the hose back into the pump. "I appreciate the offer, Miz Wheelwright, but I'm kinda obligated to Mr. Otis here. This is where I live, too."

Yvonne put her sunglasses back on and turned. "You let me talk to Otis. Where is he? Out back?"

"I wish you wouldn't…" But before Lester could finish the sentence, Yvonne was halfway to the garage stall.

"Otis! Mr. McCloud, it's Yvonne Wheelwright. How are you? You remember I bought four tires from you last year?"

Otis peered out from under the Jeep and blinked. "Uh-huh. That's right. You the pretty mama of that pretty daughter got the souped-up, low-to-the-ground sports car. How you been, sweetheart?"

"Fine. Just fine. The summer has flown by. I don't think I've been in to see you more than once or twice."

"Well, you better not be buying your gas nowhere else, or I'll put the voodoo on ya!" Otis cackled and Yvonne smiled.

"Goodness, no, we wouldn't want that. Listen, Mr. McCloud—"

"Otis. Even my enemies call me Otis."

"O-tis. I have a little proposition for you."

"Go right ahead. Don't trust no one don't got a little larceny in 'em."

Yvonne continued patiently, "Well, as I was telling Lester here—"

"Ain't he a fine little peckerwood? I can't get more'n a good hour work out of him 'cause seem like he got more goin' on round town than a fat boy at a Methodist picnic. But I do think the world of him, uh-huh."

"Yes...Well, what I'd like to say to you, Otis, is..." Yvonne paused to gather her thoughts. "My husband has been working quite hard on his boat for some time now, and I've just asked Lester here if he could possibly help him out for a few days a week. I'm hoping ultimately that Mr. Wheelwright will have a little time at the end of the season to at least enjoy his vessel."

Otis looked at Yvonne, puzzled. "Vessel."

"Yacht."

"Uh-huh. And *ultimately* speakin'...What you need from me?"

"Your permission...for Lester to come work for Mr. Wheelwright...for part of the week."

Lester grinned. "Ohhhhh, I gotcha. Well hell's bells, far as I know white people still free to rain and shine wherever they please. I ain't running no detention center."

Yvonne smiled, turning to Lester. "There, you see."

Otis also turned to Lester. "Why sure, Buster Brown, you just go on and set your grip and duds out on the curb there so you'll be ready when that 'vessel' toots."

Lester shook his head. "Now, Mr. Otis, there's none of this that's my doing—"

"You misunderstand, Otis!" Yvonne interrupted. "Lester's not going anywhere."

"He ain't?"

"Why, no. He's going to continue to stay here and work with you."

"He is?"

"Of course, say Monday through Thursday noon at the gas station, and then he can work the rest of the week with Mr. Wheelwright. Naturally, I'll be paying you for Lester's lodging here."

Otis looked bewildered. "You will?"

"Well certainly. I wouldn't expect you to run a B&B for a part-time employee."

"B and…B?"

"Of course not." Yvonne reached into her Coach bag and produced a checkbook. "Would a hundred and fifty a week be enough for Lester's accommodations?"

Otis stood with his mouth open. "Well…I—"

"One seventy-five. But you have to make sure he gets a good breakfast—something high protein, low carb, not too starchy. I'm partial to amaranth flakes and a little lactose-free yogurt myself around mid-morning." Yvonne tore off the check and handed it to Otis. "Wasn't this easy? Lester, someone will pick you up Thursday at noon sharp. Rosa will have a light lunch ready, and we'll discuss your salary then." Yvonne glanced at her diminutive Girard-Perregaux watch. "Good Lord, I still have to pick up half-and-half at the store. I think we have an account with you, don't we, Otis? Can you just add my gas to it, and I'll settle next time? Wonderful seeing you both." Yvonne trotted off toward the Jag and sped away in a blur of powder-blue good-bye waves.

Otis watched as she disappeared down the boulevard. He finally crossed his arms, exhaling loudly. "I'll just say one thing: if I don't come back a rich white lady with a checkbook in my next lifetime, there's gonna be hell to pay."

***

Melanie walked slowly along the dock, her ankle-length, orange and yellow batik skirt streaming in the breeze like the flag of an Asian potentate. With her long-sleeve cotton blouse and dark glasses, she presented a decidedly more demure visual than Saturday night's display. Since then, she'd felt mostly like something that crawled out of a compost heap. Too ashamed to see Lester, she'd stayed close to home, quietly moping and ruminating. Even Yvonne had encouraged her to drive over to Corpus and see a movie: "Get your hair done—*buy* something!" It was useless. She didn't feel like doing anything but sit by the water and think. Think till she thought her head would grind away from the friction.

Melanie stopped by the gangplank where Eddie was painting the side of a boat storage locker. "Eddie, have you seen my father around?" He stared up at her, immediately disappointed he wasn't getting more of an exhibition of those heartbreaking legs.

"He was walking around here a while back, carrying some buckets and brushes. Ain't seen him since."

Melanie nodded and started up the gangplank.

Eddie called out to her: "You going swimming later?"

Melanie turned. "I might, why?"

Eddie's face flushed, and he stammered, "I figured...you know, I thought I might go swimming during my lunch hour, too. Cool off."

Melanie stared at him. "Sounds divine. Maybe we can go together. I know a place around the cove where you don't have to wear swimsuits. I'll see if Mother and Daddy want to join us."

Eddie's smile withered, and he returned to painting.

Melanie squinted at him. "You know, I worry about you sometimes. Are you getting enough sex?"

Eddie snorted and dropped the paintbrush in a can. "All I need and all I don't want. You try being married fifteen years. That 'thrill' moved on off down the road a good long time ago."

Melanie turned around and walked back down the gangplank. She approached slowly, crossing her arms. "Eddie, have you asked your wife out on a date lately?" He looked confused. "That girl you originally had the hots for? She's still there. She's been hiding herself behind an extra twenty pounds, dirty laundry, and a lot of runny noses for some time now. Go on. What are you afraid of? You might just fall in love with her all over again."

Eddie smirked and gazed out at the bay. "Yeah, I seen that eighteen-year-old girl hiding in there. I seen her every time she puts on lipstick or sprinkles a little drug store cologne on her neck. And that eighteen-year-old girl's looking at this thirty-nine-year-old man and wondering who sold who a bill of goods. Ain't none of us exactly what we advertised, know what I mean? Takes a big bite outta the sails after a while."

Eddie went back to painting, and Melanie stared at her sandals. "I've got an idea. How 'bout I treat you and your wife to dinner over at Beulah's in Port A? Drinks, steak, chocolate cake—the works."

Eddie looked at her.

"But you gotta clean up your act: scrubbed fingernails, wear a coat, and pull her chair out. Treat her like she's some thousand-dollar-a-night French courtesan who's going to give you the most mind-blowing sex of your life—if you behave like a gentleman and be sweet."

Eddie seemed suddenly enthused. "Hell, I'd wear a tuxedo and pull her around in a wagon for that kind of sex!"

Melanie held out her hand. "Deal?"

Eddie's features suddenly clouded. "The kids. Minute we get home it starts. 'Daddy, do this. Mommy, where's my that?' We hardly have time to sit on the pot."

"You got family nearby, friends? Haul 'em off to their house for the night. This is just for ya'll."

Eddie squinted at her, still trying to decide if she was genuine or not. "Well, I'll talk to her about it…"

"No, Eddie, do it! You go home, take her in your arms, and tell her she's got forty minutes to make herself wonderful—you're going on a date."

Eddie stared at Melanie, awestruck, as if he'd just watched her pull a flaming sword from her mouth. "You think?" he asked.

"I *know*. You've got ten seconds to say yes, or the deal's off. One, two…"

"Wear a coat?"

"…three, four, five…"

"I'll do it!"

Melanie shook Eddie's hand. "You're a smart man, Eddie Frye. I'm making reservations for next Friday night." She turned and started back toward the boat.

Eddie called to her, "How come?"

"How come what?"

"Why you being so nice all of a sudden?"

Melanie thought for a second and then shrugged. "Jesus, Eddie, I don't know. I guess because being a bitch all the time causes frown lines." She grinned and waved a small good-bye. Eddie watched her climb the gangplank stairs. He felt a stirring in his jeans as he daydreamed about cupping that sweet, round ass in his hands. He wondered what it would be like to fuck her and her mother both. A little three-way afternoon delight. He dipped the paintbrush back in the can. Crazier things had happened.

Gliding through the polished teak and Honduran mahogany interior of the *Amor Descolorado,* Melanie marveled again at her father's handiwork. From the collection of nineteenth-century restored brass compasses to the Space Age weather computer that could tell you if it was raining in Zanzibar or give you the speed of currents in Galveston Bay, it was all meticulously executed by his exacting hand. She reflected on why some men completely fall apart the older they get, while others ostensibly became more whole. It seemed to Melanie that her father had never experienced a moment's hesitation, vacillation, or apathy his entire life. Or perhaps it was just a taciturn code among men his class and age to never reveal self-doubt. She theorized it might very well be the most sensible approach. Where does all this introspection and uncertainty ultimately lead to anyway? Eating alone at Denny's, that's where.

Standing in the hallway of the master bedroom, she opened a narrow door and called down to the engine room. "Daddy, are you in there?"

"Come on down and look at this."

Melanie gathered her skirt and stepped sideways, descending the narrow stairs. "Pew-w, what's that smell?"

"Industrial detergent. I'm degreasing the engine. Isn't she a beauty? Neat as a gin martini. Sweetheart, hand me that rag over there."

Melanie tucked her skirt up into her belt, carefully dodging the grungy spots, and passed Bob the cloth. Ever since she was a little girl, she loved being with her father. Whatever he was doing—

building, reading, gardening, or fishing—she wanted to be right there with him. It gave her enormous satisfaction being "Daddy's helper." It was a role that her mother and Daniel avoided like the Black Death. But not Melanie. They were the few memories of her childhood that brought her any kind of peace and delight. The rest were mostly an extended tableau of rants and mopes that embodied no origin and suggested no conclusion.

"That degreaser must really work. Smells like a burnt pine forest in here." Melanie sat on the steps, and Bob smiled at her. A milk crate crammed with scrub brushes, buckets, sponges, and squeegees lay beside him.

"Yeah well, it's probably cheaper just to buy my own forest and make the stuff. You don't want to know what this cost."

"Would it be more than a gallon of Chanel No. 5?"

Bob looked up from his scrubbing. "Now there's an idea."

Melanie smiled. "Well, for sure, you'd get Mother to come aboard more often if you could capture the fragrance of the Saks cosmetics counter around here."

Bob gazed at Melanie. "Speaking of—you suppose you and she could get through the rest of the summer without another blow up?"

Melanie frowned. "What do you think those chances are?"

"Zero to none?"

"You're an optimist."

Bob dipped the rag in the soapy liquid and went back to scrubbing. "It's not easy for your mom."

"Oh Daddy, please, not the menopause lecture again. She's been going through the change of life since I was nine."

"Your mother loves you very much."

"And this will shock you—I love her. But that doesn't give her *carte blanche* to arrange my life as a sit-down dinner for fifty."

"Your mother wants to be helpful. Can't you see that?"

"Isn't it usually better when people *ask* for your help rather than dumping it on them like a bale of hay?"

Bob wiped his brow. "So, ask sometimes. Trust me. It'll make everybody's life much easier."

Melanie leaned forward. Placing her head in her hands, she sighed. "Poor, Daddy. Am I a bad person?"

Bob looked at her and laughed. "You? You're the most beautiful, charming, dynamic, intelligent, attractive twenty-four-year-old woman I know."

Melanie grinned. "Thank you. What a delightful way of not answering the question."

"Bad person?" Bob scratched his head. "What a thing to say. Where's this coming from?"

"A place I haven't been lately—my conscience."

"Something the matter?"

Melanie stood and pulled her hair back in that tight ball at the bottom of her neck, a gesture she utilized whenever she was feeling pressure. "Daddy, first of all, I love Brian—I do. He's successful and powerful and influential and athletic and…"

"And…"

"And what?"

Bob pointed to his ear. "Must be a family thing. I'm not hearing words like 'kind,' 'good,'—'*loving*.'"

"Well, he's that, too, but that comes after the other stuff. Anyway, we were talking on the phone last night, and he asked me if I'd been seeing anybody, and I said no, which is true. And then he asked me if I'd had sex with anyone, and I said, 'No, of course not!' And then it dawned on me that Saturday night, I very much made a play for Lester Briggs, the guy who came to the party. I mean, I was plastered, but I distinctly remember thinking that I wanted to have sex with him."

Bob, flustered, began scrubbing again.

"Oh Daddy, I know you hate these confessionals, but you're all I've got."

Bob glanced up, red-faced: "What's the question?"

"The question is, if I'm in love with Brian and we're getting married and he's going to be my husband, allegedly forever, why am I thinking about sex with other men, *now?*"

Bob dropped the brush back in the bucket and thought for a moment. "It's simple. You don't love Brian."

"I *do* love Brian!"

Bob shook his head. "Honey, when you really love a guy enough to want to marry him, have his kids, put up with his moods, massage his ego, ignore the balding head and looming gut, when you really love a guy *that much*, you're not thinking about sleeping with someone else *before* the marriage!"

Melanie was completely mystified. "How can I not love him? He's perfect."

"My darling, a perfect apartment and perfect teeth do not mean love. Your photos might look good together in *Town & Country* magazine, but it doesn't make a 'three in the morning, dark night of the soul, you-and-me-against-the-world' kind of love."

Melanie shook her head. "How do you make it work between you and Mother? I've never understood."

Bob picked up a scrub brush. "Ah, now that's easy. After thirty years of marriage, we've learned to just go along with each other's individual pursuits of happiness. Your mother likes clothes, parties, interesting people, and good taste. I like boats, fishing, golf, and other things. And we're still in love with each other."

"Do you...have sex?"

Bob grinned at her, amused. "We do. No child can ever believe their parents have sex, but we do."

Melanie sighed, shaking her head. "They don't make them like you anymore, Daddy. You're a saint. The men nowadays—they're all like those chocolate bunny rabbits you get at Easter. All shiny and adorable on the outside, and then you bite into one—completely hollow."

"Brian's not a bad sort. A little self-involved, but you'll cure him of that." Bob stood, gathering his cleaning supplies. "I just don't think you love him. Not a great reason to get married."

Melanie stared forlornly at the enormous, pristine Cummins engines that hulked before her like anesthetized Leviathans. "Thanks for cheering me up. I think I'll go swallow some strychnine."

Bob put his arms around her. "Listen, you're exactly perfect the way you are, and we're all trying to be a better person each and every day. Don't be so hard on yourself. This Lester fellow—maybe you should go on a few dates with him."

Melanie gasped. "You're not serious!"

"Could be he's just what you need to understand what it is you *don't* want in a relationship. Who knows? Maybe he's lousy in the sack, too."

"Daddy! This is not what you're supposed to say to your daughter!"

"I know, I know. I'm not supposed to notice I have a fully grown, single, healthy child who might possibly have a sex life of her own. All I'm saying is, don't do this to Brian if you're not ready. Don't do it to yourself. Your mother will get over it; she always does. Just think about it, huh?" Bob kissed her on the forehead, grabbed his crate of cleaning utensils, and started up the stairs. "Have you seen Eddie? I've got to get him started sanding those decks in the stern." As he disappeared into the upstairs galley, Melanie could hear him grousing, "Never be done with this tug, never. Another summer, another fifty thousand dollars…"

Melanie looked around the cold, dank engine room and shivered. She *liked* Brian; she knew that much. They did have good conversations, and he did make her laugh, and it definitely had to be factored in: they were the best-looking couple she knew. But did he *love her*? The words were said sufficiently enough, but was there any factual heart and soul behind it? And Lester? What was *that* about? Sure, he was hot and reeked of that "country stud" thing—a major weakness of hers—but she wanted to marry Lester about as much as she wanted to marry Doctor Caraway.

Melanie stared gloomily at the myriad of dials and gauges positioned on the motors. If one could only read people like machine parts. The blessed and blurry technology of people perception. Turning to walk back up the stairs, she noticed a small book lying on the floor next to where Bob's milk crate had sat. She stooped to retrieve the paperback. Glancing at the cover, she read the title softly to herself: "*1001 Spanish Baby Names.*" Ascending the steps, Melanie began turning the pages as she flicked off the lights behind her.

chapter

EIGHT

Philip parked the Impala behind the two Harley-Davidsons stopped directly in front of him. Seated in the rear on each bike were two nearly identical, long-haired blonde women. Removing their helmets and shaking their heads indolently, they looked to him like glistening commercials for hair dye, beer, or breath mints. Piloting the powerful choppers were two strapping, equally blonde men, clad in black leather, Ray-Bans, and studied aloofness. Philip smiled. The four of them appeared to be like some assimilated organism come to spread blondeness and perfect DNA throughout the land.

The ferryboat across the ship channel from Aransas Pass to Port Aransas took no more than seven minutes, berth to berth. Since childhood, it had epitomized to Philip an exotic, transcendent journey of possibility and expectation. The choppy blue-green water, the dolphins, seagulls, and smell of pungent sea all combined to create an air of faraway contemplation. He took the ferry whenever he needed time to think. The very notion of "sailing to the island," on which Port Aransas was situated, was an act of essential escapism for him. And even if he were girdled on the tarred boat deck by overheated Suburbans, raucous vacationers, and bulging Winnebagos, the journey itself was enough to immediately transport him to a more contemplative and benevolent place.

"Excuse me, vould you mind taking the picture?"

Philip turned from his vista of blue horizon to see one of the blonde Vikings holding out his Hasselblad toward him. "Just the four, OK?"

Philip took the camera, and they quickly arranged themselves on their road hogs, looking alternately foreboding and only slightly campy. They each beamed with predictably bright teeth. He clicked. One of the Valkyries waved at Philip, "Tank you."

"Where are you from?"

"Netherlands. Ve come ever year to America to ride in the Harley-Davidson parade."

"Oh, really? I didn't know there was one."

"Yah, many. All over America. This year in Texas." He smiled boyishly. "Ve like Texas. Very 'John Wayne.'" The other three grinned and nodded in accord.

"Well, welcome. I love Amsterdam. I was only there once, but it's a wonderful city."

The blonde one's face turned to a frown. "Too crowded. Too many cars, buses, and people. Ve like the simple life."

"What do you do in Holland?"

He pointed, "Jergen and I are makeup and hair consultants. Marta and Juliana are in the adult entertainment business. Ve live together on farm."

Philip was only vaguely starting to comprehend this rather novel fusion of vocations when the ferry blasted its horn. Simultaneously, twenty-plus car engines started. The blonde man smiled and took back his Hasselblad. "Tank you very much."

"Enjoy your stay."

The four of them positioned themselves nimbly on their bikes and awaited the gangplank to drop. Philip returned to his car and waved as they sped away. If they'd asked him what he did, would it have sounded quite as intriguing? Small-town minister versus adult entertainment worker or hair and makeup consultant. The more he pondered the idea, the more it seemed largely congruent. What is a minister if not an image facilitator for grown-ups?

Philip drove slowly along Trout Street, passing the numerous cheap curio shops, seaside cafes, and bars. Docks of pleasure boats and charter fishing rentals were swarming with tourists hellbent on leisure. Port Aransas in the summer was not for the listless. Exuberant recreation was sacrosanct. All undertakings were carried out with consummate abandon: fishing the ocean bare, sunbathing until charred, Jet Skiing heedlessly, and drinking until putrefaction. It was definitely a Texas thing.

He made his way into the crowded parking lot of Virginia's. The establishment had recently undergone a change of management, and it was now his new old-favorite place to dine facing the ship channel. Sitting on the awning-covered deck, gazing out at the rusted lighthouse, feeling the sultry and not altogether unpleasant warm breeze ruffle his collar, he could feel himself starting to meld with his glass of wine. Tankers hulking past bound for Aruba or Campeche and pelicans gathered on pilings like grizzled sea prophets all made him feel like he could be elsewhere—a Caribbean isle or some Iberian seaport perhaps. His vigorous imagination was one of his more useful traits. In fact, it was his saving grace.

Ordering another white wine, he felt the fruity, astringent alcohol slowly prying open the interior door in his head marked "Lester." He hadn't allowed himself to dwell too closely on the events of the past week, partially due to a busy schedule and partially from the sheer, manifest terror building inside him. Mostly he had prayed for an immediate answer. Which way to safety, God? And as usual, the immediate answer was less than forthwith. In his long and devoted spiritual practice, he'd nearly always found a fair amount of procedure involved when it referenced God's feedback. Usually.

Had he deceived Lester? Without a doubt. Was it deliberate? Admittedly. Were there reasons—conscious ones—behind his deception? Most definitely. Would he ever in a thousand lifetimes have wanted to hurt Lester? Never. And the knowledge of that certainty pierced his thoughts like a claw digging at his brain. How did he tell him *now* that he'd already begun making plans to start visiting him in Diboll in anticipation of his release date? That he'd devised twice monthly trips, first to introduce himself as a spiritual counselor, then as a friend, and then perhaps as a potential...confidante? An early release was never even remotely in the scenario for what he'd systematically organized: acquaintance, friendship, respect, confidences shared, trust, affinity, and then perhaps...attraction? Was it so ludicrous? Had Lester not told him in his letters about his trysts with Little Ray? Were they not each "in denial" in their own categorical way?

Yes, of course he knew it was completely wrong to have instigated such a despicable ruse as impersonating another person. It was wrong to have used Luz's picture, wrong to have continued the ploy for nearly four years. He was dead wrong about many, many things—except for the legitimacy of his love for Lester. Of that he was unequivocal. From the minute he saw his picture through the prison outreach program, he knew that Lester was the one. The one he felt, quite probably, who could restore some sense of probability to his life.

But why use Luz's picture? Why not some faceless, nameless creature ripped from a newspaper or "borrowed" from an anonymous website? That was the difficult part to answer. Why indeed? As best as he could determine, Philip rationalized that, by utilizing Luz, he was delivering the closest representation of himself without risking full disclosure. If Lester could "like" Luz, could he not "like" Philip as well? It wasn't precise logic, God knows, but in his impulsive, anxious reasoning, it had sufficed.

Philip stared at the plate of boiled shrimp placed before him. They were fat and succulent, orangey-rose beauties that had no doubt taken their last swim in the Gulf only hours before. One of the true glories of living adjacent to the formerly pristine Gulf of Mexico was the seemingly endless offering of ocean produce. If the shrimp and oysters grew meager, there were snapper and amberjack. If they were in short supply, there were Spanish mackerel and grouper, cobia and pompano, flounder and sea trout—an embarrassment of quantity that even oil spills, pesticide drainage, and raw sewage couldn't seem to abate. And yet, he'd often wondered, shouldn't they—the fish and the people, that is—all be extinguished from ingested chemicals by now? On the other hand, hadn't scientists found natural fumaroles buried deep in the Pacific belching out hydrochloric acid and other toxic gases? Sea creatures were observed swimming around it no more affected than if it were pee in the pool. The ability of nature (and human nature) to adapt—for better or for worse.

Philip mindfully peeled the translucent fingernail shell encasing the savory flesh and bit into its briny, chewy essence. No cocktail sauce, no *rémoulade*, no lemon, and—heaven forbid—no tartar sauce. The naked shrimp in all its humble, boiled glory was unrivaled magnificence to Philip. Despite Luz's continual badgering that he was a rank food snob, he saw his passion for quality as nothing more than a gift, like musical ability or violet eyes, a feature given to one through no effort of his or her own, yet sensibly utilized just the same. Like athletic ability or extravagant, curly red hair...or being gay.

He took another sip of wine, savoring both sea and grape. It's true; there were some gifts more readily esteemed than others. The gift of being a dwarf wasn't always viewed as an optimal blessing. But of course it was. Just as blindness, cancer, beauty, and genius were each gifts, each with their own distinctive imperatives. And although he'd lived his entire adult life as a closeted gay man, out of professional necessity rather than personal choice, he'd always accepted his circumstances as simply another act of divine Providence. If it wasn't God's will that he be gay—whose then?

It certainly wasn't *his* stratagem. No, no—Philip Yancey was a go-along kind of guy. Rocking the boat was not his strong suit. To appear averse or in conflict with public norms was totally against his nature. He was just following the edict handed him. In actuality, he had no real issues with being gay one way or the other. It was the "others" he had to be mindful of. Christianity had given up the

124

ghost long ago on such former hot buttons as slavery, misogyny, and anti-Semitism. Even adultery, which got mentioned far more times in the Bible than anything approximating homosexuality, seemed to have lost much of its former iniquity. When divorce notably began outpacing marriage in the Bible Belt, suddenly something wasn't quite kosher in the lives of Bubba and Missy. And still, in the small towns and small minds of Middle America, homophobia hung glumly around like the proverbial village idiot: you despised the poor bastard, but you needed him in order to feel superior. And for a "Messenger of the Word of God," really, what options were there? Zip. For Philip, it was more a question of, "Exactly how accommodating can we make this closet we've purposely inserted ourselves into?" Food, wine, gracious surroundings, and good music all helped to ease his self-incarceration.

And one wrote letters—lots of them. For the first time in his life, Philip felt an unconditional kinship with another human being. The decades of repression, angst, and hesitancy burst forth in an uninterrupted flood of impassioned correspondence. It was as if he were breathing bona fide oxygen again after gasping at life from a suffocating existence. To unburden oneself at length, sharing all dreams, desires, and declarations of love was an act of unqualified audacity for Philip. The fact that the object of his affection was locked away in his own "societal closet" made it ostensibly more germane. God's will, not infrequently, incorporated some exquisite form of paradoxical symmetry as metaphor. For Philip, it was enough just to be *recognized*, even imperfectly, by another human being.

And now that the calamity of Lester and Luz's meeting had transpired without apparent bloodshed, where would this runaway love train discharge its irregular payload? Philip could only surmise. These were the facts: Lester was in love physically with a woman who didn't know he even existed until a few days ago; essentially, Luz was incapable of loving Lester physically due to her own sexual preferences; and *essentially*, Lester was in love with Philip through their exchange of letters but was unable to physically or mentally demonstrate that love. And thus, for the present, Philip remained as ever, deeply unattached.

The waiter cleared the plate of shells and tails and brought Philip another glass of *Pinot Grigio*. He'd been so deep in his head, pondering his plight, that he hadn't noticed the place had begun to fill up—the usual assemblage of hetero couples of all ages on first dates, anniversaries, having illicit affairs, about to break up, about to cohabit, and even a few apparently about to expire from sheer tedium with one another. It was still a hetero couple's world in the hinterlands. Single people stayed home. Gay couples in small-town Texas—they knew their place. If they flew low enough under the radar, they could pass unchecked. Stand out a little too boldly, however, and one courted the inevitable disapproval and umbrage of the plurality. Know your place; that was key. Of course, Philip had never experienced any personal slights himself. After all, he was "Father Phil," a regular guy. In addition to his innumerable duties as pastor and spiritual counselor, he volunteered his time with the local AA chapter, the migrant workers' council, the local Meals on Wheels, the Community Little Theater, the Rockport Arts League, and, yes, in blatant defiance of Supreme Court judicature, he continued on in his position as Boy Scout Troop leader. (Nobody else in town seemed to want the job.) No question, he was clearly one of the community's leading assets—with just one small concealment.

The waiter placed a spinach salad before him, and Philip took a bite, frowning at the bottled dressing. A good, easy vinaigrette is so simple to make. If something could be made better with negligible cost or effort, *why wouldn't you?* He couldn't understand such blatant indifference. Chewing dismally on his greens, he suddenly caught a glimpse of someone staring at him from across the deck. He stared back for a second and then turned quickly in embarrassment. It was a young man, a nice-looking young man, and he was alone. Philip studied his plate, crunching away in self-conscious distraction. Swallowing, he brought the wine to his mouth and risked another glance at the stranger. This time the young man smiled back at him and nodded slightly. Philip immediately felt his face flush. He managed a half-panicky, semi-smile and returned to contemplating his salad. There was a sliver of hardboiled egg and half a crescent of red onion left. He anxiously pushed the two of them around with his fork and reached for another sip of wine. Empty. Where was the waiter? Of course, there was no server anywhere on the floor. Not one. Philip tore off a piece of French bread and swabbed it in a saucer of olive oil. Who was this person? What did he want? Why was he staring at him? Philip let his eyes casually roll toward the young man again, and this time he saw that he had stood and walked off toward the cocktail lounge. He could see him chatting amiably with the bartender. What was *that* all about? Odd. Philip dabbed another piece of bread and stared toward the docks. A late fishing charter had just berthed, and the crew was hurriedly hanging up the day's haul for the obligatory trophy photo. He noticed some nice-sized bonitos and what appeared to be a small swordfish. Not bad. Hauling in a swordfish—the deep-sea fisherman's consummate prize. But like the near-vanquished tarpon, the swordfish was headed for extinction in the Gulf as well, and it saddened him to see such a small specimen hooked on the scales. Philip shook his head. Maybe Mother Nature would allow the swordfish another of those dramatic comeback stories she occasionally sanctioned: sturgeon in the Hudson, buffalo in the prairie, doodlebugs in the dung pile.

"I couldn't tell if you were drinking Chardonnay or a Riesling, so I got one of each."

Philip twisted around to see the young stranger from across the room standing beside him, holding out two glasses of wine. He smiled, trying not to appear fazed.

"Actually, it's a not-so-great *Pinot Grigio*."

The young man sat the glasses down on the table and turned back for the bar. "Not a problem. I'll finish these two and get you a *Pinot*."

"Hold on!" Philip called to him. "That's OK. I...I'll drink the Riesling."

The young man smiled and returned to the table.

"Are you dining with anyone? I don't mean to appear intrusive, but I noticed you across the room, and we seem to be the only brave souls venturing solo tonight. Would you care for some company?"

Philip looked at him as if Dick Cheney was suddenly stopping by for a chat. "No...no, not at all. Please." Philip motioned tentatively toward the opposite chair. "Have we met before?"

"Not yet, but I think I know who you are. You're the Episcopal priest, right?"

Philip nodded. "And you are?"

"Daniel Wheelwright—man about town. Nice to meet you." The two shook hands.

"Philip Yancey." Philip continued to stare at him, mystified.

"Yeah, I've seen you around. I don't actually live here, but my family has a summerhouse in the area. I'm in school in Houston. Do you mind if I smoke? If you do, please say so. I'm not hung-up about it or anything."

Philip stared at him, bemused. "Go right ahead. I may join you after dinner."

Daniel smiled and lit his Marlboro Lite. "So," he exhaled, "did you order the tile fish? I usually don't like tile fish, but the way the waiter described it with the shallots and cilantro butter sounded tasty. By the way, are you gay?"

Philip nearly spit out his wine. Clutching his napkin to his mouth, he stared at Daniel, wide-eyed. "I'm...sorry?"

Daniel took another drag and flicked his ash. "Oops. I do this all the time. See, in the back of my mind, I was holding that thought to ask you sometime around coffee or dessert, and then all the other questions I was planning to ask got jumbled up, and that one got spewed out first. Something to do with social anxiety. Can you pass the bread, please?"

Philip numbly handed the basket to Daniel. "Why would you...*ask* me that?"

Daniel looked surprised. "Why?" he shrugged. "Just curious. I'm gay. I'm always looking to meet like-minded family in the 'nabe.'"

Mouth open, Philip could only nod dully. The two men stared at one another until, thankfully, a waiter finally approached the table. "Decided to move on me, huh? What do you think, Father Phil? Should we let him stay?" The waiter winked at Philip who suddenly felt an overwhelming desire to be back at home, sitting in his living room quietly listening to the new Renée Fleming opera CD he'd recently bought.

Philip smiled perfunctorily. "Oh, I think stay. He doesn't look like he'd hurt anybody." But even as he said it, Philip wasn't entirely convinced of his own judgment.

Daniel instantly turned to the waiter. "Would you bring us a bottle of whatever Father Phil is drinking, a fresh glass for me, an ashtray, and some more bread, olive oil, and a place setting? And could you please lower one of those rattan blinds in the corner? The sun's hitting my eyes. Oh, and there's old lipstick on this water glass. I don't think it's a shade belonging to either of us." Daniel smiled pleasantly, and the waiter cast a weary glance in Philip's direction. He then sighed and leaned forward, whisking away the glass, bread, and olive oil in one dramatic sweep and hurtling away with a look of titanic ennui etching his face.

Philip took a sip from the Riesling and cleared his throat. "I was hoping you might mention something about needing a little more fuchsia in the sunset this evening."

Daniel looked up, surprised. "Do you think it's wrong to expect decent service from a semi-upscale establishment?"

"Absolutely not."

"I count on good service from the Dairy Queen. Why not here?"

"You're very correct." Philip smiled. "And forthright."

Daniel shrugged, hoisting the glass of Chardonnay. "Works for me. I'm rarely misunderstood. Cheers." Daniel held forth his glass and clinked it on the edge of Philip's. "So, now that we're old friends, *are* you gay?"

Philip's smile never wavered. After living a life of emotional subterfuge, he was prepped for potential onslaught at any instant, from any source. He quickly glanced around the room, observing the crowd still mindlessly huddled in their own intrigues. "Would you mind lowering your voice a little, please?"

Daniel's eyes widened. He blew a puff of smoke and hastily tapped out his cigarette, contrite. "Oh God, I'm sorry. Please. I'm really sorry. I didn't realize."

"It's all right."

"I just didn't think. I'm so stupid sometimes."

"Forget it."

"This has happened before, and I always forget that, well, you know."

Philip looked at Daniel quizzically. "What?"

"You know."

"Know what?"

Daniel leaned in, sotto voce, "The *gay* thing." He shook his head and frowned. , "*Out, In,* top, bottom, green, blue—it's all so fucking tedious." He smiled agreeably. "Are you having dessert?"

Philip now leaned forward and said in a low voice, "It just so happens I don't feel it's in very good taste, to say the least basic etiquette, discussing one's sexual peccadilloes with perfect strangers."

Daniel held out his hand, grinning. "Hi, I'm Daniel." His grin turned pensive. "Didn't we do this already?"

Philip leaned back in his chair, annoyed. "I guess I'm not very amused by all this."

"I'm sorry. Would you like me to go?"

Philip stared at Daniel, not sure of anything. He finally sighed. "No. But could we change the subject, please?"

"Of course." Daniel tore off a chunk of bread from Philip's salad plate and rolled it between his fingers. "How big are you?"

Philip immediately shot him a look.

"Five eleven? Six feet? I'd say we're probably the same size, wouldn't you?"

"I'm five ten and a half. My turn for a question. Why are you here?"

"Here in the restaurant? Well, it does have a nice view of the harbor, and the bar makes a mean *mojito,* and—"

Philip shook his head. "No. Why did you come over here to sit with me?"

Daniel gazed at him, eyes glinting with animation. "You want the 'basic etiquette' version or the bald truth?"

"I'll go with bald truth as long as I don't have to share it with the rest of the restaurant."

Daniel, his mouth a slightly leering pucker, tilted forward and drawled in a sensual, whispery murmur, "'Cause I thought you were a hot-looking closet-case I might have a decent chance of getting naked and doing the 'dick dance' later on with." Daniel eased slowly back in his chair, smiling. "How come you let me sit here?"

Immediately, Philip felt himself becoming aroused. "Mr. Snake" had crawled out of his cotton basket and begun swaying heedlessly to the tunes of the charmer and his pipe. Ludicrous! Philip was completely exasperated. Forget libidinous dolphins and promiscuous protozoa, men were the prototypal, congenital sluts of the known universe.

The waiter abruptly reappeared and plopped down a bottle of Pinot Grigio, two wineglasses, a fresh pannier of bread, and a carafe of olive oil. He poured each of them a glass and then placed the bottle in a nearby ice bucket. Turning to an adjacent table, he reached for a clean water glass and placed it directly in front of Daniel. "How we doin' now, professor?"

Daniel slowly moved the glass to the side and smiled up at the waiter. "You've done very well." He then squinted impishly and asked, "Would you say your hair is more of a reddish-brown or a brownish-gold?"

The waiter blinked and then beamed brightly as if a fresh battery had just been inserted. "My boyfriend calls it 'sun tea.'" He giggled mischievously. "I spritz a little Summer Blonde in every week or so, and he fantasizes I'm some Slavic surfer dude he just picked up. *Whaat-ever.* Ya'll holler if you need anything." Daniel grinned, and the waiter skittered off to another table.

Philip looked at Daniel. "Is he...gay?"

"Um...that would be putting it *unerringly.*"

"How did you...How could you tell?"

Daniel shook his head, incredulous. "My God, you're virtually straight, aren't you?"

"What?"

"Don't you have a gaydar? Can't you tell who's gay and who's not?"

"Well, I—"

"Our waitperson is practically a poster child for Lambda. All he's missing are white rollerblades and Richard Simmons shorts. Come on, you knew, right?"

Philip, bewildered, shook his head. "I don't judge people."

"You mean you're just the silent type," Daniel smirked. "*Everyone* judges."

Philip placed both of his hands on the table and exhaled slowly. As much as Daniel's candor and brashness alarmed him, he was obviously intrigued enough to continue bantering. "You seem to know a lot about human nature. Maybe you're the one who should be a minister."

Daniel laughed. "Yes, 'Brother Danny's Divine Temple for the Immediate Salvation and Release from Family Values, Moral Majorities, Compassionate Fascists, and all Misnomer Theocracies Worldwide.' Amen."

"Sounds like you've given it some thought."

"Only in this lifetime. How old are you, thirty-four, thirty-five?"

"Eight. Thirty-eight."

"You look good," Daniel said, smiling. "Like I said, I really didn't come over here for the sunset."

Philip flushed and crossed his legs, hoping to mitigate the persistent straining in his slacks. "So, since you've brought it up, I must look pretty gay to you then."

Daniel sipped his wine. "Not particularly. You could easily be one of those 'immaculately natty' straight guys."

Philip nodded, "Natty, huh?"

"You know. Those preppy, stylish types who care just a tad too much about their hair and their dry cleaning to get the full-on 'butch' award. I blame their mothers."

"Of course, the genesis of everyone's adversity."

Daniel shrugged.. "Mothers just enable proclivities with laser-like proficiency. They see little Elmo combing his hair in the mirror, and the next day he's got a sixty-dollar blow dryer and a subscription to *GQ*."

Philip laughed. "You may be right. I remember my mother enrolling me in tap class when I told her once, if you squinted a certain way, Gene Kelly looked a little like my dad!"

Daniel gasped, mouth open. "That's amazing! *My* father *sounds* like Gene Kelly after a couple of whiskey sours."

As both men laughed, the waiter reappeared with their entrées. "OK, boys, I'm going to need a little help here. Who had the pound of butter with the tile fish drowned in it?"

Daniel raised his hand. "I."

The waiter sat the plate down and turned to Philip. "And you're the grilled snapper. Good choice—easy on the waistline." The waiter glanced back, appraising Daniel. "Ricky Martin here doesn't have to worry about that, now does he? Ya'll need anything else?"

Daniel looked up at him, sweetly. "More butter, please?"

The waiter stared at Daniel, aghast. "Wowsy. I guess some of us don't have to worry about the old bubble butt developing into the buffalo that ate Kansas, do we?"

Daniel shook his head. "Not unless you're a size queen."

The waiter arched a sudden eyebrow and once again retreated.

Philip looked at Daniel, bewildered. "Did I just miss something?"

Daniel cut into his fish. "I dunno. But I'd suggest we seriously overhaul that gaydar of yours before you end up running off with Michele Bachmann. Mmm, good fish."

Philip put his fork down, annoyed. "OK, why do you keep inferring all this...this gay stuff?"

"Well, are you?"

"I...I don't even know you!"

"Does that change your answer?"

Philip stared at him. "I've never had sex with a man, if that's what you mean."

"Define sex."

"Define sex! You know exactly what I mean."

"Ever touch a man's cock?"

"Y—yes."

"His ass?"

"Yes."

"Ever kiss a man on the mouth who wasn't your father?"

Philip's expression resembled that of the Coyote chasing the Roadrunner over the edge of a cliff and suddenly being reintroduced to the laws of gravity: *"Oops! Three strikes, you're out!* (You know the old adage: "All guys get to suck a cock once; it's part of growing up. Twice? Hey, everyone makes mistakes. Three times? *Big old homo!"*)

Philip stared at his plate glumly. "I don't think you understand my position."

Daniel stopped chewing. "Would you like to tell me about it?"

"I can't."

Daniel reached for his spoon and stretched across the table, tapping Philip's hand. "If you ask me to keep a confidence, it's done. I'm a pretty good listener, a better talker, but I'm still a lot cheaper than a psychiatrist."

Philip, sullen, looked at him and sighed. "I minister to the spiritual needs and moral uncertainties of a congregation of two hundred eighty souls. I work with another equal amount through charity work and public institutions. My life is dedicated to helping other people get through their lives sanely, ethically, and with some modicum of dignity. My own egocentric desires are way, *way* down on the list of must-dos to save humanity."

Daniel took one last bite of tile fish and pushed the plate away from him. He swallowed, wiping his mouth quickly. "And I think that the 'martyr position' is one of the least effective ways of helping anybody do anything. Doesn't the Bible say, 'The Lord helps those who help themselves?' and 'What does it profit a man if he gains the whole world, and loses his own soul?' How can you help someone when you haven't 'helped' yourself?"

"I'll make this real simple: gay preachers are not accepted in this town and just barely in my faith. Period. End of conjecture. Can we find a different topic now?"

Daniel stared blankly at Philip, shaking his head. "Amazing."

"What?"

"I'm just amazed when I meet people who're willing to forego any possibility of personal and intimate love in their lives, regardless of the rationale. Isn't that a big reason for being human?"

"I'd say it's a reason, but not a universal calling."

"You're the second guy I've met lately who's running as fast as he can to keep his 'other' calling from catching up with him."

Philip smiled tersely. "Think so?"

"Yeah."

"Well, I'm sure there's quite a few of us out there." Philip suddenly pushed his chair back and signaled for the waiter. "It's been a very…engaging conversation, Danny."

"You're leaving?"

"Afraid I have to."

"You hardly touched your food."

"I've had more than enough." Philip nodded to a passing bus boy. "Check, please."

Daniel stared across the table, embarrassed. "I've made you uncomfortable; I'm sorry. That wasn't my purpose."

Philip quickly turned to him. "No. Your purpose was something more like making certain I understood what a hopeless closet-case and neurotic distortion of a human being I am. I think I got it. You know, I'll wager sooner or later you'll pick up on the fact that not everyone in life has the burning need *or desire* to brandish their sexuality like some cheap T-shirt bought in a novelty shop."

The waiter approached, and Philip handed him his Master-Card. "In fact, one might even think if you resisted such measures, you'd stand a better chance of doing the 'dick dance' more often, as you so eloquently put it."

The waiter, catching the tail end of Philip's remarks, cast a blank glance at Daniel, then back at Philip. He sucked in his cheeks wearily. "So—anyone up for coffee or dessert? We've got a killer tiramisu." Daniel remained silent, and Philip shook his head. The waiter smiled wanly and disappeared.

Unexpectedly Daniel's large blue eyes began to well, and his lower lip slackened noticeably. His inner "wounded child" had, unannounced, suddenly entered the polemic. Clearing his throat, he said to Philip, "Just so you'll know, I really don't have a problem doing the 'dick dance' with whomever, whenever. At all. I *might* have a slight problem finding love, but then that's a burden most of us share, don't you think?"

Philip looked at Daniel as if for the first time. What he saw before him was a big, anxious kid wearing an adult bodysuit and pretending to be the love child of Dorothy Parker and George Hamilton. And somehow, it moved him. "Look, I'm sorry. I'm usually not so rash, I guess I just—"

"Got your buttons pushed? I'm good at that. Gets people to pay attention to me."

"And you think they're not?"

Daniel shrugged, laughing. "Self-esteem's not a strong point in my family. We do all kinds of ruthless things for even the slightest regard."

Philip wasn't sure what to make of this outlandish creature grinning across the table. "Would you like to take a walk out on the jetty? I think I've had enough of here."

Daniel eyed him, suddenly reticent. "Are you sure? I might say something off color—'queer' even."

Philip stood, placing his wallet back in his pocket. He motioned to the waiter that he'd sign for the check at the front desk. Turning to Daniel, he let the corners of his mouth curl enigmatically upwards. "I'm assuming that's how most 'dick dances' begin."

chapter

NINE

Lester brushed away the spiderwebs that swung invisibly between the two large Italian cypresses and cursed their fine, gluey filaments now snarled in his hair. He'd just spent several meticulous minutes combing and shaping his wavy locks into, what he presumed, was a sexy, manly crown of glory. Only now, it resembled something sucked up and spit out by a vacuum cleaner. That's what he got for being in a hurry and taking a shortcut across the lawn from the parking lot. Jabbing his fingers through his hair, he muttered, pulling loose strands of bug silk from his mouth. He was meeting Luz after her last class at the community college. Tonight they would eat a hamburger, see a movie, get an ice cream, and afterwards officially inaugurate their mutual objective of spending the rest of their lives together. Simple. Then why was he suddenly as wet as a drowned man? Humidity, pressure, or just a flat-out, clenched balls attack of nerves?

"Excuse me. Can you tell me which way is the art building?" Lester asked.

The disheveled slacker-student leaning against his corroded mountain bike glanced up at Lester, puzzled. "Umm, I think it's like over there. Like, behind those trees and stuff." He pointed beyond some bent live oaks and scratched his head covered in an orange knit cap. He looked at Lester. "Dude, you got a second? Can I like, ask you a question?"

Lester stopped and stared at him. "Shoot."

"So, like…do you know who the governor is?"

Lester stared blankly. "Perry."

The student snatched off his cap and flung it on the ground. "Fuck! I knew that, but I couldn't remember if it was, like, his first or last name, you know?"

Lester squinted. "So, you say, 'Perry.' Either way, you're right."

The student kicked his bike. "Fuck! I knew that, but then I thought, what if it's like, his middle name?"

Lester nodded slowly and began walking toward the distant building. "Thanks for the directions," he said over his shoulder. "Good luck." Strolling away, he glanced back to see the student suddenly lunge at his bike as if it were a stray dog about to pee on his knapsack. He pondered momentarily the American educational process and then, very briefly, why people wore wool on their heads in August. He let it go. He decided to focus instead on the large, gray building in the distance behind the trees. And stuff.

Taking the steps two at a time, he pulled open the green metal door at the top and stepped inside. Immediately he was overwhelmed by the smell of…What was it? Turpentine, shellac, acetone? Whatever it was, his eyes began to burn fiercely. How did she work in an environment like this? It certainly couldn't be healthy. Or maybe it stimulated the "creative process," inhaling all these fumes. They say in prison, just being around all those ancillary "Y" male chromosomes doubled one's testosterone levels. Of course, being cognizant of that fact never benefited anyone. After a while, banging your head against a concrete wall lost its appeal.

Lester looked about for any sign of Luz. She'd said she'd meet him "outside the Ladies Room, on the first floor. It's the closest exit to the parking lot." What parking lot? He hadn't seen a parking lot on his way over. He began striding down the hall and glancing into each classroom.

The building appeared to be completely empty, and it seemed to Lester lonelier than a Sunday night mall. He supposed that if a body had never experienced any boon from academia in its past, all future run-ins with higher learning would be brief, nerve-wracking affairs. It wasn't that Lester viewed education as irrelevant or unworthy. To him it was all a question of methodology. And basically, the method reeked. Losing a little kid at six because of some shithead's control issues and "the system's" incompetence was a much greater crime than selling a lid of pot or, most definitely, stealing a church.

Looking into another classroom, Lester saw what appeared to be a store mannequin coated in glitter and colored gravel. Beside it stood a hideous clay head someone had rammed a trowel into. Suspended in front of the window was a kind of yarn flag with bits of bone and twig hanging on it, looking as if it had just been blown out from a passing lawnmower. None of what he saw appeared to be informative or a pleasing "thing of beauty." But what did he know about art anyway? Art was something other people did to pass time. Like fishing.

Rounding a corner he heard a remote voice and then another coming from behind a door down the corridor. He proceeded toward the noise and stopped just outside the entrance with the word LADIES painted above it. Luz's animated speech could be heard emanating from inside.

"Oh no, God no! I would *never* have said that!"

"Well, she said you did."

"Bitch!"

"Uh-huh."

"What is it with her? It's a blouse. It's not like, her fucking *child*."

"Um-hmm."

"I'm going to say something to her. I mean it."

"I wouldn't if I were you."

140

"She's insane. Does she really think I give a shit about some six-dollar T-shirt from Target? Please."

"It's the weight gain. She's up to one eighty, one eighty-five now."

"No way!"

"Serious. She's one big old gordita now, girl."

"Very sad. When she loses that face of hers, it's really going to be tragic."

"Like she doesn't think she's Melissa Etheridge already."

"Right. Mrs. Jody Foster."

The door opened to the Ladies Room so quickly, Lester jumped unwittingly. He blinked at the two women self-consciously. "H-hey."

"Lester! I didn't know you were here already. How long have you been out here?"

He shrugged. "Not long."

Luz motioned to the other woman. "This is my friend, Elsie. Elsie Garza."

Lester shook her hand. "Nice to meet you."

"Hello."

"I hope you don't mind. Elsie was dying to see the movie too, so I said I'm sure it'd be OK if she wanted to come with us, OK?"

Lester stared at the two women, and they stared back.

OK? Hell no, it's not OK! Why does this always, always happen to me? He bit his lower lip and looked at the tall Mexican American woman with red hair and even redder lips, and he managed to fake a half smile. "Sure, why not?"

Both women immediately grinned and began gabbing like it was the most natural thing in the world to bring along an interloper on a first date.

"I mean, it's not as if we're on a *date* or anything, right?" Luz grinned at Lester as they were exiting the building. Truthfully, he couldn't tell if she were being cruel or sincere, or maybe both.

"No...We're going to the movies, that's all."

"Luz told me you just moved here. Where from?" Elsie flashed a bright smile, and he noticed for the first time that she was actually pretty—in a tall, athletic sort of way.

"Diboll."

"Isn't that where one of the big prisons is?"

"Yep."

"When did you get out?" Elsie asked. Then she burst out laughing. "I'm kidding. *Ai-i!* Don't be so serious!"

"You're bad." Luz thumped her on the back as they walked toward the van. "I can't wait to see this movie, ya'll. I don't care what anyone says. I think Vin Diesel is good."

***

Good was not the word Lester would have chosen to describe the film. *Good riddance* or maybe *good grief.* It was depressingly more of the same Hollywood mindless crap that gets shoveled upon the gullible masses like so much piled manure. No real story, no real acting—no *real* anything. The only *real* part is the computerized portion of the film where they actually make an effort to somehow "get it right." And since *the realest* part of most people's lives was experienced through the Internet, the satellite dish, and their cell phones, maybe Hollywood was even smarter than Lester could imagine in reaching its audience.

Luz and Elsie loved the picture. Lester knew this for a fact because Luz and Elsie spent most of the picture discussing their enjoyment of it with each other. It wasn't that Luz ignored him. It was really more that she concentrated primarily on Elsie's observations and reactions rather than on his. He felt the "girl-buffer" distinctly.

After the movie, they drove to the Whataburger and sat out on the concrete tables swatting at willow bugs and eating onion rings. Elsie kept up a lively discourse concerning her large, dysfunctional family and her many disasters with men and dating. Luz laughed and laughed as if with each outburst she were slowly dislodging some annoying encumbrance wedged deep inside her. She was glowing pink with delight by the time they left.

Lester said a silent prayer when Luz dropped Elsie off first. Finally, at long, *long* last, an unrivaled moment alone together. As the two women hugged and shared good-byes, Lester stared ahead pensively. His mind gyrated through an endless combination of scenarios. What would he say to her? How would he break this all down for Luz, so that, somehow, it could be reassembled whole and expedient for both of them to work through?

Elsie extended a hand through Luz's driver-side window. "Nice to meet you, Lester. I like you quiet ones."

He stammered, "I'm not usually this quiet. I just…I guess I was a little shy this evening, or something."

Elsie turned to Luz. "Is he not the cutest thing or what?" She turned back to Lester again. "Honey, do *not* change. You just stay like you are. We got too many *pendejos* walking around here already."

Laughing giddily, Luz shifted the van into reverse and backed out of the driveway, pointing the VW for home. Riding in silence, Lester beat his brains trying to put together the elemental tenets of human discourse. Plain old everyday articulation had somehow rudely abandoned him.

"Must be a drag not having a car, huh?"

Lester's head jerked sideways. "Excuse me?"

Luz smiled. "No car. How do you survive?"

"Oh, everything's pretty much within walking distance. It hasn't been a problem," he lied politely.

"I've got an old bike in the garage I never ride anymore. Would you like to use it?"

Lester hesitated. "Sure, yeah, that'd be great. Thanks." He tried imagining himself riding a bike around Rockport. Who gives a shit? Honestly, he was tired of trucking his butt everywhere on his two bald sneakers. A bike? Why not?

"You're a real cryptogram, you know that?"

"No, what is that?"

"A message in code. It's like I can't decipher your owner's manual. I need a Rosetta Stone or something." Luz smiled at Lester. "It's this stone Napoleon's army found in Egypt when—"

"I *know* what the Rosetta Stone is. I did a lot of reading in the…" Lester caught himself. "In high school."

"Oh."

He studied Luz. "You know, you're maybe a little bit crypto yourself."

"Me?" Luz stared at the road, perplexed. "God, there's nothing mysterious about me. I'm as 'open book' as they come."

Lester smiled. "You sure about that?"

"Uh-huh." Then she frowned at Lester. "Yeah. OK—what?"

Lester shook his head. "Nothing. Just seems like you hold your cards pretty tight."

"I do? How?"

Lester exhaled, feeling slightly unwell. "How did we get off on this anyway? Let's talk about something else. I got one. Shania Twain or Faith Hill? Who's done more damage to country music?"

"Neither. 'Grooming Consultants' killed Nashville. Now tell me." Luz's voice had a tinge of irritation in it.

Lester gripped the armrest as the van made a tight left and zoomed on toward the Chevron station. Why did it nearly always end up like this? Backed against a doorway and fending off some provoked beast you were, only seconds earlier, offering a can of Whiskers to? He cleared his throat and said to her softly, "I thought…we had a date?"

Luz turned and squinted. "What? I couldn't hear you."

"I said, I thought we had a date tonight?"

Luz looked at Lester, at the road, and then back at Lester again. "Did you say you thought we had a 'date' tonight? Is that what you said?"

Lester wanted to shrink into a dirt atom and disappear into the van carpeting. Anywhere but here. Even prison seemed somehow welcoming to him at this juncture. Anywhere but here, God. "Yes."

Luz looked bewildered, answering in a childlike voice, "I… Isn't that what we just did?"

Was it his imagination, or did her inflection now carry just the slightest hint of dread? "Yes, forget it."

Luz shook her head, shifting the van. "I mean, it wasn't a 'date' date, but I haven't been on a 'date' date since, God, I can't even remember. Is that what you were asking?"

"Yes. Forget it."

They drove in silence for a few more seconds, and then Luz offered forth a sudden gush of introspection, "I've had *dates*. I guess you'd call them that. But then, what is a *date*, really? Flowers, chocolates, once around the dance floor? Does anybody know what a *date* is anymore? No, I haven't really *dated*, but I guess, you know, I've been on a *date* a few times…maybe."

Lester stared ahead, gritting his teeth. "Why did you ask your friend Elsie to come?"

Again, Luz alternated her focus between Lester and the road. "Um, because she wanted to see the movie, too? I thought you said you didn't mind?"

"I didn't."

"Then-n-n…?"

"Nothing."

"Nothing?"

They drove on in silence. When Lester finally spoke again rather abruptly, both flinched involuntarily. "Have you ever been in love?"

"Me?"

"Yes, you."

"What a question!"

"You don't have to answer."

"Why ask it?"

"I don't know. Why not?"

Luz stared straight ahead, flustered. "Yes, I might have been in love, and no, nothing ever came of it. Is that an answer?"

"Maybe."

"What about you?"

Lester turned his head to the right and gazed at the choppy bay water jerking in a spectrum of reflected light shafts. He wondered what it might be like to jump on a stingray's back and take off for the Indian Ocean on a perfect, moonlit night in the month of August. "Maybe."

The van pulled into Otis' driveway and stopped just alongside the closed garage doors. Luz shifted into park and kept the engine idling. "Well, here we are. Two big 'maybes' in a wide world of 'perhaps.' I'm sorry my inviting Elsie bothered you. I just didn't think...Look, I really *don't* date, you know what I'm saying?"

Lester looked at her with a mixture of hurt and confusion. "Not really."

Luz dug her fingernail into the steering wheel and picked at the tattered foam cover. "If you're looking for some kind of... romance thing, I'm not really available."

"You're seeing someone?"

"No! I'm just not, you know, 'dating.'"

"Why?"

Luz crossed her arms and squinted at Lester. "My God, you ask a lot of questions! You're a very nice guy, but I just met you. And besides, I'm busy with school and students and friends and the house and—"

"Can I see you again?"

Luz exhaled and smiled, putting both of her hands on the steering wheel. "Sure—as friends! I'm not into misleading or abusing people's trust, ever. This is who I am. Take it or leave it."

Lester put his hand on the door and started to open it. "OK, friends?"

Luz smiled back. "Friends."

He gazed at Luz momentarily and, without thinking, leaned forward to kiss her. Luz instantly backed her head against the window and turned just as his lips brushed the side of her mouth. Lester immediately felt both shame and elation from his impulsive gesture.

"Why did you do that?" Luz had pushed Lester back so hard that he hit his head on the window. "Don't ever do that again! I don't even know you, and I certainly don't feel that way about you."

"I'm sorry. I didn't mean to—"

"Get out! I have to go."

"Please, don't be mad. I'm sorry, really."

"Just…go." Luz stared rigidly ahead, clenching the steering wheel as if it were some wild thing about to attack her.

Lester stepped out onto the drive and turned back to face her before shutting the door. "So, the movie sucked, the 'date' sucked, the onion rings sucked, but *you*—you were wonderful." Lester smiled his little-boy grin, and Luz, unable to sustain her anger, burst out laughing.

"You…*asshole*."

He nodded. "But sometimes fun, if not downright occasionally agreeable."

Luz shook her head and shifted into reverse. Backing out onto the empty highway, she drove off, blowing her bus horn twice.

Lester nodded and rubbed his arms in the cool breeze. Prison had bestowed on him one very valuable favor: endurance. He could out-endure a fence post if he had to. If he had to, he could endure most anything.

***

"No, I don't think it's really the season for apricots, Rosa. Who even knows where these things are from? Romania?" Yvonne Wheelwright tossed a perfect-looking apricot back into the pile at the upscale H-E-B grocery store. Rosa, her arms outstretched and her stomach nearly touching the cart she was pushing, stared blankly ahead.

"The chives? Do you want the fresh chives with the fish tonight?"

Energized, Yvonne turned and marched off behind Rosa. "Yes, thank you. Mr. Wheelwright loves a fresh lime and chive zest on his seafood. But only if it's fresh."

Rosa touched her belly as she felt the baby leap inside her. Distractedly stroking her fingernails across the surface of her T-shirt, she began to feel just the tiniest bit light-headed. It was almost like a "hitting-a-sudden-dip-in-the-highway-when-your-mind-is-somewhere-off-contemplating-God-men-or-shoes," kind of startle. Spontaneous wonder. And it wasn't so much a leap as a shove. Why was the baby pushing her?

"No, I don't see any fresh. Freeze-dried, and something in olive oil. Nope, nope." Yvonne shook her head, gazing at the neatly stacked vegetables with a shrug. "We'll just have to make do with the last of the shallots. I guess that's everything." Yvonne glanced back at Rosa. "Can you think of anything else?" Not seeing her standing by the cart, Yvonne strolled back to her wares and gazed around the store. "Rosa?" Unconcerned, she began pushing the cart toward the checkout line. Studying the produce in her basket, she did a quick mental check: *lotion, thumbtacks, Ajax, spaghetti, butter...razors! Bob's razors.* She quickly turned the cart around and aimed for the drug department. As she wheeled down the "Asian products" aisle, she saw ahead a tall African American man in an apron race across an intersecting aisle. He was immediately followed by a red-faced Mr. Hinojosa, the store manager. Yvonne approached the crosscutting rows and glanced to her right to see a cluster of people gathered around an open refrigerator case. Ignoring the razors temporarily, she unconsciously directed the cart toward the crowd, half expecting to find a gallon of spilled milk and a distraught four-year-old wailing away. Stopping just behind Mr. Hinojosa, she peered around his shoulder and immediately felt the life explode from her body as instantly as a gun firing bullets. Grasping feebly for Mr. Hinojosa's shirtsleeve, Yvonne reeled sideways and flung both hands on the cart handle instead. She then turned slowly back to stare in terror. Rosa lay sprawled beside the refrigerator case, atop about a dozen cartons of smashed orange juice containers. The floor was saturated with orange juice... and blood. Rosa's thighs were stained crimson from a viscous flow seeping between her legs. Paralyzed, Yvonne stared helplessly at the assemblage gathered around Rosa's recumbent body like voyeurs at a hanging. She wanted to blind their rude intrusion, to run and carry Rosa to safety. Instead, she remained immobile as a brick wall, powerless to react. She closed her eyes in distress: *"He will give his angels charge over you...he will give his angels charge over you..."*

Scarcely audible, Yvonne found herself murmuring the Epistle from the Book of Common Prayer, "Ministrations to the Sick."

An adolescent youth spent with the Episcopal Girls League as a weekend Candy Striper had left its unanticipated mark on her character. Abruptly, a voice called out, "Get an ambulance! Did somebody call the ambulance?" As if prodded by unseen hands, the crowd immediately lurched into frenetic motion.

"She's having a miscarriage!"

"Lie her down."

"The ambulance is coming!"

"Here, put my jacket around her."

Yvonne kneeled beside a man holding Rosa's hand. She placed her own hand lightly on Rosa's cheek and spoke calmly, "You're going to be OK, sweetheart. We're getting you to the doctors as fast as we can."

The man beside Rosa slowly turned to Yvonne and said, "*'He that dwelleth in the secret place of the most High shall abide under the shadow of the Almighty.'* Why did you stop?"

Yvonne stared at him, bewildered. "What did you say?"

"You were reciting the 91st Psalm, weren't you?"

Yvonne flushed. "Yes...I guess I was. That's all I could remember."

The man half-smiled as he rubbed Rosa's hand. "That you remembered is the expedient thing. Do you know her?"

"She works for me. What happened? Did you see?"

"I don't know. I got here with the rest. What month is she in?"

"Her due date is in six weeks." Yvonne shook her head in disbelief. "Dear God, let this baby be all right."

"God has her other hand right now."

Yvonne looked at the man, still confused. She watched as he unbuttoned his cotton shirt, removed it, and tucked it around Rosa's trembling knees. She was unexpectedly moved by his instinctive act of compassion.

"Well, thank God you're here anyway. You have a very calming presence. I'm afraid I might've panicked." She extended her hand. "Yvonne Wheelwright."

He turned and took her hand. Shivering slightly as the chilled air from the display case gusted against his T-shirt, he smiled. "Philip Yancey."

***

Following behind the ambulance, Yvonne made two calls to Bob and one each to Melanie and Daniel. The only one to answer was Melanie, and she had no idea where "the boys" were. She agreed to meet her mother at the emergency room as quickly as possible.

Yvonne hung up the phone. Her mind raced through an infinite list of queries ranging from employee insurance coverage to canceling her book club meeting tonight to wondering if they could all just eat Sloppy Joe's from a can this evening. She speculated on Bob's whereabouts until she realized he was probably out on the boat testing the new fishing sonar that had arrived via Fed Ex. She shuddered at the thought of informing him about Rosa. Bob didn't acknowledge affliction with any degree of certitude. In fact, he generally refused to acknowledge any difficulty that clashed with his own version of self-actualization. For all intents and purposes, Bob hovered in a near resolute "state-of-grace" denial.

At the hospital, doctors had stopped Rosa's bleeding and, though she gazed coma-like from her snare of intravenous tubes, breathing masks, and computer monitoring appendages, she appeared to have endured the worst of it. So far.

"You're going to be *okey-dokey*, Miss Guzman. You need to rest and definitely stay off your feet, OK, shug? Try and get some sleep, OK, hon? *Dormir, comprende?*" The doctor spoke to Rosa as if she were a toddler who wouldn't eat her carrots. Melanie and Yvonne both winced. He resembled some small-town football coach rather than a member of the medical profession. Motioning for Melanie and Yvonne to follow him into the hallway, they all exited as a nurse stuck yet another IV into Rosa's arm.

Walking down the hall to just in front of a small room with vending machines, the doctor turned back to them, shaking his head. "She's had a very close call."

"What did you find out?"

"They could've both died. Easily. She had a sudden detachment of the placenta from the womb: *Placenta previa*. Happens about one in every fifty thousand or so, more so with first-timers. Is she on her feet a lot?"

Yvonne nodded. "She's employed as my housekeeper. She's on her feet most of the day."

The doctor scowled. "That's out. She's going to be in bed until the baby comes. I don't even want her getting up to go to the bathroom."

"Is it too early to just go ahead and induce labor?" Melanie asked.

"Nope, but I won't do it. Not yet. Let's just keep her monitored, and we'll see how it goes. Is she insured, or is this another Chicano welfare case?"

Yvonne stared with her mouth open, unable to reply at first. Then she thrust a hand on her hip and defiantly extended her foot toward the lumpish doctor. "*Any* employee of mine and my husband's is fully insured to whatever extent the law mandates. And for your information, she's not *Chicano*; she's from Guatemala."

"Glad to know it. It's usually 'fun and games with green cards' around here most days. Probably wouldn't surprise you the percentage of illegals we get. Through the roof. Hell of a mess when the Republicans can't even fix the system. I gotta run. Ya'll have a good day." With that, the doctor turned and plodded off down the hall. They watched as he fished a roll of breath mints from the pocket of his rumpled white jacket and popped several in his mouth.

Yvonne continued staring, aghast. "A real prince of modern healing."

Melanie shook her head. "What a waste of polyester."

Yvonne removed her shoulder purse, rummaging for her cell phone. "I think I left my phone in the car. Do you have yours? I need to try your father again."

Melanie pulled her phone from her own bag and pressed Bob's number on auto-dial. "Mother, poor Rosa, so far from her family. What if she loses the baby?" She handed the phone to Yvonne, who placed it to her ear.

"What if we lose Rosa?" she said to Melanie. An expression of grief etched her eyes. "I don't know what I'd—" She glanced up suddenly. "Bob? Can you hear me? Where are you? I've been trying to reach you for over an hour. I'm at the hospital…Rosa's in the hospital…no, no…everything's all right for now. She collapsed at the grocery store. When will you be back at the dock? I'll meet you there." Yvonne paused and stared straight ahead. "Are you OK? Are you sure? Al…all right. See you then." Dazed, she handed the phone back to Melanie.

"What's the matter?"

Yvonne appeared wholly drained of energy. "I'm not sure. I think he just started…crying."

"Daddy?"

As the two women stared at each other, a passing male nurse with a bright red box of Marlboros visible through his gauzy white shirt pocket pushed an old man wearing an oxygen mask. Whistling loudly the theme from *I Dream of Jeannie*, he rounded a corner and grinned back at the women, winking at them both.

***

Despite her lack of nautical expertise, whenever Yvonne saw *El Amor Descolorado* pulling up to the dock, it always made her slightly giddy. It was as singularly beautiful an image of man's grace, imagination, and boldness as anything she knew. That she complained bitterly about the time and expense it wreaked on her marriage had little to do with her clear approval of its flat-out éclat. Anyone could appreciate that fact. That Bob looked more in character piloting a vessel as magnificent as this one was largely extraneous. Some men were just predisposed to looking noble standing in the rain on the bows of large boats.

Yvonne waved again as the boat advanced slowly toward the pier. Even from this distance, she could see Bob's face was grave with concern. They both were attached to Rosa, no question. In a way, she felt they each thought of her as a kind of implied relative somehow. Still, she was just the slightest bit puzzled at how hard Bob seemed to be taking this.

"How's she doing? The baby all right?" Daniel called from the boat as they eased sidelong toward the dock. He stood on the deck, his shirt off and tied around his waist, massaging a sunburned shoulder. To Yvonne, he looked exactly like the ten-year-old imp that only yesterday parodied his father's every move like a veritable "Bob-clone." Where did that child go? she wondered. That carefree child who so captivated everyone with his wit, glee, and charm.

"Your husband tried to kill me out there. He had me swimming under the boat in shark-infested waters. How's Rosie?" Daniel put his shirt back on as Eddie tossed a line toward Melanie, who was now standing at the end of Wheelwright Marina.

"I'll tell you all as soon as you get ashore," Yvonne said.

Melanie tied the bow rope securely to the cleat and then hurried aft. Eddie, looking grouchy as usual, grinned slightly as Melanie tripped over a coil of garden hoses. He did enjoy seeing a pretty girl humbled occasionally. Was it asking too much that they touch earth once in a while? Besides, it did his whole outlook on life a world of good just to see those long, bare legs of hers every now and again.

Melanie straightened herself and fished around for her pitched sandal. "Dammit, Eddie, aren't these hoses supposed to be in the bosun locker?"

Eddie's eyes crinkled. "Yeah. I'll be getting round to it this afternoon."

Bob stepped to the side of the pilothouse and gently edged the *Amor* to shore. As Melanie tied the stern ropes, Eddie and Daniel both jumped on the landing and aimed for opposite ends of the pier. Daniel, wiping his forehead, approached Yvonne. "Mother, does he think I'm the hired help? Every time I offer to lend a hand on *"Das Boot,"* he ends up treating me worse than Eddie. I don't get it. I'm suddenly the new peon?"

Yvonne sighed and again studied Bob's expression up on the bridge. "I'm sure it's all character building."

"*Lines!* I'm going to look like Nick Nolte's mug shot before the end of summer."

"Wear a hat. I've warned you about the sun." Yvonne turned and walked over to where Eddie was adjusting the gangplank to the side of the boat. They stared at each other like two Rottweilers standing over the same ham sandwich. She examined his hatless, scarlet head. "I'm afraid a hat wouldn't do you any good, Mr. Frye. The damage seems to be already done."

Eddie smiled lazily. "Thanks for not worrying 'bout me, Miz W. I'm sure you've got more important things on your mind."

Yvonne glared at him a second longer and then briskly strode up the gangplank. Eddie rubbed his chin thoughtfully and watched her disappear. Yes, sir, *primo* bitch that she was, he'd still do her in a New York minute.

Climbing to the bridge, Yvonne was surprised to see Bob holding a teeming Bloody Mary. Flicking switches and adjusting dials on the equipment panel, he turned to her, face flushed. "How serious is it?"

Yvonne took a breath. "She nearly bled to death. She's all right for now; baby's OK. They just want to keep her horizontal as long as possible."

Bob took a long drink from his glass and stared at Yvonne, looking disoriented. "Jesus—how? How did it happen?"

"They don't know. The womb…it happens. I guess it's not terribly uncommon. I think she's going to be fine, it's just…Oh Bob, it was horrible. I've never seen so much blood." Yvonne reached out for him, and he put his arms around her instinctively. They leaned against each other, four legs of a precarious sawhorse threatening to buckle. She cleared her throat. "I suppose…we need to get word to the father somehow. What's the name of that offshore drilling concern he works for?"

Bob brought the Bloody Mary perfunctorily to his lips. Somewhere in the back of his mind, he envisioned a caramel-skinned child standing on the bow of the *Amor Descolorado* gazing at the waves and the sky with the exhilaration and wonder of an incipient philosopher. Somewhere in the back of his head, Rosa cradled a baby rabbit in one palm and the dismembered hand of an infant in the other. Bob blinked and stared blindly in the distance at a slow-moving dumpster chugging up on Bay Road. He sat his drink down. Placing his hand on the back of Yvonne's head, he stroked her hair gently. He said in a low murmur, "The father can wait."

chapter

TEN

Philip eased the Chevy Impala up under the covered drive-through of Otis McCloud's Chevron station and turned off the ignition. Glancing around, he looked for any sign of Lester. The place looked abandoned. Stepping out of the car, he pulled a stick of gum from his shirt pocket and scrunched it up, popping it into his mouth. Pondering for a moment whether or not to fill the tank himself, Philip eventually thought better of depriving himself of the singular occasion. Otis McCloud's Chevron was virtually the last place in Texas one could still get the "Full Service" treatment. And it was not a ritual to be idly dismissed. Check the oil, check the fluids, wipe the windshield, inspect the tires, spritz Armor All on the dash, and empty the litter bag. Mr. Otis even swept out your floor carpets with a little straw brush he carried in a clip on his belt. And it was the standard service he offered to everyone. His kind was as numbered and rare as the one hundred eighty or so revered whooping cranes that migrated each winter to the National Wildlife Sanctuary north of Rockport. The sole remnants of a once-abundant species, now meager as moondust.

Philip peered around the corner of the office door and saw Mr. Otis in a little alcove leading off the garage. Sitting in a straight-back chair, his feet stretched out atop several stacked cases of motor oil, he appeared to be dozing. Philip considered slowly retreating, but he knew Mr. Otis would scold him for sure if he discovered he'd visited the premises and departed without so much as buying a candy bar or a Coke. He scraped his feet a few times on the concrete floor. Silence. He then jingled his keys in his pants pocket. Silence. Finally, he reached over and lifted a bag of onion and sour cream potato chips. The crinkling noise of merchandise being fondled startled Mr. Otis like a poke with a stick. He scowled at Philip for a long second and then suddenly grinned from ear to ear.

"Well, Preacher! You done caught me back here saying my prayers. How the hell you been?"

"Doing all right. Not as good as some, but a whole lot better than most."

Otis stood up slowly, laughing. "That's what I like to hear. Problem with most people is they do more complaining than living. Some of 'em's got it so well rehearsed it's all downhill right after they brush their teeth in the morning." Otis shook Philip's hand.

"I've told you before, Mr. Otis, any time you want to come and give a sermon, I'll be glad to arrange it."

Otis hooted and spit out the front door with superior accuracy. "Shoot, you don't want me over there riling up those nice 'piscopalians. I'm from the old school of hellfire and damnation. I'm liable to get those folks so stirred up, they likely to fall out in the aisles all wall-eyed and foamy."

Philip shook his head. "Might be just the thing. We could use a little excitement."

"Oh, it'd be exciting all right. One time I give a sermon at a little old church down around Beaumont, and damned if one big old gal didn't jump up and yank off ever stitch of her Sunday finery and race on out the front door whooping like a bald wildcat. They pulled in a collection that day big enough to put down on a new Sunday school bus."

Philip laughed till his cheeks hurt, and Otis joined along with him. To Philip, the absence of true storytellers in the world was a sincere calamity. He himself had no gift for the talent, but at the very least, he felt people like Mr. Otis should be honored in some way as national repositories of common sense, spirit, and levity. Poet laureates of the hinterland.

"You need a fillem-up today, Father Phil?"

Philip nodded and pointed to the rear of the car. "Sure thing. I clicked open the trunk. Would you mind just checking the air pressure in that spare, too?"

"Done deal. Now you take a look around in here and see if you don't need a little extra somethin'." Otis pointed along the wall. "I got a sale on those fishing caps up there; got a nice wide brim on 'em, too. I sell two for one, or three for two. Any way you cut it, you getting an extra hat in the exchange!" Otis scurried out the door and started pumping gas.

Philip stared at the caps a second and turned to glance back toward the garage alcove. Was Lester not even here? He'd driven by on the off chance he might be lucky enough to instigate some kind of rapprochement between the two. Fat chance.

Wandering into the back storage room, he saw the cot and small duffel bag with Lester's worldly possessions all neatly folded inside. It looked like a visual aid on how to pack for summer camp. Philip shook his head, no doubt a prison memento. Picking up one of Lester's boots, he sat on the edge of the small bed and inhaled the scent of earthy, musky leather that was both surprisingly clean and redolent of Lester's fastidiousness. Tracing his fingers over the scuffed toe, Philip felt a surge of intense sadness envelop him. How did it happen *this way*? He'd never envisioned…*this*. Truth be told, he was infinitely happier with the *possibility* their prison correspondence availed him rather than any chance of actuality. Truth be told, imagination was clearly the stronger aphrodisiac.

Mildred jumped onto Lester's duffel bag and began mewing, rubbing her face back and forth on Lester's neatly folded T-shirts.

Philip reached to pick her up and, glancing to one side, he saw the edges of several worn and smudged envelopes tied together with string. He stared at the partially concealed bundle, momentarily bewildered. Feeling light-headed, he slowly reached over and lifted the letters from their partial concealment. Holding them in his hands, he studied his own handwriting and felt a form of rising atonement. Lester had indeed saved every one! Over four years of unadulterated desire bound up in a single packet of ragged exposition no wider than three packs of cigarettes. He shook his head. There had to be a consequence, some finality to all this massive outlay of human heart and soul laid bare. But what?

A car drove up out front. Philip could hear Otis' hearty hellos being flung about like vocal flower leis, homespun salutations designed to comfort the harried road warrior—another hallmark of McCloud's Chevron "Full Service" station.

Philip examined the letters a second longer, and then he placed them back in the bag. Picking up Mildred, he carried her with him to the front office. Stopping to pick up a new package of gum and some breath mints, he glanced up at the graduation photo hanging behind the desk, next to the calendar and the battery display. It was Otis Jr. looking as formal and immaculate as an egg. He placed Mildred on top of the desk and contemplated the picture. "Dr. Otis McCloud, Jr., Internal Medicine, University of California, San Francisco" read the small marker attached to the frame. With his reddish, curly hair and pale caffe-latte skin, Otis Jr. had never looked like anyone else around Rockport. A bright, observant kid, he was already wearing glasses in the first grade. By the third grade, he knew the names of all the presidents and how to multiply to a thousand without using a pencil and paper. In junior high school, he was class president, yearbook editor and, being a male in small-town Texas, an obligatory participant in at least one sporting venue, the track team. He'd been among Philip's closest friends all the way through junior high. It was in high school that things began to change between the two of them. That's when they both began having sex—with each other.

Timid and giggly stuff at first, it was more teasing than anything else. It then gradually evolved into more hormonally robust
occasions and, finally, flat-out libidinous exercises they were both
helpless to cease. Neither of them could deal with the hyper-conflicting emotions they were suddenly experiencing. Nor could
they stop doing it. It was only after Philip's mother walked into
his bedroom one afternoon with an armful of laundry and found
them both naked in the closet that they ended it. Philip was mortified beyond belief, and none of them spoke of the incident again.
Philip's mother, in particular, seemed to have developed a kind of
amnesia about the whole thing. Never happened. The tape in her
head was permanently deleted. That's how you got on. Push delete.

And Otis Jr. became the town introvert for a while, graduated
class valedictorian, and took the first scholarship to the college
farthest away from Rockport he could find. And none of them, it
can be safely stated, ever dealt with their hyper-conflicting emotions again.

"He asks about you when he calls."

Philip turned to see Mr. Otis stuffing a wad of bills in his
pocket. "Otis Jr.? Really?"

"Sure does. Says he's coming back for a visit someday soon."
Otis sighed, lowering his head and squinting at his feet. "But I
reckon he's just saying that on my account. He don't care for here.
And 'cept for maybe me and you, *here* don't care for him much
neither." Otis walked slowly to the cash register and banged open
the drawer. "All set. Full tank of gas, air in your tires, shine on the
hood—the whole damn world is yours for twenty-two dollars and
sixty-three cents."

Philip smiled and handed Otis his credit card. He watched as
the old man's gnarled and rough hands delicately tried positioning the credit voucher into the embossing machine. He then clumsily skid the indenting arm over it. The voucher ripped in half.

"Goddamn! Sorry, Preacher. I do it ever time. These hands of
mine has gotten so arthritic, I can't hardly open a can of chili no
more."

"Why don't I pay you in cash."

Otis handed the credit card back to Philip. "Hell, come by and give me a check at the end of the month. I'll keep ya in my register book. If I can't trust you, I might as well just shut 'er down and go fishing."

Philip slipped his card back into his wallet. "I'd heard you were supposed to have some new help around here?"

"Who?" Otis glanced at Philip sharply. "Oh, you mean Lester?" He grinned and spit. "Now there's a lucky little poot for you. He come to work for me not more'n a week and a half, and up drives old lady Wheelwright in that big, blue Jaggy-ar of hers saying she sure do need a man can work on her husband's *vessel* part time. Damn!" Otis wiped his forehead with his handkerchief. "You know the problem with people with money, Preacher?"

Philip shook his head, and Otis leaned in closer. "Ain't none of it mine!" He snorted, bent his knees, and did a little half-circle dance, wheezing with laughter. Philip laughed too, enjoying the exhibition as much as Otis did performing it.

"So, I guess Lester'll be back to help you on…"

Otis straightened his back and thought for a minute. "Monday? That's right—Monday. You know the boy, Preacher? Know anything about him?"

Philip shook his head, smiling. "No, no. Well, good to see you again, Mr. Otis. Glad to hear Otis Jr.'s doing fine." Philip extended his hand, and Otis held on to it, staring intently into Philip's eyes.

"I didn't say he was doing fine. I said he asks about you."

Philip's smile never wavered. "Yes, that's right. I forgot."

Otis peered more intently. "How come you never ask 'bout my boy?"

Philip felt his heart lurch in his chest. "I…I do…I mean, I thought I had. I'm sorry. How is Otis Jr. doing?"

Otis continued holding Philip's hand. "He asks about you. That's all." Otis suddenly let go his grip. He turned to rummage through a desk drawer.

Philip, clearly uneasy, ran a hand through his hair and rubbed the back of his neck. "So…does Otis Jr. have a family? Is he married now?"

Otis turned back to Philip, holding a small can of Copenhagen snuff. He inserted a pinch between his lip and gums and looked at Philip blankly. "No…He's just like you."

***

Lester edged the paintbrush down the bare plank of dull teak and marveled at its sudden transference from monotone to polychromatic—every finite vein, line, and detail of the wood transformed by the polyurethane into an astonishing palette of gold, red, bronze, and sienna manifestations. In the sun, the wet varnish looked more like honey than a chemical derivative, and the wood seemed more like bread. It was almost too illusory for Lester to fully incorporate. The sky, the wind, the JELL-O-green sea surrounding him—it all appeared to him more keen memory than any present-day reality. After Diboll, it was still problematic processing "now" from "then." Everything new continued to carry a kind of bleached authenticity concealing it: veiled, hazy, like weathered teak under fresh varnish, recovered but not completely untouched.

What he fully understood by now was the notion of self-autonomy. It felt good just to be out in the hot sun—shirt off, barefoot, and breathing in the Gulf air in long, sustaining mouthfuls. Standing, he wiped his forehead with his arm. Bob was with Eddie cleaning the side of the boat. He liked Bob. Friendly, reasonable, a "straight-shooter." They got on well. Eddie, on the other hand, was like every other guy he met in prison: lackadaisical, shifty, and too calculating to be of any real advantage to him or anybody else. It wouldn't have surprised Lester to have learned that Eddie had done a stint or two in the "system" himself. Not one iota.

He dipped the brush back into the can and started to kneel when he glanced up to see Melanie descending the hill from the main house, carrying three large glasses and wearing a pair of khaki Bermudas and a halter-top. Lester watched as she stopped on Bay Road and scanned both directions for traffic. Little Ray suddenly popped into his head. The way he used to scope out any room he'd enter at Diboll with those long, furtive, sidelong glances. It always reminded Lester of a skittish chameleon. He grinned to himself and squatted back down when Melanie caught sight of him looking. He was still feeling a bit chagrined about the bedroom fiasco. He felt sorry for the both of them. Not that they would have remotely made each other happy, but why should two bodies touching have to be such a tortured foray? So he wasn't "aroused" by her. He wasn't even sure at this point he was aroused by Luz. The only one who seemed to be winning the "pants pointer" medal was Daniel, and he for God sure was *not* hooking up with him anytime soon. It was the quandary of the age. Why do we always want what we're not supposed to want? To the best of Lester's reasoning, it was probably because we're just stupid enough to think we can get it anyway.

"Are you hiding from me or just being unfriendly?" Melanie squinted up at Lester from the dock below.

"Hey. I thought it was you, but I wasn't sure," he lied.

"I brought everybody lemonade. I put fresh ginger in yours." Melanie smiled at him mischievously. "They say in some countries it has aphrodisiac qualities."

Lester smiled back at her, playing along. "No kidding? You probably should've served some the night of the party."

Melanie laughed, handing a glass up to Lester. "Not from what I hear. You seemed to have done all right for yourself."

Lester looked at her, puzzled. Then he blushed. "Some people like to talk."

Melanie shrugged. "Doesn't matter to me. Although, I must say, your choice of my brother was a minor revelation."

Lester went back to staining the deck. "I didn't realize you were so easily shocked."

Melanie held a glass to her lips as she watched Lester's movements. "Not shocked. More beguiled, really," she explained. "Anyway, I think it was probably some kind of diversionary tactic for you rather than a 'real-life calling.' Know what I mean?"

Lester took a long swallow of lemonade and sat the glass down. "I think you may be thinking about it too much."

"Oh, no doubt!" Melanie laughed. "That's what happens to single women deprived of physical contact for too long. We turn into raging machines of hormonal calculation. That ginger doing anything yet?"

Lester laughed and stared at her. "Now how'm I supposed to get any work done here with you carrying on like this? Your dad's probably going to fire my butt."

"Oh, he won't fire you. If you'll just keep him company on his baby here, you've got a job for life. Why do you think Eddie's still around?"

"I was starting to wonder."

Melanie sat the other glasses down and began twisting her hair into a ball on the back of her head. She secured the knot with an elastic band on her wrist. Placing her hands on her hips, she said to Lester, "Hey, I want us to be friends. Really. Forget the other night. I was high, and you were"—Melanie shrugged—"a *parolee*. What do you say? Fresh start?"

Lester really looked at Melanie for maybe the first time. What he saw was a big, sunburned kid with a great smile and floppy yellow bangs hanging in her eyes. A kid who wanted to be loved in the worst possible way. A kid just like himself. He held up his drink. "Fresh start."

***

"*Fresh Start.* Isn't that the name of a toilet bowl cleaner?" Daniel asked, glancing up from his *Entertainment Weekly* crossword. He peered over at Rosa, waiting for an answer.

She gazed at him feebly and shook her head.

"Fresh Swirl, Fresh Flush—something like that. I need ten letters for "antibacterial product.""

"Fresh Touch," Rosa said softly.

"That's it! You're good, Rosie. I knew I could count on you for the merchandise stuff. Here's a tough one: 'Name of dog that torments Sylvester.' Oh God, I used to be so good at this—Pluto, Brutus...Spike. Shit, why can't I remember?" Daniel looked up and tossed the magazine to the floor.

Rosa was standing by the side of the bed, wobbling unsteadily.

"Honey, are you crazy? Get back into bed. You know what the doctor said. Are you OK?"

"I have to pee."

"I'll get your bedpan. Jesus, you nearly scared me to death." Daniel put his arm around her shoulders and tried directing her and the portable drip back into bed.

"No. I want to sit down. I don't like the pan."

"Rosie, you can't. You want to risk losing *muchacho* again?"

"I need to do the number two, and I can't do it in the bed. Just walk me to the door."

Daniel, unsure, looked at her and sighed. "If anything happens to this kid, I'll be in therapy the rest of my life."

"Hurry!"

Daniel nudged Rosa and the intravenous cart slowly toward the bathroom door. The tiny bathroom was so small, and with Rosa's large belly and drip gurney consuming all the space, it felt as if they were trying to mold ten pounds of hamburger into a three-pound skillet. Wearily, Daniel stood outside and held the door handle. "Rosie, you holler if anything funny starts moving. Rosie?"

"Quiet. I'm concentrating."

"I thought you had to go."

"Sh-h-h!"

Daniel exhaled deeply and looked around the room. Yvonne had sent scads of flowers, and most of her friends had responded in kind. One could always count on rich white ladies to respond in kind. In fact, everyone had been invariably concerned and solicitous toward Rosa—all except for Bob. He'd been to the hospital exactly one time since her arrival and, though he stayed half the day, he hadn't been back since. It puzzled and worried Daniel. Where was he during her time of need?

"Everything OK, Rose?"

"I can't."

"Can't what?"

"It's no use. I'm constipate."

"Do you want me to call the doctor? Maybe he can give you something."

The door opened suddenly, and Rosa stood there looking miserable with little half-moon plums of exhaustion hanging under each eye.

"Maybe gas. I try later."

Daniel gently eased her back into bed, straightening the tubes, wires, and blankets with the deftness of a trained attendant. "All set. You sure you don't want me to ring for an Ex-Lax?"

Rosa shook her head faintly. "You've all been so good to me. Especially Mrs. Wheelwright. I must be a very bad person...to sleep with a married man." She turned her head to the side and began to weep quietly.

Daniel took her hand and patted it, just like Nurse Anne Logan on *General Hospital*. "Now, it's going to be all right. You'll see. Everybody loves you, Rosie. Mom's excited as anybody about the new baby; we all are. Look, maybe we can tell her your husband died at sea. Or he ran off with someone. Another *man*! That's it!" Daniel said excitedly. "He was really a closet-case all along, and you're better off without him. We'll figure it out. Don't cry." Daniel held a tissue under her nose.

"Your father's going to tell your mother, before I leave the hospital. He told me so." Rosa blew her nose loudly.

Daniel bit the inside of his mouth. "Um, when did he tell you this?"

"When he was here visiting. He's so good, your father. So good. I don't deserve him." Rosa began to cry again.

"You know, I was kind of wondering. Why hasn't he been back to see you?"

Rosa stopped sobbing and looked at Daniel, alarmed. "I told him not to come! No, it's better that he stay away. I had a dream that the baby was born, and he was not there at all. The child had no father. When I told my mother on the phone, she said it was a sign that his presence was frightening the baby. He's too—how do you say?—too much 'affect' by the baby's coming. It's not good." Rosa shook her head in emphasis. "Not good."

On that much Daniel could agree. His father was on automatic "boat pilot" all the time now. He ate, slept, and obsessed about the boat. Period. Maybe he had to get it all ready for his new son. Maybe it's how he dealt with impending change. Who knew what was haunting him? The boat was his baby for now; that was certain. And when the *muchacho* arrived, *Quien sabe?*

There was a knock at the door. Daniel and Rosa exchanged looks. "Are you expecting anyone?" he asked.

She shook her head. "Maybe it's the doctor. Open."

Daniel turned and moved to open the door. It was Philip Yancey holding a fistful of crepe myrtles. "I hope this isn't a bad time?"

Daniel, mouth open, stared at him. "What…are you doing here?"

"I minister, remember?"

"Right." Daniel remained frozen. "But we're not Episcopalian. We're not anything."

Philip smiled. "And we're not picky people. Is Rosa receiving visitors?"

"Um…sure." Daniel absently stepped to the side, and Philip entered. Daniel stared after him as if he were observing an apparition float by.

"How are you doing, Rosa? Do you remember me?"

After a moment, Rosa beamed. "*Si!* You were in the ambulance, yes?"

Philip shook his head. "I was with you in the store."

"You were?"

"Right beside you. I'm so glad you're doing better."

"Thank you very much. You're very nice to come here. Are you a *padre?*"

"Well, yes, I'm a minister, but I'm not Catholic. We do have the same boss, though."

Rosa grinned. "That's nice. What beautiful flowers!" She glanced around the room. "Maybe we can put them…"

Daniel finally unhinged himself. "Um, how 'bout a water glass? We're a little short on vases."

"Excellent." Philip handed him the flowers, and Daniel disappeared into the bathroom looking acutely bewildered.

Rosa extended her hand slowly, "Rosa Maria Guzman."

"Reverend Philip Yancey. Please, call me Philip."

"*Con mucho gusto, Padre Felipe.*" Rosa lifted her head up from the pillow and stared intently at Philip. "Please," she said. "I would like to make confession."

Daniel instantly reappeared at the bathroom door, and both men glanced at one another quizzically. "Well, actually," Philip replied, "I don't do confessions."

"But you listen with your heart, no? I need to speak with someone of the church."

Philip held her hand again. "Of course. Whenever you like."

Rosa focused on him, a hint of anguish clouding her eyes. "Now?"

Philip studied her expression and then turned to look at Daniel. "Would it be OK if Rosa and I had a few moments alone?"

Daniel, mesmerized, snapped from his trance and nodded, "Sure, whatever. You...do your thing. I'll just be outside...if you need me." They both watched as Daniel backed slowly toward the door, turned, and exited.

Standing in the hallway, Daniel felt as if he'd just been steamrolled by a giant cupcake. Sticky, dazed, yet adrenalized from the encounter, he stumbled over to a nearby plastic patio chair. *What just happened?* Rosie and Philip—*acquaintances?* Bedside confessional? And, oh yes, by the way, isn't Reverend Yancey looking like a big hottie today? He'd always been attracted to the "daddy types," but Philip at first had seemed so, so...*Episcopalian.* Of course there was nothing wrong with that; still, it was a new sensation. Lusting for pastors. Daniel shook his head. What the hell? Don't men of the cloth deserve an even chance at snagging a few favors? Still, there was "something other" about this man that thoroughly captivated him. Their stroll on the levee after dinner in Port Aransas had been a thoroughly hands-off affair. Nothing unseemly, for sure. And truthfully, Daniel hadn't really given it much thought since. Until now. Seeing Philip standing in that doorway made his heart race, his palms sweat, and—why not just go there?—his dick jump. He couldn't for the life of him explain it. And whenever he couldn't explain anything, Daniel tended to fixate on said object until it "clicked" in his head.

"Is she sleeping, or can I go in?"

Daniel slowly looked upward from his reverie to see his father standing over him holding an enormous bunch of gerbera daisies.

"Wh...What are you doing here? For God's sake, who's next?"

Equally baffled, Bob shook his head. "I've come to see Rose. Is everything all right?"

Daniel stood, positioning himself between his father and the door. "She's confessing right now. She's fine, but you can't go in."

"Confessing?"

"Right. You know, sorry I did this, sorry I did that—six 'Male Harrys' and back to the pool."

Bob let the flowers slump to his side. "She doesn't want to see me, does she?"

"No! It's just that, I mean, she really is confessing right now."

"With who?"

"Father Phil. The Episcopalian minister."

"Did she ask to see him?"

"He just showed up. I think they'd actually, uh, met before."

"Met?"

"In the grocery store—when she fell."

Bob looked at Daniel, confused. "How long's he been in there?"

"Not long. Dad, why don't we sit over here and wait till he comes out—what do you think?" Daniel put his hand on Bob's shoulder and slowly led him over to the plastic chairs as though he were directing a great grandparent to his favorite bench in the park. Bob was obviously taking this much harder than Daniel had realized.

Sitting down, they both fixated on Rosa's door. Daniel finally cleared his throat and turned to his father. "So, this has been... difficult."

"I'm the father. You knew that, right?" Bob asked as matter-of-factly as asking the time.

"Yes."

"I love Rosa. You know that."

"Yes."

"I love your mother, too."

"Yes."

"I can't choose between them. I won't."

Daniel mustered his courage. Such talks were usually rare and uncomfortable ordeals for the both of them. "Then, what if you lose them both?"

Bob didn't answer for what seemed a very long time. He then coughed slightly. "I'll sail away on the boat somewhere. I won't be a burden to anyone."

Daniel suddenly felt enormous tenderness for this complex, rigid, basically decent, loving man who happened to be his father. Who would've thought at his age he'd be going through *this?*

"H...Have you told Mother anything?"

"I've decided to wait until the baby's born. Maybe if she sees him, or holds him, maybe she'll be able to..." His voice trailed off.

"Rosa mentioned you might tell mom *before* she left the hospital."

Bob placed the flowers on a nearby chair, sighing heavily. "It's not easy, son."

Daniel could see Bob's eyes filling with tears, his big, sturdy chin twitching slightly. He put his arm on his dad's shoulder. "It's OK, whatever you decide. We love you."

Without looking at Daniel, Bob suddenly reached his hand out and squeezed Daniel's neck, hard. He then rubbed his head for several moments and turned to put his arms around Daniel, hugging him tightly. "I love you too, son."

Daniel felt himself nearly leave his body. His emotions were vaulting wildly between anger, love, joy, and a vast chasm of sadness. It took every shred of willpower to keep from completely falling apart. Of all the times in his life he'd wanted his dad to hug him, to put his arm around him, to say, "I love you too, son,"—well, this was definitely a first. To think what they missed, what might have been, what friends they truly could have become, it addled his brain to even conceive such a likelihood.

Bob finally loosened his grip and kissed Daniel hurriedly on the neck. He pulled away and brushed his eyes with his thumbs. Daniel felt the sticky wetness of his father's lips on his skin. He thought of all the men in his life that had kissed him before—all the lovers, boyfriends, tricks, one-nighters, fuck-buddies, strangers, and yes, relatives. None of them had ever come remotely close to impacting his scrupulously guarded façade as surely as this one, impulsive gesture. He swallowed back the lump in his throat and took several long, deep breaths.

"The thing is…the *thing* is, I always felt I could've been a better father to you and Mel. I wanted to. I tried. I just…I just felt…inadequate. All I knew was money and numbers and machines." Bob laughed then. "And freakin' boats. And I knew how to make your mother happy. But you and Melanie—more so *you*—I just didn't have a clue really. I'm sorry for that, son."

Daniel stared at the floor praying, imploring to heaven that this please not get any more emotional. Yes, it was a boring "guy thing" not to show emotions, but he just didn't see how he could handle having a mini-nervous breakdown in front of his father right now. He knew if he let himself go, it might just become over-the-top, B-movie wacko, and he didn't think the hospital had the staff to deal with it.

Bob continued, "And the gay business? I left all that up to your mother to handle. Maybe I was wrong. I didn't know what to tell you, how to advise you. From the bottom of my heart, Dan, I just want you to be happy. I'd like you to find someone you can love and respect, but mostly I want you to be happy with yourself. To like who you are, to be proud of yourself. Don't let anyone ever take away your self-respect. You're the only *you* we've got, and that's just the way we want you."

That did it. Hoover Dam cracked like a cheap ashtray. Daniel hung his head and watched in amazement as tears poured from his eyes, nose, and mouth like his very own afternoon rain shower. He could hear weird strangling noises coming from his throat and he thought, for just a second, he might be having a stroke.

When Bob reached over to put his hand on his back, he gave in and let his head roll onto Bob's shoulder, sobbing like a three-year-old. Several nurses passed, and one of them stuffed a handful of tissues into Daniel's shirt pocket and continued on without a word. Daniel cried until he thought he might have ruptured something, and then he cried some more.

Finally Daniel wadded his Kleenex in his fist and sucked up the last remaining tears. Straightening his head, he slowly rolled his neck to ease the strain. He hadn't felt this wasted since three-for-one, 151 Rum Night at his favorite gay bar. He put his hand on his father's knee. "Thank you, Dad. I guess it was all, you know... just waiting to come out."

"That's quite all right, son. I know you must feel a lot better now."

Daniel looked at Bob. "Maybe you need a good cry, Dad? Just let it all hang out. I'm telling you, it does wonders."

Bob smiled slightly. "Maybe so, maybe so." After a moment, Bob straightened his back and concentrated on Rosa's shut door again. He was resolute: "I'm going to make it up to that little boy about to be born in there. All the sorrows and hurts, loneliness and absences. I will be a better father, to *all* my children. Wait and see."

Daniel stared at his father and considered the chances of such an avowal actually occurring. He exhaled and focused on the door as well, thinking, *Wait...and see. Wait...and see.*

chapter

ELEVEN

Luz stared at the braised pigeon with fennel heads and carda-mom *en confit* and put her fork down. Why—just once a week, once a month—couldn't they have something for dinner like tuna cas-serole? On paper plates, nuked in the microwave, and served with a tall glass of root beer? She relinquished (gladly) all rights to the kitchen years ago. Only now of late was she beginning to lament her hasty decision. Philip didn't know the meaning of words like "takeout," "Lean Cuisine," or "heat and serve." Who in Texas was eating braised pigeon at this very moment? In the entire United States? Outside of a very small region in France, who the hell ate nasty pigeons anyway?

Luz picked up her plate and exited the dining room for the kitchen. Philip glanced up from his supper and stared at her. "Anything the matter, Luz?"

"Nope."

"Is your meal OK?"

"Nope."

Philip put down his fork of *polenta* and wiped his mouth with the linen napkin. "What's wrong?"

Luz's voice echoed from the kitchen, "Not hungry for pigeon, I guess."

Philip stared toward the center of the table, gazing at the crystal eighteenth-century French candelabras their mother had purchased at an estate sale in New Orleans. He frowned. "May I ask why?"

Luz re-entered the dining room eating from a bag of Tostitos. She plopped herself back down and flung a leg over the armrest of the chair. "I have a question for you. Where does one *buy* pigeon for eating anyway?"

Philip looked at her, surprised. "I order it flash frozen from a farmer near Franconia Notch, New Hampshire. From barnyard hutch to dinner table in less than twenty-four hours. It's not inexpensive but definitely worth the trouble."

Luz shook her head, impassively. Philip's penchant for exotic foodstuffs was ancient territory. There was nothing to be gained from plowing up this picked-over field. Her parents, God rest their clueless souls, caved in to his quaint proclivities as a youth rather than just insisting he join a ball team like the rest of the boys his age. And she became the reluctant upshot, having to pay for their unwitting, tender mercies.

She stopped munching corn chips and swallowed slowly. "I think I'm going to start eating out more."

Philip looked at her as if he'd just been stabbed with a fork. "You're *what?*"

"I can't eat all this rich food."

Philip blinked impassively and traced his finger along the nubby, raw silk place mat. "It's the sauce, isn't it? I used butter and cream when I clearly could have gotten away with a little milk and some infused sesame oil. It's a bit profuse, I agree."

Luz shook her head. "It's not the sauce or the fennel heads or even the skanky pigeon. I just want to eat like a normal person again. I want Hamburger Helper and SpaghettiO's and—God help me—I'd even chow down on fried Spam with a smile on my face. I just can't keep going at it like we're the offspring of Louis the Fourteenth anymore."

Philip stopped massaging the place mat and stared at his plate, dejected.

"Phil, it's OK to every once in a while lay it on grand. I don't mind that. But every night is just too much. You're obsessing on food like it's your soul mate or something. We're Americans for God's sake; we don't live to eat. Eating is what you do between the office and the TV!"

Philip looked up at Luz and lifted the glass of early Beaujolais to his lips. "It brings me...pleasure. I don't ask you to stop painting, do I?"

"But I don't ask you to *eat* my paintings either!"

"You're missing the point. This is how I express myself. I enjoy it; it relaxes me; I'm good at it; and it's definitely not hurting anyone."

Luz nodded, sympathetically, "Fine, but I'm not willing to be your captive cohort anymore. You never ask me what *I'd* like for dinner, what *I'd* like to eat, or, God forbid, if *I'd* like to cook myself sometimes."

Philip was aghast. "You...*cook?*"

"Yes, me!"

"But I...I didn't think you cared."

Luz threw her napkin in the air. "I *don't!* But how 'bout letting *me* make that decision for God's sake."

Chastened, Philip placed both hands on the table. It definitely appeared to him his once acquiescent baby sister had begun to voice her personal convictions with a newfound fervor. Was she prepping herself for an even perhaps more harrowing showdown ahead? *Dear Lord, give me strength.* "All right. I do apologize for not taking your needs and wishes into account. It would be helpful, though, if you expressed yourself a little more regularly so we can avoid misunderstandings such as these."

"I'm *trying*, Philip! You're not exactly the world's greatest listener."

Philip's eyes widened. "What? That's what I do for a living. I listen to people every day."

"I'm your sister, *not* your career. In case you were confused, there's a difference between professional duties and family ties." Luz stood from the table again. "But since none of us *has* any family around to remind us of that fact—of course, other than our own lonely selves—I fully understand your propensity to forget one small, insignificant truth: we're all we do have, Philip! Make a note!" Luz stormed from the room, and Philip blinked at Windsor. He rationally deducted there'd be no after-dinner coffee, Cognac, or Scrabble in the living room this evening. Retrieving his plate, he walked toward the kitchen. Luz was standing at the sink eating from a box of Fig Newtons.

Philip sat the plate down, put a hand on the back of his neck, and began rubbing his shoulder. "Do you…have an extra one of those?" Luz, without turning, extended her hand with one cookie in it. "Thanks." Philip took the Newton and munched in silence. After a long pause, he asked, "So, what would you like for dinner tomorrow? You tell me, and we'll have it."

Luz looked out the window, pursing her lips. "Frito pie."

Philip winced, but only slightly. "All right. That's Fritos, cheese, chili—"

"Wolf Brand, in a can, *with* beans. Grated rat cheese only. Half a chopped-up yellow onion on top. Period. Think you can you pull that off?"

"Think so."

"Good."

Philip brushed his hands together, scattering crumbs. "Can we still eat in the dining room, or would it be better to go outside and have it in the tree fort?"

Luz tried not to smile but couldn't help herself. She picked up a dishtowel and threw it at him. "Smart ass. What am I going to do with you?"

"I was beginning to wonder the same thing myself. I'm apparently just rotten enough to curdle milk."

Luz sighed. "You're not *that* bad. It'd just be extremely helpful if you'd occasionally remember there're two of us living here."

"Roger. And contrary to popular opinion, I do. I'm consciously aware of your presence at least eighty-six percent of the time."

"Umm-hmm. Well, bump it up if you want fewer misunderstandings around here." Luz held out the package of Fig Newtons. Philip shook his head and watched as Luz walked over to the pantry, offering a cookie to Windsor along the way. He hated it when she fed him human food, but he bit his tongue. Choose your battles. Windsor greedily devoured the forbidden treat, and Philip wondered once again how all this intrigue with Lester would play itself out. How indeed? If he revealed everything to Luz, would that be the absolute, final rupture between them? If he pleaded with Lester to consider the ramifications of his vengeance very carefully, would he simply laugh in his face? How could there possibly be any peaceful, sane resolution to the turmoil he'd created? Anxiety exceeded his every expectation.

"My friend Elsie is coming over tonight. Are you going to be listening to the CD player in the living room? She's got some new music she wants me to hear."

Eureka! The *Elsie Factor*. Philip hadn't fully addressed this key component. If Lester knew about Elsie, if Luz told him about Elsie—"No, no. I'm going to do a little reading. Try not to crank it up too loud, please." He smiled. "How is Elsie? Haven't seen a lot of her lately."

Luz looked up from shoving scraps down the garbage disposal. "Probably because the last time she was over here, you asked her if she'd read *The Idiot* by Dostoevsky, and I think she took it personally."

"Are you serious?"

Luz began rinsing plates. "Philip, Elsie grew up in a mobile home with nine brothers and sisters. Her mother was a maid, and her father drove a truck. Why not ask her which of Monet's *Giverny* paintings are her favorite?"

"Poverty doesn't have to be an excuse for unworldliness."

"Yes, and inflated presumption usually doesn't endear one to others, either."

Philip shrugged. "Well, I can't seem to win any merit badges today. How are you and Elsie getting along?"

She turned to him. "Fine. Why?"

"No reason. I like Elsie. She seems very…cheerful."

Luz stared at him oddly and then turned back to the sink. "I'll tell her. I'm sure she'll be slaphappy with the news." Placing glasses in the dishwasher, Luz laughed. "I don't think my new friend Lester found her quite so cheery."

Philip froze. "Oh. Why's that?"

"I dunno. I think he was pissed she came to the movie with us, or something. Who knows?"

Philip smiled. "Did she? I hadn't realized."

"Yep." Luz ran a sponge across the countertop and turned to Philip. "So what do you think of this Lester?"

Philip inhaled a long breath through his nose. "Um…he seems…interesting."

Luz smiled. "You like him, don't you? I knew it." She turned to toss the sponge into the sink. "Too bad he's straight."

"I doubt that," Philip answered before he could edit.

Luz looked back at him slyly. "Why?"

"Because I can…tell, that's all."

"Oh please, you still think Richard Chamberlain is straight. I wouldn't go getting any ideas about Mr. Briggs, Philip. I don't think you're his type."

Philip reacted quietly. "Well, you're certainly not his type either."

Luz turned, crossing her arms. "God, this is serious. I didn't realize you had a big old crush on him." She moved to Philip, putting a hand on his shoulder. "Brother, I mean he's cute and everything, but he's not…*bright* enough for you."

Philip backed away, glaring at her. "And maybe you're wrong about that, Luz. How do you know what my type is? I may not even have a type. Maybe I like them all. Maybe I have a secret life you don't even know about. No one knows! What would you think about that? Old boring, repressed Father Phil has a totally scandalous 'other' life. Wouldn't that just be the best?"

Luz stared with her mouth agape. Something had really rattled Philip's cage, and it intrigued her to no end. Getting a rise out of Philip was as difficult as dancing with a ladder. Could she be wrong about Lester? Lester and Philip?

The front doorbell rang, and Luz smoothed the front of her cotton blouse. Pulling the elastic band from her hair, she let her brown locks fall around her face. "That's Elsie. Look, we can talk about this later if you like. Hey, what do I know? Maybe you were meant for each other. Anything's possible, right?" She aimed for the front door, leaving Philip to foment.

Luz entered the hallway and reached out to click on the front porch lights as she moved. She could make out a silhouette that appeared at first glance not to be Elsie. Reaching the door, she opened it slowly.

"I'm terribly sorry to bother you. I do hope I haven't come to the wrong house."

"Who are you looking for?"

"Father Philip Yancey. Is this his residence?"

Luz nodded. "*Our* residence. The house belongs to both of us."

The woman extended her hand. "Yvonne Wheelwright. We have a summer home here in Rockport. Is the reverend in?"

Luz opened the door wide. "Yes, of course, come in." Luz was more than accustomed to ushering parishioners into the Yancey manse at all hours of the day. At first she'd resented the usually ill-timed intrusions into her family home, but later on it became largely routine. Like it or lump it, it was their shared existence.

Yvonne, looking as slim and stylish as ever, walked inside. "Oh, what a lovely home you have. Your garden is just my favorite in town. Are you Mrs. Yancey?"

"Actually, we're known as the 'unmarried Yanceys.' Philip is my brother." Luz extended her hand. "Luz."

"Luz? Just like Rock Hudson's sister in the movie *Giant*?"

Luz nodded.

"How marvelous. So nice to meet you."

"I'll just get my brother; he's in the back here."

"Thank you so much. If this is an awful time, I can certainly come back."

"Not at all. Please, have a seat in the living room."

Luz wandered back into the kitchen. Yvonne walked over to the plush Queen Anne divan nearest the hallway and sat, gazing around the room. It certainly wasn't her thing—antique bric-a-brac and monstrous credenzas looming like grizzly bears in every corner—but she could assuredly appreciate the discernment and planning that went into pulling it all together. Someone with a sense of authority had definitely configured the whole thing. Picking up a small cloisonné bowl on the coffee table, she studied its intricate ornamentation. Again, not her style; it was too "grandmotherly dear" for her tastes. If Yvonne could live in the Museum of Modern Art, she'd be delighted. Hygienic and minimalist was her thing. She sat the curio back down and stared absently toward a far window. She wondered how on earth she was going to tell this perfect stranger what needed to, had to, be told.

"Hello? Oh yes, from the grocery store. How are you?"

Yvonne jumped slightly. "I didn't hear you coming." She rose and took Philip's hand. "I don't think we properly met before. I'm Yvonne Wheelwright."

"Philip Yancey." Luz stood alongside Philip and patiently waited for their departure to another region of the house. "You've met my sister, Luz."

"Yes, thank you. I hope you don't mind my barging in like this. I had to do a little detective work to find you. I wanted to thank you for all your help with Rosa."

"Oh my goodness, not at all. We had a very nice visit at the hospital today."

"Yes, she told me." Yvonne hesitated. Then she continued, "I was wondering if I could speak with you about a matter for just a few moments."

"Of course. Why don't we go to my study? It's more private there."

Yvonne turned to Luz, "Very nice to meet you, Liz."

"Luz."

"*Luz!* Of course. I got you confused with Liz Taylor. Same movie—"

"Happens all the time. People always confuse me with her. It's the feet. We have identical feet."

"Ha-ha! Cute. Very funny. Well, good-bye."

"Bye." Luz watched as Philip and Yvonne disappeared down the hall and into Philip's study. She puckered her mouth and inhaled slowly, emitting a high-pitched whistle that brought Windsor scampering from the kitchen. Kneeling beside him, she began rubbing his head. Shouldn't she be getting paid a little something for these recurring appearances as the "vicar's wife"? Windsor rolled over on his side, and Luz scratched his belly absently. "He owes me, that boy. Owes me big time."

***

Philip watched Yvonne as she gazed around the room, studying his expanse of books, paintings, statuettes, photographs, and assorted collectibles. Everyone always did the same thing. He'd designed his study so that people would never just plunge right in for whatever it was they'd come to see him about. He learned from an elderly reverend in seminary school, one should immediately divert their attention. It took a bit of urgency from the encounter and gave people time to gather their thoughts. Of course by now he'd stitched it together that this was Daniel's mother. He'd been as startled as Daniel was when he showed up at the hospital and saw him standing at Rosa's bedside. But then again, these random coincidental acts were hardly by chance. It had become exceedingly apparent to Philip for quite some time now that all "fortuitous encounters" were skillfully prearranged in the great, ethereal order. No doubt about it. Now, the question of *why* such meetings were designed in the first place was infinitely the more intriguing conundrum. Why indeed?

"Such lovely things you have. And so beautifully displayed. It's almost like a...museum."

"I'm afraid my sister would agree with you. She keeps telling me we're just one or two knickknacks away from residing at the Smithsonian."

Yvonne laughed. "What a darling sense of humor she has. Why isn't she married?"

The question, asked so ingenuously, threw Philip for a moment. Finally he shrugged. "I guess she just hasn't found the right one. Have a seat, please."

Yvonne sat in the leather wingback by the fireplace and folded her hands. "Actually, that's one of the reasons I wanted to see you."

Philip waited.

"My daughter, Melanie, is engaged to be married in the fall to a lovely man in New York. We're all very thrilled for her, naturally, but just in the past few days she's expressed a burning desire to marry, well, right away. Like…next week."

"Goodness."

"Exactly. You can imagine I've been a bit…overwhelmed… trying to make this all happen for her. And now with Rosa…" Yvonne sat up straight. "Well, I always say there's nothing I like better than a challenge. It will all be lovely, simple, elegant, and *perfect*. No question. And I just thought that since our meeting at the store—I'm not sure how to put this—well, meeting you was just so providential. I was wondering if perhaps you'd—"

"Perform the wedding?"

Yvonne sighed with relief. "Yes!"

"Well, let me look here…" Lester pulled a date book from his desk and flipped it open. He looked up at Yvonne. "*Next* week you say?"

"Saturday the twenty-fourth. Oh, you don't know what a difference this will make. And you needn't worry. We're mostly Episcopalian. Though to be honest, perhaps more lapsed than allegiant."

Philip glanced up, smiling. "You seemed to have a grasp of the Anglican canon when we were kneeling in front of that refrigerator case. When people say lapsed, I always think 'just on vacation, not worrying about the bills.'" He idly picked up a letter-opener, balancing it across his index finger. "I have this vision," he continued. "We all pass through that big front office one day. Dues get paid, books are balanced, the uniform is returned. In the end, all people become 'godly.' At least in their own heads anyway."

Yvonne smiled, not entirely sure she was comprehending the mini-sermon. Philip returned to the book. "Let's see. I have a ten o'clock christening. What time is the wedding planned for?"

"Four in the afternoon."

Philip nodded slowly, "Hmmm, um-hmm…yes, I think I can do it."

Yvonne exhaled audibly. "Oh—you have no idea. Bless you!"

"When can the couple come by for a brief chat?"

"Come by?" Yvonne appeared perplexed.

"Traditionally the rector meets with the betrothed couple. It's a pep talk, some sanctity-of-marriage business to discuss. All quite congenial. We usually cap it with a glass of sherry and a few biscuits."

Yvonne smiled vacantly, flicking her nails. "Well, let me see. Brian's taking off work to fly in on Friday. We're having a cocktail at seven, which I'd be honored if you and your adorable sister would attend by the way." She gazed at the ceiling doing mental calisthenics. "Would, say, five o'clock on Friday be OK?"

"Five it is." Philip scribbled in his book and then looked up, smiling. "We're all set."

Yvonne smiled back, a frozen grin lining her face. "Yes."

"Anything else I can help with?"

"Yes." Yvonne's expression remained fixed.

After several moments, Philip cleared his throat. "How may I be of service to you, Mrs. Wheelwright?"

"Yvonne, please." She snapped out of her trance. "I was…wondering. Did Rosa…mention anything to you this afternoon?"

"About?"

"About…*anything*?"

"She mentioned lots of things, yes."

"Of course, I wouldn't dream of having you divulge a confidence. I just…"

Philip cocked his head at an angle, smiling patiently.

Yvonne continued, "I just...would like to know."

"Know what exactly?"

Yvonne fidgeted with a bracelet, nervously massaging her hands. "It's about the...father...of her baby. You see, I don't believe Rosa's story about who the father really is."

Philip arched a brow, listening attentively.

"I don't feel she's been entirely truthful."

"Why do you think that?"

Yvonne stared at him, a gloss of tears filling her eyes. "I don't really know how to say this. I've been holding it inside for quite a while now. You see, I'm afraid the father is someone I know."

Philip's face remained impassive. Yvonne began to sniffle, and Philip handed her a tissue across the desk. "Thank you. Oh Father Philip, you don't know how awful this makes me feel."

"Would you like to take a moment to gather your thoughts?"

"No! If I don't get this out now, I never will." Yvonne blew her nose and took a deep breath. "I think the father of Rosa's baby is someone...I know very well!"

Philip blinked and clasped his hands together atop the desk. "Why...do you think that?"

Yvonne lowered her head. "This is the part...I'm so ashamed. I've been married for thirty years to the most loving, wonderful, kind man in the entire world. How this ever..." She wept into her tissue for a few seconds and then once again drew a steady breath. "I had an affair with the man that works on my husband's boat."

Philip's eyes grew large. "Who?"

Yvonne wiped her nose and stared at him sheepishly. "You need a name?"

Composing himself, Philip shook his head. "No, of course, if you'd rather not..."

She wadded the tissue in her fist and grimaced. "Oh what does it matter? His name is Eddie Frye. He's a married father of three with a junior high school education and a penis for a brain. It was an *entirely* physical liaison, and I felt dirty and cheap every time we did it." Yvonne groaned. "Yes, and I'm quite certain all the dime-store Freuds would agree that's exactly why I did it, too.

But in reality, I think I did it to get closer to my husband." She looked at him mournfully. "Bob's been so distant this summer, as if there were something standing between us. It's that—pardon me—damn boat of his! Bob spends all his time on the boat, and Eddie spends all his time with Bob. I don't know. In some crazy, mixed-up way, I felt I could be with Bob (if I didn't have Bob) by sleeping with Eddie. Does that make any sense at all?"

Philip made a round O with his mouth and hunched his shoulders. "It seems to me that whatever the reasons were, your contriteness and remorse concerning the affair were sufficient enough to end it. I'm assuming it is over?"

"Yes! Absolutely."

"Then forgive yourself. God already has. Learn from your experiences, and resolve to do better next time. The guilt and re-criminations and angst hardly make it worth the intrigue."

Yvonne shook her head. "You're so right. I feel like such a cheat. Never again."

"I never say, 'never again.' I say, 'Holy Spirit, let me at least achieve a little grace with each stumble and recovery.'"

Yvonne's eyes brimmed. "How beautiful. How perfectly put." She sighed. "I feel so much better already."

Philip looked at her, slowly nodding his head. "But…I guess…I'm still a little confused. How does your affair relate to Rosa's pregnancy?"

Yvonne clasped a hand to her chest. "Because, that narco-leptic erection Eddie kept warning me if we stopped being intimate with each other, he'd go sleep with Rosa. Worse than that, he threatened to seduce my daughter! Well, I knew for sure *that* would never happen. But still, you never know what kind of harassment these types will stir up in their delusional thinking."

"Why not just fire him?"

"He's my husband's only friend here! A 'paid one' it's true, but he'll do anything Bob asks him—paint, scrape, row, laugh, jump, or skip. Bob would sink into a depression he'd never climb out of if I insisted he fire him." Yvonne leaned forward, a small grin on her lips. "But I think I may just have out-smarted Mr. Frye. I hired a new fellow to come work on the boat. So far, he's accomplishing wonders. Perhaps Eddie won't be so irreplaceable after all."

Philip leaned back in his chair and contemplated. He knew more about the Wheelwrights in one day than most of his parishioners in a lifetime. What Rosa had revealed to him, what Daniel disclosed, could it be possible these familial random acts of coincidence were leading him into some unknown, hazardous territory? And, as usual, the cunning conundrum of *why?* loomed large.

"So, you *think* this Eddie fellow slept with Rosa. That's your concern?"

"Yes. She's such a sweet, naïve girl. I think he could have talked her into anything. To get back at *me!*"

"Have you asked her?"

"Oh, she denies it. She bursts into tears whenever I bring it up and runs from the room. I've just never bought into her "offshore driller" boyfriend ruse. Not once. Poor thing, and now this. We're all so fond of Rosa. She's like a member of the family. We'll love her child and help her no matter whose baby it is." Yvonne leaned forward again, jabbing her finger angrily on the desktop. "But I want to be damn sure if it's one of Frye's whelps we're managing to raise, he acknowledges his paternal responsibilities to the full extent of the law!" She then sat back in her chair calmly. "That's all."

Philip studied Yvonne's face, wisely deciding to table the "grudging ex-lover" homily for another time. "Well, I'll certainly pray on the matter, and I'd hope that you and whatever family members you can persuade to join you, participate as well. Is there anything else I can do for you, Yvonne?"

"Do you eat lamb?"

Philip blinked. "Lamb?"

"Yes, I was thinking of an outdoor Moroccan feast after the wedding. I don't want it to be too grand, but doesn't that sound like fun?"

Philip's eyes twinkled. "Wonderful! I have a knockout couscous recipe with almonds, dates, and pomegranate seeds."

"I'd love to see it."

"Have you thought of doing a traditional *bisteeya*? It's this enormous, three-layer *baklava* kind of thing with spiced chicken and lemon eggs and tons of exotic savories. A real crowd pleaser."

"Marvelous! What terrific ideas you have. You should consider running a party-consulting business on the side."

Philip nodded, amused. The demand for a party planner in Rockport was not an enormous necessity at present. Yvonne stood and offered her hand. "I can't tell you how much better I feel after having this opportunity to unburden myself. You're an absolute miracle worker."

Philip led her to the door. "It's kind of you to say so, but this is simply what I do. Always glad to be of service."

Reaching for the doorknob, Yvonne placed a hand on his arm. "Oh, by the way, are you by any chance, gay?"

Philip clenched the handle, twisting it slowly. "Am I...I'm... excuse me?"

"I hope you don't think I'm being nosy. Really, I'm not. It's just that my son, Daniel, is gay, and he has such few friends around here. So I thought, well, if you two are both—how does he put it?— 'Friends of Doris?'"

Philip frowned, unsure. "Dolores?"

"Dagmar? *Dorothy!* Friend of *Dorothy!* Well, maybe you two could get together and, I don't know, talk about old movies or whatever."

Philip's eyes glazed over. "Well, why don't you have Daniel give me a ring."

Yvonne beamed. "Oh lovely! Well, this has been such a fortunate visit. I do hope you'll come round and see us sometime during the week. Of course, it's going to be a madhouse, but I frequently do my best work when there's a smidgen of panic in the air, don't you agree?"

Philip nodded. "Frequently. Let me show you to the front door."

"Oh, you needn't bother."

"No problem."

As they walked down the hallway, Yvonne suddenly gasped, taking Philip's hand. "I just had the oddest sensation. It was exactly as if someone were whispering in my ear."

"What did they say?"

Yvonne gasped again, placing her hand to her chest. "They told me you were about to become a…family member. Good gracious, what do you think it means?"

Philip stared at her, mystified. Finally he grinned. "I have no idea. Maybe it means…'Hi, Mom.'" After a pause, they both began to laugh uproariously.

chapter

TWELVE

"What do you mean *space*? I give you lots of fucking space."

"It's not just that. It's like I don't feel like being committed right now."

"I'm not asking for commitment."

"But you like, *need* me and stuff."

"I need you for friendship. What's wrong with that?"

"Nothing."

"So?"

"So…I'm not into the physical stuff anymore."

"You're not into the physical stuff…with me?"

"Right."

"And like…what happened?"

"I don't know, but it's not you."

"It is me."

"No, it's me."

"It's me!"

"OK, I just don't feel that way about you anymore. OK?"

Luz stared at Elsie and could feel that familiar burning sensation building behind her eyeballs. *Dammit! I am not going to cry this time. I will not fucking cry!*

"Um...What happened?" Luz asked. "A week ago we were making love out at your uncle's catfish pond, on a blanket, under the trees, in the moonlight, and now...we don't *feel that way*? Just bring me up to date here. What happened?"

"Nothing happened. It was just coming, that's all."

"Coming?"

Elsie nodded.

Luz could hear Philip and his lady visitor laughing loudly in the hallway. She rose and went to the massive living room doors, sliding them shut. Turning back to Elsie, she placed a hand over the hollow squeamishness in the pit of her stomach that was making her knees wobbly. One more time, another one floats out the front door unscathed and eager to conquer new worlds. And Luz returns to scribbling in her tear-stained journal/sketch book of life's observations: wiser, stronger, braver. *Pathetic.* She twisted her mouth around the word again: *Coming.*

"Look, it hasn't really been working. You know it; we both know it."

"But I guess the difference between you and me is I know it's never going to be perfect with anyone, all the time, anywhere, anyway. You have to hang on and ride the waves. It's called 'dedication to the cause' in some obscure cultures."

Elsie stood and put her cigarette out in one of the antique bowls. Luz knew she'd have to rinse the bowl later and spritz the room with English air sachet until all traces of tobacco infraction were annihilated. She didn't give a shit. The way Elsie looked now in her tight jeans and tank top, she wanted to swallow her whole, cigarettes and all. Why was it always you want them the most when they want you the least? She watched transfixed as Elsie picked up a striped mint and removed the wrapper. "Anyhow, you know I'm moving to Houston in the fall. We'd just be going through this in a few months anyway."

"So what's the rush? Am I that awful to you?"

Elsie held the round mint between her perfect white teeth and perfect red lips and sucked it in like a particularly lewd child's mechanical bank. "You're a great girl, Luz. You really are. It's just... you're too good for me."

"Oh vomit!" Luz threw a sofa pillow at Elsie, narrowly missing the potted fern on the stand. "Even you can come up with something better than that. Come on, try a little harder."

Elsie stared at her, provoked. "What are you talking about?"

"Oh, for God's sake, Elsie. Did you hear that line on one of your TV *novelas*? 'You're too good for me.' Fuckin-A right I'm too good. Who else would put up with such wretched inanity?"

"Well look, I gotta go. I hate it when you get all bitchy and smart-ass. Like I don't know anything, and you're Miss Queen of the University, professor bullshit, *artiste*. I get treated a lot better elsewhere, let me tell you."

Luz rose quickly. "Wait a minute. Are you...seeing someone else?"

"I gotta go."

Luz grabbed Elsie's arm. "Are you?"

Elsie pulled away. "Give me a break. I see lots of people. Are you asking me if I am *dating* someone else? No. Thinking about *dating* someone else? No. *Seeing* anyone else on the planet in a casual, friendly, non-desperate, open kind of way?" Elsie nodded, "Uh-huh!"

Luz, devastated, let her eyes fall to the floor. She turned and picked up the soiled ashtray. "Thanks for telling me. It's helpful to know when your girlfriend is seeing someone else. That is, when you live in such a small dating pool. I mean, it's not like there are a million other lesbians in town and I wouldn't find out eventually, you know, so thanks for that."

Elsie stared at Luz. "It's a guy, Luz. I'm seeing a guy. It just... happened."

Luz stared at her impassively. "Oh."

Elsie slid open one of the heavy living-room doors. "So, I guess...I'll see you around." She stood for a moment longer and then turned and walked out the front entry. Luz held the bowl in her hand, twisting it round and round until the bottom of the dish left a perfect red circle in her palm. Raising the bowl to stare at her flesh, she suddenly flung it across the room into the fireplace, shattering it loudly. Ashes dispersed ethereally over the carpet like fairy filament. Luz looked at Elsie's stubbed cigarette filter, ruby shellacked and squatting obscenely atop a pile of Philip's imported *Country Living* magazines, and she suddenly burst out laughing. On cue, Philip entered.

"What happened? Is everything all right?"

Luz snickered, staring at the butt. "I'm afraid...one of the bowls broke."

"Broke? Which one?"

Luz pointed toward the fireplace, and Philip moved to retrieve the shattered pieces. "Oh no, no. Do you realize how old that one was?"

Luz shrugged, biting her lip.

"Only over a hundred years. It was one of Mother's favorites. What the hell happened, Luz?"

"I guess I...threw it."

Philip stood from where he was kneeling, appalled. "Why?"

Luz shrugged again. "I don't know. I just...felt like it."

Philip blinked in complete bafflement. "Well, you're going to have to pay for this."

Luz glowered at him. "I certainly am not. It's not yours; it's *ours.* You can file an insurance claim with that exorbitant home-furnishings rider we pay through the nose for. And when you get the money, Philip, you can go buy another one just like it. Or a hundred fake ones just like it. Or, I have an idea, why not take the entire big old check and stick it up your ass?" Luz turned and exited the room.

Looking down at the broken pieces in his hand, he once again contemplated the contingency of "random acts." He pondered as well if somehow there might be a way he could tie all of this together into a cautionary tale for the upcoming Sunday service.

***

"You're pretty quiet today. What happened?" Lester glanced over at Daniel steering silently behind the wheel of the Porsche. Daniel had offered to chauffeur Lester back into town after his spending the weekend working on the boat. The two of them hadn't said a word since leaving the dock.

"I don't know. Lot on my mind, I guess." Both continued staring solemnly ahead for another half mile or so.

"Your dad's a good guy."

"Yeah."

Another half mile went by.

"Your mom's OK, too."

"Thanks. They make each other very happy."

Several oncoming cars drove slowly past. "And Melanie," Lester continued, "I think she's doing the right thing just going ahead and getting hitched."

Daniel looked at him. "Well, that's the Triple Crown. You've got everyone covered but me. How'm I doing, Lester?"

Lester glanced back and then squinted ahead. "I dunno. You don't seem all that happy."

Daniel nodded, shifting into a lower gear. "I can truthfully say I've had jollier periods in my life. For sure."

Off on the horizon, Lester watched the line of shrimp boats come slipping into the bay from the Gulf. They reminded him of cattle, the way they always moved in single file when heading in from the pasture for water. No matter how hot, tired, or thirsty they were, no one ever got ahead of the head bull or mama cow doing the leading. There was an order to it, an invisible blueprint. Cattle, shrimp boats, prisoners—always an invisible blueprint involved.

"It's about the sex thing, isn't it?"

Daniel turned to Lester. "Beg your pardon?"

Lester continued, "You're upset 'cause we didn't have sex again after that night."

Daniel took a deep breath of soupy air and grinned. "Actually you're wrong. I mean, you're a very hot man, Lester, don't get me wrong. But you've got "Unavailable" stamped in giant, block letters all over your body. I love punishment as much as the next red-blooded American guy, but I knew there'd be zero payoff in throwing myself at you like some manic teenager. Once was enough—although, if you're thinking about a quickie, I don't have to be anywhere for a few hours."

Lester grinned. "I like that about you. Your humor and your honesty. You're a good role model."

"Me?"

Lester nodded. "Yeah. I know you like to play at being the fuck-up, but you're not. Not hardly."

"Damn. That's about the nicest compliment anyone's ever paid me. You sure you don't want to have sex?"

Lester laughed, nodding. "Yep. And it's not 'cause I didn't like it and I don't think you're good looking too and everything. It's just…" Lester thought for a moment, slouching back in the seat and staring up at the clouds. "It's just…that thing you said about 'Unavailable'? I think it's more 'Unready.' Till I figure out why I came here, my brain won't let me plug into my dick."

"Right. I guess you were just running *off battery* that night on the beach."

"Actually, and I don't mean this in a bad way at all, you helped me to reconnect with someone else."

"Oh really? Big shocker, dude. I knew that! It wasn't about me. And guess what? It still felt good!"

Lester smiled. "I wish I had your nature. Prison has a way of knocking all the easy places out of your head."

Daniel looked at him. "So, what's his name?"

Lester glanced over, puzzled.

"Come on, Lester. If you can't talk to me about it, who's left?"

Lester stared back up at the sky. "Little Ray."

"Do you love him?"

After a long pause, Lester spoke quietly, "I love someone else."

"Oh right, Laurel Jean—"

Lester immediately sat upright. "There is no Laurel Jeanette!"

Daniel kept his eyes on the road. "But, you said that—"

"She's not the person I thought she was."

"God, Lester, I'm sorry."

Lester shrugged. "Me too. I guess."

"What are you going to do now?"

Lester inhaled deeply. "Haven't decided yet. I just figure…" Lester stared ahead, "that there's some reason for all this. Maybe the thing is to just see how it plays itself out."

Daniel glanced at Lester, then back to the road, then back to Lester again. "Well, I've got some news." Lester glanced over at him. "What's it worth to you to find out?"

Lester rolled his eyes and stared out the passenger side, playing along. "Gee, I don't know. A blow job?"

"No thanks, I'm driving. You can just give me a kiss."

Lester looked at him as if he were deranged.

Daniel pointed to his cheek and leaned in to Lester. "Come on, right here."

"No thanks."

"Why not?"

"I don't want to. Keep your eyes on the road."

"My God, you were kissing me in places not that long ago that'd make a lap dancer blush."

"Go find a lap dancer."

"Come on."

"No."

Daniel frowned. "All right, I'll tell you anyway." Daniel extended his wrist toward Lester. "Kiss my hand."

"God, you're an insistent little shit." Lester grabbed his hand, kissed it quickly, and then flung it back in his lap. "There."

"I think I'm in love."

"Glad to hear it."

"Not with you, studly. I've met someone else."

Lester looked at him. "Who?"

"It's a secret. He's a very important man."

"Oh yeah? How's he feel about you?"

Daniel shook his head. "The *big* question: *numero uno.* That's what I'm working on finding out. I'll keep you advised."

As the wind blustered through Daniel's reddish-blonde hair, Lester thought for an instant he resembled some version of "Robert Redford Lite." He was a nice-looking rich kid. Genetic immunity from poor people imperfections was his birthright. "Good for you, Dan. Glad somebody's got a plan. Good for you."

***

Otis was sitting at his desk stroking Mildred's arched back when the Porsche pulled into the drive-through and shifted loudly into neutral. Starting to rise, he stared at the two men in the front seat. When he saw that one of them was Lester, he plopped back down in his chair. Daniel waved to him. "How you doing, Mr. Otis? Selling lots of gas?"

Otis called out the door, "Shit no! And you ain't bought none here since I don't know when."

"I guess I'm always someplace else when the needle gets low."

"Well, why don't you just *get* your butt over here 'fore that happens next time? How's that pretty sister of yours?"

"Getting married!"

Otis sprung from his chair and walked to the front door. "Married?"

"Yes, sir. A Yankee from New York. You think we'll survive it?"

"I don't hardly know." Otis chuckled and spit, and then he eyed Lester mischievously. "I'm wondering if old Lester will?"

Lester stepped outside the car and stood adjacent to the passenger door. "Don't you worry about it, Mr. Otis. I don't believe I'm ready for that kinda enterprise just yet." He shut the door. "Thanks for the ride. Glad to hear about your news. Hang in there."

Daniel smiled and shifted into first. "Like a Jack Russell biting a rope. Later." Daniel waved at Mr. Otis and roared out of the station, a techno CD blaring from the speakers.

Otis scratched his head and sat Mildred atop a display of windshield wipers. "Damn, if I drove a vehicle like that, I'd get arrested every third stoplight. Now why you figure rich white boys always gotta have some foreign car to haul themselves around in?"

Lester shrugged. "'Cause they can. How'd the weekend go?"

"Respectable. Not too slow and not so fast I couldn't get 'em all in and out and sell a little candy on the side to boot."

"Well, that's good news." Lester stretched. "I'm bushed."

"And here I thought you was dating the rich man's daughter, and now you back in the smokehouse stringing jerky with the rest of us peons." Otis turned and lumbered inside. "Come on in the office and sit. We need to do some visiting." Lester followed him in, a puzzled look on his face. "You need a Coke, Big Red? Get yourself something cold and sit over here." Otis pushed out a chair beside his desk.

Lester went to the refrigerator case and lifted a cream soda. "Thanks, Mr. Otis." Taking a gulp, he wiped his mouth on the back of his hand. "What's on your mind?"

Otis tugged at the flesh on his neck for several moments, staring at him. "How old are you again?"

"Twenty-eight."

He shook his head. "Twenty-eight and look at ya. Don't own nothing, don't have nothing—no car, no home, no checking account. Don't even own a hat." Otis stared at him. "You need a hat, Lester."

"Yes, sir."

"Man's gotta have a hat." Otis nodded and pointed to the line of fishing berets hanging on the side wall. "And not one of them damn 'gimme caps' neither. A real hat."

Lester continued staring at Otis, somewhat skeptical.

"See, when a man's got a hat on, it's like he's saying to the world, 'I got ideas! A plan. I know which way the road arises.'" Lester scratched his forearm idly. "You ever see a Jimmy Cagney movie?"

"Who?"

"Cagney."

Lester thought for moment. "Mmmm…What was he in?"

"Aw hell, he was in a million picture shows, but you ain't never seen him. What I'm trying to tell ya is, he was a little fella. A little Irish banty rooster. But when he'd put on one of them thirty-five-dollar fedoras and stick out his chest, he was all of a sudden nine feet tall. Nobody messed with Mr. Jimmy! For a little ol' toot, he carried a lot of rocks in his shoes." Otis grinned, pondering the vision. He then shoved himself back in the clattery office chair and propped a foot up on the desk. "An ivory straw Stetson…tight weave…turned down brim on the right. So's you can hold your fingers up to the edge…like this…when a lady passes." Otis touched his hand to the imaginary hat on his head and smiled. "That's what you need."

Lester was surprised at Mr. Otis' sudden concern about his attire. The old man had truly given it some thought. And though he didn't know for sure who this Jimmy character was, he got a distinct image from Mr. Otis' portrayal. "Well, a hat would be nice, but I sure can't afford one right now."

"'Course you can't. We'll just have to do it the old-fashioned American way—we'll take a little out of your paycheck every month."

Lester was alarmed. "B…But I don't think I need a hat. There's a lot of other things more important than a hat."

Otis pulled a toothpick out of his shirt pocket, stuck it in his mouth, and squinted at Lester patiently. "How you gonna run a gas station looking like a beggar man?"

"Excuse me?"

"You can't operate no business going round like one of those mangy surfer types that come snaking in here trying to cadge free this, free that. Some of 'em look like they ain't even scrubbed their head in a month."

"But I don't *run* a gas station. You do."

Otis thoughtfully rolled the toothpick around in his mouth. He reached over and opened a side drawer from the desk, retrieving a manila envelope. He sat it on top of a tattered phonebook. "I been knocking this around in my head, and it seems to me like the choice thing to do." Otis slowly stood and ambled toward the front door. He stood with his back to Lester, coughed, spit, and cleared his throat. "Otis Jr. called me two days ago. He wants me to come out to California and live with him. Well, not exactly with him, but nearby. He's gotta little renter house he bought for some extra income, and now he says he don't really need the cash and wouldn't I like to be closer by?" Otis turned to face Lester. "And you know, I had to think a good long while about that. I got my whole life here. People are pretty obliging to me round town, some of 'em downright hospitable. But I ain't got no family in these parts. Only family I got is Otis Jr. And I'll just be up front with ya. I don't even know Otis Jr. no more. And that's a shame. He's my boy, and now he's like a stranger to me. It ain't right."

Lester stared at Otis wide-eyed.

"We're just two old bachelors now, and we all we got." Otis moved to Lester's side, placing a hand on his shoulder. "'Tween you and me, Lester, Otis Jr. ain't doing so well."

Lester looked up at him.

Otis continued, "He been kinda sick. I don't know what exactly—he ain't told me—but I stitched two and two together, and I 'spect…I 'spect maybe he got the AIDS." Otis nodded listlessly, staring at the back wall. "Sure damn do."

Lester looked at the floor, not certain what, if anything, he could say to console this uncommonly decent man who had been a true friend to him from the beginning. He spoke softly, "Mr. Otis, I'm sorry to hear such news as that. I truly am. And I'll help you any way I can. I just…I don't really know what you need me to do."

Otis reached his arm over Lester's head and retrieved the manila folder atop the desk, holding it aloft. "I'm giving you my gas station to run!"

Lester blinked a few times, and then shook his head, bewildered. "But I don't…I mean, I don't even…"

Otis beamed. "All you need is a shittin' hat! Don't you see? You just ain't never had no confidence. All you ever needed in life is a little self-confidence. It's all anyone needs. With a hat on your head, you'll be somebody! You'll have rocks in your shoes!"

Lester gaped at him, unconvinced.

"Otis Jr. had a lawyer-friend of his draw up this contract here. They Fed Ex'd it to me today. I'll own title to the property, and you'll own the business. Sixty-forty split: sixty you, forty me. The accountant in town'll handle the books every month, and all you gotta do is sell gas and a few of those Taiwanese sunglasses by the register once in a while. And wear your new 'determination hat'!"

Lester shook his head. "You're not...serious?"

"Does a buck sniff a doe's ass in the spring? Hell yes, I'm serious. Now we got a lot to learn ya, but I ain't leaving tomorrow." Otis leaned forward, solemnly. "I'm telling ya, son, don't let fortune roll off your plate 'fore you've even had a taste of it. Those old breaks in life ain't always gonna come round regular, hear me now."

Lester was completely dumbfounded. He didn't know what to think. "What about the boat? I've got a job out there, too."

Otis spit his toothpick into the wastebasket. "They ain't here all year-round, are they? And did he ever offer you a full-time job on that ferryboat of his?" Lester shook his head. "I didn't think so." Otis folded his arms and leaned beside the front door. "Rich people ain't thinking about your welfare. It's the way it is. Rich people just worry about keeping themselves rich. And you ain't never gonna make that dog jump high enough through the hoop to change things, neither." Otis held out the manila envelope toward Lester. "You sleep on it tonight. And give this document a fine gleaning." Lester took the envelope and stared at it. Otis coughed and snorted again, shoving his hands in his pants pockets. "I'll tell you something else. I wouldn't be doing this if you hadn't of come along like you did. That's for damn sure. You got... character. I can see that. You just ain't gotten your breaks yet." Otis nodded, staring at him thoughtfully. Finally he scuffed his boots a few times and stretched. "I'm going to bed. Shut off the lights and lock her up when you turn in." Otis picked up Mildred and put her on his shoulder. She sat beside his head like a fat, fur hat and purred. "That's right, honey. Those old mice are hard to come by, I know it's so. Let's go find us some Tender Vittles." Mildred meowed loudly, and they disappeared into the back room. Lester stared at the legal-sized envelope in his hand. He tapped it on his leg a few times and then placed it under his arm. Rising, he clicked off the lights outside, locked the front door, and extinguished the office lights as well. He'd never thought about having a business of his own. He'd never thought about any particular line of work, any profession, or any job that he might succeed at. It didn't seem the most important thing to him somehow. He'd always figured there'd just be something he could "do" that would keep him alive. The only thing he'd ever truly been interested in was finding love. It was the thing that mattered most to him. And now it seemed as if those chances were growing as faint as the breath of a dying man. And still, it's all that mattered.

***

Rosa clicked the remote control in her hand over and over. There were so many stations to view. To her the only possible way to watch the TV was to keep the channels moving continuously. Occasionally she slowed her relentless pursuit to gaze at the sporadic *novela* or the *Cristina Show*, but even the familiarity of language wasn't enough to halt her electronic quest for an unknown solution. Surely, there was an answer to her quandary somewhere inside this box of so many visions. If she could only click fast enough.

Lying on her back all day made her limbs numb. Her ankles had swollen to twice their size, and her head hurt all the time. She wanted the baby to come now. Not tomorrow, not this afternoon, but immediately. It felt to her as if she couldn't carry the child a minute longer. So immense was her worry and discomfort. So immense was her guilt.

Why had she chosen to lie? What had started out as a mild conciliatory falsehood had somehow become a life-threatening deception. And the baby was insisting that she reveal all, now. It made her sick to her stomach again just thinking of the consequences. She turned her head to gaze out the window, anything to distract her from this incarcerated purgatory. Someone had planted a hedge that now rose to half the window's height. Why was there a window there if you couldn't see out? People were truly thoughtless sometimes. If she could only see out that window, she thought, perhaps she could diminish the non-stop turmoil in her head. Pushing aside the serving-tray table lurking above her chest, Rosa slowly moved her alien, lumpy feet to the side of the bed. Letting the dizziness subside, she placed one hand on the IV drip and the other on a nearby chair. Cautiously, gently, she felt for the ground. The floor was cold and peculiar to her bare skin, like some odd acquaintance she hadn't fully reconciled with. Shuffling in diminutive steps toward the window, she began to feel marginally better. Standing seemed to have a mitigating effect on her spirits. Towing the drip stand beside her, she shook her head in wonder. How did her mother, sisters, aunts, grandmothers, and the rest of the women in her extended family and village survive childbirth without all these machines and needles and satellite TVs? Did "progress" help or just confound the primordial act? She wondered if her baby would have survived being born beside the grocery refrigerator case. Surely God had originally intended this before revising his strategy. She knew of a woman in her home-town who fell from a second-story balcony while mopping the floor in her ninth month. The baby was born with bright red hair and six toes on its left foot. It was considered a good omen by everyone.

Pulling the venetian blinds fully open, Rosa blinked at the bright sunshine glaring off the cars in the parking lot. She stud-ied the neatly trimmed lawn and concrete walkways, the sprinkler system strategically watering the nondescript shrubbery, and the forlorn birdbath that appeared to her like an alien tombstone for some unlucky thing underneath. And then she saw the battered truck pull up. Eddie Frye got out on the passenger side, and a haggard-looking, overweight woman with three young children sitting beside her drove off and parked under a shade tree. Rosa blinked in astonishment. Was he…coming to see her? She lowered the shade quickly and stumbled her way back to bed. Why *now?*

She'd barely straightened the covers when she heard a knock at her door. Rosa stared at the entry, emitting a weak "Come in." Eddie stuck his head around the door and peered inside as if he were anticipating a surprise party.

"Hey. I heard about your…accident. Sorry 'bout all that. You doing better now?"

"*Si.*"

"Well, good, that's real good." Eddie glanced around the room. "You sure got a lot of flowers. That's good." The two stared at each other. Eddie cleared his throat. "The thing is Rosie, um, old Dave wanted me to come by and tell you he was real sorry about your accident, n' all. And uh, well, he's sorry he can't be here for the, uh…birth neither."

Rosie continued staring. "I know."

Eddie's eyes moved laterally across his face as he spoke, as if he were watching a horse race in the distance. "And like, since you know Dave's married and everything, he's got a lot of responsibilities with his kids and stuff." Rosa watched him in bewilderment. Eddie continued, "See, back then, that night when I asked you out? See, you were supposed to be *my* date, not Dave's. But I didn't say nothing. He's my buddy, and you two were hitting it off. And like… like after you got pregnant, and he offered to take care of your… situation…well, after you declined his offer, he just kind of felt like you were on your own after that."

Rosa lifted herself up slowly in bed. "Why have you come here to tell me this? I know. Dave does not want to be involved with the child. I accept. What do you want?"

Eddie's expression changed to one of near disdain. "Well see, Rosie, see the other day I was out on deck of the *Amor* cleaning up a buncha shit, and I just happened to overhear Mr. Wheelwright talking to Daniel down in the galley. He was telling him stuff that sounded a lot like…" Eddie smirked at Rosa. "Well, like he's thinking *he's* the father of your baby." He shook his head. "Which is it? You been telling Dave since day one he's the daddy, and now you got Mr. Wheelwright all strung out thinking he's the papa? Damn, I guess if I'd a slept with ya, you'd a hung that medal on me, too."

Rosa could hear her heart pounding loudly in her chest. She took a tiny breath and asked, "What do you want?"

Eddie cocked his head to the side, a look of sudden piety sheathing his features. "I just want to know the truth, that's all. If Dave's the daddy, then no hard feelings. But I think Mr. Wheelwright ought to know about it. And if Mr. Wheelwright's the daddy, then that other stuff'll just be between you and me. But I reckon I oughta get a little something in return for keeping your secret, don't you think?"

Rosa's face flushed, and her voice withered to a peep, "What… something?"

Eddie shrugged. "Like, I don't know. Like maybe a little cash to help out a working man and his family. Hell, it ain't much. As my wife says, them Wheelwrights go through money like it's all just one big cold Dr. Pepper on a hot summer day."

Rosa lifted quickly on one elbow. "You told your *wife?*"

"Now don't go getting riled. She's a businessperson just like me. She don't hold nothing against nobody. We're just looking out for our family, that's all. Poor Man's Golden Rule: 'You don't ask. You don't get.'"

Rosa, exhausted, let her head fall back on the pillow. "It's… *blackmail.*"

Eddie frowned. "That don't seem right. Makes it sound kinda ugly. Kinda like when a person deliberately deceives another into making them think they're the father of their kid when they just might not be. That's not very nice, is it?"

Rosa's eyes began to sting. The last thing on earth she wanted at this moment was to cry. There was simply no way she could avert it. Huge tears started rolling down her face, smarting her cheeks like rubbing alcohol. She felt trapped, angry, and very, very alone. "How much?"

"Now I ain't gonna take advantage of this situation like some other scoundrel might. I know you're in a fix. Hell, we all are." Eddie grinned. "I got some stuff in my background I ain't too proud of neither." He idly reached for a daisy in a nearby vase and began plucking petals. "Oh, I 'spect a couple of thousand might be all right to sorta quiet things down. How's that sound to you?"

Rosa closed her eyes, shook her head, and smiled bitterly. "I don't have it."

Eddie laughed. "Jesus, Rosie! Give me a little credit for some brains. That so-called 'daddy' of your baby, *he* has it and a whole lot more. Hell, I mighta pulled the same stunt as you if I'ze in your predicament." Eddie laughed again. "God knows poor old Dave Gonzalez ain't got a pot to piss in. You just say to 'daddy Bob' you're gonna be needing some extra things for the baby. He'll give it to you. Sure 'nuf will." Eddie smiled and handed her a tissue. "Now, don't go upsetting yourself. It ain't that bad—just business. We all gotta look out for ourselves. Hell, when that little *muchacho's* up and racing around the house like some wild-eyed ferret, you'll look back on this and laugh. Wadn't no big thing." Eddie patted Rosa's arm, and she flinched. "I reckon it's kinda late for this now, but if you'd a gone with me that night instead of Dave, you might not be in this jam today." He leaned in grinning. "I got a vasectomy last year! That's my ace-in-the-hole if some gal starts squawking about who the daddy is." He stood up straight and laughed, pitching the stripped daisy into the trashcan. "Well, you be thinking 'bout it. I'll check back in a few days. Don't look so down, Rosie. You got all the right cards." Eddie opened the door and exited, leaving his distinct scent of Right Guard, Marlboros, laundry detergent, and sour sweat suspended in the air like damp curtains. Rosa stared at the door for a long, long time. Then she picked up the TV remote and began flipping through the channels rapidly. She whispered as the programs flashed by on screen, "Don't...ask...don't...get... don't...ask....don't..."

chapter

THIRTEEN

Luz hadn't seen Elsie since the flying ashtray episode, but she was almost over it. Sure it hurt, hurt like hell, but whenever these unfortunate matters reared their ugly particularities, she merely receded further into her own head. At least she had her art, her music, long walks on the beach, Windsor, and, of course, Philip. They were as destined to ride out this life together as the two halves of an Almond Joy. Some things were inexorably, divinely decreed. Fact.

Luz looked around the park and saw that she pretty much had the grounds to herself, as usual. A woman was off in the far corner pushing a child on a swing, and a maintenance man was hauling away litter barrels. She liked coming here on her lunch hour, having the place to herself. It was quiet, and she could stare at the water and dream about parties on boats and water skiing and deep-sea fishing—all the things she never did. It was deeply satisfying to her, somehow, this imaginary-life-at-noon she'd contrived. Safe as a child's blanket. Safe as reading. Safe as the self-exoneration of noble intentions.

Luz reached into her brown paper bag and pulled out the wax paper-wrapped sandwich. God bless Philip. He had to be the last human in Texas who still used wax paper. It was sweet. Something their mother always did. Unfolding the vestige, she saw one perfect chicken breast sandwich on a brioche with arugula, red onions, and Dijon mustard. She held the sandwich in her lap and felt an enormous wave of emotion come over her. Her brother loved her very much, that was true. He made her lunch every day without asking. He occasionally bought her clothes (that she rarely wore); he paid for her ski trip to Colorado last winter; and he encouraged her, praised her and, in general, fussed over her as if she were something rare and splendid indeed. He was a good brother. That she loved him was unequivocal. That they were far too close was equally undeniable. What was she to make of their far from incestuous but just as discomfiting co-dependence upon one another? Where was the healthy partition between them?

She lifted the bread on the sandwich, removed the onions (as always), and took a bite. Another beautiful, cloudless, hot summer day. Another reason not to move. Just to sit quietly…with good intentions.

The Jeep appeared to circle the park twice. Luz paid it little mind until the driver pulled over to the curb nearest to where she sat and got out. She could see Lester walking toward her. What a strange one he was! Sort of sweet, sort of slow, largely too uncertain for comfort. What did he want from her? She swallowed her bite and smiled. "Hey, how you been?"

"OK."

"Where'd you get the Jeep?"

"We just put a new clutch in it down at the station. I was testing it out and saw you here."

"Caught me, huh?"

Lester smiled. "Yeah." They stared at each other with pleasant expressions, seemingly daring the other to blink first.

"Um, would you like half of my sandwich?"

"No, that's OK. You go ahead and eat."

Luz held out the half. "Go on. Get it while the getting's good."

As Lester shyly wiped his hand on his jeans and took the sandwich, Luz motioned for him to sit.

Lester smiled at her as he took a bite, chewing with his mouth full. "Thanks...good."

"Philip made it. Did you know my brother makes me a sandwich every morning before I go to work?"

Lester stopped chewing and shook his head.

"Yep. Every morning. Regular as the Today Show and the local weather. How 'bout that?"

Lester swallowed. "Pretty nice, I suppose."

"Isn't it? You have any brothers and sisters?"

"Bunch of 'em."

"Are you close to any of them?"

"Nope. I was the change-of-life baby—the accident. They're all a lot older than me."

Luz took a bite of her sandwich. "Hey, Lester." She swallowed and took another bite. "You don't know anybody I can fix my brother up with, do you?"

Lester stopped chewing and smiled slowly, shaking his head. "What do you think he's looking for?"

Luz gazed at the distant shoreline. "Yeah, you get a prize if you can figure that out. A closeted, gay minister. I don't think he can ever allow himself to want anything he'd ever actually want."

Lester thought about it. "Maybe he's one of those types that likes the *idea* of something better than the real thing, know what I mean?"

"I do. I really do." She nodded slowly. "Are you gay, Lester?"

Lester stopped chewing. "Bi maybe?" Lester wiped his hands quickly on his jeans. "You sure ask a lot of personal questions!" he laughed.

"You asked me if I'd ever been in love the other night. What's the difference?"

"There's a big difference."

"Really? OK, forget it. I thought we were friends. You've got your little mysteries; I've got mine. What time is it?"

He looked at his watch. "Quarter to one."

Luz began stuffing the sandwich wrapper back in the bag. "I gotta get back."

Lester abruptly blurted out, "Yeah...OK, I've had like...experiences. Gay experiences."

Luz looked up at him. "Was that so hard?"

"No."

"Big deal, right? Look, I'm gay, bi...whatever. Who cares? Been there, done *all* that."

"Are...you?"

"Well, yeah. Who did you think Elsie was? I thought you knew."

"She's your..."

"*Ex*-girlfriend. It's over. She thought you were nice, though, if it matters."

Lester sat back down next to Luz, shaking his head. "Holy shit."

"What's wrong?"

"I don't know. You ever have something 'big' in your head just totally turn into something else?"

Luz frowned. "Not offhand."

"Are you sure Elsie was your girlfriend?"

Luz burst out laughing. She laughed so hard, she fell sideways into Lester's lap. Lester began to laugh as well—at first gradually, hesitantly, then finally, flat-out guffawing. They both laughed so hard, they could barely breathe. Finally, gasping for air, Luz raised her head, wiping her eyes. "What the fuck was *that* about?"

Lester snickered again in hilarity. "I asked you...I asked you..." Lester couldn't get it out. He simply wrapped his arms around his sides and rocked. A passing jogger glanced at them and smiled in accord with whatever was rousing them both. Finally the laughter decreased to intermittent waves of spontaneous outbursts. They both sat in stoned exhaustion, panting in short, erratic sighs.

"I've got a headache."

"Take deeper breaths."

"I really have to go."

"Stay! Just a few more minutes."

Luz sat back on the bench and took one long deep breath. "Oh...much better."

"Told ya so."

Luz took another breath and turned. "Lester, I was just wondering..."

He looked at her expectantly.

"Why did you come here anyway?"

"You mean today? Right now?"

"No. Why did you come to Rockport?"

Lester rubbed the side of his cheek and rested his other hand on the back of the bench. "Because of...you."

"Me? What do you mean *me*?"

"I think...I think I was in love with the *idea* of you."

Luz stared at him, baffled. "I don't...understand."

"When I got out of prison—"

Luz sat upright. "*You* were in prison?"

He smiled slyly. "We've all got our little mysteries."

"But you never said—"

"You never asked."

Luz stared at him as if he'd just crawled out of the ocean.

"When I got out of prison, I had an idea in my mind somebody like you was out there, waiting for me."

"Me? That's crazy. Why me?"

Lester stared at her, amazed at this new frankness between them. He did love her, only now he thought he might even like her more. "I had a very clear picture of you in my head. I knew all about you. Maybe I was mistaken about some of it, but it doesn't change my wanting to know you, Laurel."

"Laurel?"

Lester shook his head quickly. "Luz."

"Why did you say 'Laurel'?"

Lester shrugged.

"That's so weird; that was my mother's name."

Lester couldn't help grinning. Of course it was. Philip was nothing if not consistent. Lester nodded. "Maybe she's around us, huh?"

Luz cackled. "Oh God, I hope not! She'd scream if she saw what a slob I am today. I really have to get back to school." Luz stood, methodically folding the top of her paper bag. "You know, I haven't understood a word about anything you just said. But I've got a hunch you're not through telling me your life story yet." Luz put a hand on her hip and stretched her foot out. "When are you coming over for dinner? I *don't* cook. You can relax. But, as you know, Philip is our town *Epicurean*. Come join us. Really."

Lester stood. "OK." He took her hand and then, without deliberation, slowly placed one arm and then the other around her. He held her as delicately as if he were cradling an infant. He was finally holding the crux of his conviction nearly four years later. He stood there silently embracing his love. His now only-slightly-faded love.

***

It was a first: the four Wheelwrights in church, together, on time, and in accord. The eleven o'clock Sunday service at St. Michael's and All Angels was not an insignificant affair. Those who accounted for "society" in Rockport made their obligatory appearances in a lively display of pastels, seersucker, and Ralph Lauren rip-offs. Good Episcopalians usually made some kind of effort toward being visually amenable. It was a badge of their genus approbation, their *uber-preppiness*.

Luz sat in the choir and gazed out at the congregation as she had done for most of her adult life. There was old Mrs. Tuttle, her third-grade teacher with the rotten teeth and steadfast habit of unwrapping a crinkly, endless caramel during the offertory prayer. Mr. St. Onge, a once-prominent lawyer and school board president, now a retired lush thriving on wisely invested offshore banking dividends and his late wife's inheritance. The Mapstones, a nice couple of displaced Yankees, who had moved down one spring marveling at the glorious weather and greenery and were too insensate by summer's end to realize the grievous error they'd made.

The O'Briens, the Martins, the Hildebrandts, the Jespersons—she knew them all, and they her. It was a nice, cozy, and clubby milieu, their church family. Only occasionally did Luz want to do bodily harm to any of them anymore. She'd made her peace, for the most part, with her role as "the reverend's kith" among the St. Michael's faithful. She didn't inquire into their lives, and they didn't inquire into hers. It was a tenable arrangement.

Sitting in the mid-section, on the right-hand side, was a new family she hadn't seen before. They were a natty-looking bunch, indeed. All brushed, groomed and seemly attired, she thought they must be from Houston or Dallas. Their clothes were too new, too tailored. They all had hair that hadn't been cut at the mall. Luz stared at the beautiful young woman sitting beside, she presumed, the father. She was as sleek and dewy as a moist fig. Definitely not a native of these parts. Women around here began to resemble heavy prunes after a few seasons of corrosive sun, salt air, and too many grocery runs to Walmart. Finally she recognized her as the woman from the Petronilla Bakery. How odd.

Philip stood and walked to the pulpit, his black pleated robe swishing across the dais like a shower curtain caught in a draft. He sat his notes down, concentrating on them for a few seconds. then lifted his head, beaming, "What a glorious morning indeed! The sun is shining; the birds are singing; the sky is doing its very-blue best; and all is right with the world." He gazed at his flock, probing. "No? Are there some of you here today that perhaps don't share this sentiment? I see some of you looking at each other with, 'Oh brother, here we go again with another of his "ain't life a bowl of cherries" sermons.' Well, I'm going to fool you today. No lectures on stopping to smell the roses, no ministrations to appreciate the little things in life. Today I'd just like to—and please pardon my outright candor here—kick your butts…just a little."

Mrs. Tuttle coughed on a mouthful of caramels, and Mrs. Flournoy from the pew behind patted her back with a look of alarm.

"See, I think most of us do a fairly decent job of gratifying ourselves with all the ingenuity and magnificence of God's abundance surrounding us. We have every comfort of a modern society to make our lives easier, less burdensome, but I wouldn't say a whole lot simpler really. Did getting another fifty channels on your satellite dish make your life any simpler? I think that so much of progress has simply numbed us down to the point we've basically stopped empathizing beyond a certain level. It's too much to grasp: the war in the Middle East, political corruption, pornography on the Internet, global warming, the West Nile virus, reality TV, on and on. And what we can't handle we shut out. Click. Zip. Gone. Back to the crossword, the nap, hoeing in the flowerbed. And don't get me wrong; you all know my mania for gardening. The world needs gardeners as much as it needs doctors and lawyers and candlestick makers, in my biased opinion. But at what cost the bias of one over the other? A universe of all gardeners may make for an aesthetic Eden, but who's going to service the Weed Whacker when it shatters? Likewise, a cosmos of just doctors is a hungry cosmos. A world of shutting out life for the sake of not having to put up with life is equally a hungry world. Hungry for meaning, for answers, for input…for just plain more love. And isn't part of our job on the planet to be—how to put it without the nagging exhortations surrounding it—*involved*? Oh the dreaded word! It all just leads to more misery. You can't change the world; don't even try. Go sticking your nose into the unknown, and you're liable to get it chopped off. Or punched or handed back to you in a bloody fist. No thanks. Not for me. I gave at the office. By the way, I've always been fascinated by that phrase. Exactly *what* did you give at the office anyway? A check? A pat on the back? Polite directions to the office down the hall? See, I think what holds most of us back is that sometimes, when we do dare to open ourselves up and give wholeheartedly, guess what? No one cares. We aren't appreciated; there's no pat on the back: 'Way to go, Al. Nice job, Ellen.' And worse yet, we end up being ridiculed at best, reproached at worst. It's totally disheartening. Why even bother? you ask." Philip's eyes roamed the chapel, a cheerful expression on his face. "Glad you asked. Here's why. When we get off the sofa of life and add marginally to our daily affairs a small offering of ourselves, God rewards you in ways you can't even imagine. Don't believe me? Try it. I dare you. I double dare you to make an effort this coming week. Do something for someone else, for your community, for society at large. It can be minor, insignificant, trivial. Doesn't matter. Give some small part of yourself back and watch what happens." Philip grinned. "And listen to the fourteen-year-olds: it's *awesome*! Still don't believe me? Every child on earth knows what happens when you stick a sunflower seed in the ground. You get a flower. One plus one equals flower. No mystery there. Fact of life. So take the leap with me here. 'Hmmm, if I just stop and pick up that beer can in the street down in front of the Stop and Go and throw it in the trash barrel, maybe someone else will do something similar over on Baker Street, and maybe someone'll clean up that vacant lot on Tidewater, and maybe...' Well, let's not get overconfident on our first outing. And for heaven's sake, let's not be so goody-goody about it either. Why do Christians always get dumped in the goody-goody bin? How boring. Did somebody say 'self-righteous'? Heavens, certainly not us! Sounds more like a Presbyterian thing, Baptist perhaps. I wonder how many potential believers get turned off by viewing self-important Christians out doing their humble, duteous thing with a virtual bullhorn and an ad campaign attached? I don't recall Jesus hiring a PR firm to plug the forty loaves and fishes. Can't we simply roll up our sleeves and get down and dirty without alerting the media of our righteous intentions? God and Santa Claus know when you're being good—that's all that matters. And if someone comes along and tosses a soda can in your newly weeded rose garden of life, pick it up! Immediately! Discard it! Order, purpose and grace do not attract garbage. Get on with your worthy actions. Address your community's needs! Confront your society's inadequacies! Be helpful to just one other person in one small way. In a way that only you can make the difference. And for truly God's sake, click off the Time Warner 'Super Package' occasionally and open the front door of your life. Look around and see where you might be called. I guarantee you'll be astounded by the remarkable, unimaginable rewards that will come your way."

Philip gazed out proudly at his flock of wandering sheep and swabbed the beads of perspiration on his lip with a handkerchief. *It may not be much,* he thought to himself, *but here, in this room, among these people, within this community, here is my calling.* "Let us pray."

Daniel lowered his head. He thought about goodness and mercy, charity and faith, and also about the erection that was presently expanding his britches. What was it about the Reverend Yancey that was so stimulating to him? He was nice looking, but he was no Adonis. Bright, but no Stephen Hawking. He wasn't vastly wealthy, intriguingly neurotic, or hugely charismatic enough to engage him as past conquests had. It seemed to Daniel he was just above average in exactly the right ways. Here was a challenge without the ordeal. Interesting minus the unreasonable side effects. Cozy but clever. For once, a sane adult you could squeeze hands with in the endless "Tunnel of the Lovelorn."

Immediately following the service, the parishioners gathered outside the vestry for coffee and pound cake. Yvonne made her way over to Philip, who stood shaking hands with a departing couple. Towing Bob in her wake, she touched Philip's shoulder, and he turned to greet them. "Yvonne, what a delight to see you this morning."

"We loved your message, absolutely loved it. So hopeful, meaningful. This is my husband, Bob. I understand you two met briefly at the hospital."

"Yes, briefly."

Bob extended his hand, and Philip took it. "Very motivating service, Reverend. I'm wondering if you might be willing to part with a copy of your message today? For a donation, of course. I'd like to give a copy to all my employees."

"Not at all, not at all. No donation required, but by all means feel free to come down and help us paint the church hall whenever you like."

Bob smiled after only a brief cloud of dismay marred his chiseled features. "Terrific. Uh-huh. You bet."

Yvonne turned to search for Melanie who was nowhere in sight. "I'd like for you to meet the bride-to-be. I thought she was right behind us. Daniel have you seen your sister?"

Daniel approached the gathering with an almost shy restraint, very unlike him. "She went to the powder room. She had to pluck something out of her eye, probably an iniquity. Hello." Daniel and Philip shook hands, and Daniel immediately felt an overwhelming desire to lean the reverend far back and plant a big, tasty one right on his lips.

"Yes, hello. Actually, we've met as well, haven't we?"

"Correct." Daniel blushed, again thoroughly atypical.

Yvonne looked at them both, surprised. "Well, I didn't know that. When? Daniel, you didn't say anything…"

Daniel continued his sly approbation of Philip. "Must've slipped my mind. Yes, we had an accidental dinner together in Port Aransas one night. Two stags at a largely couples-heavy establishment. Synchronistic, no?"

"Very." Philip nodded at him, his face a mask of bland repose.

Yvonne watched the two of them and a tiny, tiny *frisson* of prospect zipped across her brain. Daniel and…the vicar! But of course!

***

Melanie stood at the sink and wetted the neatly folded piece of paper towel again. She dabbed at her carefully made-up eyes and cursed. She absolutely had to pull herself together and stop these tearful, mini-outbursts of self-pity she was wallowing in. You're marrying a nice, rich, successful, handsome man. There are much worse things in life! So he's not passionate, adventurous, unconventional, or even slightly unpredictable. Too bad! And just who the hell did she think she was anyway? Isadora Duncan? Suck it up; get over it. *This is what you were born to do. You have a lovely career that you can take or leave anytime you want. You'll have lovely children, lovely vacations, lovely clothes, lovely homes. It'll all be simply…Oh God, why was it so hard to say it?*

The door to the restroom opened, and Luz walked in carrying a paper cup of punch. "Oh, I'm sorry. I didn't know anyone was in here."

"It's OK. I was just leaving." Melanie blotted her eyes again.

Luz glanced surreptitiously at her, marveling at her overall flawlessness. "I see my brother is out chatting with your family. I'm Luz Yancey, Reverend Yancey's sister."

Melanie turned quickly, looking at her for the first time. "Oh, for goodness' sake, pleasure to meet you."

"Actually, we met in the bakery a while back. Like an idiot I spilled coffee all down the front of your friend."

Melanie gasped, "Yes! That's right. I do remember you."

"I was just glad to know I didn't cause any serious damage."

"No, no." Melanie stared at her, trying to connect some missing tie-in.

"Have you known Lester long?"

"Um…no." Melanie was thoroughly confused now. "Do *you* know Lester?"

Luz went to the sink to pour out the punch. "Can't stand this stuff. It's so sweet it hurts my teeth." She turned back to Melanie. "Not really, sort of. Interesting guy. Lots of unexplored pathways in that head of his, that's for sure."

Melanie nodded, not listening. "I'm getting married next Saturday."

Luz looked at her. "Yes, I know. I'm playing the organ at your service."

Melanie suddenly snapped and stared at Luz. "You are? That's wonderful. I'm so glad. What are you doing for dinner tonight, tomorrow? I really need a girlfriend to talk to right now. Please say yes."

Luz continued staring at her. She smiled slowly. "Absolutely."

***

"Hello, I'm Melanie Wheelwright. I'm so thankful you were able to do this on such insanely short notice." Melanie took Philip's hand and beamed as if he'd just handed her the trophy for Best in Show. Others in the room were gazing at her with admiring, assessing glances. All the world stops to watch a beautiful woman simply being…beautiful. A profoundly mesmerizing act. Like watching Dachshunds fuck. Impossible *not* to stare.

"My pleasure. I'm sure you and your mother are up to your necks with all the details right now."

Melanie sighed. "Can you imagine? And with Rosa being hospitalized and everything, well, you were definitely an enormous piece of good news."

"How is she doing today?"

Yvonne interrupted. "We're heading straight over there as soon we leave. Would you join us for lunch later? We're driving down to the Town Club in Corpus."

"Yes, why don't you and your sister join us?" Melanie quickly chimed in.

Philip looked at the four slightly addled Wheelwrights staring back at him and determined today would not be the opportune time for lunch. "Very kind of you to ask, but I'm working on a piece for Episcopal Life about tithing, and I promised myself I'd try to wrap it up this afternoon."

Yvonne gazed at him approvingly. "We understand, of course. I wish I had your discipline."

"Very nice to meet you, Father Yancey." Bob shook Philip's hand briskly.

"Likewise. I'll drop a copy of the sermon in the mail for you."

"Terrific." As Philip released his hand, he saw what he thought to be a kind of beseeching aspect in his eyes. "Thank you, again, for coming to our rescue."

Melanie touched Philip's arm. "I love your sister! We're seeing each other for *girl talk* this week. We actually met before in the craziest way. We both know the same ex-con!" Melanie leaned in to kiss Philip's cheek, and his eyes glazed over.

As the Wheelwrights started to depart, another hand reached out to grasp Philip's. "I need to see you. Soon." Daniel stood there, nodding with resolute conviction.

"Um, sure. It's going to be a pretty full week, but—"

"Don't keep putting me off…please."

Philip stammered, "I'm sorry, I wasn't aware…"

Daniel squeezed his hand. "I have to make up my mind. I'm going to need your help." As the two unclasped their grip, Daniel wrapped his hand around Philip's index finger and tugged on it. "I enjoyed what you had to say today. Got me…fired up." Daniel turned and walked out the front door. Philip watched as his slender, sturdy hips bounced in his khakis like a pair of frisky colts. Handsome lad, no question. Why couldn't he appreciate him more? If he wasn't so…pushy. Was that it? Needy. Was that it? If he wasn't so much like…*me.*

***

Sweeping through the chapel, Philip, Luz, and another volunteer picked up the discarded bulletins, gum wrappers, and doodled-on donation envelopes scattered throughout. Luz stooped to retrieve a kid's white Bible in its little zippered casing. "Some child left their Bible behind. Mama's not going to like that."

Philip looked over from the next pew. "See if there's a name inside."

Luz opened it up and flipped several pages. "Nope. No name—nada." She handed the Bible to Philip.

"Odd. I always have them sign their Bibles before each catechism session." Philip examined it. "Well, it's not the ones I give out anyway. Were there some other visitors today?"

Marlene Bedichek called to them from the front where she was removing the altar flowers. "One old man from the nursing home in Ingleside. He said he was actually Catholic but preferred a rousing Protestant hymn occasionally. And then there was that wealthy family."

Philip smiled, slipping the Bible into his shirt pocket. "Good for the gentleman from Ingleside. I prefer the Catholic vestments myself. They've definitely got that show business thing nailed."

Luz handed Philip her collection of Sunday bulletins, nodding. "The wealthy family have become fast friends, haven't they? Are they here to stay or just summer commuters?"

"Definitely summer folk. They're scattered about, mostly Houston people, I believe."

Luz moved her hand over the pew back. "The bride-to-be's a raving beauty, no question about that."

Philip glanced at her. "Yes. Brides-to-be always have that special glow, don't they?" He stooped to retrieve a pencil.

"You think she's…really ready to get married?"

Philip rose impatiently. "Oh yes, absolutely. Why do you ask? And don't tell me you think she's gay, because she's not."

Marlene Bedichek stopped at the exit door by the altar, clutching her gladiolas and loitering to garner another particle of gossip from the Yancey siblings. They both paused until she coughed nervously and finally left the room.

Luz hissed, "Did I say she was gay? No. I asked you if you thought she was ready to get married. An honest, impartial question. God, Philip, sometimes you act like even mentioning the words 'gay' or 'lesbian' is an abomination."

"Please don't say 'God' like that inside the chapel."

Luz rolled her eyes and started to exit. "I give up. I'll ask her on my own."

Philip turned to look at her, wide-eyed.

She continued, "We're having lunch tomorrow. She wants to talk to a 'girl-friend.' Can you believe it, Philip? Someone actually wants my counsel and advice." Luz stood at the front entry doors and called out *sotto voce*, "Gay and lesbian, gay and lesbian, gay and lesbian! Help, I'm going mad!" She turned and exited. Philip stared after her with the weariness of a barbecue salesman in hell.

***

Backing out of the church parking lot, Philip was glad to be going home. He'd slip into his Bermudas, make himself a Bloody Mary, fix a little pasta salad, put on some Saint-Saëns or maybe Ella and just chill. Another week over. Another host of perplexity and trials afflicting his fold quietly put aside until further divine guidance on Monday morning. It was his favorite time of the week. Peace, comfort, solitude, and just a smidgen of cultural indulgence.

As he was about to turn right onto Texas Boulevard, he saw Daniel's Porsche come racing down the intersection. "Too late," Philip muttered to himself. "Escape foiled."

The Porsche pulled up alongside the opposite sidewalk, and Philip saw Bob Wheelwright get out from behind the steering wheel and hurry across the street toward the front of the church. Philip rolled down his window and called, "Hello there! Did you forget something?"

Bob turned with a startled look and immediately walked toward Philip. "I feel like such an idiot. We were leaving the hospital, and I remembered that I had brought a Bible for you to sign for Rosa's baby. I think I might've left it on the pew."

"This look familiar?" Philip asked, pulling the Bible from his pocket.

Bob beamed. "That's the one. I know this seems silly, but I'm kind of sentimental about these things. I bought this for Daniel when he was about five, and then I found out his grandmother had already bought him one, so I just kept it. You know, somewhere down the line, I thought I could give it to another child someday."

"Very thoughtful. Shall I sign it now, or would you like me to meet with the child?"

Bob hesitated. "Well, actually, I wanted to have a little visit with you myself."

Philip shifted the car into park.

"Oh, not now! I know you're headed home, and they're expecting me in Corpus. Thank goodness we took two cars today. Uh…"

Philip smiled patiently.

"Do you suppose it would be all right if I came round to see you…Well, when *would* be a good time, actually?"

"You tell me."

"Tomorrow evening?"

"Seven o'clock?"

"Right. I'll see you at seven." Bob turned toward the Porsche.

Philip called out, holding up the white Bible. "Shall I just keep this till then?"

Bob spun around and once again returned to Philip. "No, no. I want to write something in it myself. I don't know why I'm so… scattered lately."

Philip handed it to him, and Bob stared at the Bible blankly. "Or, who knows? Maybe I'll end up just sticking it back in the desk drawer…for another time." Bob then turned abruptly and walked back toward the Porsche. As he drove away, Philip waved to him. Bob ignored him, staring straight ahead with such intensity it was if he were watching God direct traffic just down the street.

chapter

FOURTEEN

The ship channel jetty in Port Aransas extended nearly four thousand feet into the choppy Gulf of Mexico. The massive granite blocks had been stacked up in an impressive jumble of brawn that resembled to Lester some great, submerged "Wall of the Sea Emperor." He never tired of walking out to the end, past all the weekend fishermen and angler fanatics with their lawn chairs, coolers, multicolored open-weave caps, and expressions of unbounded patience. He liked to sit out on those slick and mossy final boulders rising up from the briny like lost Behemoths, and think. Think about many things. The only sounds were the slapping waves, occasional gulls, and the low rumble of a passing freighter headed for Tampico or Dar es Salaam. The only view was east—east across a blue-green expanse toward Florida, the Canary Islands, Africa, and then he wasn't so sure. Beyond Africa lay more emptiness, he imagined. Perhaps there was another contemplative soul sitting on a beach somewhere in Kenya or Mozambique conjuring up the void before him or her, just as he was. Surely, there had to be.

His time in Rockport had been…eventful. No question. It had also been wearing, surprising, funny, interesting, vexing, sad, illuminating, and largely frustrating. What had once been the "sure thing" in his life was now nothing more than an expired daydream. No more flights of fancy, no more what-ifs, no more "when I finally start my life, I'll…" This was, in very fact, *it*. Life. Life concurrent. What exactly was he waiting for? He had a few friends, a job offer with some possibility, his health. What in God's holy name was he so maddeningly unsettled about? What other conceivable likelihood was there racing forward to present itself anyway?

Lester picked up a broken oyster shell and absently skipped it into the surf. A man on a small skiff was out about a hundred yards from the jetty, slowly tugging at something on his line. Lester watched him idly. He'd have to make peace with Philip somehow. He knew it. As much as he hated him for what he'd done, he couldn't stay here and have that hanging between them, mucking up all his other relationships and emotions. Especially toward Luz. He still wanted Luz in his life somehow. He knew that. He loved her still. But it was a new picture he carried with him now. One more precise, more honest, more…nonfictional. Maybe his love had never really been a passionate thing. Deeply heartfelt, yes, but perhaps never a precise erotic conviction. It was hard for him to reconstruct it all now. Somehow, Laurel Jeanette was the abstraction at the end of every sex act with Little Ray. In effect, it was a cheat to everyone, but mostly to himself. What was he thinking? Or, the more obvious question: What was he trying *not* to think?

The man on the small boat continued to lug and tug on something deep in the water. Lester studied him closer. There was something vaguely reminiscent of Little Ray in his posture. Maybe it was his build or the shape of the head. Lester couldn't quite place it, but it was there, most definitely. He squinted at the boatman. Just supposing he did love Little Ray, what could he do about it now? What would it serve by writing him in prison and tormenting him with dicey illusions as Philip had? He never even said good-bye when he left. He didn't know how. Everything had been riding on

Laurel Jeanette. She was the train, Little Ray the conductor. Lester never once considered a round-trip purchase, ever. Funny how life makes its little hypothetical points. Funny how so many of us seem to be racing for the wrong train.

The fisherman gave an odd sort of yelp, and Lester turned back again to see him pulling in a huge sea turtle on the side of the boat. Somehow the massive tortoise had wrapped its head around the fishing line and choked itself to death. Lester watched in horror as the fisherman cursed and fumed and finally cut the turtle's head off with a pocketknife. The creature's lifeless, jade carcass plunked back into the ocean like the tossed rind of a half-eaten watermelon. It sickened Lester to think of the loss. That incredible relic—no telling what age it had survived to, gone now in a matter of a few hapless minutes. And what exactly was your point, God? Was this another one of your metaphorical fabrications designed to get our immediate attention? The turtle, the fisherman, Little Ray, Luz, Philip, the ocean, Africa? Draw me a picture, God.

Sad and flustered, Lester stood and shoved his hands in his pants pockets. The sun was lowering, and a strong breeze had suddenly kicked up, sending waves splashing well over the top of the rocks. The fisherman was busily hauling in his anchor and steering his now-bucking craft back to shore. As Lester slowly edged his way back toward the beach, he instantly regretted his choice of shoes. Leather cowboy boots were not the most appropriate footwear for wet, slippery rocks being pounded by high waves. He crouched lower to give himself more balance, stepping cautiously on each rock as if somehow they might give way beneath his touch. The waves were beginning to pummel him. He stared down the long breakwater ahead. As far as he could make out, he was the sole individual still atop the jetty. Had he been out there that long? How had he not seen the gale coming in? As much as he loved and appreciated the sea, he was pretty much oblivious to its erratic nature. Clearly, he was as much a landlubber as an East Texas loblolly pine.

He now began to hobble on all fours, making his way as deliberately as he could. Clutching at non-existent crevices and digging in on surfaces slick as waxed tile, he fell and slid as much as he advanced. And then the rain began. It fell on him like a roof collapsing, peppering his back like a jillion tiny bees scaring him off the hive. Slipping again on another rock, he tore his jeans, bloodying his knee. Squinting ahead through the squall, he figured he had about another three hundred yards to go. He could do it, no problem, if he just stayed low and center and took his time. He made a mental note to wear sneakers next time. And bring a rain poncho. And for God's sake, notice the sky...

The wave hit him like an explosion. It startled him silly, knocking him so cleanly off the rocks, it was as if he'd been swimming in the sea the whole time. Coming up for air, he choked on an enormous mouthful of salt water. It tasted so nasty that it seemed to him, by far, the worst part of this entire misadventure. Before he had time to react, another wave picked him up and slammed him back against the granite crags. A last second thrusting of both legs outward saved him from having his face scraped off. He kicked off the rocks and began swimming with all his might away from the sea wall. His clothes and boots pulled on him like sandbags. He wanted to strip them off, but there was too much surrounding chaos to allow it. Another wave threw him back and, this time, he hit the side of his head squarely. Blood began seeping into his eyes and mouth, but still he didn't panic. He just needed one more determined shove off the rocks, and he could kick his way free. Life had taught him guts; prison had given him patience. God would have to fill in the rest of the particulars. And courage always came at the last minute.

The last wave knocked his thigh against something very sharp. A beam, a rod, a pipe—what was it? It stung like a son of a bitch, and he could feel the muscles in that leg contracting from the shock. Propelling his arms and one good leg against the surging breakers, he began to swim and kick with all his might. It was no use. Every few feet he'd wrench himself away, and another wave would toss him back. The great quantities of blood and seawater he'd consumed made him nauseous and suddenly weak. His hair matted his eyes, and the brine burned fiercely as he glanced one final time toward shore, hoping to signal someone, anyone. He saw that he was truly, utterly alone. He lay his head back in the water and stared up at the sky. And again, what exactly was your point, God? Rising and falling like a paper cup in the massive swells, he felt a strange calm and mindfulness come over him. It was all… OK. Everything was completely and unconditionally…all right. It occurred to him that his own life was an extraordinary, fragile illusion of joy and pain shared proportionately with every single person on the planet. And it was all completely perfect. Everything. Every single damn day, every wretched, damn moment. All perfect.

The huge roller hoisted him higher than any of the previous ones, and he inadvertently realized something had a hold of his hand. He gazed up to see the fisherman in his boat, the turtle killer, "Little Ray," holding on to him for dear life. Lester smiled just before passing out. Funny how life makes it little hypothetical points.

***

"Looks kinda like after you've slit a snapper's belly and watched all the guts fall out."

"Mmm-hmm. We had an old milk cow when I was a kid got wrapped up in some barb wire and damn if she didn't tear herself up something good. I sewed her up myself. Ever last cut. Good training for a young doctor."

"Friend of mine works up in the emergency room up at Parkland. You wouldn't believe the shit they have to try and stitch back together every weekend up there."

"Wouldn't I? I sewed a Mexican fellow's pecker back on once. Got it hung up in a cement mixer. Never could get him to tell me what his ying-yang was doing in that cement mixer."

Lester moved slightly. His head felt like a sack of burning nails was sitting on it. He dragged one eye open and could see that he was in a doctor's office. His entire body felt achy and feverish, his brain mushy as breakfast cereal.

"No, sir. I'll tell ya. I've just about seen it all in my day. The predicaments some people get themselves into, you wouldn't believe. There." The doctor made a clipping sound with scissors.

"Good as it's gonna get. What do you reckon he was doing out there anyway?"

"Beats me. I just seen him sitting up on the rocks. That's all I know."

The doctor began wrapping a bandage around Lester's thigh. "You don't reckon he was trying to kill himself?"

Lester jerked his head, coughed, and called out hoarsely, "N…no! I wasn't trying to kill myself. I was *thinking.*"

The two men looked at each other. Finally, the doctor said, "How 'bout thinking in the park, next time? That old jetty's a dangerous place when a storm blows up. Some old snowbird from Wisconsin got stuck out there last winter during a freak norther, and they had to call a dadgum helicopter to pull her off."

Lester opened both eyes. "Where am I?"

The man on the boat leaned in and stared at Lester. He most definitely could have been an older brother of Little Ray's. "You're in Doc Joe Sample's office. He just sewed up your haunch. You tore it up pretty good."

"You'll be OK. I gave you thirty stitches and a tetanus shot. You got enough painkiller in ya and on ya; you won't feel too bad for a while. What'd you get into out there? Looks like you were in a sword fight or something."

Lester shook his head. "I don't know. Some kind of pole or bar, not sure what it was."

"There's some of that nasty rebar sticking outta them old rocks. Don't know why the government couldn't a removed all that shit 'fore they throwed it out there."

The doctor finished his bandaging and rose, turning on the overhead fluorescent lights. Lester averted his eyes. "I 'magine 'cause they know fish are smart enough not to get hung up on it. It's the 'human fish' always gets in the jam." He leaned in toward Lester. "Where you from, son?"

"Rockport."

"You got a car, or can someone pick you up?"

"I rode my bike over."

"All the way from Rockport?"

Lester nodded, and the two men again looked at each other. Finally the fisherman said, "I can give him a lift, Doc. It's on my way home."

The doctor nodded, and Lester tried lifting himself from the examination table. The fisherman placed a hand behind his head and held him. "Easy. You're probably going to be a little dizzy."

Lester could feel the blood rushing to his leg and the first tingling sensation of discomfort arising.

"We had to cut your jeans practically up to the belt loops. But, like I always say, you can just about sew anything back together again." The doctor shuffled over to the sink and began washing his hands.

Lester lightly touched the floor, holding his damaged leg aloft. He could see in a mirror across the room his head was bandaged. He pointed to it with his hand. "What happened up here?"

The doctor turned off the sink and dried his hands. "You tore some chunks of hair out, scraped it up. I put a little antibiotic on it. You'll need to change those bandages daily. Come back in a week, and we'll see how those stitches are doing."

"What do I owe you?"

"Nothing. Just stay off that shittin' jetty during a storm, that's all."

The fisherman spoke up. "Old Doc takes care of all us out on the offshore rig I work for. He's our 'Company Doc.' We're just gonna call you our new 'employee.'"

Lester stared at the two men. Once again, Providence had spared him both adversity and not insignificant expense. He wondered if there might come a time when such munificence would be suspended from overuse? He shook his head and extended a hand toward the doctor. "I don't know what to say. I just feel kinda stupid. Thank you. You're a good man."

The old doctor shook Lester's hand, gazing at him. "And you're a lucky boy. You can start walking on that leg in a day or two. I'd give you some crutches, but I'd have to charge you for 'em. Big fella like you ought to be able to hop around on one foot for a day or two. I'll see you in a week."

"Yes, sir."

Exiting the office, Lester held on to the fisherman's shoulder as they made their way into the parking lot. Lester stopped skipping about halfway and turned sideways. "I don't even know your name. You saved my life—who are you?"

The man grinned and stared down at his shoes. "Naw, I didn't save your life. I was just there to make sure nothing bad would come to you." He stuck out his hand. "Royce Stevens."

"Lester Briggs."

The two men looked at each other. Lester figured he was about ten, twelve years older than him. Clean shaven, deeply tanned, he had the alert and friendly features of a rugged terrier. Royce opened the passenger side of his Chevy Silverado and patted the seat. "You hop in over here, and if you don't mind, I need to head over to the dock and pull my boat back onto the trailer."

Lester lifted himself up onto the seat and eased his hip around, staring out at the horizon. The sky had cleared, and whatever had blown in and blown him out to sea was now gone like some trifling inconvenience. He shook his head in wonder. "Not at all. I'm sorry to cause you so much trouble today. Would it be all right if we looked for my bike? It's borrowed."

Royce got in on the passenger side and shut the door. "No problem at all." He started the ignition, exhaling sharply. "Only real problem I've had all day was losing that old turtle."

Lester looked at him. Royce stared into the distance. "That Kemp's Ridley was some kind of persistent turtle, I'll say that. He just kept circling and circling my fishing line. I kept hauling it in, moving it, hauling it in, moving it. Damned if he didn't finally just get his head all wrapped around it and strangle himself. Unreal. It doesn't make any sense, I know, but I truly believe he was trying to kill himself. I really do."

They were both silent for a moment and then Royce shifted into reverse and backed up. "I cut him loose and felt pretty bad about it. Old turtles a peaceful thing. Like killing a good dog or something—no reason to it."

They drove in silence all the way to the marina, both men pondering whatever anomalies in the natural world could cause such adversity.

After winching the boat back onto the trailer, they found Luz's bike where Lester had left it. Loading it up, they began the drive back to Rockport. Royce talked about his job out on the rig in the Gulf. He'd worked as a roughneck for a Louisiana outfit for about four years now. It was hot, dirty, grunt labor, but he made good money, and he had half the month off to himself, which he appreciated most of all. Fishing was his passion, and he loved being out on the water with just his thoughts and the vast expanse of infinity surrounding him. He loved it better than anything he could imagine. He'd been in the Navy for a couple of years, living out on a destroyer for months at a time, and he'd grown quickly accustomed to the 180° horizon and a constantly rolling equilibrium. For a small-town kid from the Texas panhandle, discovering the ocean in his teens was like meeting up with a long-lost lover he'd never even contemplated missing.

Royce wanted to drop off his boat at his place first. They turned away from the highway and onto a sandy path headed toward the bay. It was nearly dusk. Lester watched the filtered twilight settling around them, and he felt an agreeable combination of elation and drug-induced loopiness enveloping him. He gaped in wonder at the green fields of coastal Bermuda and grazing Santa Gertrudis heifers that surrounded them like sleek, cherry boulders. A cluster of snowy egrets flew overhead like dispersed quotation marks. Suddenly, a young sorrel colt kicked across the road with her tail high and nostrils flaring. It was as if she were determined to remind the world such beauty was an entirely ephemeral proposition. Lester couldn't recall a time when he had felt more utterly at peace.

Royce leaned his head out the window and called to the filly. "Where you going, Isabella? You're prettier than your mama and daddy both. Yes, you are." Royce turned to Lester. "Ain't she something? I bought her mama over a year ago and bred her to a King Ranch quarter horse. No telling what I could get for her if she gets broke right. But she ain't for sale. Hell, I just like having a few animals to look at. It's that 'Texas thing,' you know?"

The truck pulled up in front of a simple wood shingled house, elevated a single story off the ground. The water's edge lay ahead another hundred yards or so. A small deck extended around half of the dwelling, and an unknown flag and some wind chimes spun loosely in the breeze. All was neat and tended to, and Lester could see a fenced-in vegetable garden off to the side. He nodded. "You've sure got a pretty place. You a gardener, too?"

Royce turned off the ignition and opened his door as two rowdy mutts came bounding down the deck stairs. "Naw, I'm not much of a farmer. That's Leland's thing." It was at that point Lester glanced up to see a blonde man in shorts and an undershirt standing above them, smiling. Royce fussed half-heartedly at the two mongrels. "Tilly and Abner, ya'll get down! Cool it!"

"What'd you catch?" asked the man from the deck.

"Nothing. Total bust."

"Sorry to hear it. I've got the hamburger patties waiting."

"Suits me." Royce walked halfway up the steps as the other guy descended. Meeting in the middle, they casually put an arm around each other and kissed, a kiss as natural and spontaneous as a wink or a sigh. Lester looked on in astonishment. Now he knew he must be high.

Royce took off his fishing cap and pointed to the truck. "Lee, this is Lester. I saved his life today."

The blonde man smiled. "There you go again." They shared a look, and Leland said to Lester, "Come on in. Have a hamburger and a beer."

Lester slowly moved himself off the front seat and stood wobbling by the door. "I appreciate the offer, but I don't want to barge in on ya'll like this."

"You're not barging. Hell, he saved your life. Least you can do is break bread with us."

Lester smiled shyly and began to feel his way around the front of the truck.

Leland looked at his bandaged leg and whistled. "Damn, you did do some damage."

Lester stopped skipping and looked up at the blonde. He appeared to be younger than Royce: smooth skinned, slender, perfect white teeth. Another generic, nice looking, Scotch-Irish Texas lad. Lester sighed, "This is what happens when you're just plain stupid."

Royce walked back down the steps. "Nah, smart people are always breaking stuff, too. It's nature's way of making sure we don't get too cocky for no good reason. Here." Royce offered his shoulder again, and Leland approached on his other side.

"I'm Leland. Royce calls me 'Lee.' You can call me anything but 'shithead' or 'Pat Robertson.'"

"Nice to meet you. I'm Lester." The two shook hands and, in one swoop, both men lifted Lester and carried him up the stairs like he was nothing more than a sack and a half of groceries. He laughed at the scene. It made him feel giddy and slightly ridiculous. And, not too surprisingly, a little excited. The grip of these two vigorous men beside him brought back a sensation he'd not wholly experienced since prison: physical desire.

After the two men set him down inside their living room, Lester looked around, taking in the surroundings. The room was small but neat and well planned. Someone had obviously thought it out in a clean, pragmatic, and simple approach. The furniture might've been second hand, but it was obviously of good quality. A sand-colored sailcloth sofa, several huge canvas club chairs, sea grass rugs, white wooden louvered window blinds, rows and rows of books, model boats, CDs, and jars of sea glass. It was the perfect beach house—cool, comfortable, and easy. Lester turned to them. "This is a great room. Who's the designer?"

Royce pointed to Leland. "He is. It's all his. We get along 'cause I don't care what it looks like long as I can put up my model boats I make." Royce lifted an elaborate Tall Ship and handed it to Lester. "This here's the 'Pride of Baltimore,' a nineteenth-century Clipper Ship. Took me six months to finish that little number."

"Beautiful."

Leland nodded. "You can get high from all the glue just walking across the room sometimes. Why don't you stretch out on the couch and rest your leg?" he suggested.

Lester handed the ship back to Royce and sat slowly on the sofa, propping his sore leg up. "Thank you. Wow, much better."

"How 'bout a beer?"

"Sure."

Royce walked off toward the kitchen and Lester smiled. "What do you do, Leland?"

"I teach school in Corpus. Junior high social studies."

Royce called from the kitchen, "And he's a good one, too. He gets letters every year from students and parents thanking him for being such a good role model."

Leland pulled a joint from inside a small metal box and lit it, nodding. "A good 'gay' role model. Whether they realize it or not." He sat in the chair beside Lester.

Royce re-entered and handed both men a beer.

Lester stared at the two of them. "So, ya'll are a couple?"

They both looked at each other, grinning. "Oh yeah," Royce said. "For like six years. We met in a bar in Houston. That was it. So long to my wild, wild days."

Leland handed the joint to Lester with a look of conferral. But Lester hesitated. He wasn't much of a pot smoker. "Thanks, but with all those painkillers, it might not be too wise."

Leland snorted. "Hey, when those painkillers start to wear off, you're gonna be crawling around here looking for this sucker. Go on, a few hits aren't gonna do any harm."

Lester took the joint and inhaled. The acrid hit was like a sweet and only slightly schizo friend you didn't mind occasionally hanging out with. He tilted his head back and let it occupy his throat fully before exhaling. He looked again at the two guys before him. Here he was in the home of two seemingly well-adjusted, happy, sane, and *normal* gay men, smoking a joint and acting like it was all just another day at the factory. He laughed loudly, unable to contain himself. "Hey, I gotta ask. How come you kissed like that in front of me? You guys don't even know me." He handed the joint to Royce.

Royce nodded slowly and inhaled. "I know you. You can usually tell."

"Tell what?"

"About certain people."

"What?"

"If they're gonna be cool or not. I just had a feeling about you."

"Like...like I'm gay, or something?"

Leland took a sip from his beer. "You're not?"

Lester blinked, "I...I just don't like labels. That's all."

Leland smiled. "That's cool. When you find someplace that doesn't type you in some way as a twenty-something blank, religious background blank, last-year-of-education blank, blood type blank, ethnicity blank, political preference blank, drinking habits blank, drug usage blank, diet restrictions blank, marital status blank, tax status blank, credit rating blank, good old red-blooded American type male—*blank!*—you let me know. Everyone labels. Consciously, subconsciously. Seems to be the way of the world." Leland took the joint from Royce and imbibed.

Lester shifted uneasily on the couch. "But I don't see why a person's sexuality has to enter into it?"

Leland looked up dreamily and smiled. "Was there some other reason you asked if we were a couple?"

Lester stared at him, feeling slightly ridiculous. "Yeah, OK. I just get a little uncomfortable around all that stuff."

"Ever ask yourself why?"

Lester shrugged. "Sure. I guess I don't want to feel what I'm feeling a lot of the time."

"And not thinking about it makes it go away?"

"No. Not thinking about it keeps me from beating up on myself."

Leland nodded, eyebrows raised. "From feeling what you feel?"

238

"Right." Lester plunked his beer down and sat up. "Hey listen, we don't have to play psychiatrist right now. There's a lot of other things we could talk about."

Leland smiled. "OK."

They all stared at each other expectantly. Finally Lester spoke haltingly, looking at the coffee table. "That's a…nice ashtray. Where'd you get it?"

"Tulsa Marriott."

"Nice."

After a brief moment's contemplation, the three of them burst out laughing instantaneously. It was as if some unaccountable constraint had risen up and flapped out of the room. They were cohesive again.

"Hey, I don't mean to bust your chops. Sorry. Everybody has their own comfort level. Whatever." Leland handed the joint to Lester.

"I'll tell ya something. I'm not running around on that rig shouting, 'Gay Pride! Gay Pride!' Fuck 'em. Each his own. And I don't want anybody else's shit dumped on me neither." Royce reached down to scratch one of the dogs.

Lester inhaled the pot and felt his damaged leg twitch. He couldn't tell if the weed was having a mellowing or mildly paranoiac effect, or both. What he felt certain was he liked these two. "So, no problems with you guys? Nobody gives you any shit around here?"

Royce smirked. "We don't give 'em an opportunity. We pay our taxes, keep the property up, volunteer with the fire department. Lee coaches Little League in the summer, and I take the old geezers in the nursing home out on the boat to look at the whooping cranes ever winter. They either love us, or they ignore us."

"We're not exactly hanging on each other in front of the post office, you know what I mean? We don't have anything to prove to anybody."

Influenced no doubt by the cannabis, Lester was feeling all of a sudden philosophical. "So like, when you see straight couples making out and holding hands and doing all that stuff in public, what are you thinking?"

"Bully! Have a nice day! We do that when we go line dancing at the gay bars in Corpus or Houston. It just wouldn't occur to me to grope Royce in public. Now private's a different matter." Leland moved his foot over and rubbed Royce's leg. "He's a pretty sexy guy, don't you think?"

Lester flushed. They were both well beyond agreeable in the looks department. A little voice shouted out somewhere deep inside his head, *"But I still like women, even if I don't have sex with them anymore!"* Lester almost wished he were back in prison where only his thoughts were real, and the deeds were the fictional part. He glanced at Royce and then pulled a stray string from his ripped pants leg. "Yep. Sexy guy."

"How 'bout you, Lester? You ain't told us nothing much about you." Royce scratched at his sinewy arm.

"Oh...there's not much to tell. I did a little time with one of our fine Texas penal institutions. Got out not that long ago. Came down here looking for my true love and wound up a respectable old bachelor...with prospects. All I need now is a hat."

They both looked at him slightly confused. Leland shook his head. "About that 'true love'—male or female?"

Lester grinned. "Both!"

Royce jumped right in. "Hey, I know just who you're talking about. That old dyke runs the dry cleaners on Main! I 'magine she's got a pair of balls you could knock pins over with."

Lester laughed. "No, it was somebody else. Someone I just had the wrong idea about, that's all."

The two men waited to see if Lester would be more forthcoming, but he only stared at his beer stone-faced. After a pause, Leland stood. "Well, you don't have to tell us who it is even though we're dying to know. How do your prospects look now?"

"For?"

"Finding true love?"

Lester swallowed some beer, feeling his head empty out. He gave an offhand shrug. "I guess I'm still investigating that possibility."

Leland laughed and patted Lester's shoulder. "Good man. It ain't over till it's over. Nice-looking guy like you, don't sell yourself short. Hell, after work and whatever hobbies you're into, I mean, what's left? Everybody needs someone to stick their cold feet next to at night." He took one last toke on the joint, handed it to Royce, and headed for the kitchen. "How you like your burger, Lester?"

"Medium's good."

"You got it. Babe, you need another beer?" Royce shook his head. "Lester?" Lester held up his hand, and Leland exited the room. Royce leaned over and stroked one of the dogs again, and Lester studied him. What would it be like to be with that person every day for the rest of your life? How do you do something like that? Can you go on loving the same person, the same man, year after year, and still—*love* them?

"That happened to me, too," Royce said, sliding back in his chair. "Prison, I mean."

"Really? When?"

"Shit, I was barely out of high school. Spent a year for possession of a controlled substance. They say I was lucky to get the lighter sentence. I say I got fucked. Anyhow, it was a long time ago."

"How was it for you?"

Royce looked at Lester. His big, brown eyes were as calm and resolute as those of the colt running out in the pasture. "Same as for everybody. Same loneliness, fear, shame. Same roller coaster of experiences you never thought you'd go through. The good, the bad, and the dead all at once. "

Lester wanted to ask him if he had someone like Little Ray to confide in, to trust, someone to help preserve his sanity and sensibility, someone to feel for. He wanted to ask him a lot of things about his prison experiences, but he couldn't get the words sorted out. The painkillers, the beer, the pot, the leg injury, the entire day had worn him down to the point of numbness. He merely nodded at Royce. Royce continued looking at him with the same wide-eyed, guileless expression. Slowly, Royce stood and walked across the room toward Lester. After a moment, he placed his hand on Lester's neck and began rubbing. As he massaged his head and shoulders, Lester closed his eyes and let himself fall into a state of unconsciousness. He hadn't experienced such undiminished contentment since…since ever. Royce spoke softly as he manipulated the muscles in Lester's neck, "I know you…I know you.…"

chapter

FIFTEEN

Melanie stared at her nails with a look of indecision. "I hate my job. I really do. You know what PR is? Selling people on the premise that not being aware of something they could care less about is regressive, deficient, and harmful to their general well-being." She held up her hand. "Does this look too 'Help, I'm trapped at the mall'?"

Luz looked at Melanie's pinkish-purple immaculate nails and shook her head. "Perfect. It says, 'clever but not too insouciant.'" The two women sat on matching stools at the Korean Manicure Salon next to the Blockbuster Video in Corpus. So far, they'd done lunch, checked out accessories at Julian Gold Apparel, discussed appetizers with the caterers, done a quick fitting with the dressmaker, and made appointments for shiatsu massages later on. It was the perfect "girls' day out." Luz couldn't remember the last time she'd spent an entire day just paling around with anyone. With summer school over and the "dog days" of August acutely upon them, it seemed the decidedly germane thing to do: chill, schlep, schmooze, and dish—and particularly with someone as strikingly glamorous as Melanie. It was like being on holiday with Michelle Pfeiffer. Everywhere they went, people stared at them as if they were toting the Holy Grail of inner peace and fabulousness in their shopping bags from the Limited.

Luz lifted her left hand from the bowl of warm, sudsy water and stared at her cuticles. "These look like they belong to someone who installs roof shingles for a living. I wish I was a PR executive. You'll never appreciate the significance of the word 'stoicism' until you've taught art in a junior college."

Melanie laughed. "You are so much fun, Luz! I knew when I saw you, you'd be perfect."

Luz shook her head. "Perfect for what?"

"For this! Hanging out, having fun, being a bud." Melanie was suddenly somber as the woman with the name tag reading "Cho Yon" applied a last layer of protective sealant. "This has been *such* a trying summer. I've never felt so completely alone in my whole life." She looked at Luz. "You know what it's like when it just feels you're going to break inside if *someone* or *something* doesn't immediately come along and release you from the apathy of your life?"

Luz shook her head, mystified. "I didn't know there were people available for that position."

"Of course! What else is there in life but spontaneous circumstance? I live for it. Jesus God, if it hadn't been for Lester coming along and shaking up the boredom around here, I'd have withered. Absolutely expired!"

Luz stared intently as the woman with the name tag reading "Min Hei" diligently snipped away at her ragged nails. "So...you and Lester dated?"

Melanie frowned. "No, no. I think maybe Lester's gay, or bi, whatever. But he's so cute and sweet and sexy. God, it's just a hot flash being around him sometimes, don't you think?"

Min Hei pinched a little too much flesh, and Luz winced. "Well, why do you think Lester's gay, or bi?"

Melanie held a graceful hand aloft to admire. "I still can't decide. This color over a plain glaze for the wedding. I mean I want to look pure, but it doesn't have to be Mother Teresa-ish, you know. Why do I think it? He slept with my brother, that's why."

Luz continued concentrating on Min Hei as she carefully trimmed each of her digits with the skill and precision of a bonsai botanist. Such fastidious and exacting work made her dizzy with wonderment. If she applied as much diligence toward her own life as Min, she'd be picking up a MacArthur genius award by now. If wishes were horses. "Um…your brother slept with…Lester?"

Melanie shrugged. The two manicurists continued mindfully in their labors, oblivious—or indifferent—to their clients' conversation. "It was just a guy hormone thing. I don't think either of them gave it too much consideration. My overall theory is, sex is *not* what it's all about. Unh-unh. You can have sex with a doorknob, right? I mean it's just *there*, everywhere. Like cell phones. What you want is their minds *and* their damaged little hearts. *Then* you control the entire synergistic universe."

Luz made a face. "Sex is pretty damn significant in my orbit. Who wants to be with someone that's sleeping around? That wouldn't exactly make me feel *special*, you know?"

"Exactly. It's not *special* until they *love* you! Surely you don't think sex is love? That's the hollandaise, not the filet! Love, love, love—that's what I want!"

"But people fall out of love. It happens all the time. I speak from experience."

Melanie turned sideways in her chair to face Luz. "Listen to me," Melanie said. "People can never stop loving you as long as you let them be *free* to rise and fall of their own accord. Who does a child run to when they scrape their knee? Mommy. Why? Because it's a guaranteed kiss and a hug, no questions asked. When you have their hearts and their minds, *sans* judgments, they never leave."

Luz blinked at her, smiling slightly. "Can you handle one small observation?"

"Shoot."

"I think maybe you're steeling yourself up for the wedding. I don't even know you, Mel, but I feel like you're probably a little scared silly by what you're about to do."

Melanie stared at her, mouth open, speechless. "You know something? You're absolutely right!" Melanie reached over and hugged Luz. "Oh God, I'm so lucky to have found you. I really appreciate that." She then turned back to face Cho Yon. "Doesn't change anything, however. Sometimes you just have to will your life to work out. And you know what? It usually does."

Luz couldn't argue with her insight. Purpose follows desire. Conclusion follows plan. Form follows function. It all made sense if you were a computer programmer. And when exactly did the human heart ever follow accordingly? "About Lester," Luz said. "Are you sure?"

"Yes, why? Oh God, did you fall for him, too?"

"No. But I think, never mind."

"Tell me."

Luz looked at her sheepishly. "Well, I got the distinct impression he...liked me. Like...a lot."

Melanie stared at her stunned. It was as if she'd been abruptly exposed to something truly alarming, like geriatric porn. Finally she smiled. "That's adorable! I can see it, of course. He's totally enamored with you."

"But why?"

"Because, because...because you're such a mystery to him."

"Me?"

"Yes. It's sweet really. I'm getting the whole picture. You're both like—I don't know how to put it. You're both like so *unadulterated.*"

"What does that mean?"

"Pure, real, and I mean this in the most positive way...*simple.*"

"We sound like bars of soap!"

"Not at all. You're just less neurotic than the rest of us." Melanie pointed to Cho Yon's nails. "That's such an interesting color. What's it called?"

Cho Yon grinned. "Firecracker Limeade! *Ver-r-ry* different."

Melanie nodded thoughtfully. "Reminds me of a toothbrush I used to have." She turned back to Luz. "What I want to know is the mystery part."

"What?"

"Are you?"

"Mysterious?" Luz shook her head. "Yeah, like a can of Beef-aroni."

Melanie squinted. "I'm just going to take a stab here. You're not really into Lester, are you?"

Luz shook her head slowly.

"Another leap into the abyss—you're not all that hung up on guys either, right?"

"Correct."

"Thought so. Well, too bad we're not in New York. I could introduce you to some great girls."

Luz looked forlornly at Melanie. "Story of my life. All the 'great' ones are somewhere else."

"Poor baby. You know, it's not that desperate. There's the Internet, after all."

Luz looked at Melanie and smiled. It was a lot of information to process all at once. Lester, gay? How odd. But then, why not? People are so strange. Why always this fixation on the most inopportune thing? She and Philip were two of the most compulsive romantics on the planet—her love worn as a Day-Glo banner in a meadow of army fatigues and Philip's an ocean of prodigious need compressed and repressed into some tight, sunny veneer of normalcy.

"Well, at least it's worked out for you. You're getting married to the man you love. You have a life mate, a partner, someone to share every remarkable, mundane, and ridiculous detail with. It's what everyone wants."

Melanie turned to Luz with an equivocal expression. "I never said I *loved* him. I wouldn't go that far. I said he *loves me*. It's good enough."

Luz stared at Melanie's golden, creamy faultlessness and determined that for the first time in her life, her own personal dilemmas weren't such awful things after all.

***

The two of them sat on the aft deck of the *Amor Descolorado* and watched as the sun hunkered low over the beach houses of the upper-upper-middle classes lining Bay Road. They each clutched ample old-fashioned glasses of Maker's Mark, and each propped a foot up on the exterior railing. Philip marveled at the drop-dead dazzle of the Wheelwright floating manor house. It was ostentatious in the extreme, but not exactly a disagreeable invitation. On the contrary, he was just glad he didn't have the job of keeping it all 'shipshape.' That was somebody else's job, somebody at the moment who was nowhere in sight.

Daniel sampled his bourbon and smiled at Philip. "So, what do you think of my father's idea of spiritual fulfillment?"

Philip shook his glass, toppling a bank of ice cubes. "Well, I certainly don't feel the enjoyment of beautiful things is anathema to Christianity, if that's where you're going."

"What I mean is, we're sitting on a million-and-a-half-dollar barge that the man circles the bay in a few times a year and toots his horn. Maybe just a bit indulgent, no?"

"I don't know. They said that about the Taj Mahal, the Parthenon...Radio City. Lots of people think St. Peter's in Rome is a colossal squander."

Daniel laughed, shaking his head. "You Episcopalians. You're all such *accommodators*."

"I thought your mother told me you were raised Episcopalian?"

"Yes, between the Country Club and Neiman's, we managed to do a drive-by twice a year."

Philip looked at Daniel, trying to determine if his resolute flippancy was a mask, a cry, or a flat-out 'fuck you.' He decided it was probably something innate. "So, what did you want to talk about, Daniel? It's very pleasant enjoying the sunset with you, but I know you have other things on your mind."

Daniel held his glass to his lips and peered at Philip. He braced himself. Now or never kid, take your best shot. "Yeah. Well, I was just wondering…" He suddenly sat up straight in his chair. "Boy, this feels strangely cumbersome."

Philip studied him, puzzled. "Go ahead. I'm sure we can handle it."

"I…feel, I mean, I think…You know, just for curiosity's sake, are you seeing anyone right now?"

"Me?"

Daniel nodded at Philip.

"Um…" It instantly materialized before Philip like fast-forward windowpane frost in a high school science film. Daniel was more than a little interested in…him! He flinched, even as he spoke. "Why…are you asking?"

"Because, for some reason, I mean it *is* ridiculous. You've become someone that I…care about." Daniel watched him pensively. "Does that make you crazy?"

Philip didn't know where to look. At Daniel? The sunset? His shoes? There was no convenient resting place for his unanticipated apprehension. He couldn't remember another man, woman, or child ever saying to him "I care about you" in precisely the same manner. It was such an abrupt and intentional sneak attack. He'd never allowed the possibility of such awkward divulgences to occur in the past. He was the past master of "heading them off at the pass," and it frightened him silly, such manifest vulnerability. "When you…uh…say 'care 'bout,' do you mean…?"

Daniel whirled around in his chair to face Philip head on. "Come on. This isn't 'me and the minister' right now. We're two grown, adult men discussing feelings. I said I care about you, Philip. I have feelings for you. Please don't analyze this for some discourse you can incorporate down the road."

Philip looked at him askance. How had this *kid* managed to break through the massive, painstaking wall-building he'd implemented to keep himself safe and whole from people *exactly* like Daniel? "Thank you," Philip replied. "I appreciate your…feelings. I think you're a very interesting and clever—"

But before Philip could finish, Daniel kneeled beside Philip's chair. Daniel looked into his eyes with such intensity, it stunned Philip. "You're the only man I've ever wanted to know better before actually seducing and instantly having sex with. In the grand plan of things, I know it doesn't seem like much, but it's a first for me. I really would like to know you better. There's just something... There's something about you that touches me. I want to protect you, help you, heal you. I'd like to love you, if you'd let me. I think I could do that." Daniel then leaned slowly toward Philip and kissed him softly on the mouth. Nothing more than a touching of lips. Then Daniel sat back on his haunches, and they looked at one another. Philip's heart was racing so fast, it was as if he were straining on a treadmill. Without warning, Daniel leaned in to kiss Philip again. This time, a slower, more savoring gesture.

The two parted and Philip felt his face flush from embarrassment and excitement, confusion and angst. Daniel smiled at him, and Philip slowly placed an unsteady hand behind Daniel's neck, speaking in a whisper, "I'm just...I'm afraid I don't know...how."

Daniel shook his head, his words filled with compassion. "What's the worst that can happen by letting yourself love and be loved?"

"Everything."

"Have faith! God did not put you here to be alone and confused."

Philip looked at Daniel's bright, earnest face and smiled. He gently rubbed the back of Daniel's head and then pulled him closer until their lips met again.

***

Lester tightened the oil filter back onto the engine of the Dodge Caravan and slid out from under the car. The sunlight was directly in his eyes as the young mother holding the toddler stood above him. Lester rose up gradually on his still-bandaged leg.

"That's it? Already? Gosh, I thought we'd be here another hour or so."

"No, ma'am, all set. Changed you oil, new filter, checked your fluids, tires, battery, wipers—you're good to go."

"Gosh you're fast. Are you always so fast?" Grinning, she stood there with her legs spread wide, clutching her baby like it was a pillow someone had just tossed to her.

Lester shook his head. "Nope, not always. Just today. Got two more to do right after you."

"What a shame. I've got a twelve pack of beer in the cooler in the backseat. I was really hoping to share some of it about now."

"Thanks. Not while I'm working."

"How 'bout later?"

Lester squinted at her. She was maybe twenty, cute in a cornflakes, small-town, Texas-girl way. You could read her current frame of mind by the way she held that baby: careless, bored, impatient.

"Naw, I appreciate it, but I better not."

"Aw, come on. I don't bite. One beer, just to be friendly."

Lester wiped his hands on a rag. "And what would the baby's father say if I did?"

"Not a fucking thing. He's offshore working till next Friday. Fuck do I care anyway?"

Lester stuffed the rag in his back pocket and sighed. "Tell you what. You pull up after five, and park over on the side there. We'll set some folding chairs out, and you, me, the baby, and Mr. Otis'll all sit in the breezeway and have a good visit. What do you think?"

Her grin withered as she shifted the baby to her other hip. "Some other time. What do I owe you?" She dug in her shoulder purse and handed Lester a credit card.

"The full service oil change is thirty-one, ninety-five."

"How come ya'll charge five dollars more than the Jiffy Lube?"

Lester went to run her card through the machine. "'Cause we're better, quicker, more thorough, and we don't try to sell you stuff you don't need."

"I bet I could find someone over at Jiffy Lube to drink my beer."

Lester nodded. "I bet you could, and a few other things, too." He handed her the card back. "You have a great day, and come see us again." Lester took hold of the baby's chubby foot. "You're just as pretty as your mama, you know that?" He smiled, turned, and hobbled back into the office leaving pretty mama and her tow-headed toddler both blinking in the sunlight.

As he walked into the back storage room, he looked around for Otis. He had two more cars in the bay to service and, with people whizzing in and out like bees on cake, he needed some help. Come to think of it, he hadn't seen Otis for several hours. Walking out into the garage again, he returned to the office, puzzled. It wasn't like Otis to just disappear like that.

Lester took a Big Red from the cooler and started to exit again when he noticed a foot perched just inside the barely-ajar washroom door. He held the soda next to his mouth and stared. Finally he called out, "Mr. Otis, that you in there?" He walked slowly to the door. Knocking lightly, he called again, "Mr. Otis, you OK?" The door creaked open a little, and Lester peered inside. Mr. Otis was sitting on the toilet holding Mildred in his lap, stroking her head. He looked up, his eyes filled with grief. "Miss Mildred's... dying."

"What?"

Otis continued caressing her motionless body, "She's old. Miss Mildred is old, old. She got some kind of tumor on her belly. Vet told me one of these days it'd kill her."

Lester interrupted, alarmed. "Let's take her back to the vet! There may be something he can do."

Otis didn't move. He lowered his head as if listening to Mildred. She made a faint growling sound as he traced his finger down her neck. "She's tired. She's ready to go on now. I know Miss Mildred. She's been my most loyal friend for near fourteen years. And I know she don't want to be strung along on no pills and shots neither." Otis slowly conveyed his gnarled hand down Mildred's side as if reading a braille text. "She just wants me to hold her a while longer, that all."

Lester's voice grew panicky. "I'll get the vet to come here. It may just be something temporary. She'll be OK. Let him look at her."

Otis lifted his head, eyes glaring. "We gonna let her go on her own with peace and honor. You wouldn't treat your best friend with nothing less than that."

Lester stared at them, both vulnerable as chicks knocked from a tree limb. He wanted more than anything to be able to fix it. Fix their pain. Fix everybody's pain. He couldn't stand to see suffering. It was as if all that grief got wedged into his soul somehow. All he wanted was to fix it.

Lester leaned down to touch Mildred's head. He whispered, "It's OK, Mildred. Your best friend has you." Lester placed a hand on Otis' leg. "You stay as long as you need, Mr. Otis. I'll take care of it out here." Otis nodded and Lester slowly pulled the door. His leg was throbbing again. He absentmindedly traced two fingers lightly alongside the stitches on his thigh, and the pressure helped ease the irritation some. Passing by the desk, Lester picked up the envelope of an unpaid bill and scribbled on the back of it, "Out of Order." He tacked it to the bathroom door and stepped outside as a truckload of fishermen pulling a sixteen-foot outboard breezed into the sally port, loudly jangling the arrival bell.

**

Philip opened the front door and smiled. Bob Wheelwright was standing there looking like the burnished prow of the Tommy Hilfiger armada—a distinguished patrician one didn't have the opportunity of viewing every day. Philip silently affirmed the seeds of physical grace he'd deposited in both his children. Abundantly so. "Well, welcome. Right on time. Come in. Can I get you something to drink?"

Bob pumped Philip's fist. "No, no, I'm fine. Awful good of you to see me like this. I know how hectic your week must be for you."

"Not at all. Why don't we go down the hall here to my office."

"Great, great." Bob's eyes darted about the hall. "Wonderful place you have."

"It was my parents' home. I'm just the 'keeper of the flame.'" Philip motioned toward his office door. "Please come in; have a seat."

Bob, as expected, surveyed the office and pronounced it "refined" and sat in the same Chesterfield wingback his wife had occupied. Philip contemplated if either spouse knew of the other's visit to his office. He then wondered for a nanosecond what it would be like to have them as in-laws. He scratched his nose impulsively. "What can I do for you?"

Bob rubbed his hands as if warming them before a fire. "I'll get right to the point, Phil. I think the woman who works for us—Rosa—well...I don't believe she's been...faithful."

Philip raised an eyebrow. "To...whom?"

"Well, to her boyfriend. The father of her baby."

"Why do you think that?"

Bob stared at Philip earnestly. "Because...she's been sleeping with me."

"Uh-huh."

"And possibly...others."

"Others?"

Bob looked down at his hands. "I think—I'm reasonably sure—there were others."

"Why?"

"I've...heard as much."

Philip rested his palms on top of the desk and cleared his throat. "As I'm sure you know, Bob, gossip isn't the most reliable source when we're dealing with a sensitive matter such as this."

Bob leaned forward, solemnly. "This is someone that I trust."

The two stared at each other for a moment. "What is it you'd like my help for?" Philip asked.

Bob nodded slowly. "I love my wife...and I love Rosa. And I can't bear the thought of not having either of them in my life. Yvonne is terribly fond of Rosie, almost like a daughter. But if she found out the child was fathered by me—"

Philip interrupted, "Or...not?"

Bob looked surprised. "Or not. It doesn't matter. Whoever the alleged father is, he hasn't shown any interest. He hasn't come forward. There's no one else to take on the role but me."

"No one?"

"No one."

Now Philip looked confused. "And?"

"I'd like to adopt the baby. I want you to help me talk with Rosa…and with my wife."

Philip sat back in his chair, resting an ankle on his knee. "I see. Then you're going to tell your wife about the affair."

"Not exactly. I'm going to tell her I want to adopt this child."

"And what has Rosa said?"

"She hasn't. I haven't asked her."

"Why not?"

"Because I honestly don't know if she knows who the father is. Look, I'll take care of her and the baby exactly like my own family. No question. What's the need in tormenting her? She's a good person, a long way from home, who may have made some hasty decisions. I want to help her, that's all."

"You know they have DNA tests now. Wouldn't you at least like to know?"

Bob sprang forward in his chair. "It doesn't matter! I don't care who the father is. I care about the child."

Philip rocked his foot, gazing at Bob. "You do know that I've spoken with Rosa, your wife, and now with you. I may know some things that I wouldn't be permitted to reveal, you understand?"

Bob nodded, slowly sitting back in the chair. "Of course. That's why I'm here. I'm relying on your moral integrity."

Philip idly picked up the letter opener on his desk and balanced it on the tip of his index finger, his standard diversionary tactic. He watched it seesaw in jerky synch with his pulse. Why did he have to evoke such a messy codicil as "moral integrity"? It was the sole miscreant that thwarted his immediate compliance with Bob's request. "Moral equivocator" was more to the point. Everything seemed gray, mutable—all issues, contrivances, and misdeeds surrounding acts of love bleached to near obscurity. Wasn't the *wrong thing* quite often the *right thing*? He folded his hand around the letter opener. "I'll talk to them, Bob, if you'll answer me one question?"

"Yes."

"Why do you want this baby so much?"

Bob continued staring wide-eyed and then heedlessly plowed a hand through his blanched, amber hair. He spoke carefully, as if reading from a chart across the room. "Because...I want another chance. I don't want to leave this earth without having at least tried to correct a few oversights. Because I know I can make a difference in at least one life that would gain much through my involvement. Because I messed up with my own kids. I was too busy 'driving' the corporation to realize I'd forfeited their trust and faith. Because you can have a person's love out of obligation, but without *attachment*. Because it's a blank feeling knowing your worth is measured in stock portfolios and bond funds. Because nobody wants to accept the fact they're largely extraneous in their own descendants' lives. Because all I've ever known how to manage successfully was a business, a boat, and maybe...a spouse. And there can be—and damn well should be—something else. And because I love Rosa very much. I want that child to *legally* have everything I can give it."

Philip pictured Rosa in his head as she lay in her hospital room, when she had absently rubbed her stomach through her cotton nightgown and turned to him, smiling. "This one is a fighter. I can feel him wanting to come, to show the world his courage, his determination. I feel him so much. He's a strong one!"

Philip opened his fist and let the letter opener roll onto the desktop. "*We'll* talk to them both. It won't be easy. A woman doesn't readily give up her child for adoption no matter what the circumstances. And a wife..." Philip rubbed his fingernail on the desk mat. "A wife will usually do whatever she pleases."

Bob stood, extending his hand. "Yvonne is a bright, sensitive woman. Her dignity is everything to her. Just follow my lead, and together I think we might be able to reason with her."

Philip nodded, a small smile on his lips. "I may know of a way to enlist her sympathies."

"I realize this is a hell of a week, but I appreciate your help. I'll call and we'll set something up with your schedule, OK?"

"Fine. Oh, and by the way..."

Bob had moved to the office door, stopped, and turned back to Philip.

"I think you're wrong about one thing. Your children love you more than just out of obligation. I think it's pretty apparent."

Bob smiled, genuinely surprised. "Thanks for saying that."

Philip followed Bob down the hallway toward the entry. They shook hands and Bob exited down the steps. Philip stood momentarily at the door pondering why so many acts of love are of approximate virtue at best? He turned and glanced at Luz's picture on the wall, the one that he'd sent the copy of to Lester in prison. He thought about how Luz had always hated the photo. She'd declared it cheap and cheesy and had it taken only under duress for a Teacher's Newsletter deadline. Philip felt it was one of the few where she hadn't "dressed the part" of some good girl/bad girl image revolving in her head. In its artlessness, it remarkably captured her sincerity and warmth. The perfect picture to send a lonely prisoner. Again, when *was* the *wrong thing* the *right thing*?

Windsor padded up behind him, dropping his sock doll at his feet. Philip picked it up and patted Windsor's head. It was the first time since he could remember he'd gone *almost* a whole day without thinking of Lester.

***

Rosa finished writing her letter to Bob. Her English was still not great, but the words she couldn't remember she wrote in Spanish. Bob had a good enough grasp of the language to make sense of it. She picked up the first page and stared at her neat, schoolgirl script. It was immaculate: not a cross out, smudge, or illegible scribble anywhere. She wanted it to be perfect. She began re-reading the first sentence again:

> My Dear Sweet Bob,
> I have not been honest with you, and I know this has caused complications. You are the most kind and gentle man I have ever known. But I have only known you—and one other. Why certain things in life happen together is a very great *acertijo* for me (a confusion we cannot understand).

I did not love you in the beginning. You were the first man to share my bed. But I did not give you my heart. I was angry about so many things. It seemed my life was like a room *desordenado,* too much mess. I did not want to belong to you or anyone. I felt much wiser than you. You, who was always so trusting and kind. Your love was like a child's. But for me, a young woman in this country for the first time, I want to explore, to see, and to know for myself what is life, what is freedom—what is, maybe, a love of my own.

And that is how I meet Dave. Just a date, *una cita,* very common in my country. Nothing formal, nothing bad. A friend of someone (I thought) was a friend. I had a nice time, too. To dance like an American girl in a big club with cocktail and beautiful shoes. I cannot describe the feeling, the crazy happiness of such *freedom.* And I fell for this handsome Mexican American man, Dave. He treated me so nice, so special. I felt different with him. Like a woman who knows her own worth. *Comprendes,* Bob? I never knew that before. To be independent and free. And to have something that someone wants, like a sock for a shoe. Needed!

I went with him. I was drinking, but I knew what was happening. I wanted to go with him. I was doing the choosing, *si!* To be honest, he was not tender like you. To be honest, I don't remember much. To be honest, if it had ended that night like a nice movie, it would have been only an interesting memory. But of course, it did not.

We like to play a game with God—"If you let this happen," "If you don't do this," or "If you make this go away." We make little *promesas* to be good, to change, to never fall again. And God tires of our little game, and then he lets us face ourselves. It is the greatest act of love. Without it we can never be anything more than children playing games. We can never be anything more than our own *melancholia.*

When you discovered I was pregnant, your face became all light, like a birthday cake with a million candles! This was such a surprise to me. Such an unusual reaction. I didn't know what to feel at first. How could I tell you that I slept with another man? How could I hurt you? Mrs. Wheelwright? The shame and sadness, the fear that I experienced, I put it all in a box in my head and hid it away. Dave would be my *husband*, and you would be the *father*.

The sad part is I felt, for a small time, Dave would come for me. That the man who needed me actually wanted me. But to *lose* my child was all that he wanted. So I let you believe you were the only one. I'm sorry, Bob. I wanted you to know all of this if, for some reason, anyone should tell you before I do. I don't know the exact word in English for when a person takes advantage for money, but in Guatemala we call them *chantajista*. Such people are like moss under the boat. They do not assist in your journey.

I just want you to know, with all my heart and soul, I say to you, "this child to be born is yours." There is no doubt or question anymore. How could it not be? The one who needed most is also the one who wanted most.

Love, happiness, and peace always,
A new mother! Rosa G.

Rosa folded the letter and stuck it inside the card that the nurse had purchased for her in the hospital gift shop. On the cover was a picture of a Midwestern farmhouse, a horse, a dog, a red mailbox, and a beautiful sunrise. It read, "Oh What a Beautiful Morning." And on the inside? "Now get your sick ass outta bed and back to the office!" Rosa smiled. Bob would laugh. She was certain of that.

chapter

SIXTEEN

Otis held the Raytheon battery box close to his chest. Inside the cardboard receptacle was an expired rabies tag, a ripped-and-faded pink hand towel, a plastic bowl, an old black-and-white photograph of himself wrapped in plastic—and the coiled corpse of one fourteen-year-old "confrere" named Mildred. She was departing this world with considerably more than she came in with—that was a fact. In addition to her select worldly belongings, she would forever hold the unclouded memory of one ardent devotee who saw to her every need with the zeal of an unrepentant idolater. Few anywhere had ever known such veneration.

Otis stood beside the hole in the sand that Lester was digging and clutched the box tightly. He cleared his throat and squinted toward the horizon. "Reckon we oughta be up on that sand dune over yonder. This here looks like it may be too close to the water."

Lester stopped digging and wiped his forehead on his shoulder. The stitches on his leg were finally removed, and maneuvering became routine again. What remained was a striking red lightning bolt scar on the inside of his thigh that aimed squarely for his crotch. Royce and Leland mischievously labeled it the "Helpful Hints for Drunk Tricks" indicator. Whatever its purpose, it was still a sensitive enough region that only baggy shorts felt truly agreeable.

He fanned his pants leg as he spoke. "Now, Mr. Otis, this is the third hole you've had me dig. Anywhere you're liable to bury Mildred out here, she stands a good chance of being dug up by every coyote around for thirty miles. I'll put her wherever you tell me to: on the dunes, on the beach, out in the surf even. But let's stick to one hole, OK?"

Otis frowned. "Leave her there. Don't matter what happens to her after she's buried. I just want her to have a nice view of the water is all."

Lester scratched his head. "Why?"

"'Cause." Otis reached into his back pocket and pulled out a red hankie, blowing his nose. "I never did take her to the beach, and she always wanted to go. She always did want to see the dadgum Gulf of Mexico." He continued gazing off into the distance. "A cat on a beach…it's just no damn good. They don't know how to deal with such *boundlessness*. Cats need borders, familiar places, routine. They get too much freedom, and it just tears 'em to pieces." He blew his nose again and stuck the handkerchief back in his pocket. "Still, she always did want to see the friggin' beach."

Lester hoisted the last shovel of sand and hopped atop the three-foot-deep hole. He rested his hands on the spade handle. "Well, now she'll be here in spirit for all time. She'll be chasing those crabs up the dunes, giving all the seagulls hell." Lester motioned around him. "Lookahere, Mr. Otis. She's got Texas' largest sandbox to call home. I can't think of a better resting place for Mildred. I really can't."

"Thought you said she'd end up coyote bait?"

Lester twisted the front of his T-shirt into a sweat rag and mopped his face. "You can't argue with the natural order of things. In *spirit* she'll be Queen of the Sardine Festival out here."

Otis peered at Lester with a look of resignation, and then slowly held the battery box before him. He closed his eyes and began reciting in his best "preacher voice":

"Dear God and Jesus, we gather here this afternoon to return your beloved four-legged daughter, Mildred Dorothy Dandridge McCloud, to your waiting arms as she ends her long and honorable roam amongst your earthly sway."

Otis inhaled deeply: "She was a good mouser, God. The best. Wadn't no rat, roach, horny toad, frog, or sparrow ever rested easy within her dominion. On cold nights she was a reliable foot warmer; in summertime, she was thoughtful enough to remember it was your bed, too. She liked old people, moths, cheese crackers, and Purina. She hated dogs, kids, and any kind of wet with a passion. She loved being held by the *just right* person, and she gave many, many hours of peaceful contemplation just sitting by your side. She was rarely quarrelsome, frequently considerate, and always cleaned her bowl. She was a good friend, God. Best I ever had." Otis was silent, and Lester opened an eye. Several long tears were lining Mr. Otis' face.

Otis continued: "Mildred wadn't big on possessions. She's taking her tag from the veterinarian's office, her old sleeping towel, her food dish—and if it ain't too proud on my part, I'd like her to have a picture of me so she can show her new friends up there the one person what loved her more than anyone else. If that's OK... that's what I'd like. Amen."

Lester raised his head and murmured, "Amen." The two men stood for a moment, and then Otis slowly bent forward and placed the box into the ground.

"I'll be seeing ya, sweetheart." He stared at the battery box at the bottom of the hole for a moment and then tried standing. "Damn rheumatoids got me stove up. Gimme a hand, will ya?" Lester put his shoulder under Otis' arm. "I ain't feeling myself. I'm gonna go sit in the truck. Just throw some sand on her, would ya?"

Lester watched as Mr. Otis hobbled off up toward the beach road. Poor man. Poor Mildred. Poor everybody, everywhere who

264

ever tried to love someone or something on this cold, cold earth. In the end again, you end up with you again.

Lester picked up the shovel and began throwing sand until the last thing he saw of the box was the word "Ray" staring back at him.

***

"Is everyone always this god-awful friendly?"

Melanie stopped leading Brian by the hand through the crowded room and turned to him with a fixed smile that was strangely redolent of someone else's smile he couldn't place. "We're Texans, sweetheart. You know it'd kill us to be rude to your face. Of course, we hate everyone as much as you Yankees do. We just have better manners, that's all."

Brian laughed. "Yeah, I keep forgetting that 'manners' part. I'm sure it must be something to do with the way my uncouth Yankee parents raised me." He kissed her cheek. "But I did tell you how beautiful you look tonight though, didn't I?"

Melanie's smile widened. "A few times. We have another little idiosyncrasy down here: the ability to believe anything anyone tells us as long as it makes us feel better. Very helpful, that one."

Brian stared at her, grinning. He then leaned in and bit her ear lightly. Melanie yelped, and he whispered, "That's called 'Yankee flattery.' Sometimes it hurts to be nice."

The Wheelwright home had been turned virtually overnight into a Moroccan palace (or Arab whorehouse if you were conferring with Daniel). Yvonne, with the help of two dozen assistants from a pricey Houston party service, had managed to transform the entire property. The overall effect was a hodgepodge between Osama bin Laden cave, the lobby of Las Vegas Dunes Hotel, and a food court in Dubai. Odd as a Charo bar mitzvah, but festive *por dias.*

Yvonne couldn't have been more euphoric. She was back in the saddle again, herding doggies like she'd never left the ranch. It had been cruel of Melanie to even think of denying Yvonne her expertise in these affairs. Cruel, yes, but probably necessary. In the end, lessons were learned, boundaries delineated, treaties avowed.

The lives of WASP mothers and daughters were tense, perplexing affairs at best. It was definitely not a thing for strangers to try and decipher.

"And here's that adorable man everyone's *ma-a-d* about!" Yvonne floated through the backyard sheik's tent in a tailored gold and silk caftan that broadcast, "Oscar de la Renta Meets the Cairo Country Club!"

"Martin Caraway, if you don't dance with me at least *twice* this evening, I'll absolutely expire!"

Dr. Caraway, on cue, sat his scotch down and began whirling Yvonne about in an estimable Lindy Hop. Onlookers fawned and hubbub'd around the two as if Bobby and Cissy from the *Lawrence Welk Show* had just appeared.

Inside the tent, Melanie spied her mother gamboling away in blissful abandon. She shook her head in wonderment.

Brian leaned in. "Your mom certainly knows how to have a good time."

"Mother knows when to let everyone *know* she's having a good time. Calibrating mood is key."

Brian nuzzled her neck. "How'd you get to be so smart?"

"I was raised by an American geisha."

Yvonne finally spun to a stop, saw Melanie and Brian, and immediately called to them, "You two! Bring Brian over to meet Dr. Caraway!"

"You've been petitioned." Melanie dutifully pulled Brian through the swarm.

"Who's Dr. Caraway?"

"Rockport's answer to Cesar Romero."

"Who?"

Melanie stopped walking and wrapped both her hands around Brian's, gazing into his eyes. "Would you mind if I asked Danny to give you a fast Gay 101 primer?"

Brian looked puzzled. "No. Why?"

"It'll be so helpful. You can't imagine."

Brian smiled, looking only slightly confused. As they approached, Dr. Caraway's eyes shone. "Well, well, well. Look at you two! Yummy!"

"Dr. Caraway, this is my soon-to-be-wed inamorato, Brian Dinsmore. Brian, Dr. Caraway."

Brian extended a hand, and Dr. Caraway immediately engulfed him in a bear hug. "Now, none of that Wall Street jazz. We're practically kinfolk down here." After a moment, Martin released a startled Brian and then stood back to appraise the new relative. He nodded thoughtfully, "Nice, nice. Clean-cut, earnest, virile—reminds me of a fraternity brother I once had." Dr. Caraway suddenly cackled. "Oh well, I never *had* him, you know. Really, you people are going to get me in trouble!" He then glanced down and gasped, "And *look* at those hands!" Dr. Caraway immediately hoisted Brian's mitts like they were two Golden Globes. "My God *in himmel*, you *must* play the piano. Look at the size of those fingers. I don't even *dare* peek at those feet of yours!"

Immediately, everyone focused on Brian's rather large feet. Instantly, he felt as if his shoes were on fire.

Dr. Caraway grinned. "Why don't you come round my office tomorrow? I'll be glad to arrange for a little 'honeymoon' foot alignment."

Daniel stepped from the back of the cluster, looking very Rudolph Valentino in a flowing cloak and burnoose. "Yes, Brian, your feet will absolutely be in the clouds by the time Dr. Caraway is done with you."

Brian's expression was unreadable. "Well...I've been feeling a little something in my big toe anyway. Hard to put my finger on it."

Dr. Caraway patted his shoulder. "You leave those fingers to me, Van Cliburn."

Daniel studied Brian's hands for a moment and shook his head. "Pianist? Not hardly. I'd say those hands were designed for handling more delicate things. I'd say they were perfect for taking care of one of the most precious objects I know. My big sister."

Melanie instantly felt an emotional gush. She placed an arm around Daniel, squeezing him. "You rat. Here I was determined to make it through the evening without a Barbara Walters bath."

"Honey, you're getting married! If that doesn't make you burst into tears, nothing will."

Yvonne nabbed a glass of champagne from a passing server and held it aloft. "All right everybody," she said. "For the first of about nine hundred of these to come. To my darling daughter and her darling fiancé, whom we welcome with loving arms into our humble and delighted family, a toast! May you always know love, never forget happiness, and strive eternally for kindness, *à la votre!*"

"And if the sex gets tiresome," Daniel added, "may you each develop an all-consuming passion for bird-watching." Then he ducked as his mother feigned swatting him. The crowd tittered in hilarity as the faint dinging of a doorbell chimed in the distance.

***

"When? It started a half hour ago? Yes…absolutely. I'm on my way." Bob slowly hung up the phone and listened to the partygoers reveling outside the second-floor bedroom. Rosa's labor had begun. Of course tonight, why not tonight? Is there ever a "perfect time" for a baby to come? He stared at his reflection in the mirror. Yvonne had found him a velvet fez to wear with his Sydney Greenstreet *Casablanca* linen suit. He slowly removed the fez from his head and rubbed his eyes wearily. Tonight he would, at last, tell Yvonne. After the baby's arrival. The "new" Wheelwright family status would become manifest. After tonight, he could breathe again.

***

A maid with the Party Planners staff opened the front door. "Good evening. Welcome to the Wheelwright *casbah.*"

Philip and Luz stood there looking sheepish. Luz wore designer hot-pink harem pajamas that Melanie insisted she buy at the Charity Resale Shop, and Philip wore a gold lamé turban. Except for their height and a few gray hairs, they could've easily passed for suburban trick-or-treaters.

"Hello. We're from the SPCA. We have information you're roasting a camel out back." Luz grinned at her own joke. The maid stared at her, appalled.

"You shouldn't joke about camels like that. I was a veterinarian's assistant at the Houston Zoo for five years. We lost the oldest camel in North America on my watch. He ate a disposable camera somebody threw in his pen. You shouldn't joke about camels like that."

Mortified at her failed attempt at humor, Luz stammered, "Oh God, oh, I am...*so* sorry. Forgive me. It was a dumb joke. Really. I'm such an idiot."

"People always make fun of camels because they're not smart like horses, or beautiful like tigers. If you could've seen how Sinbad suffered at the end, how he died a slow, agonizing—"

Philip quickly reached for the maid's hand. "I'm sure it was a terrible experience for you, just terrible. I'm a minister, and I'd be glad to talk with you at some point during the party about Sinbad's passing. I know he must have been a very fine...camel."

The muffled sound of choking laughter was heard rising from inside a hall closet. The maid, unable to control herself, began giggling. Luz and Philip stared at each other. Luz stepped in and reached to open the closet door.

"Oh...thank you!" Daniel said. "I was about to pee my pants in here. God, that was *priceless*! Fucking great!" He stepped out of the closet, fanning his cloak for air. "You both get the Sport-of-the-Evening award. True-blue."

A tiny smile formed on Philip's lips. "You set us up, didn't you? You're really that rotten."

Daniel, still gasping, held on to Philip's blazer. "I swear, it was so totally last minute. When I saw my friend from Houston, Alexis..." Daniel pointed toward the maid. "When I saw that Alexis was working the party, we had to have some fun."

Alexis finally drew a deep breath and stuck out her hand. "Hi. Alexis Weissman. This is my weekend gig. I do stand-up at the Improv when I'm not in school. You two were *fa-a-abulous*. Nice turban."

Philip grinned. "You're good. *Really* good."

"How can you not get great material at a party like this?" She turned to shake Luz's hand. "Hi, Alexis."

"Please tell me there is no dead camel named Sinbad at the Houston Zoo."

"There is no dead camel. Repeat after me: *no...dead...camel.*"

Philip placed a hand on Luz's shoulder. "Daniel, I'd like you to meet my sister, Luz."

"Actually, I think we've seen each other at church."

Luz turned to him. "This was your idea of a joke?"

"Uh-huh."

Luz sized up Daniel for a second more and gave him a hug. "Cute. Shitty, but cute."

"Thanks. Don't go giving me a swollen head or anything, I may just move in with you."

Luz smiled, keeping her arm around his neck. "Oh, I'm sure that'd make some of us real happy. So, what have you got to drink around here?" Interlocked, they marched toward the living room. Daniel turned back, winking at Philip.

Alexis crossed her arms, sighing. "Why can't I ever meet a woman like that. 'Water, water everywhere...and nothing to drink.'" She turned and disappeared back into the kitchen. Philip started to say something, but stopped. Somehow, in the back of his mind, he suspected he might just see her again. And again.

***

Bob hadn't bothered to tell Yvonne where he was going. This was her night. It would only confound things at this point. He didn't tell anyone. At some moment during the party, Yvonne would call him on his cell phone, and he'd break the news then. About the birth anyway. The rest would come after she'd seen the child. That would probably be best.

Standing outside the small nursing station, Bob waited patiently for someone to direct him. Which hallway, which room, which baby? As no one appeared forthcoming, he wandered down an empty side corridor. Suddenly an orderly turned a side corner breathlessly. Bob called out to him, "Excuse me?"

"Yes."

"I'm trying to find out where your patient Rosa Guzman is? She's having a baby."

"She the Guatemalan girl?"

"Yes."

"You the father?"

Bob looked at the orderly, flustered. "Fr...friend of the family."

"Can't see her. Only next of kin allowed. She's in very serious condition. She may not make it."

The orderly immediately began hurrying away. After a second, Bob shouted at the top of his lungs, "Wait!" Lurching erratically toward the orderly, Bob grabbed him by the neck and lifted him up. "I *am* the father, you unfeeling, moronic shit. Don't they teach sensitivity training around here?"

"You're...choking...me."

Bob immediately let the man slide back to the floor. "I'm... sorry. The woman is the mother of my child."

The orderly, badly frightened, straightened his glasses. "Why didn't you tell me the first time? Fuck's sake. I'm not a mind reader."

"Where is she?"

"Still in the delivery room. There's been a lot of bleeding. A lot."

"The baby?"

"The baby hasn't come yet. They're trying to save the baby."

Bob's eyes expanded. "Where? Which room?"

"I told ya, the delivery room—but you can't go in there."

Bob immediately turned and raced off.

"You can't go in there, sir!" The orderly rubbed his neck, muttering, "Asshole."

Bob scanned the Formica plaques above each door: Room number, Exit, Cafeteria, Maintenance. Where was the God almighty delivery room? Passing an open cubicle, he glanced in to see a female doctor bent over a laptop. "Can you point me in the direction of the delivery room? It's urgent."

She gazed up at him from behind her bifocals and immediately recognized the panic in his voice. "Who are you looking for?"

"Rosa Guzman. She's having her baby *right now.*"

The woman stood and led Bob over to a small sofa beside her desk. "Let me call down there and check for you. Please." She motioned to the sofa.

Bob exhaled with a gust, "Finally, someone who helps."

As she dialed on her cell, she studied him. "Are you family?"

Bob glanced up. "The father."

"I think I know her. Twenties, petite—sweet face."

Bob nodded. "That's her."

"By the way, I'm Dr. Ferrell." She suddenly held up her hand to Bob. "Dinesh? It's Ellen. Can you give me a stat on patient…?" She looked at Bob.

"Guzman," Bob said.

"Guzman." A long pause followed, and the doctor's face remained absolutely expressionless. Bob studied her features as if she were an impending NASA launch. Finally, she uttered a monosyllabic "Mmmm," and she turned to face an exterior window. She removed a shoe as she listened and idly massaged her lower shin with a foot. It seemed an eternity before she spoke again.

Suddenly, her soft voice broke the silence. "Here…correct. Yes, thanks." She clicked off the cell phone and placed it on her desk. Carefully removing her glasses, she placed them in her coat pocket. Pulling a nearby chair, she sat directly across from Bob. She took a breath. "You are Mr. Wheelwright, correct?"

"Yes."

"That's the name we have on the hospital paperwork."

"How is she? How'd it go?"

She continued staring with the same, almost serene expression. "Dr. Surati is on his way down. Rosa lost over three and a half pints of blood. The bleeding started this afternoon, probably while she was asleep. As a result, she slipped into unconsciousness. By the time the nurse checked in on her, she'd nearly bled to death. The doctors immediately got her into ICU and began transfusions, and it looked for a while she might rally. I'm very sorry, Mr. Wheelwright…" She glanced briefly at her watch. "The time of her death was recorded at eight thirty-seven."

Bob looked at her as if he were somehow trying to remember how they knew each other. He glanced up at the wall clock behind her. "It's…eight forty-five. She…died while I was…in the hospital?"

Dr. Ferrell folded her hands in her lap, her gaze remaining constant. "The doctors did everything in their power to keep her alive. It's almost as if she willed herself to live until you got here." She leaned toward Bob, touching his hand. "She knew you were here, Mr. Wheelwright. For some reason, they always know."

Bob couldn't think, couldn't move, couldn't react at all. His entire physical being was suddenly ripped apart and filled with wet sand. A shroud of emptiness choked him. He felt himself fading, diminishing toward complete, welcoming nothingness.

"Bend your head down, Mr. Wheelwright. Take a breath, hold it, and take another." The doctor's hand was firm on Bob's shoulder, coaching him back to alertness. "Deep breath, good." Bob stared at the floor and experienced such crushing sadness, he truly felt it might stop his heart at any second. He'd been a miserable human failure his whole life. No tangible connection to any warm-blooded *anything* at any time on this planet. His "connections" were machines, tools, blueprints—a boat. His existence was utter veneer, nothing supporting the sham structure he'd managed to haul himself through life with. He tried swallowing, and saliva dripped to the floor. Perhaps they were tears; he couldn't tell. Didn't matter. The longer he stared at the floor, the more luring his own passing death became.

And then…discernment. On the white tile floor before him, he could see Rosa's face. She was smiling as if in a Victorian photograph one sees in museums. The effect was preternatural, yet familiar and intimate at once. And there, in her arms was the most beautiful child he had ever seen. Angelic, radiant, precious. A child so beautiful he was sure he'd never seen another like it. Bob tried to speak as Rosa slowly held the child up toward him…

"Mr. Wheelwright, I want you to open your eyes now. Can you hear me? I'm Dr. Surati. Can you hear me all right?"

Bob slowly opened his lids to see a tall, thin man in a white coat standing next to Dr. Ferrell. He was now lying flat on his back, and Dr. Ferrell was checking his pulse. "Mr. Wheelwright, I want you to nod if you can hear me."

Bob opened his mouth and a breathless voice that sounded wholly unfamiliar said, "Yes."

"I have something to tell you, Mr. Wheelwright. We're all deeply, deeply saddened by Rosa's passing. She was a wonderful, compassionate girl, and all of us were very fond of her. Mr. Wheelwright, can you still hear me?"

Bob nodded slowly.

"Mr. Wheelwright, you are the father of a beautiful baby boy! Six pounds, seven ounces. He's perfectly healthy, has all his fingers and toes. Just a magnificent, healthy child. Did you get that, Mr. Wheelwright?"

Bob lay there motionless. He then rapidly began blinking his eyes. "Baby…OK?"

Dr. Surati and Dr. Ferrell nodded in unison.

Gradually the tears began, then more, till finally he reached up to cover his face with his hands. His sobs could be heard down the hall, all the way to the waiting room.

***

"There you are! Where the hell have you been all night?" Melanie looked over to see Lester who was semi-hiding beside the garage on the far edge of the lawn. She waved at him. "What are you doing? Come here and meet my man."

Shyly, Lester peeled himself off the wall and ambled over toward them.

"Look at you, Mr. Aladdin! *Muy caliente!*"

Lester was bare-chested, wearing green harem pants and a tight gold vest that barely covered his nipples. Of course, he felt ridiculous.

"Don't tell me. Mother found you an outfit?"

"And the shoes." Lester held up one sandal with a hyper-elongated curly toe. "She said it was *job requisite*. If I didn't show up in costume, she'd dock my pay."

"Well, I think you look *sha-zaam!* How 'bout a hug?"

They embraced and Lester offered a hand toward Brian. "You must be that lucky guy I've heard about."

Melanie turned. "Brian, this hot man is Lester Briggs, the one and only. Lester, my other hot man, Brian."

"Pleased to finally meet you, Lester. Mel's been telling me to hurry up and get down here all summer, or she was going to have to jump your bones."

"Ha-ha." Lester's not-so-enthusiastic laughter was matched verbatim by Melanie's.

"So, what do you think of my big, strong suitor?"

Lester smiled. "Well, I think you two are going to be very happy."

Melanie took a sip of her champagne. "Why's that?"

Lester smiled again. "'Cause. You deserve it, don't you? Look at you two. You're young, healthy, got money. I'd say your chances are outstanding."

Melanie stared at Lester for a moment longer, and then she suddenly burst into tears. She threw her arms around him. "Sweet, sweet Lester. No one deserves to be happier than you, no one."

Brian gently placed his hand on Melanie's back. "Hey, hey. What'd you tell me about the waterworks, huh?"

Melanie turned, wiping her eyes. "I'm sorry. Too much to drink already."

"We gotta pace ourselves this evening."

"I know." Melanie took a deep breath and ran a hand through her blonde mane. "Will you come see us in New York, Lester?"

He stared down at his feet, grinning. "Now come on. I've hardly been out of Texas. You can't expect a frog to chew with his mouth closed when he's just learning to sit at the dinner table." Lester shrugged. "*Quien sabe?*"

Melanie tugged at his vest. "I never told you this before, but I feel really lucky we stopped to pick you up that day."

Lester nodded, embarrassed. "Well, I don't know if *lucky* is the word, but as somebody I know likes to say, 'Everything right happens at the just right time.'"

A natty, elderly man abruptly called from across the lawn: "Brian, your Aunt Marian is here! Come say hello."

Brian waved back and then extended his hand toward Lester again. "The old man. Great talking with you, Les. You really should come visit us in New York. I can fix you up with some choice babes. Think about it."

Melanie looked at Lester dolefully, and then she leaned in to hug him good-bye. She whispered in his ear, "OK, the sad part is, he doesn't know any 'choice babes.' Come anyway, for my sake."

"Let's go, hon. They're waiting."

Melanie kissed Lester's cheek, and then she turned and walked off with Brian. He watched as they merged into the party. He figured they probably would be all right together. Long as they kept on seeking each other's endorsement, they'd probably do fine.

Lester prowled the perimeter of partygoers, not certain he was up for much more revelry. The gathering was fine, people were fine—everything was fine. He just didn't feel particularly festive. All he really wanted was to make an appearance before Mrs. Wheelwright so he could avoid getting chewed out for not showing up—and then quietly disappear. Actually, the whole production was starting to make him uneasy: this headlong, fierce attempt to secure two people's confinement. Sure, it could all be viewed as the optimal choice for everyone concerned. Or, it could even be seen as a mite coerced. Whatever the version, one had to wonder who Melanie might have become had she remained single. Or, at least single for a few more years. In truth, Lester's feeling conflicted was probably due to his own response to "solitary confinement." On and on, no foreseeable conclusion to his own quest for a loving accord. Just more and more...deferral.

He stood outside the kitchen door and continued debating whether or not to enter the hoopla. He started to turn back when he glanced over and saw them. Daniel, Philip, and Luz conversing with each other on the side veranda as matter-of-factly as if they'd been doing so their whole lives. He grew intrigued watching them. Who were these people who had so directly/indirectly altered his life? How did he really feel about them? Much as he tried, he couldn't summon any true feelings of aversion. Even toward Philip. After all, Philip had brought him to Rockport. To this night, to these people. Philip brought him to Luz and Otis, Melanie and Bob, Yvonne and Daniel, Royce and Leland. He'd been the catalyst behind his meeting Mirtie from the post office, the woman who'd slipped him the "fiver" his first day in town. He'd indirectly facilitated his crossing paths with the cake lady and the redheaded waitress who called him that old movie actor he couldn't remember. Even the head-trips he'd encountered like Elsie and Eddie—it was all congruent to something approaching a distinct and verifiable life. *His* life. No question about it.

"Hey," Lester spoke.

The three were so absorbed in conversation, they hadn't seen Lester approach. Immediately Luz put an arm around his waist. "Look at you! God, I think we're wearing the same pants!"

Lester smiled. "How can two people be so lucky?"

Daniel put a hand on Lester's shoulder. "Look at him; he looks like the Rock from *The Mummy*. It's not fair. I'm going to turn in my gym membership. I get bigger muscles from reading *Vanity Fair*." He then turned to Philip. "Do you guys know each other?"

Lester looked at Philip. Whoever he originally thought Philip was, he clearly wasn't that person anymore "Actually, we have met." Lester extended his hand, and the look on Philip's face startled him. It was as if Philip had been wearing a too-tight pair of shoes his entire life and had just now decided it might be OK to slip them off.

"Les…Lester. I'm…happy to…" The two men shook hands. The energy surrounding them seemed to dissolve whatever acrimony had once existed.

"Why do I get the feeling there's something more 'behind the headlines' with you two?" Luz asked, shaking her head.

Philip and Lester laughed.

Still holding the other's hand, Lester finally spoke: "He did me a favor, that's all. A favor I didn't understand or appreciate. It's done."

"What favor? What's up with you two?" Daniel reached for a cigarette on a side table and lit it. He glanced at Luz while holding up his cigarette. "I know, I know—it's going to kill me. But first I get to kill it."

Then Philip turned to Daniel, putting an arm around his back. "I can't think of a better time or place to do this. I have a small announcement I'd like to make." The others turned to listen. Philip continued on in his reserved manner: "Well, for the first time in my life I have something...something I've always wanted very, very...*very* much. At the tender age of thirty-eight, I'm very happy to say, I'm in a relationship! I'd like you both to meet my... my boyfriend."

Lester and Luz stared blankly.

Daniel smiled and began patting Philip's back. "He's not kidding, you know. I love this big lug." Daniel's face beamed. "Who'd a thunk it, huh?"

Luz emerged from her trance. "Oh my God. Oh...my...God. It's finally happened. Philip, I'm so happy!" Luz threw her arms around his neck, squeezing him. "I always knew this day would come. I just figured I'd be gray-haired and in a wheelchair when it got here. Oh God, this is so wonderful!" She turned to Daniel and hugged him. "Now," she instructed Daniel, "we have to have lunch immediately. He's *impossible* to live with, but I can save you at least ten years of therapy. I know exactly what works, and more importantly, what doesn't. By the way, what's your sign?"

As the two of them chattered on, Philip and Lester once again glanced at one another. Lester spoke first. "Congratulations."

"Funny how things...work out."

Lester nodded. "Funny. He'll take good care of you."

Philip smiled knowingly. "Yes, I know. He's been a...*provider*... for many. It's a gift of his, kind of like being a preacher, you know? Anyway, he doesn't believe in keeping secrets. I think I need somebody like that, don't you?"

Lester nodded again, and this time his own eyes began to fill. Slowly Philip extended an arm, and Lester reached over to pat his shoulder. They both clumsily embraced. Luz and Daniel turned to look at them. As if prompted by some uncontrollable urge, the four of them were soon clinging to one another in a group hug.

"My *God*, it's a Quaker meet-up!" Yvonne had stepped out onto the veranda, weaving slightly. She saw them huddled together and called out. They immediately stood apart, embarrassed. Yvonne handed Daniel her cocktail napkin. "Somebody's eyeliner is running," she told him.

"I don't wear eyeliner...anymore."

Yvonne started adjusting Philip's headdress. "*Padre*, you look like you've been forced through a garden hose; you're all unraveled."

Philip sniffed. "We were all just...reminiscing."

"How depressing! We'll have no more of that. You should be out on the dance floor doing the *lambada*, or whatever they're doing now." Yvonne downed her umpteenth glass of champagne and threw her head back in admonishment. "Live kids, *live*! You'll only be thirty-nine once! Speaking of sixty-four going on thirty-nine, has anyone seen Mr. Wheelwright? I've looked *everywhere*."

***

Bob stood outside the nursery room window and watched his son sleep. How unbelievably small he was. Just a tiny lollipop face peeking out of a yellow coverlet. From what he could see, he already appeared to have a full head of hair. Bob smiled. Mel and Danny had been bald as lemons for almost a year after they were born. This was going to be something new for everyone. In every way. A death, a birth, and a marriage—all at once. How to proceed? Which way to safe harbor? He knew he could pilot everyone to acceptable moorings; it was just getting *everyone* on board that seemed momentarily daunting. Bob had never really given much focus toward a spiritual life. He believed in God, of course, but to him, God was more like an old college roommate. A familiar face, but they didn't speak much anymore. And now, he wanted so much to connect—he *needed* to connect—with some form, any kind of greater mindfulness than his own. Was Rosa OK? Was she in some kind of protected, secure place, free from pain, hurt, and need? He wanted so desperately for her to know how much he loved her, how much he missed her, and especially to know that their baby would be fine, completely all right. Bob leaned his head against the glass, shutting his eyes.

"God, if you hear me, take care of my Rosie. You took her too soon, and I needed much more time with her. Please let her see this child, God, how beautiful, how absolutely perfect he is. Thank you for every precious moment we had together. But right now, God, it feels like all we had were just moments, and my heart is breaking for the time we will never have. Talk to Yvonne, work with her, God, *reason* with her. She'll come around. She must. Her heart is big enough for this. Remember, I know her as well as you do."

Bob continued, "God, if you can hear any of this, I wouldn't dream of asking for some kind of stunt like sending me a sign. But if you could just help with this…sadness, I'd be very grateful."

Bob exhaled, rubbing his temples. After a moment he opened his eyes. The baby was still asleep. He assumed it was probably time to accompany Rosa's body to the funeral home. God help him indeed; he was dreading it more than he could imagine.

"'Scuse me. You know which way is the going-out door?"

Bob turned to see Otis McCloud standing a few feet away, holding a white paper pharmacy bag. "I…I believe it's up these stairs, down the hallway, and to the right. Aren't you…Mr. McCloud?"

"That's right. And you are?"

"Bob Wheelwright. Your employee Lester's been working for me part time."

"Yes, yes!" Otis chuckled softly and offered a hand, his grip not more than a frail gesture. "Didn't recognize ya. Don't see so good like I used to."

"Everything all right? You're not sick are you?"

Otis growled. "Just getting old! I lost a good friend here few days ago, and I ain't been feeling worth killing, no how. They gimme some pills here in the 'mergency room to make me feel a little better. I'm heading out to California directly to live with my boy. Need something to keep me from getting all stove up on that long bus trip."

"California? Who's gonna run your place?"

Otis blinked at Bob. "That boy ain't told ya yet? Well, Mr. Lester Briggs is gonna be running the place. Made him my partner. But I don't see how he gonna work for you and me both."

Bob scratched his neck. "No, no—that might be a problem. Well, I guess he's saving the news for later."

"Prob-blee. No tellin' what that boy's got in his head." Otis squinted at Bob. "And you? Your people all right? You sure do got a pretty wife and daughter. And that boy of yours, ain't he some kind of pistol?"

Bob smiled. "Yes, they're all fine." He stroked his Adam's apple methodically. "Well, to tell you the truth, Mr. McCloud, it's kind of a long, drawn-out story, and I could sure use someone to talk with right now."

Otis perked up. "Well, ain't no better listener than me. No sir, I shut up when I'm supposed to, and then I chatter about it when that seems to be the just right thing, too. And sometimes I even say something worthwhile!"

Bob put his hand on Mr. Otis' shoulder. "I've got a long night ahead of me. Why don't I run you over to your place, and we can talk in the car."

"Sure, sure."

As they started to leave, Otis glanced in the maternity window. "Ain't those some fine-looking little papooses in there? Lord, Lord—got their whole, young lives ahead of them. Makes you feel kinda humble just thinking about it all." Bob nodded silently as Otis turned to walk up the stairs. "I 'member when my boy was that size. He wadn't big enough to fill a soup pot. But he fooled me! He growed up to be six foot three. You ever meet my boy, Otis Jr.?"

"I don't believe so."

"Oh, he's quite a man. He a doctor, you know. Moved on out to California and made a real success for himself. Got hisself the nicest house you ever seen—pretty little town called Santa Rosa. Up above San Francisco. Ain't that a sweet name?"

Bob stopped on the stairs. "What did you say?"

Otis turned. "What? The town? Santa Rosa. It's Spanish for Saint Rose." He continued walking up the stairs. "It's supposed to be a fine little city. Well, you know I 'spect I like anything with a rose in it. I'm just happy to be going someplace where we can be a family again." Mr. Otis continued talking as he turned the corner in the stairwell. Bob stood, shaking his head. Ask God a simple request—and then stand back.

chapter

SEVENTEEN

Royce and Leland carefully unloaded Mr. Otis' World War II army trunk from the bed of their pickup. Lester stood beside Otis as he paid for his bus fare from the Valley Transit Bus Company. One way to San Francisco: ninety-nine dollars. Lester pondered the significance of whatever it was that had originally stood between Otis McCloud and his West Coast reunion with Otis Jr., ultimately amounting to a lousy ninety-nine bucks. That, and of course the long-delayed invitation. Still, in the end, their reunion would be as sweet as lemon pie. Bittersweet lemon.

Mr. Otis folded the ticket and placed it inside the cloth band circling his charcoal straw fedora. He was wearing a shiny blue western suit Lester had never seen before. From the distinct smell of camphor, he doubted many had. With his new simulated alligator belt and checkered nylon tie, Otis McCloud looked every inch a man with substantial "rocks in his shoes."

As they stood in front of the convenience store by the highway, Otis glanced toward downtown Rockport. "Well boys, I can't say I won't miss it here. I will. On the other hand, I can't say I'm sorry to be done with it neither. The Good Lord put me here for a reason, and now the Good Lord gonna put these 'Tony Lamas' elsewheres."

Royce slid the trunk up alongside a row of missing payphones. "Reckon when you'll be back this way, Mr. Otis?"

Otis continued staring off, a small smile on his face. "Probably never. I seen and done it all. Nothing more going on here but more seagull shit on park benches."

Leland smiled. "Well, we're all gonna miss ya anyway. You're kind of an institution around here."

Otis retrieved a toothpick from his coat pocket and stuck it between his lips, "That's right, somewhere between dog catcher and Port-a-Potty driver. Well, every institution gotta retire one day or another. Why you reckon we don't see Captain Kangaroo no more?"

Leland shrugged. "I think he died."

Otis snatched the toothpick from his mouth, alarmed. "There it is! That's the 'Big Retirement.' Ain't nobody sneaking under that old red light. I'll be *damned* if they find my dead carcass lying upside a gas pump with a nozzle in one hand and a Mountain Dew in the other. Hell no! Get-to-getting while the getting's good."

Lester stuck his fists in his pockets, staring at his feet. "Institution, dog catcher…I'm just gonna miss you, Mr. Otis. You were my first friend and my best friend here. I owe you everything."

Otis smiled, twisting the corner of his mouth higher. "Damn right you owe me. You screw up my business, and I'll come back and kick your skinny butt all the way to Mexico." Otis turned to Royce and Leland. "You boys excuse us a minute while I have a word with my 'successor.'" Taking Lester's elbow, Otis led him toward the highway. Leaning in secretively, he muttered, "I didn't want to embarrass ya in front of your *compadres*. I just want to tell ya one thing." They stopped walking, and Lester stared as Otis pulled out his hankie and wiped the inside band of his hat. "I want you to remember, no matter what happens to the station, no matter what happens anywhere else in your life…" Otis put his hat back on and tapped his index finger over Lester's heart. "In here, you're good. You're all right, Lester. I don't mix with trash, and I knew from the first you was cut from something way above average. Don't you ever let nobody turn your head round on that. I seen the comedown of many a fella in my day, and most times they ain't no ladder back up. You gettin' me?"

Lester nodded.

"You my boy now. You my only white son." Unexpectedly, Otis threw his arms around Lester and kissed his neck. He quickly stood back, "You do me proud, you hear?"

Lester nodded. No one in his whole life had ever said he was "good." Good at anything. Not even his own father, who'd been absent for so long now, it was as if he'd never had one. He'd never allowed himself the notion that he was capable of being anything more than just mediocre his entire life. Why? Why had he denied himself? Why had his own parents deprived him and his siblings of that basic gift of approval? He felt his stomach knotting. Now, more than anything, he hated to see Mr. Otis leave. How many times does a person show up in your life affirming your existence? He placed an arm around Mr. Otis' shoulder and squeezed. "I won't let you down. Never."

Leland whistled loudly and motioned to the bus advancing toward them. Lester waved back, and he and Otis began walking in that direction. Reaching the curb, the motor coach growled to a halt, and a burst of refrigerated air spilled from the open door. Otis stopped, turned, and extended a hand. "You take care of yourself."

"I will. Yes, sir."

"And get a hat! Nothing I hate more than seeing a man go through life with a naked head." Otis then called out to Leland and Royce, who were stowing his trunk in the luggage carrels. "So long, *muchachos*! You look after my boy Lester here." Otis suddenly grinned mischievously, winking at Lester. "This peckerwood's goin' places he ain't even imagined yet!"

With that he turned and boarded without a glance back. As the bus edged away from the curb, Lester could make out Mr. Otis sitting next to another man and throwing his head back in sudden laughter.

***

Yvonne stirred her tea and watched as Mrs. Guzman adjusted little Roberto's bib. Mrs. Guzman was as natural around babies as a breeze to a flag. She'd only been in the Wheelwright home a few days now, and already she'd taken on the role of *abuelita mayor* as some postulated decree. Of course, she'd been an emotional wreck when they picked her up at the airport. She sobbed inconsolably at Rosa's grave. And since she spoke no English, and Bob's and Yvonne's Spanish was rudimentary, it'd been a confounding welcome for all of them. But when she saw her new grandchild, she did an amazing transformation. Life goes on emphatically. They were like two halves of a cracked saucer now rendered whole. And she took to Bob—*El Papa*—like her long-lost son as well. Somehow, she even managed to incorporate Yvonne into the overall scheme of things. Sort of like a step-grandmother to little Roberto. Whatever the design, at present, everything seemed to be working out for all.

And it did please Yvonne to see Mrs. Guzman fussing over the baby. It helped to ease her own fears. Somewhat. In truth, little Roberto's arrival had been both expected *and* of course, a cataclysmic bombshell as well. Despite everyone's initial shock, the wedding had gone off without a snag. Amazingly smooth. Melanie and Brian postponed their honeymoon in Fiji to help Yvonne with the funeral. And the funeral, of course, had been wrenching. Getting visas and tickets for Rosa's large family had been impossible to pull off in such a short time. Still, a sister came from California, so at least someone from her Guatemala family was there.

Brian and Melanie were now back in New York busily doing whatever newlyweds do. And thank God Bob had waited to make his "baby announcement" until after the funeral. He confided to her that he'd wanted her to know the night of Rosa's death, but Daniel convinced him otherwise. Bob's grasp of timing in these matters was fundamentally marred. Rosa's death, Melanie's wedding, Bob's disclosure—it had all nearly pushed Yvonne reeling into a yearlong collapse at the Golden Door. And then she discovered something highly pragmatic about herself. She was bigger than any of it. Not stronger, mind you, for it had been immensely problematic. It was just that she'd somehow become more proficient at managing tremendous upheaval than she'd ever imagined possible. After all, what choice did she have, really? Leave Bob? After the initial hurt and shock, it all made a kind of sense when you thought about it. Her marriage had never been a grand, consuming passion kind of thing anyway. Why presume otherwise? It was more comfortable, compatible, congenial—*gemutlichkeit.* Bob was her cozy, best friend. And really, what can one expect when a darling, sweet, young girl is deposited practically beneath your bedroom door? Did *she* not have her own ill-fated affair with the contemptible Eddie? And one couldn't disregard the overwhelming relief of knowing that Rosa's offspring was ultimately not one of *his* demon seed. No, she'd resolved at the outset that she wouldn't make him pay for it. Not too dearly anyway.

Still, staring at Mrs. Guzman cooing at the baby with a bottle, she did question once again her commitment to their agreed-upon arrangement. Motherhood anew? At this age? What of the sunset years of travel and culture and social diversion she'd long ago charted for them? What now? Carpooling to Cub Scouts between trips to the gerontologist? Could she do this, really? Could anyone, really?

Mrs. Guzman laughed suddenly and held Roberto up for Yvonne to see. He was grinning from ear to ear. Mrs. Guzman giggled again and nodded. "Happy...*ba-bee.* Happy *ba-bee!*" Yvonne rose from the table and walked toward them. Roberto waved his tiny fists and gurgled. She held his hand with her fingertips and resolved once more to herself, she was bigger than all of it! Bigger than Roberto, bigger than Bob, bigger than *Senora* Guzman—bigger than the Houston Country Club!

Yvonne patted Mrs. Guzman's shoulder and heard herself say, "Thank God we have lots of money."

Mrs. Guzman, beaming, picked up on the word *money*. As she rocked Roberto in her lap, she repeated again, "Happy *ba-bee*... happy *ba-bee*."

***

"I will never live in the guest room. Ever!"

Luz and Philip stared at Daniel who stood before them, arms crossed, chest extended, and feet spread wide on the kitchen tile. He looked as if he were about to burst into a Gilbert and Sullivan aria. Philip eased forward on his stool and cleared his throat. "It's not that you'd be *living* in the guest room. It's just where we'd keep your things."

"No, Philip, what it is, is a ruse to explain my living in your home to nosy people whose business it doesn't happen to be anyway."

"Again, you do understand my position, don't you?"

"Exactly. And my position is, I'm not interested in having intercourse with you on the courthouse lawn. But in the privacy of *our* home, we will live out, we will live open, and we will live—"

Luz raised her hand. "Can I just ask that we please not use the word 'proud'? That poor adjective has been so thrashed to death lately. It should go on life support for about a decade."

"I wasn't going to say 'proud.' I was going to say...'grand.'"

Philip rose and walked over to remove dead geranium leaves from the window greenhouse. He stared into the backyard. "You know my setup here, Dan. Luz knows better than anyone. The parsonage, even though it's not legally connected to the church, is still thought of as an extension of the church. It's the rector's home. People come here at all hours, at all times for help."

"And how many of them end up in your bedroom? Philip, I'm not asking you to stop being who you are. I'm asking that you *include* me in your life. What people don't know, they don't know. What they assume, they assume. What they can and cannot accept, it's totally not in our control. Let it go!"

Philip blinked at Daniel and turned to Luz, bewildered. She folded her arms and idly stretched a leg before her. "So, I'm watching *Please Don't Eat the Daisies* on Turner Classic Movies tonight. Anybody mind?"

Philip appeared annoyed. "Help us out here. What would you do?"

Luz comically fell sideways on the stool. "Philip Yancey asking *me* for advice? My God, do I have time to run upstairs and scribble in my diary?"

Philip took a long, patient breath. "Please?"

Luz rose slowly and stared at them both. "Right. Philip, you asked Daniel to come live with you (1) *after* you asked me if it'd be all right first, so (2) thank you; (3) Daniel, you accepted his offer knowing full well Philip's professional status, un-out-ability situation, and current fragile emotional condition; (4) you both need to get over yourselves; (5) Daniel, your crap will never fit into Philip's room anyway; (6) Philip, you need to throw out half of your crap to make room for Danny; (7) Danny's right: what you do in your own bedroom is nobody's business; (8) Philip's right: you don't have to advertise anything to anybody—just live your lives and fuck 'em; and (9) Is your stand-up comic friend, Alexis from Houston seeing anyone right now"

Daniel and Philip stared at her. "I gave her your number last week," Daniel replied.

Luz beamed. "Oh goody!" She suddenly grew worried. "Why hasn't she called me?"

"I don't know, but I'll find out. Promise."

Luz reached for an apple on the counter. "I'm taking Windsor for a walk. Why don't you invite Alexis down next weekend? The four of us. It'll be just like two old married couples getting together for a little canasta." She snatched Windsor's leash hanging by the door and exited down the hallway.

"She's a genius, your sister."

Philip shook his head. "Don't say anything. We're still trying to get her over being chosen salutatorian instead of valedictorian in high school."

Daniel leaned his head against Philip's shoulder. Philip placed an arm around him. "Sorry."

"*I'm* sorry."

"We're both sorry. Be patient with me. I'm new at this."

Daniel lifted his head. "And how many men have I lived with?" Philip started to speak, but Daniel interrupted. "I said *lived* with."

"We're both virgins. Of a sort. When are you going to tell your folks?" asked Philip.

"They know."

"About your moving in here? And college? Do they even know you're not going back this fall?"

Daniel groaned and turned his face into Philip's chest. "No. My dad'll…Who knows what he'll do. With everything going on, there just hasn't been a right time." He turned and stared glumly at the wall clock. "God, I miss Rosie. Roberto has *so* got her eyes, exactly."

Philip rubbed his shoulder. "What does he have of your father?"

Daniel thought for a moment. "His smile. He's just a very happy little kid."

"I bet he's just like you were at that age."

Daniel listened to Philip's heartbeat. For the first time in his life, he was with someone who felt safe, sane, and sheltering. He wondered if Rosa had ever felt that. He smiled and thought of the time they gave each other pedicures on the back deck. She was so funny and sweet. So alive! Where does it go, a life gone so early? He knew Philip would answer "heaven," but in his own mind, he could only imagine her dancing somewhere in a big nightclub, wearing fancy shoes, and holding up an extravagant American cocktail. Crazy happy!

***

Royce stood atop the tire rack, and Lester tossed him up the final wrapped tire. They'd spent all day rearranging the back room of the service station straightening out forty years of Otis McCloud's "organizational methodology." Lester found tools, displays, and piles of junk that would have no doubt brought top dollar at any antique store. He even found an old cigarette machine with a mirror and John Wayne's picture on it, holding a Lucky

Strike. They moved it beside Lester's cot. The thought of waking up alongside John Wayne every morning made him grin.

"Damn, how much shit can a person stockpile in one lifetime?" Royce jumped down from the racks and wiped the sweat from his eyes.

"A *hell* of a lot." Lester dragged a bucket of axle grease and parked it against the wall. "I owe you big time. You think a few beers might go toward paying off my debt to society?"

Royce smiled. "I 'magine it would. You get me drunk, and I'm liable to stick around and paint flowers on the sidewalk."

Lester laughed and walked into the office. He pulled two Shiner Bocks from the mini-fridge and returned, tossing one to Royce. "Let's go sit out in the garage and see if there's a breeze." They both found milk crates and hauled them out to where the shade bumped up against the afternoon sunlight. Sitting, they waited expectantly for any kind of gust to stir the air.

Royce took a long gulp. "Oh man, what in hell did people do before cold beer?"

Lester laughed, and Royce took another swig. "You ever quit your job out on the yacht?"

Lester held a cold mouthful and then swallowed. "Not yet. Mr. Wheelwright's kind of put things on hold. Why?"

Royce shook his head. "Just wondering. I got a buddy got laid off on a rig. He's looking for some part-time work. Figured since you're running things over here, maybe Wheelwright might need another hand."

Lester dragged his crate further back into the shade. "Tell you the truth, I imagine they're gonna be boarding up and heading back to Houston pretty soon. Summer's over; season's gone." Lester pressed the cold bottle to his cheek, musing randomly, "That's...all she wrote."

"Well," Royce drained his beer. "Thought I'd ask anyway. Gotta look after your buddies."

Lester looked over at him. "Hey, you and Leland have been the greatest. I mean it. Anything I can ever do for you guys."

Royce stood, placing the bottle on a nearby ledge. "Forget it. I gotta be heading on."

"Stay! Have another one."

"I'd like to, but Lee's got some schoolteachers coming over for dinner, and I said I'd help straighten the place 'fore he got home." Royce grinned and shrugged. "Married life."

Lester stood, holding out his hand. "I couldn't have done it without you, Royce. Thanks."

Royce held on to his clasp, gazing mischievously. "So, why don't you let me fix you up? It ain't gonna be no fun being here alone all the time, is it?"

Lester stared into Royce's pale-blue eyes and suddenly felt himself rise. Unexpectedly, he was swaying like a kite tail. He felt Royce's strong grip holding him tight as he jigged against the wind. The touch of another human, this human, made him dizzy with longing. He wanted someone to hold again. To hold him.

"There's this pharmacist over in Corpus. Great guy. Divorced, two kids. He hasn't been out long, but I think you two would hit it off. Why don't I call him and have you both come over some night?"

Lester's mouth moved slowly. "Wh...What I'd really like, Royce, is to meet someone like...you."

Royce, still gripping his hand, squeezed it harder. His thumb gently brushed against the top of Lester's. Royce pulled Lester toward him, holding him tight. He kissed his neck, stroking his head. He then suddenly released his embrace, stepping back. Lester opened his eyes and the kite skittered back to earth. "You're a beauty, Lester. You know that. I could eat you up right here. Only, Leland and I made a deal. A deal's a deal. To me anyway. It'd kill me if Lee ever screwed around on me. So, I keep my end of it. Try to anyway." Royce then slowly leaned back toward Lester and kissed him fully on the mouth. His kiss tasted like beer and sweat, both cool and peppery. He pulled away, turning to leave. "You think about that pharmacist, Les. Great guy. You two could have a good time. I know it. Give a shout."

Lester watched as Royce hurriedly got into his pickup and backed out of the station. He waved from the window as he turned onto the boulevard. Lester felt the air around him sucked out like a tornado pulling off the roof. He turned slowly and pushed the milk crate further into the shadows. Sitting down, he watched Royce's green pickup disappearing into the traffic. After a moment, he folded his arms across his knees and rested his head. Even at the *just right* place, at the *just right* time, sometimes there's no one.

***

Bob held the baby in one hand and the diaper bag, bottle warmer, portable bassinet, sack of formula, and stuffed rabbit in the other. They were going home, at long last. Yvonne would drive the crammed Jaguar behind them, and Bob and Mrs. Guzman would ride with the baby in the equally squeezed Suburban. Another summer come and gone. So much left behind, so much ahead.

"Bob, did you get the baby swing?"

"It's in here."

"And the toy chest?"

"Here."

Yvonne stopped and peered into the back of the overflowing Suburban. "The clown lamp? He'll never get to sleep without his musical clown lamp."

"I got it. I think."

"I'll go back upstairs and look."

Senora Guzman suddenly produced the clown lamp from her shoulder bag. *"Aqui esta El Payaso! Si. Si."* Mrs. Guzman smiled and patted the lamp.

Bob and Yvonne stared at each other. Then Bob smiled, slamming the rear-door shut. "How did we ever have two kids without her?"

"Gracias, Senora Guzman, gracias." Yvonne smiled and petted the clown's head. *"Muy bueno. Muy bueno para Roberto."* She placed her hands in a praying position and laid her head horizontal on them. "Baby no sleep without…*Senor* clown."

Yvonne turned to Bob. "You think she understands me?"

Bob nodded. "Does a circus lion understand a chair and a whip?"

Yvonne frowned. "That's not funny. We have serious communication issues ahead of us."

"Here, hold the baby." Bob handed Yvonne Roberto as he strapped down the rest of the luggage atop the car. "Mama Guzman understands beautifully. The important thing is she understands babies better than Dr. Spock."

Yvonne smiled apprehensively at Mrs. Guzman, who was now sitting on the steps by the mailbox, fanning herself. Yes, she was faultless with Roberto, no question. What in heaven's name would they do when and if the time came she had to return to Guatemala? Green card, green card, green card—Yvonne resolved to make it her new mantra for the coming year. She bounced Roberto against her shiny calfskin Hermes belt and scanned Bay Road. "Doesn't Danny know what time we're leaving?"

"He said he'd be here." Bob stood back and studied his handiwork. "What else?"

"Ya'll have a safe trip now."

Bob and Yvonne both turned at the same time to see Eddie holding out a string-tied box. He held it out to them. "The *Mrs.* made some ya'll sand tarts and something else, I can't remember what all."

Bob reached for the box. "Thank you, Eddie. That was very thoughtful. You tell her thanks for us."

Yvonne, unsmiling, stopped bouncing the baby and motioned toward the house. "I've turned off the water heater, but you need to drain it in a few days. And don't forget about putting the storm windows up."

"I won't forget."

Yvonne shifted Roberto to her other hip and turned back toward the Jaguar. Eddie watched her and the baby depart. "He's a smiley one, ain't he?"

Bob looked up. "Roberto? Oh yeah. Born that way. Best little baby in the whole world."

Eddie stared at Bob with large, sad eyes. "You know, Mr. Wheelwright, Rosie was a great gal. She was. And, well, the way things worked out, I'll bet she's got a big smile on her face right now—seein' all of ya'll happy and everything."

Bob, surprised, placed his hand on Eddie's shoulder. "Thanks, Eddie. I appreciate that."

Eddie stared at his shoes, struggling for words. "You know, not everybody's ever completely bad or completely good in this world. You know that, don't ya?"

Bob looked at Eddie puzzled. "Uh-huh. You tell your wife we really appreciate the cookies. I'll give you a call in a few days to check up on things."

Eddie scratched at his beard and glanced again toward Yvonne. She was busily rearranging boxes in the trunk. Eddie extended his hand toward Bob. "That baby's the spittin' image of ya, Mr. W. Ya'll have a safe trip home."

Bob looked over at Yvonne and the baby and smiled. "You think so? I can really see Rosa, but me…?" But before he could finish his sentence, Eddie had turned and walked away. Bob stared after him. Poor bastard. Was it dumb luck or just plain inertia that kept him mired in his own particular purgatory? He sighed and placed the box of cookies on top of Rosa's old suitcase, shutting the door.

Yvonne banged the trunk shut on the Jaguar and called to Bob, "I don't think Danny's going to make it. Let's circle by Philip's on our way out."

"Fine." Bob stood beside the Suburban and ran his hand through his hair. "I know I'm forgetting something. What?"

"You always forget something. It's your most consistent characteristic."

Bob reached for Yvonne's hand, smiling. "I've never forgotten you, have I?"

Yvonne looked at him. "No, you haven't." She then held Roberto toward him. "Here, 'O Thoughtful One.' Your son's getting heavy."

Bob took Roberto and nibbled on his ear, causing the baby to giggle. "Vonnie, look at this child. Have you ever seen anything so perfect in your life?"

Yvonne looked at them both. Truthfully, at that exact instant, father and son were probably the two most satisfied beings with each other she'd ever witnessed. She nodded, "Perfect."

"*Aqui Dani! Aqui viene su hijo.*" Mrs. Guzman was standing and pointing at Daniel's fast-approaching Porsche down Bay Road.

Yvonne shook her head. "Did *she* know we were waiting for him?"

"I'm telling you, she's like a cat that can tell which chair you're going to sit in before you do." Bob waved as Daniel and Philip pulled up alongside the drive.

They parked and Daniel got out motioning toward the encumbered roof of the Suburban. "You're not already packed?" He reached for Roberto from Bob, cradling his head against his shoulder like a veteran nanny.

"Completely. Your timing's impeccable." Yvonne took Philip's hand. "Good morning. If you're mad for potted cannas, I've got a row of them out on the back deck. They're just going to burn up in this sun. Take them all if you'd like."

"Thank you. Looks like you're all set here."

Bob yanked on a tied-down hibachi. "All set. I like to get the bulk of the driving done before lunch. Get a little drowsy afterwards, you know?"

"Of course."

Yvonne watched as Daniel kissed Roberto's cheek. Odd. Deep down inside, she suspected he'd make a much better parent than Melanie ever would. More caring, more concern, more "child friendly" overall. Very odd, the little swindles life plays on all of us. "I guess we'll see you sometime the first week of classes," she said.

Daniel turned from Roberto's cheek and looked at her apprehensively. "Um, actually, no."

"No?"

"I'm...staying here. With Philip."

Bob and Yvonne stared at them both.

"When did this happen?"

"A while ago actually."

"And you're just now telling us."

Daniel nodded. "Was there a better time in the last few weeks we could've all sat down and had a family chat?"

"What about school?"

"I may take some classes at the college in Corpus. Right now, I'm just going to help Philip out at the church."

Yvonne and Bob both answered simultaneously, "Church?"

"Groundskeeper, maintenance, carpenter…"

Bob looked stunned. "You're not a…*carpenter.*"

"Phil's going to teach me. And I'm going to teach him…" Daniel looked at Philip. "What am I teaching you again?"

"Patience."

Daniel and Philip both smiled.

Mrs. Guzman walked up to Daniel and held her hands out for Roberto. "*Quieres comer ahorita, nino. Si, mi hijo, si.*" Roberto fussed only briefly as he waited for *Abuelita* to produce a bottle from her bag. She sat back down in front of the mailbox and rocked him slowly in her arms.

Yvonne, nonplussed, placed a hand on her hip, unwilling to give in. "And the three-and-a-half years of college behind you? What was that for?"

Daniel shrugged. "Life, growth, training, wisdom. I learned to read *The New York Times* on Sunday, and also that beer is the unknown vitamin."

Yvonne shook her head and Philip stepped in. "If I may add something here. The job at the church is only temporary. I want Daniel to finish his education, too. I want him to do whatever it is he needs to do to in order to fulfill himself as a successful human being. And I'll support him in that goal one hundred percent."

Philip glanced shyly at Daniel. "I love your son. I think we can both help each other in a great many ways."

Bob slowly unlocked his crossed arms and scratched his cheek. "Well, your decisions are your own from now on, son. You're the man. Be wise, be smart, and remember what I always told you."

Daniel shook his head. "What was that?"

"Clean your brushes with a good-quality turpentine. You're throwing your money away on anything less."

"I'll do that." Daniel smiled.

Bob reached out to shake his hand and then pulled him forward for a hug. "Stubborn as your mom, that's for sure. I guess that's why I love you."

Yvonne threw her hands up in surrender. "Phil, you've got your hands full. I will say I'm eternally thankful he picked you instead of Cher." Yvonne gave Philip a peck and then turned to Daniel. "So, when are you coming to Houston to let me throw an engagement party?"

"Oh mother, thats so Marriage Equality of you!"

"There's a key to the house on the back post. Check on things. And don't let Eddie rob us blind."

Daniel nodded and Yvonne hugged him. His wiry, compact body was truly a man's. His unshaven cheek scratched her face. Where did the time go? Gone with that little scamp in the striped sunsuit who used to follow her in and out of every store in the mall, wearing a silly grin and humming songs from the radio. And now another one to raise? *God help me!* She took a deep breath and steadied herself. *You are amazingly bigger than* any *of this, Yvonne Wheelwright!*

"OK, here's *my* advice for you." Yvonne whispered in his ear, "Think long and hard about your life. Then do exactly what I wouldn't." She winked. "Except hold on to your partner like me." She kissed his cheek and turned quickly for the Jaguar. Getting inside, she started the ignition and turned on the air conditioner and classical music station simultaneously.

Mrs. Guzman handed the sleeping baby to Bob, and he strapped him into the car seat in back. *Senora* glared at the contraption as if it were some *norteamericano* torture mechanism. Connecting the last strap, Bob looked up and asked, "Where's Lester? I told him on the phone we were leaving this morning. I thought he was coming by."

"Don't know. He's been pretty much to himself since Mr. Mc-Cloud left. Why don't you drive by the station on your way out?"

Bob sighed. "You know how your mother gets. Once the convoy's rolling—"

Daniel finished the sentence: "No stopping till we hit Dodge City!"

Daniel and Philip both hugged *Senora* Guzman good-bye and, with a honk and a gunning of engines, the Wheelwright caravan pulled out at 9:07 a.m. sharp.

As he watched them drive away, Daniel felt a tiny pang of melancholy. His father had stuck a waving *Nino* on board sign in the Suburban rear window.

***

The Wheelwrights pulled under the porte-cochere at the Chevron just long enough to say "hi" and "bye." The baby had begun crying about something, and Senora Guzman was trying to insert herself into the un-insertable backseat. Mrs. Wheelwright complained about getting a "radiant" headache, and Bob spoke hurriedly about coming to see them in Houston, checking on Danny, making sure Eddie wasn't sleeping all day, and "See you next summer!" Away they drove on a haze of premium octane.

Just as well they didn't have time to visit. Lester didn't feel much like visiting anyway. He just wanted to sit in his gas station, sell soft drinks and fishing caps, and work on people's cars. People, as objects of necessity, were clearly too risky to aim for anymore. Give 'em half a chance…Sure, maybe sometimes late at night he might wish things had turned out differently. Tough. He'd just have to roll over and suppress it. What's the use? God gave the world cash-friendly whores for those with no luck, no capability, and no faith. A highly sensible trade-off if there ever was one.

And then they started calling. Luz was the first to invite him to dinner. Then Daniel, same thing. Then Philip drove up one afternoon and asked him to supper at their house on Saturday night. When Royce and Leland pulled in at half past five Saturday afternoon and said they weren't leaving without him, he testily washed up in the sink, put on a clean shirt and pants, and hung the closed sign in the window. Why are people so damned insistent when it's clearly obvious you're not dealing with people anymore? What really ticked him off is that Royce and Leland didn't even know the others! Daniel had gotten Royce's number and called him when they accidentally bumped into one another at the gas station. Small towns, small phone books, and even smaller social circles.

They turned into the Yancey driveway and stopped. Lester got out of the truck and slowly began making his way up the walk of the light-green house with the wraparound porch on Agarita Street. Inevitably, his mind wandered back to that first trek he'd made to the familiar front door. Was he even one second closer to understanding any of it, really?

Philip opened the door, smiling. He introduced himself to Royce and Leland and took Lester's hand last. "Glad you could make it. Really glad."

"Is that my boy from Hoot?" Luz stepped out of the kitchen munching on a barbecued chicken wing. Behind her was a vaguely familiar looking woman. Luz approached and threw her arms around his neck, extending her fingers to keep from getting sauce on him. "Hey handsome, you look great, as always. Pardon my messy hands, Philip's letting me do the barbecuing tonight." Luz turned halfway. "Lester, this is my friend Alexis Weissman from Houston. She is a knock-down-laugh riot! Funniest person you will ever meet. Isn't she a cutie?" They shook hands and as everyone introduced everyone else, Lester looked up to see Daniel descending the staircase in a long, burgundy velvet dressing gown. He was holding a lit candle and speaking in a stilted English accent:

"Last night I dreamed I went to Manderley again. It seemed to me I stood by the iron gate leading to the drive, and for a while I could not enter, for the way was barred to me..."

Leland immediately shouted out, *"REBECCA!* Alfred Hitchcock. The *second* Mrs. de Winter!"

Daniel turned, beaming. "Bingo! I couldn't decide on her or Mrs. Danforth. Isn't early Hitchcock just beyond sage?" He blew out the candle and slid off the robe to reveal shorts and a T-shirt underneath. "You're good, you knew that?"

Both men immediately began disseminating film minutiae, and Royce leaned toward Lester. "Don't worry. I don't get any of it either. I just play like I do."

Daniel caught his breath and put an arm around Philip's neck. "How could I resist? I saw that dressing gown in your closet."

Philip loudly intervened, "It was my *father's*."

Daniel continued, "It's just that I've been having this 'Joan Fontaine' other life since I got here." He suddenly switched back to Movie British. "Everything's so...*perfectly perfect* here at 'Manderley Parsonage.'"

"Welcome to *my* life," Luz dryly interjected, causing everyone to laugh.

Philip interrupted, indignantly, "Well, if any of you think I'm going to start running around here doing bad Laurence Olivier, *you're right!*" Placing a hand on his hip, Philip thrust his other hand high in the air and barked in his best clipped English: "*Go to your room immediately, you ungrateful, dungy child! And stay there till I ring for you. I shall instruct the cook: no porridge for a week!*"

Everyone collapsed in tears of laughter at Philip's flawless imitation.

Luz wiped her eyes and took a breath. "*Where*...did you learn to do that? All these years I've been living with Rich Little and didn't know it?"

Philip grinned. "I've been known to sneak downstairs and watch Turner Classic after you've gone to bed."

Daniel suddenly whistled loudly, clapping his hands. "OK, listen up members of the Robert Osborne Fan Club! We're moving to the backyard. There's beer and wine and margaritas and, please note, it's Yancey National Day of Observance. We're eating on paper plates tonight!"

Luz stuck her fingers in her mouth and whistled loud enough to rattle the crystal chandelier.

***

After dinner, they all scattered about the pristine lawn, too sluggish from food and alcohol to speak. Luz and Alexis collapsed into the hammock. Leland stood behind Royce with his hands stuffed in Royce's jeans, and rested his chin on his shoulder. They stared up at the stars silently. Philip and Daniel were side by side at the kitchen sink, rinsing pots and pans. Lester rose from his seat by the tub of iced beer, pulling out another Corona. He glanced around the yard. OK, he was glad he came. He had a nice time. These people liked him and, truth be told, he liked them, too. He moved over beside Windsor and knelt down to scratch his head. He leaned in, singing softly into Windsor's ear, "You and me against the world..." *God bless Helen Reddy, always the right song for any occasion.*

The beer was giving him a nice, cozy buzz. Plopping beside Windsor, he crossed his legs and continued humming. He felt an arm slide around his neck.

"Hey." He looked around to see Luz. "How you doing?"

"Great. Really great. Have a seat."

Luz hunkered down beside him. "How you liking it here?"

Lester nodded woozily, "Love it. Greatest place on the planet."

Luz smiled. "Wow. It usually takes a lot of beers to get to that realization." She squeezed his arm. "I want you to know something...I'm glad you're here."

Lester looked at her amused. "Why?"

She squinted at him. "I wish I could answer that. I just know somehow you're meant to be here. With us."

Lester nodded and turned his head. "Probably right."

Philip stepped out onto the deck carrying a citronella candle and approached. "Can anyone join this club?"

Lester patted the ground beside him. "Sit."

Philip crouched beside them and offered each a fresh cigar. "May Rosa Panatelas. They're American, rolled in New York. Inexpensive but not ordinary at all. Sweet, pungent—both."

Philip lit their cigars with the candle, and they all savored their first puff. Gazing up at the sky, the three of them sitting there resembled only some slightly irregular aggregate. After a pause,

Lester put his arms around both of them and laughed. "Thank you!"

Philip pulled a flake of tobacco from his lip. "You're welcome. For what?"

Lester burst out laughing. "God, I wish I could answer that!"

They all laughed. It was as close an approximation to true affinity Lester had felt for any two people in a long, long time.

"Lester!" Daniel called from the back door. "There's someone at the front door for you."

"Who is it?"

"Not sure. Says he's a friend of yours." Daniel disappeared back into the kitchen.

Lester shook his head, bewildered. "I don't have any friends here."

"We'll accept that statement as a testament to the *stupidifying* effects of beer." Luz waved her hand, motioning Lester toward the house. "Go! See who it is."

Taking another sip of beer, Lester stood with a slight wobble. Aiming for the back steps, Royce called out to him. "Hey sailor, come check out the constellation Orion. You can almost hold it."

Lester waved, "Be right back. Don't go anywhere."

Entering the kitchen, Lester looked around for Daniel. Not seeing anyone, he stepped into the darkened hallway and saw the back side of a hazy figure standing behind the screen door on the front porch. Lester squinted but couldn't make out who it was. He started walking toward the door when the figure turned around to peer inside. He was holding a duffel bag. Lester immediately stopped walking. He didn't speak, didn't move—didn't appear to even breathe. The man behind the door stepped under the light and spoke in a low voice, "They told me down at the convenience store there was a preacher named Yancey who lived here in a green house with a wraparound porch." He held up a tattered envelope in his hand. "I kept one of your letters to Laurel Jeanette." Lester remained frozen. The man placed his palm against the door. "They gave me an early release. Look, if you're with someone, that's OK.

If you're married even, I understand. I just...I had to see you one more time, Lester. I had to."

Lester slowly walked toward the door again and then stopped. "Is that...really you, Ray?"

The man smiled, "Yeah."

Lester ran and pushed open the screen door picking up Little Ray in his arms. He kissed and held him so tight he thought he might break him in two. Lester shouted and swung Little Ray around till he was hot and dizzy and nearly faint.

They both sat, laughing and crying, unable to speak. By the time the others had gathered on the porch to see what all the commotion was about, the two of them were holding each other so tight they appeared, in the evening light, to be pressed into one person.

Luz clicked off the porch lights and waved the others back inside. As she closed the screen door behind her, she saw the dropped envelope lying on the floor. Picking it up she noticed a name scribbled on it: Laurel Jeanette Yancey. Her mother's name. Startled, she held the letter in her hand.

Philip called to her in a loud whisper, "Luz, come on! Let them have some peace."

Luz glanced at the letter again and then idly tossed it into the pile of other unread mail on the hall table. *Later*, she thought. Softly, she tiptoed in the dark behind the rest of the group until they had all reached the backyard. One by one they each looked up and commented on how exceptionally clear the night sky was this particular evening.

Other works by William Jack Sibley - ANY KIND OF LUCK
(Kensington, 2001)

Insightout Book of the Month Club Bestseller 2001
LAMBDA LITERARY AWARDS, Finalist 2001
TEXAS INSTITUTE OF LETTERS Runner-up, John Bloom Award, 2001
FOREWORD MAGAZINE, Book of the Year Finalist, 2001

"ANY KIND OF LUCK is lively, funny and moving. Sibley is off to a good start!" - *Pulitzer Prize (LONESOME DOVE) and Academy Award winner (BROKEBACK MOUNTAIN), Larry McMurtry*

REVIEWS:

"One of the best from 2001!" – Book Nook, Gay Today, Jesse Monteaguado, 12/01

"Sibley's tale is humorous and full of memorable characters and laughs. (His) vivid writing style is fresh and unique; his use of unusual metaphors and descriptive text sets him apart from the ordinary. (The) story is thoroughly entertaining, and readers will easily identify ..." – Inside The Cover Book Reviews by Amy Brozio-Andrews

"Energetic, delightfull ... right on the money. Sibley's bouncy story line ... conclude this light, humorous book ... shot through with campy one-liners and happy endings." – Publishers Weekly, 7/30/01

"Hilarious characters and breezy but comically entertaining plots that don't strain the brain. Enticing and nutty ... an energetic, frenzied take ... wildly funny ... charming material ... spicy, endearing characters. (It) will certainly make you giddy, an emotion we could use more of these days." – James Piechota, The Bay Area Reporter, 8/17/01

"Sibley has written a valentine to his home state (Texas)." – John Griffin, San Antonio Express-News, 9/5/01, Section G, Page 1

"If you've forgotten what it's like to read just for fun, pick up Any Kind of Luck ... a very affectionate look at life in a small Texas town (and) Sibley captures it so well, you might feel as though you've been home again." – Ella Tyler, The Houston Voice, 9/7/01,

"What a first novel it is! The author has a grasp of the metaphor that rivals Tom Robbins. Sibley creates a story so fresh and new that it blows past the reader's expectations." – Graham Averill, The Fort Worth Weekly, 9/20/01

"To mix serious fiction with laugh out loud humor is a difficult task, but William Jack Sibley has succeeded in doing just that ... strong characters and inspired dialogue ... marvelous ability to create believable characters facing trying situations with dignity and humor." – Juliet Sarkessian, Lambda Book Report, September 2001

"Deals humorously with coming out, coming home, and coming to terms with one's identity. It's a lot of fun." – P. J. Willis, Unzipped, September 2001

"Sibley has a knack for the apt phrase ... (he) plunges gleefully through his first novel, pulling the reader along in his wake on a hilarious and breathtaking ride." – F. B. Boatner, Lavender (Minneapolis), Oct. 5, 2001

"... a book that has some muscle to it. A touching story and one I definitely recommend!" – Joe Hanssen, Gay Mans Guide, Oct. 3, 2001,

"... Funny, engaging and all around delightful ... Sibley's writing is honest, refreshing, reflective ..." – Kim McNabb, Chicago Free Press, 10/24/01

"... delightful characters ... captivating plot and sparkling dialogue ... this book teaches us some valuable lessons about family, friendship, our hometown and ourselves." – Jesse Monteaguado, The Weekly News (South Florida), 10/25/01

"Witty, charming and spiritually touching. If Noel Coward had been a novelist, his book might have read something like this" – Film Director (LOVE STORY) Arthur Hiller